**"Shane, you're not my type.
You're much too nice for me."**

"Were you not turned on the other night?"

"I don't need you to remind me."

"I think you do need me to remind you. I think you need to be reminded of all the passion and fire that exists beneath that cool exterior. No one sees how out of control you get when the right button is pressed. Maybe it's just a whisper of my hand across your breasts..." He dropped his gaze to confirm that what he was saying had some effect on her and, yep, to look at her lovely cleavage. Through the erotically thin material of that dress, he found her nipples primed to hard points.

Her tongue darted, making her lips moist, almost begging him to swipe that pouty lower lip with the pad of his finger.

"Still think I'm not your type? Because your body says different. I bet if I were to run my hand down..." He trailed his fingertips down the placket of her dress, between her breasts, along her clenching stomach, until he sensed with his fingertips the band of her panties. A sexy thong, his Braille-for-underwear skills told him.

"I bet I'd find you're as wet for me as I'm hard for you. Nice? Let me tell you, what I'm thinking about you is the opposite of nice."

ALL FIRED UP

Also by Kate Meader

Feel the Heat

ALL FIRED UP

Kate Meader

FOREVER

NEW YORK   BOSTON

Copyright © 2013 by Linda O'Dwyer

Excerpt from *Feel the Heat* copyright © 2013 by Linda O'Dwyer

Excerpt from *Hot and Bothered* copyright © 2014 by Linda O'Dwyer

All rights reserved. In accordance with the U.S. Copyright Act of 1976, the scanning, uploading, and electronic sharing of any part of this book without the permission of the publisher is unlawful piracy and theft of the author's intellectual property. If you would like to use material from the book (other than for review purposes), prior written permission must be obtained by contacting the publisher at permissions@hbgusa.com. Thank you for your support of the author's rights.

Forever

Hachette Book Group

237 Park Avenue, New York, NY 10017

HachetteBookGroup.com

Twitter.com/foreverromance

Printed in the United States of America

OPM

Originally published as an ebook

First mass market edition: September 2014

10 9 8 7 6 5 4 3 2 1

Forever is an imprint of Grand Central Publishing.

The Forever name and logo are trademarks of Hachette Book Group, Inc.

The publisher is not responsible for websites (or their content) that are not owned by the publisher.

The Hachette Speakers Bureau provides a wide range of authors for speaking events. To find out more, go to www.hachettespeakersbureau.com or call (866) 376-6591.

To every woman who thought she wasn't good enough for the unconditional love she deserved.

Acknowledgments

Thanks to my agent, Nicole "Tigress" Resciniti at the Seymour Agency, who never stops working for me and all her authors.

To my editor, Lauren Plude, who pushed me to mine Cara and Shane's story, and make those kids suffer even more. She's a cruel mistress but I made her cry, so we're even. And to the rest of the team at Grand Central, I salute you.

Thanks to Angela Quarles, Donna Cummings, and Amber Lin for reading and making this story infinitely better.

To my family and friends, who have never wavered in their support, even though some of them might be a touch scandalized by what I write.

Finally, thanks to Jimmie, from whom I steal kisses, bedcovers, and half the jokes in my books.

ALL FIRED UP

CHAPTER 1

It was the most beautiful wedding cake Cara DeLuca had ever seen. Three architecturally perfect layers of frosted purity designed to make women drool and men feign disinterest as soon as it was rolled out on a wobbly serving cart to the center of the harshly lit ballroom. Undoubtedly, a slice costs thirty, maybe forty-five extra minutes of kicking the bag at the gym.

Cara checked that thought to the tune of screeching tires in her head. In a previous lifetime, she had measured every bite in push-ups and treadmill minutes, piling on laps in the pool to punish the slightest infraction. Old Cara would be looking for an excuse to slip out of a wedding reception before the cake so she could work off the chicken or fish entrée, and she had several options for how she did that. New Cara—healthy Cara—shouldn't need to count every bite and worry if she had passed over onto the wrong side of the fifteen-hundred-calorie border.

But only an amazing cake could tempt her.

Cutting into the slice on the Limoges dessert plate, Cara slipped it past her lips, chewed slowly, and swallowed.

Ugh.

Dry, pedestrian, uninspired. No one knew better than Cara the truth behind that old adage about looks being deceiving. This cake might have been the bride's dream, but a single bite confirmed the suspicions Cara had formed the day she was roped in to salvage her cousin Gina's wedding. About ten minutes after the official planner had finally thrown up her hands in despair and gone running to the nearest sanatorium—read: palm-tree-lined, sandy beach.

This wedding was cursed.

It wasn't so much her cousin's insistence on the stab-your-eyes-out pink, fishtail-hemmed bridesmaid dresses or her requirement that she must have both a Neil Diamond string quartet for the cocktails *and* an all-girl Neil Diamond tribute band, the Sweet Carolines, for the dancing. Neither did Cara mind organizing last-minute fittings for a wedding party of twelve, or a reception for two hundred ravenous Italians. As for corralling the ovary-explodingly cute ring bearers? Child's play, though Father Phelan had drawn the line at chocolate Lab pups traipsing down the aisle behind ankle biters who could barely stay upright.

No, that was manageable and managing was what Cara did best. Where it all went undeniably south was at the joint bachelor-bachelorette party in Las Vegas. This type of thing had become *de rigueur,* and as much as Cara would have liked to put down the poker chips and back away slowly, she'd felt it incumbent on herself to manage that, too. A gaggle of drunk-off-their-butts DeLuca women needed her superior wrangling skills to make sure they had a wild and crazy, but safe, time. Unfortunately, her usually sober view had been crusted over by one colossally stupid mistake. A six-foot-tall, amber-eyed, mussed-up-haired mistake.

She should have stayed home in Chicago.

Thinking on those events of one week ago sent renewed fury roiling through her body. She could fix it. She *would* fix it. As soon as she got through this day.

Slowly, she surveyed the room and tried to breathe herself to calm in the face of the happiness onslaught. Her father—Il Duce to his daughters—held court at the elders' table after spending most of the meal bounding in and out of the hotel kitchen. Ensuring his menu was followed to exact specifications, no doubt. His queen, Francesca, rocking regal now that her corn-silk-blonde hair had returned to its pre-cancer glory, wore a familiar upward tilt on her lips as she viewed the dance floor high jinks. Cara tracked her mom's gaze to a flash of flailing arms among the writhing bodies.

Oh, you've got to be kid—

"I'm beginning to have second thoughts." A crisp, British voice intruded on her internal scold.

Jack Kilroy, her boss and future brother-in-law, wrinkled his patrician nose and laid down his fork primly.

"If you can't even get the cake right, Cara, I'm not sure I should be entrusting you with the most important day of my life," he added with just enough of that divo tone to remind her why she was glad he was marrying her sister, Lili, in six weeks, and not her. Having worked with Jack as his TV producer when he was *the* Jack Kilroy—ragingly successful restaurateur, cooking show icon, and tabloid meat—and now, as the private events manager for his Chicago restaurant, Sarriette, she was comfortably familiar with his moods and tics. Jack was almost as controlling as Cara, and that type never made it onto her dance card. The one that had turned yellow from disuse. At least until Las Vegas.

"The cake was a done deal before I became involved but don't fret your pretty head," she said, enjoying immensely how his face darkened at her patronizing tone.

Gun. Fish. Barrel.

"You've requested the most spectacular, stylish, knock-'em-dead—"

"Artistic, poetic, avant-garde," Lili picked up, a little breathlessly.

Cara smiled up at her sister, newly arrived after cutting a rug on the boards.

"Wedding to end all weddings," Cara finished while Jack pulled his fiancée onto his lap despite her whiny protests. It was a cute playact they did that would have turned her stomach at its sheer preciousness if it had been anyone else. The ache she felt in her belly could only be that cardboard cake talking.

"You shall have the wedding you've wanted since you were a little girl, Jack," continued Lili, touching his forehead in the style of a fairy godmother before dropping a kiss on his lips.

"You're so cheeky," Jack said. "Engaged for almost a year and still no joy. I'm told I'm very eligible, you know."

"Been reading your old *Vanity Fair* fluff pieces again, Jack?" Cara asked. There was a time when you couldn't turn around without seeing Jack's handsome mug on a magazine, billboard, or TV screen. Cara wondered if he missed it. Achieving her goal of becoming Chicago's events queen depended on him missing it.

"Most women are dying to walk down the aisle…" He coasted a hand along Lili's thigh, clearly appreciative of her va-va-voom figure. Even in the bridesmaid dress from Hades, Lili looked like an advertisement for real women with those generous curves.

Thin women are just as real, Cara's inner therapist whispered.

"But this one has no interest in the fairy tale," Jack went on. "Complete with Prince Charming."

Lili rolled her eyes affectionately. "I'm happy to go quietly to city hall, but if you insist, I'll indulge you."

"Sweetheart, indulge me a little now," Jack said and pulled her in for a kiss.

Cara loosed a sigh and tried to reel in her envy at how Lili and Jack stared at each other to the exclusion of anyone else, the secret messages that needed no words, and their unmistakable joy at being in each other's company. Just seeing how much Jack loved her sister made Cara's cynical heart grow larger. Not three times, but maybe one and a half.

If anyone deserved the fairy tale, it was Lili. Her younger sister had carried the weight of family obligations during their mother's battle with breast cancer while Cara had folded up like a Pinto in a head-on collision with a semi. Cara owed Lili, and she was going to repay a fraction of that debt by planning her dream wedding down to the finest detail—even if her sister didn't know she wanted it yet.

"How's the cake?" Lili asked Cara once Jack let her come up for air. Her gaze slid to the slice, lying listlessly on the scallop-edged dessert plate.

"Not so great," Cara said. "Don't worry, we'll have something much better for your big day." She already had an artiste in mind and if he was good enough for Oprah's farewell do—

"Cake's sorted," Jack announced.

"What?" Cara asked, but the tingle she felt as the word spilled out told her she should be asking "Who?" She didn't even have to hear his name; her traitorous body was already on board.

"My secret weapon." Jack chuckled and nodded to the dance floor.

Cara followed his gaze and by some Moses-like miracle, the tangle of bodies parted to reveal the weapon himself.

Shane Doyle. He of the Irish eyes, devastating dimple, and incredibly dorky dance moves.

The Sweet Carolines were playing the eponymous tune and Shane was waving his hands in the air, alternating between an interpretive dance featuring a tree and the old mime-trapped-in-a-box routine. Maisey, one of the servers at Sarriette and Shane's dance partner, was holding tight to her side because apparently Shane wasn't just bustin' moves; he was bustin' guts as well. From twenty feet away, Cara could hear him hollering about how good times never seemed so good.

The well of anger bubbled in her chest again. Shane shouldn't even be here, but after just a couple of weeks in Chicago, he had made himself right at home and finagled an invitation to the wedding as Maisey's plus one. Well, she could have him.

Cara was gearing up to drag her eyes away—any moment now—when a rather daring pivot landed him in a face-off with their table. One eyebrow arched. He held her stare. And then he winked. Which he had no damn right to do after what had happened between them a week ago in Sin Freaking City.

"No," she said firmly, turning away from those chocolate-drop eyes set in that ridiculously fine face. Not just fine, but friendly and cheerful and, oh hell, mostly fine.

"No, what?" asked Jack.

"No, we can't use Shane." When Jack's expression turned curious, she hastily added, "He's too new and he's got far too much on his plate trying to get up to speed at the restaurant.

Let me remind you that you've given me a very tight time-line here. Less than two months to plan the kind of shindig you want means I can't leave anything to chance."

Though Jack and Lili had been engaged for close to a year, Lili had only recently pulled the trigger on the wedding planning now that she was settled into her MFA program at the School of the Art Institute. Jack was champing at the bit to make Lili into Mrs. Jack Kilroy, but her sister refused to be pushed. That summed up their relationship in a nutshell.

Jack and Lili shared a meaningful glance. Cara hated when they did that.

"Something happened in Vegas and it clearly hasn't stayed there," Lili said. "We all know you slept with him."

Recrimination simmered in Cara's gut. If only it were that simple. Not that sex was ever simple, but at least they could put that in the ancient history column and move on.

"I didn't know." Jack's brow knitted furiously. "Cara, tell me it's not true."

"It's not true," Cara repeated, sort of truthfully. She hadn't slept with anyone in too long to recall and even then, she, or he, never stayed overnight. It was one of her rules, or it had been until a week ago when she woke up with a screaming hangover and a big lug of an Irishman twined around her body.

"You destroyed my last pastry chef," Jack said. "Shane's been here only a couple of weeks and you've already got your hooks into him."

"Now, now, Jack," Lili soothed. "You can't tell your em-ployees who they can and can't be with."

"Oh, yes, I can. She made Jeremy cry. The poor guy left because Cara stomped all over him."

Cara bristled, then covered with a languid wave. Every-one's impression of her was of a woman who took no prisoners when it came to life and love—an impression she did little to dispel.

"Don't be ridiculous. Jeremy and I went on one date and it didn't work out. Can I help it if you employ weak-willed mewling kittens just so you can surround yourself with yes-men who'll bow down and kiss your ring?"

The man *had* cried, though, the wuss.

Lili's unearthly blue eyes zeroed in on Cara, making her shiver with their perspicacity. "So if you didn't do the deed with Shane, what happened? You hightailed out of that Vegas hotel like you were auditioning for Girl Being Chased Number Two."

"Nothing happened. We just had a few drinks and that's it. Nobody got stomped on." Much. She felt her head cant slightly in Shane's direction. It completely sucked to have no control over her body.

And then as if she had summoned him out of thin air, he was there. The distance from dance floor to table should have given her a decent interval to adjust but Shane had bounded over like a big Irish setter, throwing Cara off-kilter. Any farther and she'd be listing like the *Titanic* in its final moments. His hip-shot loll against the table's edge made his ancient-looking jeans cleave fondly to his thighs, prompting Cara's own thigh muscles to some involuntary flexing of their own.

Who wears jeans to a wedding? While everyone else wore tuxes and dark suits, Shane was embracing the American Dream with button-fly Levis, weathered cowboy boots, and a sports jacket that stretched a little too tight over his annoyingly broad shoulders. Only after that snide thought had formed did it occur to her he had probably borrowed the jacket, likely from one of the other chefs.

Unavoidably, her eyes inched up, up, up, taking in overlong, mink-brown hair that just begged to be raked. The melty mocha eyes with a hazelnut corona ringing the iris. The jaw scruff that hadn't made acquaintance with a razor in a couple of days. The...oh, she could go on and on.

So she did. Down, down, down she traveled that granite-hard body before resting her gaze on his large hands, not that she needed visual verification of their size. She distinctly remembered how big they were because she had awoken with one spread possessively across her stomach a week ago. Worse, she remembered just how devastatingly erotic Shane's hand felt on her bare skin.

"Sure, I'm looking for a new dance partner," Shane said with that Irish musical lilt that did wondrous things to large segments of the American female population. Cara liked to think she was immunized against all that *faith and begorrah* malarkey, but she reluctantly acknowledged Shane's accent was one of his most appealing features. Like the guy needed more help to sell the goods.

Shaking off her appreciation, she tried to draw on all the reasons she was mad at him. "What happened to your last one?" She looked to see where the cast-off Maisey had landed but the poor girl was nowhere to be found. "Did you make her ill with all that jumping around?"

"Ah, I'm just too much for one woman," Shane said, exploding into that cheeky smile that had caught her attention the moment she'd entered the bar at the Paris Las Vegas Hotel. A patchwork memory of numerous drinking establishments flashed through her querulous mind. In every one, the guys had got there before the girls. And in every one, Shane Doyle had been first on his feet, motioning to his seat as soon as the lady mob arrived to meet up with the bachelor's posse for the tandem shenanigans.

A nice mama's boy, she had decided. Polite and mannered. The kind of guy she usually liked to date because they let her call the shots. Where to go, what to do, how to please her. A few tears might be shed when they parted—not by her, of course—but so far it had worked out swimmingly.

How had she messed up so spectacularly with Shane?

The band took a break and the music switched to DJ-determined wedding classics. First up, the oom-pah booms of the "Chicken Dance," and Cara found herself a tiny bit curious to see Shane's interpretation.

"We were talking about the cake," Jack said, defaulting to his one-track mind. Marriage to Lili or bust. In telepathic communication, both chefs' gazes slipped to the slice of maligned cake now insulting everyone by its mere presence on the table.

Shane scoffed. "Whoever made this rubbish should be shot for crimes against pastries."

That pulled a deep laugh out of Jack and a juvenile eye roll out of Cara. Ah, chef humor.

"So I'll expect something amazing for my wedding." He squeezed Lili's waist. "We both will. You up for it?"

A weird look passed over Shane's face, clearing his cheer. If Cara didn't know better, she would have thought he was annoyed, even angry. Which made no sense, considering what an honor it was to have Jack choose the new guy for such an important commission.

"I would think you'd want to bring Marguerite in from Thyme," Shane said, his voice as tight as the set of his mouth. "She's your best pâtissière."

Thyme on Forty-Seventh, Jack's New York outpost and Shane's stomping ground until two weeks ago when he transferred to Chicago, sported any number of culinary stars, and Marguerite was the brightest of them all. Cara was with Shane on this. It wouldn't have surprised her in the least if

Jack wanted to fly the talented Frenchwoman in for the occasion.

Shane's mood change appeared to have passed unnoticed by Jack. "Yeah, she's great, but I want you. You're a wizard with desserts, and after chasing me around for months trying to get a job, I think you're ready for the big leagues."

Shane smiled but it was as if the effort might result in the death of a puppy. There *was* something. "We could do angel food and pistachio cream, or maybe a rosemary lemon to keep the Italian theme."

"I like how you think," Jack said, smiling broadly. "Keep it up and we'll talk next week."

"Sure," Shane said with a dimple blast in Cara's direction. A return to charming, sunny Shane.

Flustered, she felt her hand move to the still-full champagne flute she had been shunning since the toasts, but before her fingers made contact, he cocked his head. One of those *Need a chaser of impaired judgment with that bubbly?* head tilts that decelerated her brain. Damn the man and his caramel-hued eyes, now narrowed and holding her captive.

"Back to the dancing," he said.

Cara had important things to say to Shane. Very important things. And avoiding him wasn't going to get it done. After years of unhealthy denial, she had vowed to meet her problems head-on, so she wasn't entirely sure why she had let a whole week go by without pulling Shane aside and telling him how it was. How it will be. She'd put it down to how busy she was ensuring Gina's wedding wouldn't be a complete debacle. Declining to examine that closely was about the only thing preventing her from losing her everloving mind.

Before she went off on him, it might be easier to soften him up on the dance floor. Besides, there was something just so adorkable about his enthusiasm. She uncrossed her legs and flexed a perfectly pedied foot clad in a Jimmy Choo peep toe. Her feet looked stunning in fuchsia.

Shane's gaze brushed fire across Cara's skin as he reached for her sister. "Lili, would you do me the honor?"

Lili slid out of Jack's lap and Cara's heart slid into her stomach.

"That's if you don't mind, Jack," Shane added.

"Oh, you wouldn't catch Jack dead on the dance floor," Lili said. "He's much too image conscious."

"I'm not afraid of looking foolish. You've heard me sing," Jack said blithely. "I draw the line at the 'Chicken Dance,' though."

"It's ironic," Cara said, aiming for levity after being snubbed by Shane because there was no doubt that's what had happened here.

"Ironically stupid," Jack replied. "Just make sure I see daylight between you two."

Laughing, Shane led a willing Lili out onto the dance floor and jumped into flapping his arms with gusto. Lili fanned her hips with both hands and then moseyed into the fray with jerky hitches more appropriate to a Taser victim.

Cara's heart boomed at ten times the beat of the music as she fought to recover her aplomb. It was easy to see why Shane would prefer to dance with Lili, who was never afraid to get into the spirit of things. Unlike stuck-up, no-fun Cara, who needed to drink her weight in vodka to go a little bit wild.

A buzz of her phone alarm reminded her that the next wedding planner task was imminent and that she had more important things to worry about than the mistake that had followed her home from Vegas. She would deal with Shane Doyle later.

* * *

If Shane were to look up "pissed off" in *Roget's*, he had a feeling Cara DeLuca would be one of the synonyms.

Damn, he wished that didn't turn him on so much.

Every time he so much as dared a glance in her direction, he got the brittle-blonde stink eye or a nice dose of dismissive ignoring. Exactly how long could she stay mad at him?

She's a woman, Doyle. There's no expiration date on female fury.

The ballroom of this swanky hotel was filled with everyone in their Sunday best, save the horrific bridesmaids' garb, but Cara stood an elegant head and shoulders above the crowd in a classy black number that exposed one of those beautiful shoulders to the world. That same shoulder his lips had grazed when he'd wrapped his body around her a week ago and slept the sleep of the tired, drunk, and stupid.

Scout's honor, his lips were only resting on her silken skin. Lying beside her in that Vegas hotel room, he hadn't dared to kiss any part of her—beautifully curved shoulder or otherwise. Well, he was far too plastered to make a decent job of it and there was no sense in ruining the moment, not when there would be plenty of time for that later. The morning after had a tendency to throw the brilliant decisions of the night before into sharp, rueful relief.

Instead of returning to Cara's frosted-over table at the end of the dancing, he headed for the bar. Not to order a drink, mind you. After a childhood spent with a constantly wasted father, he'd vowed not to fall into that cycle or become the stereotype of the Irish drunk. So much for his vow of moderation. One night in Nevada had kicked his principles to the curb, leaving in their wake a night of idiotic mistakes, a throbbing head, and the wrath of a beautiful woman.

He really should have kissed that shoulder.

At least then, he might feel justified in his role as the fall guy, because the way Lemon Tart was carrying on, you'd swear it was all his fault. For the past week, she had known exactly where to find him—elbow deep in pastry dough at the restaurant where they *both* worked—but not a whit of effort had been put forth by those killer gams. She'd been avoiding him since Vegas, click-clacking in to pick up something from her office and click-clacking right out again before he could catch her. And now Miss Perfect had the nerve to look down her nose from her seat and make him feel like rubbish? Hell, he had enjoyed wiping that sour look off her face when he'd asked Lili to dance. Let her stew a while.

Which would give Shane time to stew on Jack giving him the royal nod on his wedding cake. Shane was a great pastry chef—a stellar, award-winning pastry chef—and there was no doubt he could create something jaw dropping with both hands tied to his feet, but he had still felt blindsided by Jack's request. This was what he wanted, wasn't it? To prove himself, to show the arrogant, limey prick that he was worthy. A woman's fury might have no expiration date but this job at Sarriette did. Two months max, then on to London to open his own pastry shop and start his life proper.

More than enough time to satisfy his curiosity about the great Jack Kilroy. There was no room in the plan to take pleasure in Jack's compliment. There was no room for any pleasant thoughts where the man was concerned at all.

He needed to stop thinking so much. Stop being so maudlin, so melancholy. *So Irish.* Time to hit the head for a slash.

A strong hand on his shoulder arrested his progress.

"You're going to miss the best bit," Jack said, bowing to an all-female congregation now forming in the middle of the ballroom. Shane had attended and catered enough weddings to be well attuned to the signs, and today the ramp-up was as quick as he'd ever seen. Gentle nudges swiftly turned to less-than-subtle jabs as the ladies jockeyed for position.

"Now, girls, no need for violence," Cara said in a firm yet seductive cajole that sent a ripple to every nerve ending in Shane's body. Silky with hints of bossy. Bet she used it in bed, or she would if she wasn't passed out in a drunken stupor.

"But if you really hope to be next in line down the aisle at St. Jude's," she continued, "remember your weapons. Nails, elbows, and, of course, heels."

She turned to her cousin Gina, or the munchkin bride as Jack called her, usually to her face. Gina clutched the purple and white posy bouquet, a remarkably elegant floral arrangement considering the bride's proclivities toward the tacky. Shane's mind scooted back to that night and recalled sharing several laughs about Gina's "special requirements." Cara must have slipped the sophisticated bouquet past her during a drunken moment of weakness.

"Ready, bitches?" Gina called out and twisted away from the madding crowd, whose nostrils flared and feet pawed the hardwood floor like the bulls behind the gate at Pamplona. The dark-haired throng of Italian women was broken by Jack's blonde half sister, Jules, who had wisely elected to hover on the edges with one eye on her six-month-old, Evan, now cradled in the arms of Cara's mother. But like all women in thrall to the marriage scent, she inclined her body in readiness for the prize. Even cute-as-a-button Maisey with her purple-streaked hair was getting in on the act. Serious business, this.

An amused snort from Jack let it be known the fun was only beginning. Cara's aunt, the one with the bouffant that added a foot and change to her height, manhandled Cara from her role on the sidelines and placed her directly in the line of fire. Just as Gina's bouquet arced over her head and landed in a shocked Cara's hands.

"Oh, that's not good," Jack said, and for not the first time in the last couple of weeks, Shane wanted to work over that *GQ* magazine cover face of his. Because he agreed and Shane loathed being in agreement with Jack Kilroy on anything.

There was no way Cara could have known Shane's position about thirty feet kitty-corner from the main action, but somehow her ice-blue gaze found him like a heat-seeking missile, binding his chest in knots tighter than the hold she had on that bouquet.

No, not good at all.

The ladies groaned, a rather mean-spirited response to a supposedly fun end to the wedding festivities. Cara's expression changed from pissed to pondering as she turned the flowers over in her hand, her chilled gaze no longer on Shane.

Gina cocked her hips, all bridezilla spunk. "Probably wasted on you, Cara. Should I throw it again?"

The shadow that crossed Cara's face was impossible to miss, but it was immediately displaced by a slice of sun. Cara had a gorgeous smile, even when it was forced.

"Sure, cuz. Go for it. Though there's probably some bad luck associated with throwing it twice."

She crushed the bouquet into Gina's hands and stalked off. Looked like a case of bygones that were never gone. Cara's connection to her family had struck Shane as being a little warped, not that he could claim bragging rights in that area. His own history was proof enough that families were fundamentally untrustworthy.

"Christ, these women. Weddings turn them into crazy people," Jack muttered, which, reluctantly, Shane found amusing given how gung ho Jack was about joining the ranks of the smugly married.

"What's that about?" Shane asked. "Cara not big on marriage?"

"Cara's not big on relationships." Jack leaned against the bar and rubbed the weathered grain before meeting Shane's eyes, his expression flinty. "She's very career-focused," he added, as if that explained everything.

Shane kept his peace. Silence usually got better results.

"Don't get me wrong, I'm very fond of her," Jack continued. "But she's so tightly wound that I pity the guy who takes her on, even for a short-term thing." There was steel behind his words, sharp as a blade in that accent that made everything sound like an order. His eyes softened slightly, once he decided his message had made an impression on Shane.

Message received all right, but not in the least bit understood.

* * *

He found her in the foyer near a large potted plant, her smooth, golden back diagonally bisected by that classy dress. Her shaking shoulders could mean only one thing: she was crying.

Before he could touch her, she spun on her killer heels and the look she speared him with said she'd been expecting him. He'd got it wrong, though. As upset as she was, there were no tears, just frost turned to fire.

"You took your time, Paddy." She crossed her arms beneath her breasts, which plumped them up from B to double Ds, or that was his best guess.

"Are you all right?"

The morning after their night together, she'd been more embarrassed than annoyed. Too busy calling for a cab despite the never-ending train of taxis outside the hotel. Too busy looking for her shoes so she could put as much distance between them as possible. Now anger shimmered off her in waves, leaving a mottled swatch of pink across the exposed skin of her chest.

"No—no, I'm not all right," she hissed. "We have to fix it. It's bad enough Jack thinks I'm some sort of man-eater with my claws embedded in your hot Irish ass. If my family finds out about this, there'll be hell to pay."

Hot Irish ass? Huh, he kind of enjoyed that. He opened his mouth to make a joke, then closed it because it didn't seem like the wisest course of action. Besides, she was right. They did have to fix it. Put it behind them and return to normal or whatever the hell passed as normal in his lately complicated life. The animosity prickling the air around them sizzled, making a nice counterpoint to a distant, low-rumbled rendering of "I Am...I Said," one of Neil's schmaltziest numbers. Guilt that he had dismissed her so cavalierly ten minutes ago constricted the space around his heart, because now he wanted nothing more than to lead her to the dance floor and hold her tight.

Jesus, Doyle. Get your head out of your hot Irish ass and focus.

Taking a firm step forward, he placed his palms on her golden shoulders. Might have let his hands wander over a few inches of her soft, sleek skin. Just to stop her trembling. The raw rash on her chest was fading now along with the wild-eyed fury, but her eyes were still as big as headlights. He gathered her close, willing her stiff, slender frame to soften.

"Cara," he said. Quiet. Soothing. As if dialing the volume down might keep her from bolting like a wounded doe. "It's going to be okay."

She lifted her head and those sapphire blues knocked his heart out of his stomach and into his mouth.

"Yes, it is," she said, her chin strong and proud. "As soon as we get a divorce."

CHAPTER 2

Lake Shore Drive was a smooth ride this morning, but Shane still cursed the forty-five-mile-per-hour speed limit that stopped him from opening up the Harley full tilt. Man, he loved this machine. The vibrating hum between his legs, how the low center of gravity kept him within kissing distance of the road, the life flashing by and through him. Pastry chefs, even great pastry chefs, didn't make much in the way of readies to start out, so blowing close to ten grand on a used Dyna Super Glide had seemed like crazy cakes, but he'd never regretted it. Needing all his money for his future business endeavor, he couldn't afford a brand-new top-of-the-line Harley and the low rider with its wrinkled black paint and lashings of chrome made it as close to factory custom as someone in his position could get.

Neither did it hurt that it was a PM of the highest order. Pussy Magnet.

Angling the bike deftly, Shane narrowly avoided the danger accompanying a zippy roadster's last-minute signal change and quickly got back on track. The last thing he needed was to be laid up for six weeks with a broken arm or worse. His oscillating sanity would not be down with that.

Sanity was definitely at a premium these days, as was focus. Hard to focus on the road when all he could think of was Jack's text message, which was a welcome respite from dwelling on Cara. When it rains, it pours equatorial-strength torrents on your sorry arse. He was trying to keep his cool but it was becoming ever more difficult considering the bucket load of dilemmas in his possession.

He'd finally achieved his goal: get a job in Jack Kilroy's restaurant. That became a reality almost a year back when he'd rolled up his pastry mat and practically begged for a pâtissier job at Thyme on Forty-Seventh in New York, the flagship of Jack's restaurant empire. Taking a pay cut from his position under the great Anton Baillard at Maison Rouge had been a given and provoked a healthy scintilla of suspicion, but his credentials—several years in increasingly more responsible positions as pastry chef in Ireland, the UK, and beyond—had swayed Jack's notoriously hard-to-please sous-chef Laurent Benoit. Only when he'd been hired on did he find out the bad news.

Jack was leaving New York to move to Chicago.

So breathing the same kitchen fumes as Jack was put on the back burner. No matter, Shane was used to simmering on the fringes. For more years than he cared to admit, he'd followed Jack's explosion of popularity as he escorted stunning actresses to film premieres and struck male model poses on glossy magazine covers. He'd read every single interview and sopped up every juicy morsel of gossip, all with the goal of knowing more about Jack than the great chef knew about himself. Starting with the public face of Jack Kilroy was the best Shane could manage until he had a chance to person-

ally learn about the man behind the image, which had finally
come with this transfer to Jack's Chicago restaurant, Sarriette.

Over the last two weeks, Shane had been tossed like a rag
doll inside a tornado. Working his first dinner service with
Jack, he'd been so nervous he got three pastry orders wrong
and suffered the pointed gaze of his boss. Intimidating for
sure, but he held his own. Then for some unfathomable reason, Jack had invited him along to the stag do for his future
cousin-in-law in Vegas, had even paid for it. "Team building" he'd called it, though that idea had taken a hike as soon
as they hit the wall of Nevada heat. Not much team building
when you're slamming grappa all night while you wait for
your girl to arrive with the rest of the *famiglia*.

Jack had definitely landed on his feet with the DeLucas,
all right. They were one of those typically close-knit Italian
clans and Jack's passion for Lili clearly extended to the rest
of them. Family life seemed to suit him, especially now that
he had Jules and Evan under his wing. Giving them his protection.

Protection. Ha! Shane dropped a gear and hit the acceler-
ator, leaping ten miles over the speed limit.

As a kid, *protection* and *family* were alien words to
Shane. A drunkard father who showered him with fists instead of love. A system that was supposed to protect a child
but couldn't see the signs spelled out in the language of broken bones. He hadn't even known the meaning of family and
now he was connected to Jack's new family by marriage.
Oh, the irony.

And it was all because of Cara DeLuca.

Her name had been bandied about the restaurant during
Shane's first week, spoken in hushed tones by the servers or
derisive jibes by the guys on the line. It didn't take long to

figure out that the mysterious Cara had turned all the chefs down for a date, a crime enough to label her as either stuck up or lesbian, usually both. Nicknamed Lemon Tart by the brigade, she not only refused to mix business with pleasure, but apparently thought herself too above the crew to sit down and share family meal, the communal gathering that brought the full complement of staff together before service. She had taken the week off to work on her cousin's nuptials, so he hadn't been ready for that tall streak of sunshine to blow into the casino bar in the Paris Las Vegas Hotel and knock him off his stool.

Cara DeLuca was the most beautiful woman Shane had ever seen.

Strange to think such a thing when he'd worked in Paris, London, and New York, cities where you can't jerk off without hitting a gorgeous woman, but Cara was something else. Structurally flawless from platinum blonde head to designer-shoe-clad toe (he didn't know shit about designer shoes, but he felt it in his bones), legs a mile past eternity, narrow hips that still managed to sway with menace, and breasts that looked like they would fit his palms just right.

She had looked at him. Well, not really looked, more like an assessing arc that took in the whole room, including the murder of dark-haired cousins she was leading like a very patient chaperone. Standing apart, her aloof pose might have been taken for snootiness, but then she did this lip snag thing with her teeth. A move more nervous than erotic, it changed her from a cool Hitchcock blonde to someone who didn't fit in quite as easily as her beauty promised. Her gaze made the return trip and settled on him, and the empty seat he had vacated for her. And that was all it took.

He wasn't supposed to be drinking, not after the promises he'd made to himself, but Jack's gift to the happy couple was a nonstop booze cruise down the Sunset Strip. Another round was always there with alarming frequency and Cara's shotgun blues were usually raised in challenge. His first mistake.

Shoving those memories to the back of his brain, he hauled back to his current problem. The signaling ping of Jack's text message had awoken him from a restless sleep on Tom's sofa, an old chef pal who had put him up for the last couple of weeks. *Meet me at DeLuca's restaurant, 11 A.M.,* it said. No why, please, or thank you. Must be nice to know your word is God.

The cool May air made for perfect bike weather on the thirty-minute ride from Chinatown to DeLuca's Ristorante in Wicker Park, one of those trendy neighborhoods where every other business was a wine bar or a dog groomer. Jack owned a share of the veteran Italian restaurant, and the rest belonged to his future in-laws, or more specifically his future father-in-law, Tony DeLuca. Now Shane's father-in-law, since a guy in a Hawaiian shirt had presided over his nuptials to the man's eldest daughter.

Nope, not weird in the slightest.

Jack leaned against the hood of his car, some black deal that wouldn't have looked out of place in a presidential motorcade. His eyes were peeled to his phone, his thumbs moving feverishly. Shane had never met anyone who worked as hard as Jack. When he wasn't at the restaurant, he was checking out his other places in Europe and the US. He still showed up most mornings to receive the deliveries and he was the last one to leave at night after close down of service. No, Shane couldn't fault him on his work ethic.

The boss looked up and shoved his phone into his jeans pocket. "I hope I wasn't interrupting anything," he said, the tone one of not really giving a fuck.

"I usually like to take a ride on my day off. Coming to this neighborhood is as good as any." Shane busied himself removing his helmet and tearing open the zipper on his leather jacket while Jack just stared. Alrighty, then.

"So what's up?" Shane asked after the uncomfortable pause had joined forces with a downright awkward one.

"You should have told me," Jack said, his expression still grave.

About Cara? It had to be about Cara.

"Told you what?" Shane fronted.

Jack scrubbed his hand through his thick, dark hair, making it stand on end in furious spikes. A very specific memory invaded Shane's brain, and he forced it deep. He was so like...Looking at Jack and not being reminded was a downright impossibility but that's the path Shane had chosen. Gotta take the bad with the good.

"I had to hear it from Lili." An edge of vexation had crept into Jack's voice.

So Cara had finally confided in her sister. Made sense, though the sisters hadn't struck him as being all that close.

"It just sort of happened," he muttered.

"Well, you should have come to me." He raised his gaze to the building behind him as though pondering some great question. Pulling a jangle of keys from his pocket, he moved up the stoop toward a big oak door, about fifteen feet from the main entrance to DeLuca's restaurant.

"Come on up," he said with weary resignation.

Shane's mind raced a mile a nanosecond. Was that it? *You're married to my future sister-in-law, so come on up?* Not how he pictured his welcome to the family. He had a whole raft of other images in his head about that.

Jack was already inside and had left the door ajar. When Shane made it to the top of the inside stair, Jack had disappeared through another doorway. He followed into a comfortably cluttered apartment, walled with an array of funky art pieces.

"It's a bit of a mess and I can move the furniture into storage if you don't need it." He surveyed Shane with a quick up-down as if he were assessing his armchair requirements. "Although I imagine you probably need something given how you've been living the last few weeks."

Realization clobbered Shane like a kiss with a two-by-four. "You're offering me a place to live?"

There was that mouth twist again. Uh, maybe not. Jack arced his arm around the space, taking in a large living room with a decent-sized kitchen.

"I purchased the building about six months ago when I bought out the previous investor in DeLuca's. Lili and I used to live here before we found the townhouse a few blocks over and I haven't gotten around to fixing this unit up. She said you needed a place."

Shane's brain was starting to settle with the knowledge that, one, Jack didn't know about Cara and, two, he was offering him a place to stay but he didn't seem too happy about it. Relief and confusion got tangled up in his head, refusing to comb straight so he could make whatever he said next sound coherent.

"Is there a problem with me living here?"

"No," Jack said in a tone that rhymed with *yes*. "Lili said that sofa you're sleeping on now is bad for your back. Not that it seems to have affected your dance moves."

Shane tried to swallow the horse-pill-sized lump in his throat, but it refused to budge. The last thing he wanted was for Jack to think he was angling for some kind of advantage. The last thing he wanted was to owe Jack Kilroy *anything*.

"I wasn't trying to wrangle a bed out of you," he said

sharply. "I was just making conversation after we danced at the wedding. I didn't even think she was listening."

Jack held up both hands in a placating gesture. "Oh, I know. Lili likes to take care of people and it looks like you're her next victim. You know how Italians are. No stray left unfed. Or unhoused."

Shane took a few steps toward the kitchen and trailed his fingers along the edge of the sturdy farmer's table that would be great for making pastry dough. The corner of Jack's mouth tipped up in a half smile.

"Are you worried about the rent?"

"No." Shane took another look. It was hard to find a furnished flat in Chicago and this was so bloody perfect, he didn't know where to start. The crazy-looking art above the living room sofa might be as good a place as any. Apparently, someone had stuck egg shells onto a rug sample and daubed it with wood varnish.

"Is the art included?"

Jack's lips twitched. "Sure. What do you think of it?"

Oh hell, that backfired. What the fuck was he supposed to say that wouldn't offend the man's fiancée?

Shane tilted his head like he was taking in a *Playboy* centerfold and held his response for a couple of beats. "It's interesting. Almost Dadaist in its commentary on social connections and the interior life."

Jack laughed, a robust sound that transformed the flat into a home. "Don't worry, mate, Lili's medium is photography. That belongs to one of her whackadoo artist pals, but good move all the same."

Shane couldn't help his smile nor the way his heart lifted at the easy way Jack drew him in. Still, there was something all wrong about this. He had to refuse.

"We'll sort out a manageable rent. The place has a lot

going for it—the best Italian food in the city downstairs,
parking around back for that sweet ride of yours, only a ten-
minute drive to work." Jack leaned back against the table and
folded his arms, a move that made Shane think he might be
planning to stay awhile. A few moments clicked by, the silence surprisingly comfortable.

"You play rugby?" Jack asked.

"The sport of the oppressor? More a football man, myself."

"Don't tell me, you're one of those clover-blooded Irishmen who trots out the misty-eyed rebel songs after five pints
of Guinness. The Irish have as long a rugby tradition as the
British, you know. Besides, I'm Irish, too. On my mother's
side."

Shane knew all about Jack's mother, but he was more interested in what Jack hadn't said. The man's father was also
Irish but apparently, that connection wasn't to be acknowledged.

He turned to take another gander at the apartment as if he
needed time to make up his mind. Jack blathered on, which
was another thing he found surprising. The guy could talk
the hind legs off a herd of mules.

"I'm in a league that plays in Lincoln Park on Saturday
mornings," Jack was saying. "We get muddy, then hit a local
pub for a full English and Premier League footie on the big
screen. You should join us the next time."

A confetti bomb of—Jesus, *joy*—exploded in Shane's
chest, and he swallowed to get a grip. Rolling around the
mud, a greasy breakfast, and the match on the telly sounded
like an excellent way to spend a Saturday. *Control yourself,
boyo.*

"Sure," he muttered, as noncommittal as possible.

Jack answered with a nod and a smile, the warm, approv-

ing one the brigade waited on the balls of their feet to get
every dinner service, and Shane knew then the fuzzy feeling
a puppy must get when petted by his owner.

Shit, he did not want to feel this way. The sooner Shane
extracted himself from this murkier-by-the-minute situation,
the better, because after only two weeks in Jack's kitchen,
the worst had already happened.

Shane was starting to like his brother.

He could tell him now. Spill it out while they were having
this little moment. Two chefs—no, two friends—enjoying a
laugh about sports and nut-job art. Two brothers from different mothers finally united after years of not knowing the
other one existed. Well, one of them had known. Shane had
found out twelve years ago that he had a half brother nine
years his senior. And not just any brother.

Jack fucking Kilroy.

Already a big fish in his small British pond, Jack was
about to take New York by storm when Shane's father had
dropped the bomb. He'd knocked up Jack's mother twenty-
odd years ago, leaving her no choice but to hop the night
boat to Liverpool and raise her kid the best way she could.
The eerie similarities to his own situation had gripped
Shane's thirteen-year-old psyche. John "Packy" Sullivan
hadn't married Shane's mother either and only acknowledged Shane when she died five years after he was born. The
old bastard was no more interested in Jack than he was in
Shane, at least not until he saw an opening. An opportunity
to make an easy Euro.

His father had laughed about how much of a pushover
Jack was, how he'd forked over the cash without a word,
but Shane knew there was more to the story. Not long after,
when deep in his cups, a version closer to the truth emerged.
Jack had paid up on the condition his father never showed

his weathered, whiskey-pored face again. A bitter and twisted man, Packy had corkscrewed the knife into Shane's heart, making it clear that Jack wanted nothing whatsoever to do with the man or his no-goodnik family. Any hope Shane harbored about finding a real connection with one of the men who shared his genetic code had died during that revealing conversation.

Yes, their father had sullied any possibility for a heartfelt union of brother and brother. Every interview Jack had given after he surrendered his TV shows had told Shane the same thing. The man didn't appreciate being used for his fame. An ex-girlfriend had sold him out to the tabloids and there was no end to the hangers-on looking for a piece of him. He never came out and said it directly, but Shane read between the lines how jaded Jack had been by that whole scene, what a relief it had been to get out of it and make something real with Lili. To get back to what he cared about—the food. His *real* family. If Shane spoke up, Jack would see shades of Packy Sullivan all over again. Just another guy on the make. Another user with an outstretched hand.

Shane didn't need Jack's help to succeed and he sure as hell wasn't here to ask for a handout. He had traveled the world, worked with some of the best chefs on the planet. He had earned his kitchen stripes, and damn, he deserved his place on Jack's brigade. So what the hell was he doing here trying to prove something to a guy who, even if he knew Shane existed, wouldn't give a flying fart about him?

Simply put, he was curious. Packy was dead now, which made Jack Kilroy Shane's only living relative and Shane interested enough to put his life on hold for a while because what he didn't know was likely to kill him. He had to know what Jack was like without all the noise of the tabloids and interviews.

He hadn't reckoned on Cara, but then that was his father's dominant genes coming up trumps. Shane didn't look like the man, but apparently he had inherited his worst traits. The drunken, selfish, impulsive ones. Once he'd sorted out the Cara problem, confirmed his brother was an arsehole, and made the wedding cake to end all wedding cakes, he'd move on to the next phase.

Unfortunately Jack was not playing his part and Shane's oh-so-brilliant plan was suddenly fraught with risk. Working with the guy was bad enough. In the last five minutes, he had signed on as his rugby teammate, though he knew dick about the game, and a dangerous camaraderie was simmering to a boil. Camaraderie led to friendship and respect and other dangerous, unnamable emotions.

Accepting an offer to live here was a terrible idea. He opened his mouth to say so.

"Oh, you're here," a soft voice husked out behind him.

Shane turned to find Lili dumping a passel of shopping bags in the hallway before stumbling over them to come inside. She touched his arm gently and Shane's maudlin musings faded in the brightness of her smile. Soft, curvy, and warm, Lili was impossible to dislike.

"You're going to take it, Shane?"

"Sure he is. He loves the artwork." Jack shone a conspiratorial smile in Shane's direction.

Man, couldn't you at least try to be more of a dick?

Lili plunked down on the plush, well-worn sofa and kicked off her shoes. "I found this in an alley two blocks from here. Tad almost broke his back trying to get it up those stairs." She chuckled, pleased that she'd put her cousin through such torturous exercise. "Good times."

She tilted her head up to Jack, who was still leaning against the kitchen table.

"Good times here as well," he said, his voice so low Lili's face flamed the color of steamed lobster.

"Jack," she murmured.

"Lili," he murmured right back.

Shane rocked back on his heels, realization dawning.

"You guys have christened every stick of furniture, then?"

"Shane!" Lili's hand flew to her still-pinked cheek.

"Well, the coffee table wasn't really conducive," Jack said to Shane. "Not that we didn't give it the old college try."

Lili's embarrassment gave way to a laugh, and as Jack joined in, Shane felt he had earned the right to as well. A warm glow filled him up, washing through his veins, tapping into wells of emotion he had thought long dry. *This is a terrible idea,* the voice of reason repeated, but it was a faint echo now.

A movement in the hallway caught his attention.

"Lili, there are still eleven million bags in the car— Oh, what's going on here?"

The laughing tableau was shattered by the appearance of Cara, her slim silhouette between the doorjamb exuding enough tension to splinter the frame. On seeing him, she gripped her shopping bag handles tight and launched into a toe-tap, one of those I'm-waiting-for-an-answer bits that Shane thought you saw only in movies. Anticipation and dread sloshed over him, and he looked to Jack for confirmation.

"Shane, if you run out of sugar, Cara will be happy to oblige," Jack said dryly. "She lives across the hall."

* * *

Inside her walk-in closet, Cara hung her new Nicole Miller lace sheath dress and tried to look on the bright side, but all she could see was shadow.

Shane. Shane Doyle. Her neighbor.

Her husband.

Instead of dragging Lili around Nordstrom, she should have been on the phone to a lawyer. Two days ago at Gina's wedding, she had told her husband—gah!—that she would handle it because, damn, that's what she did. She handled, she managed, she overcame. Yet an entire week had passed as Mrs. Shane Doyle. She was a busy woman but this was absolute insanity.

The first-year wedding anniversary was paper, and Cara speculated on what kind of celebration should occur after a mere week with a ring on her finger. Oh, right, she didn't even get a ring out of the deal!

Not that a girl should be in it for the bling, but Cara as blushing bride had certain expectations: a flowing gown, smiling friends and family, a sober groom. But more than that, marriage was supposed to be about common goals and compatibility, finding that soul mate who got you and, if not completely understanding of your weirdness, was man enough to deal with it.

As the likelihood of Cara finding this paragon was negative ten thousand, she had apparently hit upon the perfect solution: ply a stranger with hard liquor and when she had him soused to perfection, drag his catatonic ass down the aisle. Perpetuating fraud was her only option because there was no way she could get a husband by fair means. What sober guy in his right mind would want a freak like her?

Certainly not a friendly, gorgeous guy like Shane.

Now here they were, living under the same roof. Like man and wife. An illicit thrill fluttered in her chest at the thought, but she quickly punched it into submission.

No, not like man and wife. He would lead his life—late

hours at the restaurant, later hours at the dank speakeasy all the chefs gravitated to after service—and she would lead hers. Working from her perfectly appointed office above Sarriette's kitchen, organizing bachelorette brunches and wedding rehearsal dinners before hitting the gym and kicking the shit out of the rock-hard abs of Mikhail, her personal trainer. There was no reason she would have to cross paths with Shane Doyle, either at work or at home.

Shane Doyle. Her husband.

"Everything okay?"

She jolted at Lili's voice, though she'd known she was here with her in Cara's bedroom, pulling exquisite shoes and stunning designer clothing out of even more beautiful bags. Sometimes, Cara thought she was paying a premium for the fabulous packaging. She looked down at her hands, now filled with shredded tissue paper.

Lili's liquid blue eyes met Cara's. "Are you upset about Shane?"

"I'm not upset. Why would I be upset?" She fought hard to dial down the hysterical hitch she imagined in her voice.

"I didn't realize how much you dislike him."

"Don't be silly," Cara snapped. "Of course I don't dislike him."

Lili picked up one of Cara's tops, a celadon silk halter in a size six that old Cara would have considered a sign of the impending apocalypse, and sighed.

"This looks like something a doll would wear."

Not exactly, but it was sweet of Lili to say so. Going up three sizes from her usual zero was an achievement Cara was trying to be proud of. Fear of gaining weight was a constant for women like her, but her recovery demanded she look at all the positives associated with gaining. With added weight came added confidence, spontaneity...and a new husband.

Not a positive per se, but somehow she doubted old Cara would have acted so instinctively.

Reverently, Lili placed the top down on Cara's silver-gray coverlet, the only splash of color in her all-white, Hamptonesque beach-style decor. Embalmed in such purity was supposed to help center Cara after a bad day at the office or an unsatisfying bout at the gym. Or, you know, finding out your secret husband is living less than ten feet away from you. Right now, the serene surroundings were doing nada for her nerves.

"He needed a place," Lili said. "He's been crashing on a friend's couch for a couple of weeks."

Grabbing the halter, Cara beelined to the celadon section of her walk-in closet. Yes, she had a celadon section, slotted between hunter and jade. The closet's ordered rows and vicious categorization appealed to her rigid personality, and after living in a studio the size of a prison cell in New York, it had been first on her list when she moved back to Chicago six months ago. Jack had given her carte blanche to rehab the apartment and she'd spent three months overseeing its transformation into a space worthy of *Architectural Digest*. A space worthy of the life she had always imagined for herself.

"So it's okay that he's living across the hall?" Lili called in after her.

"What?"

"Shane. Is it okay? You seemed a bit surprised when you saw him."

Cara hung the top, careful not to crumple it as she slid it between a Jason Wu and an Isaac Mizrahi. A real Mizrahi, none of that Target dreck.

"It didn't take him long to get his feet under the table," she said on exiting the luxurious comfort of her closet. "I

can't believe Jack would be on board. Isn't he worried about
me corrupting poor, innocent Shane?" She tackled the next
bag, extracting a slender box that held Chinese slippers in a
lovely shade of pomegranate with silver-bound jewels sewn
into the shimmering fabric.

"I can handle Jack. You're going to have to tell me what
happened some time. Did you turn Shane down?" Lili raised
a dark brow and pushed back her voluminous shock of hair.
"Oh God, did *he* turn *you* down?"

Cara could feel the imminent eye roll but she managed to
suppress it. "Nothing happened, Lili."

"Did you scare him off? You are sort of scary."

"You mean I'm a bitch." Cara knew exactly what her coworkers and select members of her family thought of her.
"Lemon Tart," the brigade at Sarriette called her, though they
probably didn't realize that she embraced the moniker. So
apt, a light-as-air confection with an acerbic bite. Not part of
the kitchen or waitstaff, her status apart was compounded by
her aloof manner and her rejection of practically every request for a date.

Practically. Jeremy, Shane's predecessor at the pastry station, had widened his puppy dog eyes and she'd taken him
for a quick turn to stretch her legs. Her first date since she
had returned to Chicago six months ago. He had been so-
licitous, polite, as interesting as wood paneling, and finally
wet-eyed when, at the end of the night, she told him thanks,
but no thanks. A month later, he was gone, leaving behind an
open position for pastry chef and a sticky rumor that she had
taken immense pleasure in punching holes in his heart with
her four-inch spiked heels. Lemon Tart's reputation had been
set like a Jell-O mold, reinforcing what everyone thought
they knew about her.

Snooty Cara who won't join the brigade's meal before

service because eating with the plebs was so beneath her. Hard-as-her-manicured-nails Cara, so focused on her career that she barely came home to see her mother while she battled cancer. Never mind that the thought of eating with others turned her stomach to knots of fear and her mother's frail, gaunt form served as too potent a reminder of Cara's mistreatment of her own body. Breaking free of other people's misconceptions was harder than it looked.

She flipped on a smile for her sister's benefit. "That's what people think of me, isn't it? I'm a bitch." She tried to take pleasure in the word, but it got clogged in her throat.

Lili's eyes softened. "No, I mean that you can be a bit intimidating to guys. Maybe Shane's not your type, too nice for you."

"Hmph. He's not so nice. I can't believe you're falling for all that leprechaun and shillelagh crap from Mr. Just-off-the-boat."

Lili scooped up a throw pillow from the bed and picked at a stray thread. "He seems like the kind of guy who'd romance a girl," she continued as if Cara hadn't spoken. "Give her flowers. Wine and dine her. Hold her hand. Yeah, much too nice for you."

"Clearly," Cara muttered as she walked back into the closet to deposit her slippers safely in plastic shoe boxes. Of course Shane was too nice for her. She knew it as surely as she knew she hated lasagna and she didn't need to have it drilled into her skull by her loved-up sister.

"That's what I would normally have thought," Lili threw out, the words muted in the layers of plush fabric draping her closet rails. Cara was just about to ask for clarification when a shadow fell across the doorway. Lili with arms folded beneath her pin-up breasts, cocking one of her rounded hips. Willing away her envy of Lili's amazing figure, Cara tried to focus on what her sister was yammering on about.

"He seems like the kind of guy who'd hold hands on a first date."

"What are you getting at?"

"Oh, nothing." Lili studied her nails and Cara's body clenched. She knew that avoidance stratagem like the back of her... nails. She'd invented it.

"Lili..."

"Just something odd that happened in Vegas. But I'm leaving it there."

Damn, she had to ask because ignoring it would be as good as dousing a flame with paraffin. "Liliana Sophia DeLuca, out with it."

"Well, you know how we had that elephantine-pink limo as we cruised the Strip?" She laughed that husky giggle that sounded like a torch singer from the forties. "Angela was already passed out, and I was left pulling Gina and her cronies down from the sunroof because a certain wedding planner had gone AWOL."

"I told you I was tired. I went to lie down."

Lili tilted her head. "Was that before or after you took a walk down the Strip holding hands with a cute Irishman?"

Oh. My. "God."

Lili's eyes sparked into puckish joy. "You sneaky girl. I couldn't believe it when I spied the two of you taking a leisurely stroll, gazing up with open mouths like you'd just hopped off the Greyhound from Podunk. Lights! Fountains! Hookers!"

Cara pushed past her sister and occupied her trembling hands with folding shopping bags. "I was just showing him around. He'd never been to Vegas and he was acting like a kid." She stole a glance back at Lili, who leaned against the closet entrance, looking like she had a shovel at the ready but would much rather let Cara break ground first.

Which she proceeded to do.

"You know how it is with these rubes. He probably grew up in a peat bog without electricity so the Vegas lights blew his country-fried mind."

Memories of Shane's wide-eyed wonder burbled to the surface of her brain. His infectious enthusiasm. His earnest curiosity. His large, warm hand interlocked with hers. She couldn't recall the last time a guy had held her hand. Usually, it was a sweaty palm at the small of her back as she left a restaurant or a movie theater after a first date, a subtle pressure that every woman understood.

I've paid up, now what can you do for me?

The hand holding hers that night had felt dry and safe. Occasionally, he'd let go to point at something outrageous like escalators on the street. *On the street, Cara!* Or he'd walk backward to tell a story, bumping into strangers whose surly expressions would turn cheerful in the face of that charming brogue and megawatt smile. There were only friends on the Strip for Shane, and Vegas, a tacky monstrosity blossomed into something magical when seen through his eyes. The rest of the night was a blur of bars and cab rides and silly jokes. She had made the biggest mistake of her life but the abiding memory was the warmth of Shane's hand.

"Is it because he's a few years younger than you?" Lili's soft words yanked Cara back to chilly Chicago.

"He is?"

"Yeah, he's the same age as me. Twenty-five." And five years younger than Cara. Shane Doyle, her boy-toy husband. The gift that keeps on giving.

Cara held her sister's gaze, as if focusing might help

make what she had to say next sound more definitive. "We had a few drinks, we walked around, that's it."

Lili matched Cara's blue-steeled look with a challenging one of her own. "And now he's across the hall. Turning on the lamps, enjoying all that American electricity. A biography of Thomas Edison on his nightstand. Wishing his dream guide would give him another tour of the sights. The sexy sights."

"Oh, shut up," Cara said above a laugh. She couldn't laugh at this. Not yet.

"Maybe I should ask him to Sunday lunch with the parental units."

"Why would you do that?"

Lili gave a half shrug. "I think he's lonely. Anyway, what do you care? You haven't been to lunch in weeks. I thought you moved back to Chicago to get back to your DeLuca roots yet you hardly ever come to the house."

That was just one motivation for gracing the shores of Lake Michigan once more. A while back, she had figured something out: her life in New York, comprising her so-called friends, her dangerous dieting, and the unattainable goal of perfection, was killing her slowly. She had surrounded herself with like-minded women who despised their bodies and delivered fake sympathy when you mentioned your own weight gain and malignant rejoicing when you dropped an ounce. Queen bee of her clique—the Skinny Bitches, they called themselves proudly—she presided over liquid lunches where the only topics of conversation were the latest fad diets and ways to keep the pounds from the door. Drinking Diet Coke like it was going out of style and engaging in a constant game of one-upmanship over who had the lowest BMI.

She never lost that one.

Until almost a year ago, she might have gone on in the same fashion, but something happened. Her sister fell in love, and Cara lost her chance to produce Jack's network show when he gave it up to focus on a life with Lili and his once-estranged sister, Jules. Seeing their joy had inspired Cara to a closer examination of what the hell she doing with her life. In winning the war on appetite, she was losing so much more. Her chance at contentment. Her chance at normal. Now, at the long-in-the-tooth age of thirty, she was trying to remake herself.

This wasn't about finding happiness. That was a touch too abstract, too pie-in-the-sky for Cara. A chance to connect with the family she felt so separate from—that she could focus on. Not men, not relationships. Certainly, not a Vegas mistake husband.

But she'd forgotten she had good reasons for leaving Chicago in the first place, like how hard it was to be the odd one out in a family that planned dinner at lunch. If she never ate another plate of Aunt Sylvia's baked ziti again, it'd be too soon.

"I'm usually too busy for lunch at Mom and Dad's. Gina's wedding took up all my time and now with yours—"

Lili cut her off with a look. "Don't use my wedding as an excuse for not stopping by. You know if Jack wanted to get married tomorrow, he could make it happen with or without you. You don't need to be spending every minute on this."

"But I want to. I want it to be special for your big day. It's important." She tried to keep the reedy note of entreaty out of her voice, the one that said, *I need this. You owe this to me because I owe it to you.*

Lili delivered the smile of the oppressed younger sister. "I know. You and Jack are going to drive me mad with its importance. Just come to lunch next Sunday. I could do with some buffering."

"Why?"

"Because now that I'm almost an old married woman, you know what comes next?"

Cara nodded as awareness of where Lili was coming from dawned. When food and marriage had been exhausted as topics of conversation, there was only one option left for the Italian table. One that Cara, the sharp-angled career girl for whom the idea of family was supposedly anathema, was never expected to partake in.

The production of heirs.

CHAPTER 3

"Cara DeLuca for Mason Napier." She made sure to inject a shot of steel into her demand so it was clear she meant business.

"Just a moment, Ms. DeLuca," the well-trained receptionist replied smoothly, though Cara imagined her making a face on the other end of the line. She didn't need to be in this woman's presence to get her back up. She'd graduated summa cum laude in getting on the wrong side of other women.

Ms. DeLuca. Wasn't that hilarious? She was tempted to correct her. *I'm Mrs., bee-atch.* A married woman, demanding all the rights and respect due her new status. Sure, if she were living in a Jane Austen novel.

She cast a gaze about her office, not much bigger than her walk-in closet but with room enough for a yoga mat and a pony. One wall housed a giant bulletin board for menus, party ideas, and images torn from lady mags and glossies that struck her fancy. The other sported an Adventcalendar-style grid with colorful Post-its representing the next month's private-event bookings. Most of the slots were full, some with two events per day.

She could do this job with her perfectly lined peepers closed.

When Jack hired her to run the events side of the business, she'd expected a challenge. A job more suitable to someone of her considerable organizational skills. She'd produced television shows and managed enough grousing talent to be able to write a book on it—and a rather unflattering one to some of the more famous names on her résumé.

Chicago might be the Second City but it still had its fair share of glamorous socialites looking to throw a charity brunch or a high tea with martinis instead of Earl Grey. Her work with some of the city's most well-known cancer charities had put her in touch with its social elite, contacts she wanted to use as she ramped up the event planning business. It had also put her in the path of several ambitious mamas offering their sons up on a silver platter. Mostly preppy types eager to brag about their big portfolios, though the lasting impression had been small minds, smaller dicks.

A long sigh shuddered through her body. This wasn't how she had envisioned her return to Chicago. Once you've seen one second-tier trust-fund baby dancing on a table, you've seen them all. She wanted to take on bigger events and more prestigious parties, but Jack continued to push back. And she knew why.

He didn't—in his parlance—give a toss.

Oh, he recognized that the private events were a nice little earner and kept the restaurant front and center, but he'd opened up the party rooms only because Lili had asked him to. So Cara would have a job. Cara wasn't the only one who felt she had a debt to pay her sister.

Jack had invented the position for Cara because he had left her in the lurch when he threw over his network deal. It had been Cara's ultimate goal to produce that show. They had been the dream team in cable culinary television, and that Jack had packed it all in without a second thought had hurt more than Cara would have imagined possible. Now she harbored brittle hopes they could bring back the gang and strike gold. Every day, she fielded calls asking for Jack to design a menu for a society wedding or a hedge fund manager's birthday. Not two weeks ago, she had spoken with a representative of the star pitcher for the Cubs. And every day, she turned business away! With her superior wrangling skills and Jack's creativity, they could be raking in a fortune planning weddings and special events for Chicago's movers and shakers, but Jack refused to see beyond the friendly confines of the Sarriette kitchen. For someone who was once the most ambitious guy she knew, he could be remarkably myopic.

"Cara." Mason's deep baritone echoed over the phone, pulling her back to the reality of her tiny job and her tinier office. There was also the reality of her marital situation but she already had a plan for that. "What can I do for you?"

Mason Napier. Scion of the Napier banking group. Art collector and opera lover. Triathlete and all-American. And son of Penny Napier, chairman (never call her "chairwoman") of the Napier Foundation, Chicago's most prestigious charity. People bruised their shins to be in her proximity. Cara liked her shins the way they were, thank you very much, hence her more indirect gambit.

"Oh, Mason, isn't it always what *I* can do for *you*?" She schooled her voice to a breathy, Marilyn Monroe gush. As well as being one of Chicago's elite, Mason was also a man's man, and he liked women who conformed to a certain stereotype.

He chuckled. "I'm enjoying this conversation already."

"Hm, well, I'm filling up my spots for December and I was wondering if your mother had given any thought to choosing Sarriette for her annual Pink Hearts Appreciation Dinner." Madame Napier threw a party every year to thank her foundation staff. It was a relatively small affair but it would serve nicely as a gateway for the more prestigious foundation events.

A slightly evasive cough warned her she wasn't going to like the next words out of Mason's silver-spoon-filled mouth. "The dinner is going to be bigger this year, maybe sixty or more. I think you said you could only accommodate thirty."

This was exactly why her job sucked. Jack's reluctance to give her free rein meant she was stuck with the Mitzies and Betsies and their bachelorette lunches.

"Well, Sarriette's dining room has seating for close to seventy." Of course, Jack would never let her close it down for one event, especially during the busy holiday season. He insisted it created the wrong impression for the regular punters. "And we've also taken over the lease on a new space. Right next door." Please God, don't strike her down, at least not until she'd had a chance to talk to Jack. She'd had her eye on the defunct space for the last three months; it fit perfectly with her plans to double the seating for Sarriette.

"You know restaurants and hotels practically fall over themselves to get this gig," Mason said. "And I've heard your boss isn't really interested in the big stuff." Every refused booking came back to bite her neck. Trust Mason to know about that. "I'm pretty sure my mother's just going to go with the Peninsula like she did last year. It's a known quantity."

Cara could feel her face crimping. Once these banker

types brought out the corporate speak it was usually all over but the shouting. Hard to get a businessman to plump for the new kid on the block over the establishment.

But he wasn't hanging up. Willing to let him lead, she waited it out. Her eyes wandered to the seating plan for Jack and Lili's wedding reception. Colored stickies circled a map of pie charts as she tried to figure out who should go where. Uncle Aldo might be persona non grata but she would find a way.

"I'd have to talk to her," Mason said in a brighter tone. A lightbulb tone, she might have called it. She had something he wanted and he was thinking of how to ask for it. Was she really going to have to date this guy just so she could get his mother's business?

Yes, she would, because she needed this to start something—*anything*—and if that required breasts blazing and eyelashes batting, then so be it. A nagging voice reminded her that she was still Mrs. Shane Doyle. *Not for much longer,* she sniped back a few seconds too late. The "Mrs." had already created a soul-deep rut in some forgotten corner of her brain, one that had been masked in dusty old cobwebs since she was a girl. Good Lord, it didn't sound half bad. She would need to shore that up PDQ.

"I did ask what I can do for you, Mason," she prompted, wishing he'd just get on with it.

"I want Jack."

She almost dropped the phone. "Jack?"

"I want to eat in the kitchen."

Cara flipped through her mind's nostalgia Rolodex while she tried to get to grips with the fact Mason didn't want to date her or, shudder, anything else. Chef's tables, popular about ten years ago, were lately back in vogue if last month's issue of *Restaurant Magazine* was to be believed. Clearly

Jack's celebrity still counted for something, and if that's all Mason wanted, she would make it happen.

"You want a chef's table?"

"Yes, a chef's table. I'd like to have dinner with a couple of friends in Jack's kitchen."

The temptation to mutter "Is that all?" was so close to spilling she had to mash her lips together to keep it in.

"You can make it work, right, Cara?" Mason purred down the line.

"Leave it with me," she purred right back.

* * *

It is a truth universally acknowledged that he who rules the kitchen rules the iPod, and this was especially true at Sarriette where Jack Kilroy ruled with a velvet fist and heaven help the man tempted to ask for alternative tuneage or, shock, a peaceful backdrop to dinner service. Watch that the door to the alley doesn't smack your arse on the way out.

Last week, it had been sixties Motown while Shane made his summer fruits bread pudding and the week before that, seventies funk played backing vocalist to his more experimental forays into flavored madeleines (hazelnut was a winner). This week, Jack was on an eighties Manchester kick, starting with the entire back catalog of New Order. And now, as they counted down to dinner service, the Smiths with their working-class dirges interspersed with teenage angst seemed as good an accompaniment as any to that most basic of staples, bread. Like a fine Bordeaux to Chateaubriand, the jangly guitar of Johnny Marr on "Big Mouth Strikes Again" was the perfect pairing to Morrissey's mournful wail.

Knead and pound. Pound and knead. Shane enjoyed the rituals inherent in baking, more so than cooking, which had always been a touch haphazard for his liking. Too much art, not enough science. He loved the exactitude of making bread, the minute differences a quarter teaspoon of cinnamon could make to a pastry.

To a casual observer, Shane's life outside the kitchen was without ritual and measurement but casual observers didn't know shit. So he didn't accumulate belongings, he lived out of a duffel bag, he came home at all hours, and slept until midday. It didn't seem all that disciplined. And when you go do something crazy like marry a girl within hours of meeting her, accusations of carelessness might be justified.

Pound and knead. Knead and pound. Bread dough was also the perfect punching bag for his frustrations right now. Last night after moving in, he'd knocked on Cara's door but she wasn't home. Two hours later, he knocked again. Then an hour after that. She still wasn't home by 1 A.M., which twisted his mind in a direction it wasn't prepared to go.

His wife was on a date. With someone who wasn't her husband. Which he shouldn't give a rat's arse about, but which really stuck in his craw.

That they needed to talk was the under-fucking-statement of the century. Three days ago, at her cousin's wedding, she had made it abundantly clear she wanted out, and he agreed. Wholeheartedly. It had been a whacky night fueled by alcohol and topped off with a whacky wedding, and there was no reason why they couldn't get it resolved with a few bucks and a couple of signatures.

Why they hadn't already sorted it out was beyond his ken. It was almost like she *wanted* to be married to him, though in truth, there was nothing stopping him from printing off those magical get-out-of-jail forms himself. Before his shift was through, she was going to talk to him if he had to nail those sexy stilettos of hers to her desk. But for now, his personal problems would have to take a backseat to a more important issue. What's for dinner.

Shane had worked at some great restaurants and some not-so-great restaurants and his opinion was often decided by what the sous- or executive chef did with family meal. The prevailing custom at most places was to take the rubbish leftovers, bung some cheese on it, and bake it for forty minutes. In a Jack Kilroy joint, that was not an option.

Running the show today, Sarriette's sous-chef, Derry Jones, was whipping up a cassoulet, its generous, meaty scent already driving everyone mad with the hunger. With his vibrant skin ink and close-shaved head, Derry looked like he should be cooking in a prison kitchen, except the tats were all French wine and cheese labels, which Shane had to admit was pretty hard core for a guy who wasn't even classically trained.

Unlike Thyme in New York, the kitchen at Sarriette was small and intimate, and the crew's movements reflected it. Whereas the brigades in other behemoth places Shane had worked operated like fifty-piece orchestras with one tuneless instrument heralding a discordant service, Sarriette's was more akin to a jazz ensemble. Easy, laid-back, sexy. Jack had handpicked his tight team, a positive Murderers' Row of culinary talent, for good reason. Everyone knew his job but no one was afraid to jump in and help out. Rock stars without the ego.

But right this minute, the lead singer was confusing the hell out of him.

Shane slid his gaze to Jack, who tended a solitary chicken breast at the grill. One of the most amazing chefs Shane had ever worked with and the most boring piece of white meat Shane had ever seen. No marinade. No frills. Nada.

"Shane. Move all your stuff in?" Jack asked as he transferred the chicken to a cutting board to rest. Grabbing a dinner plate from the shelf above the alley, he arranged some baby spinach on it. If Shane didn't know better, he would have sworn Jack actually counted the number of leaves on the plate.

"I didn't have much." He didn't have any. Just a couple of pairs of jeans so faded and worn they were starting to hole up and a few shirts that might crumble to dust the next time he did laundry.

"Cara roll out the welcome mat?"

"Haven't seen her." Unless you counted fluorescent-pink sticky notes with prescriptive instructions affixed to his door.

A few quick cuts with a Forschner turned the chicken breast into half-inch strips, which Jack arranged in a fan beside the spinach. Something in Shane's brain clicked. The careful selection down to the predetermined number of leaves? A piece of meat so plain it read like a recipe for denial? He didn't need three guesses to figure out who was on the receiving end of this dish.

"I guess our hours don't really match up," Shane said.

"Best to keep it that way."

Shane's jaw muscles bunched so tightly there was a good chance he might crush his teeth to bone dust. This was the second time Jack had warned him away and, no siree, Bob, he did not like it.

When Shane didn't respond, Jack folded his arms and lasered him with an acute look. "Listen, you've got a real future here but if you mess around with Cara, you might not. I don't want a barrel load of awkwardness if shit goes down between you two and there's an atmosphere. It's not exactly good for morale. *Comprenez-vous?*"

So that's why Jack had been reluctant to hand over the keys to the apartment. What had happened between him and Cara was already creating an atmosphere and Jack had picked up on it. Those startlingly green eyes zoned in on him. Shane could hardly believe how alike Jack was to their father. It had almost knocked him on his arse the first time they'd met at Thyme a year ago. He'd traveled all the way to the States so he could meet the ghost of Packy Sullivan.

"Not sure how it's anyone else's business," Shane said.

Jack's expression was one of disbelief; he was clearly not used to having his authority challenged. "She's a ballbuster, mate."

"A masticator," Derry added.

"She'll chew you up," Jack said. "Major mastication. Your predecessor learned the hard way. Don't go there, all right?"

The guy before him had fallen victim to Cara? Did she have some kinky thing for pastry chefs? Not that they'd even got to that level yet. Getting naked was usually a prerequisite for kink, whether with pastry chefs or otherwise.

"New guy thinks he's got a chance with Cara?" Aaron Taylor, Sarriette's maître d' had just walked in and elected to throw in his unsolicited two cents. "Uh, no."

What the hell? Shane was sorely tempted to disclose his marital status with the out-of-human-league Cara, though the amount of alcohol involved meant that defense probably wouldn't hold up in a court of law.

"Sorry, mini Bono," Aaron went on. "Maybe we could get you up to snuff with a *Queer Eye* makeover. My man would work wonders with you but as it stands"—he gave a flashy hand flourish in Shane's general direction—"Cara's a ten and you're a sketchy six at best."

"If even," Derry added, like it was any of his damn business.

"Hey, guys, go easy," Jack said with an indulgent smile

that set Shane's teeth on edge. "I'm sure that accent gets him lots of skirt."

He shifted his attention to Aaron. "What's up?"

Aaron tore his disapproving gaze away from Shane and reworked it for Jack's benefit. "We have a problem. Rahm's office called and the mayor needs a table tonight."

"Exactly how is that a problem?"

The maître d' looked distinctly put out. "Tonight's seatings were booked out a month ago."

"So the mayor can take his chances like everybody else," Jack replied. Sarriette had a policy of two-to-one: two-thirds reservations and one-third open to walk-ins, which most nights resulted in long lines down Fulton Market in the trendy West Loop. Just like Jack had planned.

Aaron's mouth worked. "Jack, it's bad enough you refuse to raise the prices but if we can't make exceptions for important customers—"

"Shane, what do you think?" Jack lobbed the question over his shoulder like a practice softball and then turned to follow up with that hardball gaze. As with everything Jack did, it felt like a test.

"Tell him we'll call one of the taxpayers who already reserved and ask them to give up their table," Shane tossed back without missing a beat.

"Fuck, yeah." This from the laconic Derry.

"Really?" Aaron whipped his gaze from Jack to Shane and back again, his face filled with hope.

"I didn't vote for him," Jack said. "And until the city of Chicago deigns to stop screwing me over on my property tax assessment, then the mayor will have to line up with everybody else. Dennis!"

That punctuating bellow was for the extern commis who had started a week before Shane came on board. Clanging metal crashed from inside the walk-in fridge, followed by a very inventive string of swear words. Jack looked heavenward for inspiration.

"Would you treat the president of the United States this way?" Aaron asked in a huff.

"If he didn't bother to make a bloody reservation," Jack replied smoothly.

Disgruntled, Aaron stormed out, muttering something about how Cara was right and Jack was a Neanderthal about the business.

Jack opened his mouth again. "Den—"

"Yes, chef?" The gangly, ginger-topped extern also known as Dennis hovered at Jack's shoulder, shivering from the cold of the freezer.

"Christ, don't creep up on people like that." Jack motioned to the chicken-and-spinach-leaf dish. "Take this up to Cara and do not drop it."

Dennis shuffled forward, his hands trembling, and not from the freezer this time. The poor kid had been dropping stuff right, left, and center since he had arrived. He really wasn't cut out for a busy line but Jack was going to let him work out the rest of his three-month-long externship to let him have the experience. Shane got the impression Dennis would rather be sacked but he was too afraid of Jack to give his notice.

"Hold on. Shane, throw me a lemon from that basket."

Shane obliged, and Jack sliced the Meyer into eighths and placed a wedge on the side of the plate. He pulled his buzzing phone out of his pocket. The plunging octaves signaled to anyone within earshot that Lili was on the end of the line. He shooed Dennis away with the plate.

Shane followed the extern out through the swing doors.

"Hold up, D. I'll take that."

The kid looked terrified. "But Jack said—"

"That's okay. I got it," Shane finished, taking the plate from the rookie's death grip. The porcelain would probably have shattered while Dennis did his best not to drop it. "Go take a leak if you need something to occupy your hands."

Breathing deep, Shane headed upstairs and readied for an altitude change. While Jack's office and the locker rooms were downstairs at kitchen and dining level, Cara's was on the second floor, next to the private-party rooms. They had two, one that seated a dinner party of twelve and another that could accommodate up to thirty guests. Cara's job was to keep the rooms booked and she fulfilled that function admirably. Almost every night since Shane's arrival there had been an event to be catered upstairs and a crap load of grumbling from the brigade behind Jack's back. The staff hated special events. They created a lot of extra work for the kitchen and were notoriously bad sources of tip income for the servers.

There was an oppressive stillness to the air as Shane made landfall on the next level. Cara's office was ajar, so he pushed in without knocking.

Shoulda knocked.

She was halfway through pulling a T-shirt over her head, a lavender stretchy material that set off her golden hair and enhanced the cornflower blue of her eyes. The flash of skin covered by a whisper of pink lace sent a shot of awareness racing through him where it settled very comfortably between his legs. A comfort that lasted mere seconds before it became tight.

Okay, so he was glad he didn't knock.

"Lost your manners?" The accusation drew her brows together into hash marks.

"Sorry," he said. *Not really.* "Your door was open and I brought up your"—*boring*—"meal."

He took her silence as an opportunity to drink her in. Pink sweatpants made her arse look even curvier than the tight skirts he'd seen molded to her. At least, he assumed so because she hadn't actually turned around, but he'd been thinking of her heart-shaped behind for the last week and he had a pretty good idea. She wore cute girly trainers that looked like they were only suitable for indoor pursuits. Was she planning to jog around the dining room?

Her hands flew to her hair and she smoothed it back into a ponytail that was all business. The move stretched her shirt tight over what he now knew were lace-covered breasts—barely covered at that—and he imagined he saw the textured design embossing the tee's fabric. Or maybe it was a nipple that was making the push. Damn, he was staring at her nipples, now jutting like bullets through that too-thin tee. His dick jumped in acknowledgment of the imminent danger.

He set the plate down and took a step back as if he'd just served the royal personage. Not far off with that snooty look she was giving him.

"Did you cook this?" she asked, her eyes darting to the plate and back to his again. Weird. Not snooty, more like skittish.

"No, Jack did. Seems kind of plain. Do you have dietary restrictions?" The guys said she never ate with the crew, that she considered herself too above them. There was a story here.

She let out a sigh. "I'm just careful about what I eat."

Careful about what she eats, careful about a lot of things. But not in Vegas, where she had let go, opened up, got down. That boring lunch didn't suit a woman who vibrated with such barely banked passion he could feel it twenty feet across a bar.

If he had his way, he'd feed her golden-pink, butter-drenched prawns. Slices of rare roast beef covered in au jus or rich gravy. For dessert, he'd smear a decadent raspberry chocolate parfait on their bodies and they'd take turns licking each other clean like hungry kittens.

If he had his way.

"You going for a run to work up an appetite?"

That tugged one corner of her mouth up into the barest of smiles. "I was going to do some yoga." At her gesture to a mat on the floor, images of stretching, supple Cara-limbs flooded his brain.

So not helping.

"I got your note this morning," he said. "I knocked on your door last night but you weren't home." That sounded like he was interested in where she spent her time. Not interested. Not in the slightest.

"I think the note said it all," she said, passing deftly over his less-than-subtle probe as to her whereabouts. "There are two parking spots out back and you need to make sure your death machine doesn't take up both of them. I almost crashed into it."

"I'll be careful about that."

"Good." She folded her arms beneath the breasts he wanted to touch with his flour-streaked fingers. More than just his fingers. "I'm sure you're very busy," she added with a pointed eyebrow raise toward the door.

He really needed to get back to the kitchen, especially now that Jack had imposed his no-fraternizing rule. If push came to shove, he had no doubt whom Jack would choose: the family he knew over the family he didn't. Shane wasn't supposed to care about that, though, was he? He wasn't supposed to give a crap about what Jack Kilroy thought, and the idea that Jack had a problem with Shane breathing the rarified air around Lemon Tart's pretty blonde head made him feel a touch rebellious. Anyway, they had important things to discuss.

He took a seat in the red-and-white-striped armchair opposite her desk, and when she looked aghast, he draped a leg over one of the arms. She was so easy.

"We need to talk."

She opened her mouth. Closed it immediately. Surely, she wasn't going to protest a civil conversation about their situation? *The* situation.

"I googled it." She moved behind her desk, sat in one of those fancy ergonomic chairs, and flipped open her laptop. It had a pink cover that matched her sweats and the Post-it note on his door this morning, the one that had told him to move his damn bike out of her damn space before she took a damn baseball bat to it. Except it wasn't that nice.

"We can get an annulment. Just fill out a form and it can be done and dusted in about three weeks." She sounded pleased with herself, downright smug in fact. That frosted him a bit.

He stood and moved to her side of the desk, leaning against the edge. "So not a divorce, then?"

"We can get an annulment because we didn't... Well, it wouldn't have mattered if we did." She hesitated, and he could see the gears going round as she rethought her position.

"What if we did?" he asked, tamping down on the glee in his voice.

"What if we did what?"

"What if we did sleep together? What if we had sex?"

The way he said it could be construed as past sex or the promise of it. The promise of can't-walk-for-a-week good times between a man and a woman. "That wouldn't make a difference?"

"But we didn't." Her brow creased in puzzlement and horror descended to her mouth. "But we didn't," she repeated, less sure now.

He couldn't keep it up but every inch of him—every hardening inch—wished it were true. "Nah, we didn't."

"Shane!" She socked him in the side and broke into that laugh that he'd fallen in love with the minute she'd graced him with it in the third bar of the crawl. It had taken him that long to get it but it had been worth every bad joke, every cheesy pun, every flash of the dimple Aunt Jo said would be a woman's downfall. The old girl had neglected to mention it would be his downfall as well.

The laughter faded, and she turned serious again. "It wouldn't matter if we had...well, you know. People make these mistakes all the time, so they have procedures in place."

"Procedures to clean up idiotic mistakes?"

There was that crease between her brows again. She didn't like that she'd made a mistake and lost control of a situation. That was so not Cara.

"Right." But her expression didn't match the word's surety. "I'll take care of the papers, then?" she prompted with a couple of quick nods. The swallow in her throat was so pronounced it made the slender column of her neck expand. It also made him feel like prodding her some more. See how far he could take it.

"What if I don't sign?"

She shot up out of her seat, her lemon fall of hair swishing vehemently behind her head. He got a whiff of herbal shampoo and sunshine. "Why would you do that?"

"Just tell me what would happen, LT."

The nickname slipped from his lips without thinking, as if his brain had been waiting for her to get into a sexy hissy fit.

That night he had abbreviated Lemon Tart for expediency's sake and found that it suited her bossy, military-style hauteur. Lemon Tart, the Lieutenant, LT.

She wasn't so haughty or self-possessed now. Her hands flailed, at complete odds with cool Cara. The more riled she got, the more his attraction to her burned.

"Well, if one party doesn't sign, it'll still happen. It just takes longer. Six to eight weeks."

If one party doesn't sign. So cold. So clinical. He nodded, thinking about how he wanted to phrase the next sentence. The silence drew heavily between them and he worked it for a few seconds because, shit, he was starting to enjoy himself now.

"Paddy, you're not seriously thinking of not signing those papers. I mean, what would be gained from that?"

"A marriage, Cara. The marriage you wanted." He hauled in a deep breath because he had a feeling he was going to need it. "After all, this was your brilliant idea."

CHAPTER 4

Cara's brain splintered and thoughts scattered about the office. She couldn't have heard him right. Never mind the crazy accusation of who exactly was responsible for this mess, he wouldn't sign the papers. The papers that bound them together.

"But that's—that's just nuts."

Folding his arms across his chest caused his biceps to bulge indecently against the short-sleeve hems of his chef's jacket. He ignored her distress and studied the events board behind her.

"Looks like you'll be busy the next month or so." With a slow brush of his fingertip, he rubbed one of the Post-its. It took all her strength to tear her gaze away from that slow, provocative slide and the faint trace of flour he left behind.

"Did you not hear what I said? You have to sign those papers. We can't be married."

"Yet, we are."

His voice traveled low and serious through the air, landing on her with such force that she slumped in her chair. Paralyzed by his words, her body solidified into deadweight. She tried to push off from the floor and send the Aeron chair into a safer zone beyond the orbit of this lunatic Irishman. It got stuck. Her personal trainer said he'd never met a one-hundred-and-ten-pound woman with more defined muscle tone than Cara, that her feet were powerful enough to be classified as lethal weapons, but they couldn't find any traction against the plastic underlay.

"What did Uncle Aldo do?" he asked.

"What?"

He waved at the seating plan for Jack and Lili's wedding, the one that required all her diplomatic skills to ensure years of infighting and grudges didn't explode into a bloodbath. "Uncle Aldo's off to the side with what I can only assume are the rest of the troublemakers. Can't find a place for him?"

"It's a long story involving a second cousin's wife and a leg of prosciutto. He's also a butt pincher—stop trying to change the subject."

Leaving off his thousand-yard stare at the wall, he leveled her with his brown-eyed gaze. "We can't deny that it happened, Cara."

"I'm not trying to deny it, you crazy peat-bog dweller—"

"Flatterer."

Agh!

"I'm trying to deal with it," she finished. Somehow, she managed to pull herself to a stand, which had the unfortunate effect of bringing her closer to him. The smell of baking bread and virile man sent her stomach into a loop-the-loop.

"It happened for a reason," he said, in a rational tone that was starting to bug the hell out of her.

"A one-hundred-proof reason."

"Perhaps, but there had to be underlying factors, don't you think, LT?"

LT. Her silly heart went dunkity-dunk. In Vegas, he had taken her nickname and turned it into something personal and familiar between them.

He was just trying to distract her, though as to the "why" she had no earthly idea.

"You wanted to see where Paul Newman was married," she said, straining for patience. "Not Elvis or Sinatra like a normal person. Paul Newman." Cara wasn't given to broad Italian gestures of exasperation but right now, her DNA was primed and ready for an explosion.

"What we got here is a failure to communicate," he said with a faraway look in his eyes.

"Come again?"

"*Cool Hand Luke.* It's one of my favorite movies," he said, still as reasonable as all get out.

"I know. You wouldn't shut up about it until we went to the chapel."

Shane laughed, and his eyes clouded over in recollection. Crap, he was remembering something nice when she could recall only snatches. She wanted to remember everything. A girl should have some special memories from her wedding day, shouldn't she?

He sat his fine Irish ass on her desk, crumpling up her invoices. She wanted to dig her hands into that ass and push him off—so she could uncrumple those invoices, of course. His houndstooth-check pants, standard issue for the kitchen, stretched tight against his muscular thighs. Thighs that had slotted against hers in perfect symmetry when he rocked her to sleep...Huh, her cherry-picking brain remembered that all right.

"We were drunk," she said, grasping on to this undeniable fact like a shallow-rooted plant at the edge of a cliff.

"True, but you can't entirely blame the alcohol. We were upright enough to go get a license from the clerk. Which was your idea, by the way."

She shoved him hard in his surprisingly resistant chest. There he went again with the ridiculous blame game. "What an outrageous thing to say. Take that back."

There was pity in his smile. "No, I won't. You asked me to marry you and I said yes. So there must have been some part of you that wanted this to happen. That wanted us to happen. And we need to respect that."

"There is no part of me that wanted this to happen, Shane." The words sounded wrong as soon as they tumbled out. Realization stung the air around her eyes like she had blinked in a cloud of pepper spray. She fell back heavily in the chair, her outrage fizzling in the face of something she couldn't even name.

"I did ask you." *Oh God.*

He nodded once, and his eyes, soft buttons of melting chocolate, grew larger in acknowledgment of her admission.

"I had some sort of brain malfunction and asked a complete stranger to marry me."

"Yes, you did. And I'm inclined to think it's not your usual MO."

It was not. Control was her watchword. Controlling her mind, her body, her life. It got her a fair amount of ribbing from the people she knew but the perimeter she had set was enough to keep most of the barbs at bay. A necessary electric fence so she didn't spiral into the destructive behaviors that had marred her teens and twenties.

But there was something inside her, something that didn't agree with her carefully wrought life and her struggle for Zen-like balance. A part of her would always be that stupid girl primed to revolt against the strictures of her Italian family and the exacting standards she had set for herself. On the wrong side of thirty, she was a little old to be a rebel.

"I did ask you several times if you were sure," he said. "And you kept saying yes, and you seemed so enthusiastic, and well, I got swept up in it. You're a very persuasive woman when you set your mind to something."

Thinking more clearly now, she had a better explanation. By the second bar in Vegas, Shane's interest had been obvious and Gina hadn't liked it one bit.

Near in age, the cousins had never been close. They could blame it on the unfortunate incident of the peroxide and the hair curling iron that left Gina with bald patches or the countless times they'd one-upped each other with stolen clothes and fickle boyfriends. Cara's last-minute assistance with Gina's wedding should have helped to ease the tension but that wasn't enough for the toxic midget.

Her cousin's sniping had begun the moment they got on the plane after Gina had already downed several vodka tonics in the departure lounge. The jibes about how Cara wouldn't need a bachelorette party of her own so she should try to enjoy this one. How a hotshot career girl like her wouldn't need a wedding. Over the years, Cara had loaded the shotgun with her own defensive pronouncements against marriage; it just needed a few adult beverages for Gina to curl her fingers around the trigger. Outside the third or maybe fourth bar, her cousin pulled her aside and told her to lay off an eligible piece like Shane. *Give the rest of the girls a go, Cara.*

She had let a keg's worth of vodka and a few bull's-eye comments push her into doing something crazy. Something she had always craved. Normality, relationships, marriage. But only normal women get to experience these things, and that night, freak-show Cara had taken a shortcut and headed straight for the minister in the Hawaiian shirt.

She had tried to cheat fate.

Part of her had wanted to flip those bitches the bird. Not only was she getting married, but she was doing it without fanfare and before the rest of them. Before Gina.

Before Lili.

No, that couldn't be right. She couldn't possibly have done this to feel superior to Lili. Gina, perhaps, but not her baby sister, who deserved nothing but the best after everything Cara had put her through during Mom's bout with cancer. Cara beating Lili to the altar was just another example of big sis putting herself first. Was her brain so marriage-addled that she would try to upstage Lili like that?

Now, a week later, it was impossible to know what her state of mind was when she'd held hands with a cute guy and let him dimple her defenses to death. But she knew her mind now.

She wanted out.

"It was a mistake."

He leaned closer, his forehead almost touching hers, his breath warm on her cheek. "How do we know it was? Maybe it was supposed to happen this way."

She moved back, away from that knee-weakening scent of man and bread. His dimple winked at her. For God's sake, not the dimple. "Maybe we should try it on for size."

"Try what on for size?" Her voice pitched high in protest. "I don't know you. You don't know me."

"Then we get to know each other."

He was insane. Absolutely insane. And she was absolutely insane to be listening to another word out of his crazy, gorgeous mouth.

Her plain old lunch lay at the edge of the desk, cooling,

and she wanted to eat. She had a plan for expanding the events business. She had figured out how to extract herself from this insufferable situation with Shane. It was a good day and she wanted to eat.

"You're not going to sign the papers."

"Not yet."

Her heart beat like a wild thing, and she swallowed to send it a message to calm the hell down. "I'm still going to get the lawyer to draw them up." *So there.* She could print the generic forms off the Web but she'd rather get her lawyer, Marty, to handle it. There could be no loose ends.

"Go for it, LT." He skirted her desk and headed to the door, then turned and tilted his head. A delinquent lock of hair fell across his forehead and was answered by an uptick of her pulse. First the dimple, now the man-bangs. She was toast.

A gentle, yet irritating smile touched his lips. "So, what are you doing later?" His eyes flicked to the big board over her shoulder, then relocked on hers. Tonight's schedule was event-free and that crazy peat-bog dweller knew it.

"Not making my marriage work," she said sourly.

"Okay, I'll pick you up at six thirty."

* * *

Cara stepped out into the hallway of her apartment building, pondering the etiquette of canceling a date by Post-it note. Maybe it wasn't a real, honest-to-God, chance-of-nookie date but it had certainly sounded like one.

She never missed her Tuesday-night Pilates class, not even when she'd had stomach flu and the thought of contorting her body was enough to make her more ill. An office yoga session might have made up for it but she didn't even have that on today's regimen.

Damn Shane.

Her equilibrium was shot; that was certain. Left behind in Las Vegas along with her single-girl status and a very expensive pair of Christian Louboutin leopard-print pumps.

Sorry, something came up, the note said in her very neat script, penmanship Sister Mary Margaret had said was the envy of the entire school at Casimir Pulaski High. Envy of the nuns perhaps. The other kids didn't seem so envious when they pulled her hair for being so perfect. Her gaze fell to the note once more. Emily Post would not approve.

Heart thumping madly, she took another step toward Shane's apartment, only to get the fright of her life when something furry glanced by her bare legs. She looked down and saw...it.

Because it couldn't possibly be described as anything else. The sorriest bundle in the world stared back up at her, all eyes and fur and defiance. A broken, scrawny thing. Too big to be a kitten, too small to be a cat, it coughed out something plaintive from its throat, then devolved into a sneezing fit.

"Who are you?" she asked, while looking around for a possible source. There were only two apartments in the building, hers and Shane's, but sometimes the front door was known to stick. Her husband—no, her neighbor—probably left the door open, an invitation for all manner of riffraff to make themselves at home. Standards were definitely slipping.

Gingerly, she picked it up. Its eyes locked on to hers. A small, not insignificant gash on its nose appeared to be on the mend. It sneezed again, right in Cara's face, and her heart broke on the spot.

Cara didn't possess a mushy bone in her body, but lately she had felt itchily sensitive, as if a whole layer of emotion was hovering beneath her skin's surface waiting for an open vein. Or a gawky stray with missing patches of gray fur and what looked like the remnants of an alley fight marking its sad little body.

They were meant to find each other. Two creatures buffeted like corks in a cruel and unfeeling sea. She smiled to herself at that thought—she'd always had a knack for melodrama. Raising her hand purposefully, she jumped when Shane's door opened as if it had been waiting for her touch. Her world suddenly became smaller as a mess of hot male crowded her senses.

"Hey," Shane said. His gaze dipped to the package in her arms. "Ah, grand, you found him."

Him? Cara was sure he was a she. "He's yours?"

Before she could adjust, Shane extracted her charge and dropped her—or rather, him—to the floor inside his apartment.

"When I moved in, he moved in with me. Just walked in off the street and made himself at home."

Oh, definitely male, then. So much for thinking they had a connection. Pushing her disappointment down deep, she refocused on her current problem. All six feet of him.

"I was just—"

"I'm afraid this isn't going to work, Cara."

Shock froze her in place. He'd better not be canceling. "It's not?"

He made a sweeping motion with his hand that took in the line of her body, still bedecked in her gray pinstripe suit, coral silk shell, and four-inch Manolos. She'd changed from her sweats to business attire for a late-afternoon appointment with a client.

"Well, you look wonderful as always." How he could make a compliment sound apologetic, she had no idea. "But that outfit's not suitable for where we're going." He stepped into the hallway and closed the door behind him. Gripping her elbow, he gave an unsubtle push back toward her apartment. "You need to change."

"I do?" Jeez, she couldn't think straight. Only single-syllable words were making the cut today.

"Where we're going is pretty casual."

Her chest constricted at how fluidly he tossed out that word. *Casual.* There was no such thing in Cara's regimented world. Did he mean a casual bistro? The taqueria on the corner? Mickey D's?

"About that. I've already eaten and—"

"That's okay. I won't be hungry until later anyway."

Relief loosened her muscles, allowing her lungs to fill to capacity. With narrowed eyes, he assessed her crazy overreaction but didn't question it.

"For now you need to change into something more like what I'm wearing."

If that wasn't an invitation to look, she'd eat her heels. Starting at his neck, she drank him in and took her fill. A faded gray henley beneath an even more faded blue button-down shirt with sleeves rolled up to the elbows accounted for the top half. Butter-soft jeans, torn in inviting places, molded taut against his thigh muscles, reminding her of how they had cradled her while they slept the sleep of the dumbass ten days ago. The outfit was topped off, or bottomed out, by those cowboy boots he must take showers in. She knew for a fact that not even his wedding night was worthy of their removal. They looked like they were ready to split where the soles met the uppers, their mileage competing with the rips in his denim for supremacy.

"I don't think I have anything like what you're wearing," she said seriously.

He stalked her and she backed into her apartment like a sleepwalker.

"Just throw on some jeans and meet me out back. I'll give you five minutes." He turned to leave, then double-backed with a jaunty turn similar to his dance steps at Gina's wedding. She loved how he moved. It was the first thing she had noticed about him as they walked down the Sunset Strip. A loose-limbed insouciance, lithe grace in every sinuous stride, so languid she wondered how he stayed upright.

His dig into his pocket pulled her gaze to his burrowing hand. He passed something off, brushing his fingers with hers. An electric shock sizzled through her as her hand closed over a small metal object, still warm from its heated cocoon.

"My spare key." From her other hand, he extracted the crumpled Post-it note and scanned it. "Something's come up all right."

Without waiting for a reply, he bounded off down the stairs to the street. He made a lot of noise while doing it, too.

Lithe grace? Ooh, that clodhopper had some nerve.

Fifteen minutes later—it had taken her only six minutes to change, but she sat on her sofa for nine—she walked around back, clad in Rock and Republic dark wash stuffed into calf-length red cowboys with a stacked heel. She'd countrified her white waffle weave Oxford by turning up the sleeves and tying the shirttails at her midriff.

Shane leaned against the hood of her royal blue BMW Z4 roadster, giving it a wary examination. On her approach, his gaze swept over her, making her tingle.

"You look beautiful," he said in a tone Barry White might want back.

"Thanks," she murmured, as if she'd never heard it before, and in a way, she hadn't. Not like that. When Shane said it, the compliment sounded new and meaningful. That Irish accent had a lot to answer for.

Stepping away from her car, he plucked a helmet from the seat of his death trap, known in some circles as a motorcycle.

"Put this on."

She gave the helmet her most dismissive glance. "I don't think so."

"You can't ride the bike without it."

"Fine by me. I have no intention of riding that thing. My cousin Tad has one and he's already wiped out twice on it."

"I'm not your cousin." He delivered an insolent grin, making it clear that they were in no way related, at least not by blood, and her stomach fluttered madly. More likely, the thought of placing that steel time bomb between her thighs was making her jumpy.

The motorcycle, she insisted. *The motorcycle.*

"We can take my car," she said, thumbing behind her.

He looked unimpressed. "It's cute, like you. But I'm not riding in a girl's car." Before she could muster a response, he placed the helmet over her head. Its heaviness stopped her in her tracks.

"I know it's probably a touch big, but you should be okay." He adjusted the strap, his knuckles brushing against the underside of her chin.

She gestured to the bike again, feeling discombobulated by the weight on her head and the nearness of him and, oh yeah, the fact that she was headed out on a date with her husband. The means of transport seemed like the least of her problems.

"I've never done this before," she said, having no clue to what she was referring. The motorbike, the man, the marriage.

His fingers grazed her jaw. "Don't worry, LT. I'll take care of you."

The sincerity in his voice and his use of that nickname brought back the flutter. Well, it had never left, but now it felt like her stomach housed a swarm of butterflies attacking a mango. He straddled the bike, and her body fired in appreciation at how his jeans stretched tight over his most excellent ass.

Cut that one out, frame it, stick it in the Art Institute.

He threw a glance over his shoulder, and his lips hooked up at one corner. Because she had been noticing his assets and he had noticed that she noticed.

"You ready to have fun?"

"I don't know."

He grinned broadly. "That's my girl."

* * *

Cara gave a cautious sniff. There must be some rule that said all church basements had to smell like musty socks, as if the nuns' revenge was to be derelict in their duty to keep the parish priest in fresh, laundered smalls.

"Shane!"

A unified cry of mixed voices went up *Cheers*-style as soon as they descended from the last step into a large room, poorly lit and uncomfortably stifling. The solitary box fan in the corner wasn't fooling anyone.

On the fifteen-minute drive, Shane had told her nothing about where they were going, though conversation would have been pointless as they zoomed down Western Avenue. Between the fact she couldn't hear the sound of her own thoughts (good) and all her must-not-die energy was focused on holding on to his strong, tight torso (excellent), small talk didn't seem to be on the menu. Something far more terrifying was, though.

"You've got to be kidding," she muttered, wondering

to which particular hell she should attribute the jellied shake in her legs. The wobbliness could be from the most exhilarating thrill ride she'd ever taken while molded to Shane's body at unsafe speeds through the city streets. But it could just as easily be laid at the feet of the sight before her.

Shane had brought her to a line-dancing class.

Her date was already making the rounds with the other dancers, a strange mix of young and old, and by the sounds of it, mostly foreign. Everyone had an accent or spoke another language, and there seemed to be a preponderance of ladies compared to men.

From the preponderance, a squeal went up. "Shane! I got you a present."

Shane ducked his head in that aw-shucks way he had that Cara was no longer buying. "Maisey, you didn't have to do that."

Maisey. One of the servers at Sarriette and Shane's enthusiastic dance partner at Gina's wedding over the weekend. The effervescent Maisey, with her purple-punk coif, a cut-off top that revealed taut cheerleader abs, and a denim skirt that barely skimmed her pert ass, drew a cowboy hat from behind her back and put it on Shane's head.

"Ah, that's just perfect." Toothy grin flashing, he pulled it down over his brow and rocked back on his heels. Stroking the brim, his eyes crinkled with joy. Something darkly feminine curdled in Cara's gut.

"Hi, Cara," Maisey said, as if she'd just noticed her. "I wouldn't think this is your kind of thing."

"Oh, I'm game for anything," Cara said. *And I've got more game than you, little girl.*

"Well, it's great to see you joining in," Maisey added, the dig about Cara's propensity to keep to herself at the

restaurant not lost on her. "Though our Shane could probably persuade the dogs off the meat truck."

Shane's grin stretched wide, taking in both of them, and
Cara balled her hands into fists. In her office today, there
had been tungsten behind his cute smile, and again when
he dictated their manner of transport. While the female
of the species had more leeway in the realm of contrary
behavior, no woman wanted that in a man. If she was in
the market for a man—a big *if*—she would want a clear-
cut, straight shooter who didn't play games, not a guy who
confused the hell out of her with his farm-boy demeanor
one minute and his rip-roaring certainty the next. He was
both the good cop and the bad cop in one delicious law en-
forcement package. And now that he had the hat, he was
rocking small-town sexy sheriff.

Go easy on me, Officer Shane. It's my first offense.

"I can't believe you brought me here," she gritted out
while they rattled through the introductions. *Padma. Kumar.
Vladimir. Esme.*

"If I'd told you, would you have come?"

Maybe. "Probably not."

Roberto and Corinne. No, Corina.

Shane flashed that cocksure grin. "I get the impression
you don't have a lot of fun."

Taken aback, she fought to keep her defensiveness in
check. "I have fun. I have plenty of fun. You don't want to
say that to a woman whose body could crush you."

Introductions abandoned, his gaze made a lazy trip down
the body she claimed was lethal. "It could?"

"Hell, yeah. My kickboxing skills are legendary."

A short, ruddy-faced man with a pink fringed shirt and
a ten-gallon hat was fiddling with a boom box, sending out
tinny snatches of country. Good grief.

"What else do you do when you're not kicking the crap out of people, LT?" Shane asked.

Her volunteer work at Lurie's Children's Hospital took up most of her spare time, but it was too special to share with anyone even if that anyone was a someone like her husband. Not even her family was any the wiser.

"I work a lot so I don't have time for hobbies."

"Except kickboxing."

"And spin class, Pilates, yoga."

"So all your leisure pursuits involve the gym?"

Leisure? That made it sound as though she enjoyed herself, which wasn't right at all. The gym was a studio, her body was a project, and every class she took brought her closer to the goal of perfection. Working out fed that primal need while reading to the gorgeous kids on the sixteenth floor at Lurie's fed something deeper. Her soul. Between those pursuits and reforging the connection to her family, she had no time for anything else.

Especially dates with her husband.

"I like to keep in shape. You have your…" She gestured around the room and swallowed her rising panic. People were starting to line up in a rather professional manner. By now, she should be used to feeling like the odd one out but each new situation produced its own difficulties. "I have a personal trainer."

"There are better outlets for your energy." Shane's fingers brushed against her elbow as he nudged her a few inches to his right. She pretended it didn't send a blood-hot rush through her. Sure she did.

Cara had never encountered a man with such a devastating effect on her body. With that torrent of sexual awareness came heat that seeped into her skin and warmed her muscles, making her feel protected. This was how she had felt when they had collapsed in a drunken heap on the bed of his hotel room in Vegas. With Shane she felt horny *and* safe.

Her mind blurred in confusion and she turned to eye the position of the dance line behind them. They were right up front, which meant everyone had a prime-seat view of how many steps she was going to mess up. Ten years of ballet was probably not going to help. Why hadn't she signed up for those Zumba classes?

"I thought you just moved here. How come you're Mr. Popular?"

"Took my first class last week after Maisey invited me. Everyone's so friendly. It's a great way to meet people." He smiled, a slow burn that made her light-headed. She should have had a yogurt before she came out. "It can be tough in a new city."

It can be tough in an old city, too.

He thumbed the brim of his hat, and a secret smile played on his lips. Cara's insides turned pea green with the knowledge of how much pleasure the perky Maisey's gift had given him.

"You know you look ridiculous, right?" Her heart sank at the emergence of her inner mean girl. She could never stay down for long.

"Why thank you, darlin'," he said with a twang that went straight to the fork of her legs. The music started, an up-tempo number worthy of some hootin' and hollerin' from the cheap seats behind her. She could have sworn she heard a "Howdy, partner" in a thick, Indian accent.

Shane turned on that cornpone grin, cocked his head, and took a step to his right.

"Let's dance."

CHAPTER 5

Shane didn't consider himself a good dancer. He tended to forget the steps or lose himself in the music's beat so completely that there'd been times he started out with a partner at a club and then found himself spinning alone like a gobshite by the closing bars. Most women preferred their dance partner's undivided attention so his lack of focus on what he was told was the true purpose of dancing with a woman—make her look good—usually resulted in a hissy fit or worse. Like a glass of Southern Comfort and 7 Up in the face. That shit stings.

But line dancing wasn't like real dancing at all. Even Kumar was rocking the Casbah like nobody's business and if an old Pakistani bloke with a turban could get the hang of it, anyone could.

Except Cara.

She was hands down the most elegant, poised, knock-him-over-and-call-him-Stanley woman he'd ever met but she couldn't dance for toffee. He'd turn to the left and she'd turn to the right. He'd bend at the hip, only to see her pitch forward precipitously and then right herself with a surreptitious glance to see if anyone had spotted her.

Shane couldn't help but spot her. He had been spotting her all night, from the minute she'd walked out in those jeans that fit her like snakeskin. If he'd thought she looked good in yoga sweats or tight little skirts, she owned him in those jeans. And then there was that white shirt she'd hitched up over her belly button. It billowed like a breezy sail around her slender frame and when the light caught it just right as she gave a wobbly turn, he could see her breasts' silhouette framed like a truck's mud flap cameo.

She was trying, though. Lord, how she was. Her teeth dragged along her plump bottom lip that looked kiss-swollen without being kissed. A patch of perspiration on her forehead broadcast her effort. The heat of her skin had gotten all jumbled up with her perfume, creating a brand-new floral-hot woman scent that drew his body in with every pivot.

He'd only asked her out to rile her up, see if he could crack that cool façade of hers. In her office, he had spouted some claptrap about alcohol giving fate a helping hand. Neither of them had bought it, but the minute he'd seen her cradling the bloody cat in her arms, a certainty about the unabashed rightness of it had conjured up strange weather patterns in his brain. That night in Las Vegas, he had experienced hope for the first time in forever, and now, with Cara at his side, his gut bubbled with it again. After years of feeling like his existence was one big old mistake, how could a drunken lurch down the aisle feel so right?

"How're you holding up there?" he asked, sending her a look that he hoped she understood. The one that said they could leave at any time. He might even have meant a little more by it. She wanted out of the marriage and forcing her to maintain this charade as a prop to his self-esteem was the ultimate in dick moves.

Her tight smile broke into a wider one and his mind flipped like a flapjack. Damn, he was going to push his luck as far as he could because that blast of winter sun was worth it. And while pushing his luck, he'd push his guilt about his dishonesty down deep.

The instructor, Big Mac, who was actually five foot nothing and not in any way deserving of the moniker, came over to see how his child-sized hands could be of service.

"Quick turn, sugar," he said with both hands on Cara's hips. She quick turned her way out of his grasp like she'd been scalded. Good thing, too, because Shane was about ready to deck the little shit.

"I just don't have any rhythm," she said with a wide-eyed stare of sky blue that hit Shane in the chest with the force of a cannon ball.

"Everyone has rhythm, sugar."

"It might be better if I could stand farther back and see how other people are doing it. When I'm looking at you, I'm just seeing it done backward," she said to Big Mac. "No offense. Sugar."

"Let's head to the back row, darlin'," Shane said in his best cowboy. It sounded pretty damn good, actually.

She arched one skeptical brow. "Back row? You trying to take advantage of me?"

"Any chance I get."

That drew her singular laugh, a naughty giggle that warmed him through and made him wish he was funnier. With a quick pivot, she was already barreling to the back of the room, leaving him no choice but to follow her.

As they started up again, she watched the line in front,

her focus avidly trained on their feet. "Hey, look, I've got it," she said, starting on the wrong foot. "Oh, don't look."

A deep laugh rumbled through him. "Ah, you were so close."

He loved that she wasn't giving up, the unexpectedness of it. It took a lot to surprise him and Cara had managed to surprise him. More of that, please.

"Do you mind if I..." He sidestepped behind her.

"Be my guest," she murmured, but he was already fanning her waist with his hands, her girth so narrow that his fingers almost met at her navel. She released a little whooshing sound that he felt in his groin—maybe he had surprised her, too. The complicated-looking braid in her hair had flopped to one side, leaving the slender column of her neck exposed, her pulse pumping out that sexy scent that made him glad he was holding on to her. He was supposed to be teaching her about balance but was having a hard time maintaining his own.

"Bend as you place your right foot forward," he said in an unintentionally husky tone.

"Like this?" She pitched forward, and her stellar arse smashed right into his stiffening dick. *Yeah, exactly like that.*

"More like this." He placed his hand on her belly, his other on her spine, and pushed her over a couple of inches. "Not at such an angle. No need to jerk so much."

"Hm," she hummed, sending his balls into red alert. Just that beautiful little sound, low in her throat, and he was a goner. They were in a church basement with a host of people learning to dance and all he could think about was slipping his twitching fingers below the waistband of those second-skin jeans until they were clamped by her tight, wet—

"Shane?"

"Yeah?"

She twisted her swanlike neck so his lips brushed against her cheek. Painfully late, he realized that his entire body was flush against hers, but especially the harder-than-concrete part barely contained by an overworked zipper.

He pulled back, unable to let go completely. Not yet. "You got it?"

"I think so," she said, a smile in her voice. A few more tries, without his favorite part meeting his favorite part of hers, and she seemed to be getting the hang of it. They separated and returned to the line.

"Thanks for being so patient," she said with a slice of brightness that boosted his heart through to the church nave above their heads. "I know I'm not the easiest student."

"No problem. We'll teach each other."

* * *

"Bye, beautiful Cara."

"Oh, bye..."

"Kumar," Shane whispered.

"Kumar," Cara called out to the elderly, but surprisingly spry gentleman with the moves like Jagger.

The rest of the class trickled out on a wave of burbling chatter and laughter, leaving Cara with Shane and a few stragglers. She couldn't believe how much fun she'd had tonight, and she owed it all to Shane's patience and good humor. No one knew better than Cara how difficult she was to be around, how uptight she was. He brought out a part of her she'd forgotten existed or maybe had never existed. The part that didn't care how she looked or what people thought of her. More important, she hadn't needed alcohol to get here.

She turned back to Shane, who, in that Stetson, looked every inch a Nashville god only to find him locked in Maisey's tractor beam. Perk-in-boots laid her fingertips on his chest every time he said something funny—well, it wasn't all that funny but she thought Shane was Mr. Hilarious. That he did nothing to resist Maisey's charms didn't escape Cara's notice either.

"We're all going for a bite to eat," Maisey said to the small group remaining, but her gaze never left Shane. She gave her eyelashes an extra vehement batting. "You said last week you wanted to try Sunita's Kitchen up on Devon Avenue."

Shane's eyes brightened as Cara's heart sank. "Right, they do that head-blowing red curry everyone raves about. The one that's supposed to make you blind."

"Better you go blind doing that than something else," Maisey said with a bedroom giggle.

He gave a warm smile in response. *Oh, come on.*

Encouraged, Maisey turned on a high-wattage grin and tilted her head up to her target. It was incremental but he moved his body slightly in Cara's direction, and she couldn't resist a mental high-five. Shades of high school all over again.

"Oh, you should come, too, Cara," Maisey conceded. No flies on her.

"What do you think? Danced up an appetite?" He laid his hand at the base of Cara's spine, sending a heated flush across her body. His gaze held hers steady, but as the seconds ticked by, panic evicted pleasure and took up residence in every cell.

This was usually the point in the proceedings where things turned tricky. Maybe if it was just the two of them, she could muddle through, but she was no good in groups. All that "try this" and "split this." Wondering if people were judging how she looked when she chewed or why she had eaten only a third of what was on her plate. Plus, Indian

food was so far outside her wheelhouse that she'd undoubtedly make a fool of herself. Best to cut off the inevitable
weirdness about sharing a meal, that eminently normal ritual, the cornerstone of dating and relationships. A normalcy
she could never hope to attain.

"I don't really like spicy food, and I have some work to
do at home. You go ahead."

He hesitated just enough to send Cara's heart to crypt
level, but then his innate manners kicked in and he turned
back to Maisey with a tip of his hat. "Next time perhaps."

"Shane, you should stay." Cara made a move to the door,
every step like she was dragging through treacle. Evidently,
he wanted to head out with the bubbly, interested, *normal*
Maisey.

Behind her, she heard Maisey murmur, "Too stuck-up to
eat with the help."

*Cara, you stupid, stupid girl. Did you think it would be
that easy?*

Unable to stop her shaking, she pushed through the exit
and arrowed for the steps up to the street. *Run away, freak,
run away.* Hot blood pounded in her ears and drowned out
everything around her.

Except the harshness of her name on the warm night air.

She felt her neck prickle. With one foot on the lowest
step, she turned and her breath trapped in her lungs at the
sight of Shane silhouetted in the doorway, still wearing
that hat slung low over his face. Gone was the boyish expression and playfulness. His face was hard, his jaw rigid,
his gaze burning into her like a brand. Back to that other
personality, the one that projected intensity and strength
beyond his years. No matter, he would never be old enough
for her.

"Don't walk away like that," he said, sharp enough to

slice through her like a blade. "I thought you had a good time."

"I did," she pushed out. "I have to leave."

"Is Maisey right, then?" Closer now, his body eclipsed the light from the hallway. His hat eclipsed his expression, but she knew without seeing that his eyes were wide with something. Anger, perhaps. "Are you too stuck-up to eat with your coworkers?"

Her mouth had stopped working, but who needed words when he continued to talk. To needle.

"Or maybe you just want to be alone with me. Is that it, Cara?" Amusement enriched his tone, as if he didn't quite believe what he was saying.

Finally, she found her voice. "Sounds like you need a ladder to get over yourself, Doyle."

He smiled, seemingly pleased at her answer but then tension crossed his mouth again so quickly she almost stepped back. With one long stride, he closed the gap between them.

"I think I know what the problem is."

She'd bet dollars to doughnuts he had no clue, but she held her breath all the same.

"You're hiding, Cara. There's something happening here and you're scared because it doesn't fit into that neat box you've constructed. You thought you got the lid back on after Vegas but now the edges are straining and what you're feeling in here"—he touched her forehead, then coasted his fingertip down her cheek, her jaw, her neck until he reached the top button of her shirt—"and in here is too big for that box."

"Let me go," she said, the words out of her mouth before she realized how ridiculously melodramatic they sounded. As if he were somehow keeping her prisoner on this step in this quasi-relationship. She was free to leave any time.

Then why couldn't she move?

She backed up, but her heel caught on the step, and her vision filled with a wide-brimmed hat and shining brown eyes. Warm fingers hooked around the bare band of skin between her shirt and her jeans. His scent settled inside her, smoking through her blood.

Please, oh, please.

"Don't hide from me, darlin'. I'll just find you." He brought his mouth down on hers and stole her breath, balance, and any chance she had of keeping that lid screwed on tight.

His tongue stroked hers hungrily, an insistent push that left her greedy for more. Had they kissed when they got married? Surely she would have remembered this warmth, this color, this feeling. Surely she would have remembered the bristled rough around his lips sparking her to life. Whatever happened, its imprint was lost in a sea of competing tastes and sounds from that craziest of nights. Now, she had time to savor, to taste, to enjoy a true consummation of hunger, unlike anything she ever felt for food. Who needed a full stomach when her heart was brimming to ripeness in Shane's kiss?

Her improved dance moves stood her well as she pushed him back into the stairwell and then flipped against the wall of the church, the support of the brick necessary until the anchor of his body could kick in and hold her fast. Their slanting mouths twisted, mapping untrodden paths of pleasure. The push and pull of tongue-on-tongue ramped up her desire. His hard body pressed against her, slotting in from neck to knee, and she almost cried out at its perfect symmetry.

Skin. She needed to feel it. Just to check if those hard muscles contouring that henley were as defined as they looked. Yanking up his shirt, she trailed her hands across his abs and a corresponding thrill trailed across her skin as his stomach tautened under her touch. Maybe those abs were tight before but she liked to think her fingers were giving his muscles a nice workout.

At her exploration, he groaned a deep, chest-filling sound, which she took as an invitation to take things to the next level. Gripping his shirt, she tugged it higher. The shadows kept him safe from her grasping eyes, so her imagination filled in the blanks. Not an inch of fat marred that terrain. Her investigations ended at his nipples, already erect, inviting her to rub and stroke. And lick. Bending, she flicked her tongue across one stiffening bud.

So maybe she'd skipped a couple of levels.

Her gaze crept up to meet his, now trained on her mouth just scant millimeters from his chest. He was holding his breath, a forever breath she recognized because she was holding one, too. His tongue skated across his lower lip, a little puffy after their kiss.

"Please," he rasped, needful and low.

Her hot mouth sealed over his nipple and sucked, her ears alert for his reaction, needing to know this felt good to him. When both his hands cupped the back of her neck and held her fast, she knew he liked it. When a very male sound escaped his throat, one he had been clearly shoving deep, she knew he loved it.

"Your mouth, Cara. God, your mouth."

Now she knew he was hitching a ride to heaven right with her.

His rough fingers massaged the nape of her neck, and she moaned. And he moaned, a sound so heartfelt she felt its pulse between her legs. A feedback loop of pleasure. Gently, he drew her back and shaped her head to his palm, directing her up to face him. He was smiling, a big crescent of a grin. Making a guy smile during an intimate moment was not part of her usual skill set.

"Do you like that?" She'd always been a get-it-in-triplicate kind of girl.

His smile stretched wider. "You have no idea."

Oh, she did. Good thing she was wearing a dark-rinse jean because her panties were so drenched she could feel the damp. He brought her in for a kiss, a long plundering one. Her blood bubbled like champagne. Drunk on him, her senses lurched toward chaos. Just like in Vegas, except tonight, there was no alcohol to blame, only an acute case of dirty lust outside a church.

Yes, she was on a fast train to hell.

Suddenly aware of the shocking inappropriateness of her behavior, her brain crashed and she pulled away, but it got her nowhere except the brick wall behind her. He was on her again, possessing her mouth, destroying her for all others. It was madness. Pure, unbridled madness, and she loved every second of it.

The basement door flew open, casting a wedge of light that penetrated Cara's eyelids and forced her eyes open. Shane pushed her farther into the shadow of the stairwell just as a few class stragglers emerged, walking slowly up the steps before stopping to laugh about something. Cara recognized Maisey's giggle.

Her head was crammed into Shane's hard chest, her hand trapped at his navel as six feet of rock-hard muscle covered her like a granite curtain. They were exposed—a look their way would reveal their position—but Cara felt strangely safe. She managed to inch her head up until it was nestled in the crook of Shane's shoulder. His breathing was serrated, and his abs pulsed in time with her heart. Against her hip, she felt the ridge of his erection. Maybe she could...no. Stop that.

She slipped her free hand into his back pocket, not because she was worried he might move away from her but because it was either that or she was going to cup his cock. The muscles of his hot Irish ass flexed against her palm. He drew his head back and gave her an eyebrow hitch of *naughty, naughty*. The voices faded out as she focused on his eyes, still big and lust-blown under the shade of his hat.

Unable to stop herself, she licked his throat. It was crazy, but that train had run express and she was only human. His skin tasted of salt and bread, man and desire. She could live here, be happy here, feel safe here. Alternating between kisses and licks, she moved her mouth and tongue over that rough swatch of territory and claimed it for her own.

All hail the conquering Cara.

He was struggling not to react, his throat convulsing under the velvet nap of her tongue. But he must have figured that the prospect of discovery was so arousing that it was worth it to play at her game. She had just registered the growing thickness of his erection as it stroked her hip when he brushed the side of her breast and rolled her already-primed nipple with his thumb.

It was so intimate. So sensual. So intimate and sensual that she moaned her approval.

"Hello?" One of the chatty trio on the steps turned in their direction. "Oh, sorry."

Maisey's mouth gaped as she took in the scene before her. Lit by the overhead security light, a flush of garish color rose to her cheeks. Shane stepped out of Cara's grasp and his loud swallow cut through the silence. He pulled his shirt down to cover his exposed skin.

"Oh, it's okay." Maisey backed away, stumbled a little, and Cara felt a twinge of guilt. Only a twinge. She already had enough baggage; she wasn't going to take on any more. She almost wished Maisey had blundered in while she was in full-on Vampira mode.

Cara, you are an evil, evil girl.

Maisey disappeared up the steps to the street with her friends following close behind.

"Ah, shit," Shane said, adjusting his hat. "We upset her."

Cara supposed she should be glad he wasn't a complete asshole who cared nothing for the hurt feelings of a burgeoning crush, but she had never been one for conventional thinking. "She'll get over it."

A shadow crossed his face. "Yeah, I know."

"Do you want to go after her?"

That hesitation again. "No, of course not. I don't like to upset anyone, that's all."

She was mad to think this could work. That a toxic cynic like her could be right for a nice guy like Shane. His easygoing charm would only last so long in the face of her unbending personality.

"You and Maisey would make a cute couple. All that perk with your farm-boy shit."

Pulse accelerating, she pushed him aside and clattered up the steps. A block east would take her to Broadway and a plethora of cabs and, most important, away from *him*. Panic clawed at her insides, fear sucker punching the confident woman who had almost jumped a hot guy's bones outside a church. Because that wasn't really her, was it? It was a facsimile, a hopped-up-on-hormones version who was letting her body call the shots again. Pleasure and guilt went hand in hand. If her body wanted it, then it was one hundred percent bad for her.

Indulging in Shane might make her feel good, but those empty calories would be a killer.

She scurried toward the busy street up ahead, praying Maisey wasn't lying in wait behind a car with a tire iron.

A strong hand landed on her waist.

"Cara," Shane said, turning her back the way she had come. "Talk to me."

"About what?"

"About what you're thinking."

Oh, he didn't want to know what she was thinking. Guys pretended they did but they couldn't handle a woman's truth. "I can't do this again."

"Which? The dancing or me?"

"Both."

His hand splayed on her denim-clad hip, sending a dangerous ripple of pleasure through her. Could he not feel the sharpness of her bones jutting like a coat hanger through the rough fabric? Did he not realize that stroking her, no matter how gentle, might slash him to pieces? She was a barbed weapon, hazardous to the touch, a danger to anyone who dared to come close. And yet, when he had kissed her and held her in his arms, she didn't feel the awkwardness that accompanied every fumble with previous guys. She felt those barbs inside her retracting, her body blooming into a voluptuousness she had never experienced with anyone else.

Shane's hands scared the hell out of her.

He cocked his head, still magnificent in that hat. "Did you have fun tonight?"

"Yes—"

"So you have something against fun?"

"No—"

"You had fun tonight but you'd hate to repeat the experience?"

What did he want from her, other than to torture her and make her feel like the worst kind of fool? A woman who had no control over her life, a woman so needy she had jumped at a guy who was all wrong for her. Not that any guy was right for her. With all her hang-ups, she couldn't inflict her crazy on any guy.

She let go of a long, dramatic sigh. It seemed easiest all round to play up her worst qualities. Cara, the princess. Cara, the Lemon Tart. Best to push him away so he understood what he was dealing with and that she was doing him a huge favor.

"Shane, I'm trying to let you down gently. You're just not my type. There's no future here, so let's not drag it out."

A slow, good ole boy Texan nod was his response or maybe she was just reading into it because of the stupid, sexy hat. "Is this about Maisey?"

She coughed out a mirthless laugh. "Oh, Irish, that's cute. You think I'm jealous."

"Well, you were sending her the stink eye, LT. Got any gypsy in you?" He was laughing at her now, not outright but she could hear the mockery warming his voice.

"I was not sending her the stink eye. Believe me, if I was, she'd know it." Damn, that sounded like she was jealous. "This should never have happened. None of it should ever have happened." Over his shoulder, she spotted a cab on a crawl-by to Broadway and she stuck her arm out. With shaky fingers and a couple of tries she got the car door open.

He held the door, blocking her entry. "Cara, I know you think I took advantage of you in Las Vegas—"

"I'm going to stop you right there." She pressed her hand against his chest, then curled it into a ball because the flat of her palm felt unaccountably intimate against all that vitality.

He was as hard as Sheetrock. Sheetrock with wonderfully sensitive nipples.

Stop. It.

"No one takes advantage of me," she said, smoothing her voice to a businesslike tone. "I cannot be played. You're not the first mistake I've made and I can guarantee you won't be the last, but I'm owning it and now I want to move on. It happened and we can un-happen it. It doesn't say anything about who we are or who we want to be or what we mean to each other."

A strange look passed over his face, as if he had come across a puzzle that needed to be solved. He needn't bother. She couldn't figure herself out; she certainly didn't need someone to "understand" her.

"Are you trying to convince me or yourself?" he asked.

She had no answer for that, or more likely, she was just tired. It had been a long couple of weeks. She slipped by him into the cab, careful to avoid his hard body. Through the window, her eyes lifted unavoidably to that brute streak of male with his arms crossed over that sturdy chest, scene of her last meal.

He continued to stare at her in a way that made her uncomfortable. Usually that was her job, eroding the balance of the enemy so she could stay on top. She didn't like this new feeling, this squall of unease whenever she was with him. She especially didn't like that he no longer felt like the enemy.

She tried not to watch him in the cab's rearview mirror as they pulled away but even now, the sight of him riveted her. He didn't move an inch, as though the act of waiting for her to drive away was some statement of intent. A refusal to back down. She wished he would because she wanted the decision to be taken away from her. Let Shane make his choice—let him confirm hers—so Cara wouldn't have to consider it.

But when you let outside forces determine your decisions, you may as well not bother getting up in the morning. For years, she viewed herself as a number: on a scale, a measuring tape, a clothing tag. The tyranny of digits, the bane of every woman's existence, but especially Cara, who had had lived her life as a constant negotiation.

When I lose another ten pounds, I'll have more friends. When my waist is twenty-two inches, I'll find a man to love me. When I'm thin, I'll finally be happy.

Bargaining for perfection had gotten her nowhere. Negotiating was for losers. Today, she was healthy, more secure in herself than she'd felt in years, maybe not entirely content but she had the means to grasp it. Not by being married to some guy she'd met ten minutes ago but by changing the terms going forward. She whipped out her phone and did what she should have done the moment that early morning Nevada sun had streaked across her pillow.

Her first call went to voice mail. And the second. She tried again until she got through to a human, though that was debatable. Insert lawyer joke here.

"Marty, I have a legal problem I need taken care of yesterday."

CHAPTER 6

Cara accepted her award for parallel parking queen on a busy residential street in Andersonville, steps from Lake Michigan on the city's far north side, and braced herself for the afternoon ahead. Sunday lunch at Casa DeLuca. Oh, joy.

She had read somewhere once that those we most love are the most alien to us, and nowhere did this seem truer than when she spent time with her family. That she loved them, she had no doubt. That they loved her, she didn't question. She just never felt like she measured up.

Led by her nose, she entered the kitchen and was greeted by a whole lot of doing. Her father and Jack stood at the stove, arguing over how best to divvy up the burners so as to ensure everything would be ready at the same time. Aunt Sylvia busied herself coating a cookie sheet with olive oil for the pillows of gnocchi. Stuffed with asiago cheese if her senses served. Off in the corner, Lili furtively picked at something on the granite countertop. Cara didn't need X-ray vision to know what her sister was up to—she was sneaking surreptitious bites of Jack's truffle-oil focaccia. Cara smiled. Some things never changed.

"Hi, Cara." A willowy blonde carrying an even blonder child shuffled into her orbit. Jack's sister Jules. She offered the beatific smile she used to calm the world around her and Cara found herself responding with a press-on grin. They weren't particularly close. Jules's particular brand of helplessness held little appeal for Cara. She liked to play the victim, wearing her single motherhood like a badge of honor and wrapping everyone around her little finger, including Cara's parents, who had taken her in when she crashed a taping of Jack's show at DeLuca's Ristorante. The one Cara was producing at the time.

She'd since made herself at home, a perfect substitute daughter for the DeLucas. A soft, fertile version of their oldest one. It was bad enough Cara felt like an outsider with her food-obsessed family, standing next to Jules always made her seem…less. But Cara had a soft spot for Jules's six-month-old son, Evan, who invariably left her reeling and broody.

"He's getting so big," Cara said, surprised at the tremor in her voice. She stroked his wispy hair gently, absorbing his breathy sigh and sighed back at how her body morphed into this tower of need around children. Since moving back to Chicago, there had been moments when she thought anything was possible—a relationship, a child, a future— but every step forward was met with two steps back, reminding her that she wasn't normal enough to expect those things. A woman who was holding on to the ledge by her impeccably manicured fingernails could hardly be expected to provide adequate care and sustenance for a helpless parcel of humanity. Her hips were made for Prada, not for childbearing.

Which is why she really shouldn't have asked, "Could I hold him?"

"Oh, please," Jules said, her London accent dragging the words into a singsong. "He's getting so heavy."

Handoff made, Cara enjoyed a moment's bliss as the infant's scent washed over her, leaving all the kitchen smells in the dust. Evan burrowed in the crook of her neck and Cara knew if she was taken now, she'd die in ecstasy.

At Jules's curious expression, Cara realized that Evan had caused her world to come to a standstill and several moments had passed when she should be carrying on some sort of adult conversation.

The younger girl bit down on her lip. "I know you work a lot but if you have a night free—"

"I'd be happy to babysit anytime," Cara cut in, far too quickly. "If you ever need to get out of the house, don't hesitate to ask."

"Thanks for offering, but actually, I was thinking about the two of us going out some time. Just you and I," Jules said, her green-gold eyes smiling. "Us single girls have to stick together."

Stifling her surprise, Cara swallowed hard. Whatever would they talk about? Who was the blondest of them all? However, Jules lived with Jack and Lili, and if she had to witness that love fest every day, she probably deserved a night out. "Sure, let's do that. I'll text you."

Jules's face clouded over. "Might be better to call. I'm not big on texting."

Weird, but whatever. Cara nodded and then felt her lips shaping a grin at the sight of another blonde, lately arrived from the backyard where lunch would be served beneath shady linden trees.

Though several inches taller than her mother, Cara mirrored her in coloring with golden-girl northern Italian looks. All evidence of Francesca's bout with cancer a couple of years back had been relegated to the past now that her hollows had filled out and her hair had long since grown back, but Cara's heartstrings still plucked with guilt every time she saw her. There had never been any recrimination from her parents over Cara's fade-out during that awful time, only understanding that no two responses to fear are the same. Lili's was the correct response, of course. The Italian response. Her baby sister had dutifully accepted the mantle of caring for their mother, running the restaurant, and absorbing Il Duce's dictatorial moods. Between the sisters, a strained truce had been reached but it could be better. With the wedding, Cara would make it better.

"Cara, ciao," Mom said with a warm embrace that took in Evan. When her mother pulled away, she had somehow managed to extricate Evan at the same time. Woman was as tricky as they come. "I've got him, *tesoro*. He'll spit up all over your lovely blouse."

"Oh, I don't mind," Cara murmured to deaf ears. Evan was already comfortably nestled on Francesca's hip, clearly used to his de facto nonna's ample curves. Poor child was probably glad to get away from Cara's bag-of-antlers sharpness.

Speaking of sharp, her mother's gaze honed in on the bottle of Syrah Cara had placed on the sideboard.

"Californian," she said in the same disappointed tone she might use to describe overcooked linguine. "You know your father won't approve."

"Let's see," Tad jumped in, taking the bottle and applying his eagle-eyed scrutiny to it. Steward of the DeLuca Ristorante wine cellar, her cousin was never afraid to wow everyone with his erudition. "Good choice, Cara. One day,

Uncle Tony will have to admit that it's possible the New World might have something to offer viniculture."

"Glad you approve," Jules said. "Of course, you always know best, don't you?"

Whoa, Nelly. What happened there? Tad's face sharpened, and he flattened his lips, but Jules had already refocused on Evan.

"Thanks, Frankie. I think he needs to be fed." She scooped him out of Francesca's arms and moved off to the fridge.

"What did you do?" Cara asked her cousin. Those two had been airtight since Jules arrived in Chicago, though they'd yet to run with it. Whatever their connection, it hadn't stopped Tad from plying his bad-boy charm credentials on anything in a skirt. Perhaps that was the problem.

"Why do you assume it's my fault? I mean, you try to be the good guy…" He trailed off in his grumble and then slid a dark look to Jack. Aha. So Jack had laid down the law with Tad about laying hands on his baby sister. Made sense.

Tad returned his troubled gaze to Cara, but not for long. "Hey, Shane. Good to see you."

Cara spun around a little too hastily and then compounded it by choking out a testy, "What are you doing here?"

"Lovely to see you too, Cara," that devil-lipped demon of her dreams said.

The smell of his leather jacket wafted under her nose, a perfect addition to Evan's baby scent. Good Lord, that was the stuff. For the past five nights, sleep had been a stranger as she twisted up her bedsheets thinking about that frustrating man a couple of walls away. The night of the line-dancing class, her apartment had benefited from her insomnia as she vacuumed every inch her Dyson could reach.

Then again the next night when she still couldn't catch any Zs. That kiss...that kiss had shocked her entire body to life and even now she buzzed with the memory of his mouth on hers, the taste of his skin, how not-numb she had felt. Because numb was her default when it came to sex.

For so long, she and her body had been barely on speaking terms and only recently had she felt the opening overtures of a renewed understanding. Emerging from hibernation, she found herself relearning how to relate to her body's basic functionality. Enjoying food. Enjoying sex. Enjoying life. Appreciation for food had returned in fits, though she still had issues with eating around others. Appreciation for sex was something else entirely. With Shane, her appreciation was off the charts. Hell, the chart hadn't been made for how combustible the heat was between them, and that was the problem. No way, José, was she ready for a Shane Doyle assault on her senses. That kind of pleasure required effort and devoting it to a man was not on her agenda.

"You must be Shane," her mother said brightly. "Lili said you'd be joining us. *Benvenuto*."

Shane hooked those kiss-me-deadly lips up, sending his dimple into a two-step. Every uterus within a ten-mile radius probably felt a disturbance in the Force.

"Thanks for inviting me, Mrs. DeLuca. I hope it's okay that I brought something sweet. A blackberry cheesecake." He held out a plastic-domed tray to her mother. Dimples, deference, and dessert. *Brown nose.*

"We never say no to dessert, and please call me Francesca. Taddeo, get our guest a drink," her mother ordered as she got busy crafting a spare square foot of counter space for Shane's offering.

"What do you think you're playing at?" Cara asked in a

low voice that only Shane could hear. "I think I made it very clear—"

"Now, why do you have to be like that? Let's try a little small talk before we get into the less-than-charming back and forth." He accessorized another dimple blast with a dirty wink. "Fine weather we're having."

She clenched her fists at her sides. The man was impossible.

"Gorgeous," she ground out.

"How about that local sports team? Think they've got a chance this year?"

She sighed. "I'm sure they can go all the way."

He leaned in and she almost folded in half as his warm, comforting scent washed over her. "How've you been sleeping, LT?"

Caught off guard by both his question and his knee-weakening closeness, she flashed her pearly whites and lied her excellently toned butt off through them. "Wonderfully well."

"Oh."

"What's that mean?"

Eyebrow quirk ahoy. "You still have the spare key I gave you?"

"Yes, about that—"

"The next time you need to work off a little frustration, feel free to take your vacuum for a spin around my hardwood. It'll relax the hell out of that lethal body of yours."

Having waded through the dating sludge of New York, Cara was used to double entendres but most guys stuck around to enjoy the fruits of their innuendo. Not Shane. He brushed by her on his way to chat with Lili, leaving her to get her racing pulse under control.

Tad passed her a glass of the—Saints preserve us—Napa Valley Syrah she had insulted her lineage with.

"Are you guys doin' it?"

"How old are you? Ten?" She chugged half a glass because apparently the mere mention of "doin' it" with Shane was enough to drive her to drink.

"Ah, you're not doin' it," Tad pointed out helpfully. "But you will be soon enough. I called it on Jack and Lili. I'm calling it here."

"I overestimated your mental age. Make it six."

Undeterred, Tad carried on with enthusiasm. "I've found a location for the wine bar and I could do with your help. Marketing, interior design, all that Cara know-how."

"Tad, that's awesome." Her cousin had been boning up on his business smarts in preparation for opening his own wine bar, even going so far as to get certified as a sommelier. "Does Dad know?"

"Not yet, but I'm going for it. Can't be a bartender all my life, got to take the bull by the horns."

Cara smiled. She and Tad hadn't always seen eye to eye—their relationship was best described as "quippy"—but he was family and she was happy to help him make his dream come true. She also knew exactly what he meant about striking out and making something happen. Her gaze fell on Jack, the key to her own lofty ambitions—she still hadn't worked out how to approach him about Mason Napier's eat-in kitchen needs—then slid predictably to Shane, the man who impeded her path to serenity.

She turned back to her cousin. "Give me a call tomorrow and we'll talk."

"Cara, come here." Dad's stern voice cut through the chatter. It didn't usually bother her, but when he used it in the kitchen, it never boded well.

"I'm going in," she muttered to Tad, who sent her off to battle with a smirk.

"Taste this," Dad said, raising a wooden spoon coated in thick, bloodred marinara sauce.

Her laugh spilled out as a nervous rattle. "Can't I enjoy my glass of vino first?"

"Tony, leave her be." Her mother's calm voice soothed behind her.

With a tut, Aunt Sylvia added, "She never eats. That's how she keeps her girlish figure."

Cue hollow laughter.

Her father arrowed in on her with his steel-blue gaze.

"Cara," he warned, just as her eyes met Shane's, curious and mocking.

Tony must be obeyed or she'd never hear the end of it. Inclining her head, she took the edge of the spoon in her mouth just enough to coat her lips. She sensed rather than tasted the sweet and pungent tang of tomatoes with the piney-woodsy overlay of rosemary. *Oh, thank God.* Relief flooded her chest and relaxed her wire-taut muscles. It was all good, and she didn't want to run.

"*Bene?*" her father asked, but there was no missing that familiar flicker of disappointment in his eyes, the one she saw whenever they shared an awkward moment like this. In a family as crazy about food as the DeLucas, it was a capital offense not to enjoy every taste, every morsel, every meal. When his efforts to encourage her to cook as a girl were met with disinterest, he had transferred those aspirations to her younger sister. Tony and Lili had forged a bond over food that Cara could never replicate, and now her sister had found in Jack a man who understood how important food was to her and relished every one of her pasta-molded curves. The way to a man's heart, or a woman's as Lili demonstrated, might be through the stomach, but that road was riddled with construction and dead ends for Cara. Having a, shall we say, complicated relationship with food ensured complicated relationships all around, especially with men.

"It's good," she said, compelling her voice bright.

When she looked up, Shane had already returned to his conversation with Lili.

She often questioned why she was drawn to that thing that caused her so much heartache. First as a producer for Jack's cooking show, now as his private-events manager, all the roads of her career—of her life, if her marital shackle to, of all things, a pastry chef, was any indicator—brought her back to food. In masochistic moments, she said it was her way of challenging herself. Surround yourself with temptation, with the thing you want, with the means to break you. Resist, reject, rise above.

But in her heart of hearts she knew that wasn't it at all. It was for the same reason people gravitated to the kitchen: a pot of bubbling sauce was as magnetic as a warm fire in the hearth. It tapped into the limbic system, scattering troubles to the four corners. Bills to pay. Relationships to repair. Hearts to mend. All took a backseat to the security of the kitchen and the memories it invoked.

Because even though she dreaded those family mealtimes during her teen years and the obscene excess of platters of pasta and mountains of bread, she still sought out the comfort and camaraderie that only food could bring. Pleasure and pain at once.

How screwed up was that?

* * *

"Shane, have you met Tony?" Jack asked, nodding to the DeLuca paterfamilias who stood at the stove.

Tony, his father-in-law? That Tony? "We met briefly at Gina's wedding. Thanks for inviting me today."

Even more imposing than his six-foot-two frame, the man wore that classic air of the well-lived, urbane Italian. The silver tips at the edges of his temples winged a face that couldn't be older than fifty, which meant he had been barely out of his teens when Cara was born.

Leaving off stirring a fragrantly scented sauce, Tony applied a measuring stare. "Jack says you are to make the cake at my daughter's wedding." The cake that Shane had better not screw up, was the unspoken undertone.

"Yeah, I'm excited to be a part of it." And he was, truly. Shane was coming round to the notion that Jack had entrusted him with a very special task.

"Of course, Jack's confidence is so often misplaced," Tony said, pulling Shane up short. The older man waited a long beat. "Anyone who would choose me as a collaborator for a cookbook cannot possibly have his head on straight."

Ker-ist, a joke.

Jack laughed, clearly used to Tony's quirks. "Our opus on the synergy of French-Italian cuisine will be out in time for your Christmas gift buying. If Tony would stop arguing with everything I say."

Tony lifted his shoulder in a lazy shrug and turned back to his pot like a warlock. They had been dismissed. With a nod to a platter of steaming gnocchi, Jack picked up a couple of colorful bowls of salad and headed out back. Shane scooped up the pasta and followed.

"Tony's a bit—"

"Intimidating?" Jack finished over his shoulder.

"Uh, yeah. How'd you ever run that gauntlet?"

Jack set the bowls down on a large picnic table in the backyard, then nudged them a couple of inches to the right. Shane let him take the gnocchi, knowing Jack would just move it around to his liking anyway. Ever the perfectionist.

"It was touch and go for a while, especially with how public things were with Lili and me at first. Believe me, I got it from all sides with every DeLuca. Tony, Cara, Tad. Only Frankie was on board." He shook his head. "Hooking up with an Italian woman definitely does a number on your balls. In more ways than one."

Shane laughed, the sound falling flat. "You love it."

His brother smiled and answered with a simple, "I do."

As the rest of clan DeLuca piled around the table amidst good-natured joshing and laughter, something dark and hungry clawed at Shane's chest. He hadn't wanted to come here today, but Lili had already been so kind to him that it would have been rude to refuse. This wouldn't have been the first family meal he had joined on his travels, only the most dangerous. Getting close to these people was dangerous because it was built on sand.

Curiosity to see how Jack fit in with his new family had played a part, but mostly he wanted to see how Cara acted in her natural habitat. From what he'd seen so far, it could be more aptly termed her unnatural habitat. He had already spied an interesting moment between father and eldest daughter when she tried her father's marinara sauce. She had been panicked but then the tight knot of fear on her face had unfurled in relief, as if she had woken up from a nightmare where she'd forgotten the answers to the big test.

Now at the communal table, she seemed more relaxed while she smiled and joked with Lili. Hot damn, she was looking fine in a silky top and slim white pants that cut off before her ankles. Confirming his suspicions that she was a bit of a health nut, she stuck mostly to the tasty summer salad of arugula, golden beets, and goat cheese. No bread, no pasta, and just the half glass of wine.

Maybe she was worried she'd make a toast to the wrong happy couple.

Lost in his thoughts, it took him a moment to realize that Francesca was asking him a question.

"Do you have family back in Ireland, Shane?"

Shane's heart jerked to a stop. "Not anymore."

"County Clare or thereabouts, right?" Jack cut in. "You talk like my mother. I recognized the accent as soon as I met you."

Another fluffy pillow of gnocchi made it into Shane's mouth while he chewed himself to calm. These Italians sure knew their stuff.

"Yeah, Ennis." It was the closest big town to where he had actually grown up in Quilty, a three-pub backwater battered by the Atlantic Ocean winds with a solitary general store and a rundown post office to keep it relevant. The town Jack's mother had left in the salt-soaked mud.

He had always assumed that Jack had never visited Quilty and that he knew nothing about John Sullivan's family. He was sure someone would have mentioned a visit from a famous native son. Panic that he had miscalculated tightened his skin. Luckily he didn't have time to think too hard on that as Tony's sister-in-law, Sylvia, took up the interrogation slack.

"Shane, are you Catholic?"

A collective groan went up around the table at Sylvia's words, the aunt with the hair tower that looked like several birds' nests interlaced with a complicated ribbon lattice. Up until now, most of her conversation had started with "so-and-so went to the deli to get a pound of Italian sausage" and ended with "and now he's dead."

"Welcome to the trenches, DeLuca style," Tad said affably.

"It doesn't hurt to ask. There are still plenty of nieces to go round and the Irish are more Catholic than the Italians, I'll tell you." Sylvia licked her lips, a gesture in oddly lascivious contrast to the topic.

"Don't answer, Shane," Lili called out. "You'll be on her matchmaking spreadsheet before the end of the day if she thinks you might be eligible."

"I'm not really in the market for a girlfriend," he said, keeping his eyes focused on Sylvia, though they itched to gaze in another direction entirely.

"Why ever not? A healthy young man like you?" Sylvia leaned over, flashing a scary expanse of wrinkly bosom. "Is there something wrong with you? You're not one of those homosexuals, are you?"

Mild protestations from the peanut gallery quickly lapsed into silence as everyone leaned forward. Typical behavior in families who pretended offense at their embarrassing relatives but were happy to let them ask the burning questions.

"It's okay if you are, Shane," Cara offered, her eyes glinting at him from across the table. "Lili and I have a lot of gay friends. We'd be happy to introduce you around."

"That's very kind of you, Cara, but I'm not gay. In fact, I've already got my eye on someone. She's an awful lot of trouble but I'm confident I can persuade her to play ball."

Cara flushed a golden pink that made her even more beautiful and then tried to counteract it with a late scowl that did nothing to minimize his attraction. Before that explosive kiss outside the church, he'd spent inordinate amounts of his time fantasizing about his neighbor-wife. Those long, tanned limbs wrapped around his hips, her herbal-scented hair falling into his face as she covered him with her body like a sex blanket, her tight heat enveloping and milking him to bone-shattering release.

None of his fantasies had involved nipple sucking.

Now he was living under the same roof as that batty bundle of woman and it was all he could do not to rip her door off its hinges and make her his. He should be staying away from her because of the whole FUBAR situation with Jack, but there was something about this woman that made him want to mess her up, ruffle her knife-straight hair, make every part of her curl. Even if the frost she was blowing his way might freeze his dick when he came into contact with her.

Sylvia plowed on with her efforts to pair him off with another DeLuca cousin. "Angela makes terrible choices in men. That last one was the worst. Never brought a bottle of wine or a box of cannoli to the house."

All eyes fell to Shane's blackberry cheesecake sitting in the middle of the table like a barometer of good manners and DeLuca mate potential. It also reminded Francesca that it was time for dessert. As the slices of creamy perfection were passed around, Cara's refusal didn't pass unnoticed by Shane.

"None for you, Cara?" he asked, a touch peeved because it was one of his favorites and if she wasn't going to at least try his creations, they had a bigger problem than a wedding under the influence.

"Thanks, but no. I never put anything in my mouth I don't know the full calorie count for." She held his gaze and again, something flashed between them. His body hardened as he pondered exactly what he'd like to put in her mouth, calories be damned.

"What about Nicola? She just broke up with that boy who works for the Streets and Sanitation," Sylvia continued, her focus unwavering.

"Cara's not seeing anyone," Tad said mischievously. "Are you, Cara?"

Sylvia waved a dismissive hand. "Oh, he's much too young for Cara." She shot a dagger of a glare at her niece. "You're the oldest cousin. At thirty, you should be married and settled by now before you lose your looks or your eggs go stale."

From the other end of the table, Tony growled his displeasure at the turn of the conversation. There's only so much of this kind of chatter a man can take in his own home. *Hear, hear.*

Francesca frowned at her sister-in-law. "Sylvia, Cara's very happy with her life the way it is. Not everyone is interested in marriage and motherhood."

Shane was sure the maternal smile she delivered to her daughter was intended to put her at ease, but that's not how Cara took it. She blinked rapidly, her discomfort flitting like a dark-winged bird across her face. But then she recovered with a bright smile that almost made the grade.

"Stretch marks and a man's stinky socks on the bedroom floor?" She smirked at her aunt. "Think I'll give it a pass."

* * *

"You know, Jack could afford better than this." Cara fingered the silk organza sheath hanging on the rack at Ann Taylor. Better quality than she expected but still not really what she had in mind for Lili and Jack's big day.

Lili expelled another world-weary sigh, only her fiftieth in the last hour. Whereas Cara had been born without the food-loving gene, Lili had missed out on the double-helix shopping DNA. Her younger sister liked funky, vintage outfits in keeping with her artistic leanings. Take her down Michigan Avenue to buy real clothes and she reverted to a bored ten-year-old being dragged from store to store by her mother.

"If I'm required by the wedding gods to have three bridesmaids, then we need to find something affordable. I know Jack's offered to cover the cost of everything, but the bridesmaids should pay for their own. What about this one?" From the rack, she unhooked a full-skirted *Mad Men*–style taffeta affair. "Hides a multitude of sins."

"I suppose. Hold it up." Cara snapped a photo with her phone and made an annotation. *Hideous.* "About the three bridesmaids..."

Lili speared her with a look. "I'm not going to like this, am I?"

"Well, there's me and Jules, of course. And you can't pick Gina without picking her conjoined evil twin, Angela. We'd never hear the end of it."

Lili returned to sighing. Fifty-one. Or was it fifty-two?

"Zander called me, too," Cara said, referring to Lili's studio stablemate and weirdo artist buddy. "He didn't want to bother you."

"Zander a bridesmaid? Oh, for heaven's sake."

"He's one of your closest friends, Lili. He wouldn't wear a dress—well, unless he really wants to—but he doesn't know Jack well enough to be in his party. You don't want to get on the wrong side of the gays."

With great prejudice, her sister scrubbed a hand through her voluminous hair. "So, that's five—that should be enough."

"It's bad luck to have an uneven number, so we'd need someone else but we can't pick another cousin because it would open the floodgates."

"*Madre di Dio*, Cara. I know it's going to be big, but I'm kind of relying on you to rein in Jack's wilder impulses."

Cara schooled her expression to blank, praying it wasn't obvious that the only impulses on display here were Cara's to go as big as Aunt Sylvia's skyscraper bouffant. "You mean you haven't discussed it with him?"

"No, he's working a lot these days and I've been focusing on my graduation portfolio. When we see each other, we're not talking about cummerbunds and wedding favors." Her eyebrow jumped. "If you know what I mean."

"I've never met a couple who can't keep their hands off each other like you two. Surely, it must have cooled off by now."

Lili's smile made it clear cooling didn't even enter the picture. "I thought someone who wasn't getting any would love to be living vicariously through the sister who's getting schtupped on a regular basis. In very hot ways. In very interesting places. Only yesterday—"

"Sure, the old maid loves to hear about the endlessly fascinating sex lives of others. Should I be avoiding the kitchen at the restaurant now?"

"Oh, no. Jack won't allow sex in the kitchen," she said with a giggle that spoke to her having tried. "Something about health codes. But you might want to knock before you come into the office." She angled Cara a look, somewhere between pity and bafflement. "I don't know why you don't date more. We've been out for only an hour and you've already had two guys trying to chat you up."

"Right, while they wait for their wives to come out of the fitting rooms."

"So you attract your fair share of losers, but they're not all losers." Lili had that wicked gleam in her eyes.

"He's my neighbor."

"I was talking about that cute guy over there." She gestured to a hot nerdy type who was acting as a personal clothes rack for an elderly blue-hair. Maybe it was his mother, or maybe it was one of those *Harold and Maude* situations. Hard to tell. "But interesting how your smutty mind went straight to Shane."

How could it not? A week ago, she had made a banquet out of his chest and every night since, she had fantasized about gobbling up every tasty inch of him.

Each word out of her mouth during her rejection had sounded ostensibly right. *You're not my type. It should never have happened.* But now the words she had so emphatically spoken bounced around her skull like ghostly taunts. She should be rejoicing at the recovery of her singledom. In a couple of weeks, she would be free to see anyone she wanted. Scratch that. She was already free to see anyone she wanted. She and Shane Doyle were linked by nothing but a piece of paper, and tomorrow, she would pick up the annulment papers from her lawyer and hand deliver them to her neighbor. Her legal status might be a form of bondage, but her mental state proclaimed her independence.

There was a song in there, somewhere.

"Hey, where'd you go?" Lili said, waving a hand before Cara's eyes. "Thinking about Irish Stew?"

"He's my neighbor," she repeated.

"Exactly. Maybe you should just be neighborly." Lili licked her lips. "You have this smokin' guy ten feet from your door and you're telling me you haven't devoted a smidgen of gray matter to what it might be like?"

Cara took a moment to savor the visual of a naked Shane. He looked wonderful.

"Actually, I know you have because there was, you know"—Lili grasped Cara's hand dramatically—"dun, dun, dun. All that innocent hand-holding in Vegas. What's the problem here?"

"So you think I should go for it because it's geographically convenient? Never mind that we work together. Good

God, Lili, rule number one: you don't make honey where you make money."

Lili looked like she had her own opinion of that rule but thankfully her phone rang before she could voice it. While she chatted with Jules, Cara caught the smile of Cute Accountant. He seemed pliable, quiet, safe...and nothing like Shane.

Her sister finished her call on a sigh. "Poor Jules. She was so looking forward to going to this hot restaurant opening with us tonight but Mom's got to work. Gina was supposed to be back from her honeymoon rampage-slash-George Clooney stalker tour around Lake Como, but her flight got delayed."

Cara's mind whirred at the possibilities. "I'm free. I'd be happy to babysit for Evan."

"Are you sure?" Suspicious surprise lit up Lili's eyes. "Thought kiddies weren't your bag, baby."

Cara tried to lose the hurt expression she knew was soldered to her face. As elder aunt, she had looked after several DeLuca cousins and the little scamps had escaped without major injury every time, but her family always acted like Cara might run screaming into the street at the first sign of a baby crying.

"I love playing at glamorous aunt," she said with a pressed-on smile. Beads of desperation trickled between her shoulder blades. "I get to hand them back and it gives me a chance to wield my nefarious influence while they're young."

"Well, if you're sure," Lili said slowly, and called Jules back.

Cara didn't do a lot of things: relationships, all-you-can-eat buffets, and camping, to name a few. Yearning was definitely on the list, yet here she went again hankering after things she had no right to.

Shane was to blame. Las Vegas and Stoli were co-conspirators. This morning, she had finally fallen asleep at three A.M. only to jolt awake an hour later from a dream in which she was nursing a devil-haired infant with a dimple. She couldn't have standard erotic dreams like everyone else; her dreams had to be about birthing Shane Doyle's spawn!

The sensual dreamscape was reserved for her waking hours. Since telling Shane they were over before they started, her whole body had been in heat like an alley cat, and Lili's encouragement to go for it was not helping her oversexed brain. Under no circumstances did she want to revive the corpse of their marriage, but a little electroshock therapy wouldn't go amiss. Just a pleasant release of the building tension with her neighbor...her coworker...*her husband.* Oh rats, when she put it in those terms, it sounded like she should be making a reservation for the nearest padded cell.

In recovery from her disordered eating for almost a year now, Cara had no illusions. She was a ticking time bomb. She knew she could relapse, descend into that spiral and become that woman she hated. The bad daughter, the worse sister, unworthy of her Italian card. Hell, it had already happened. She had lost control and tied the knot with a stranger, a move that could only be described as stupid and selfish. Not so different from old, self-absorbed Cara who bailed when her mom needed her. Her family could never know.

Taking it a day at a time, keeping her life on an even keel, this was what Cara had to focus on. She needed all her love for her family. For herself. There was none to spare. Shane Doyle might have the best-tasting nipples on the planet and his warm, dry hand wrapped around her as they stumbled down the Sunset Strip might have been the best feeling in the world, but it was an illusion. An alcohol-fueled illusion.

Cara wanted Shane more than she wished she didn't and that was exactly why she couldn't have him.

CHAPTER 7

Shane wasn't sure what he'd expected as he glided quickly up the steps of Jack and Lili's brownstone on Evergreen Street. Something more palatial, perhaps, not quite so welcoming and cozy. After all, this street, only a few blocks from his flat but far enough off the main drag to be peaceful, boasted two-million-dollar properties. A perfect location for the millionaire rock star chef. He rang the doorbell and then turned to the street so he wouldn't look like a sad-eyed orphan with his nose to the glass.

The prickle he felt between his shoulder blades as the door opened was his first clue tonight was not going to go as planned.

"What are you doing here?"

Ah, the dulcet tones of the old ball and chain.

He spun around. "I'm here to see Lili."

His neighbor-wife looked cool and sexy in a dusky pink dress like a man's shirt that wasn't much longer. She also looked less than pleased to see him.

"She's gone out with Jack and Jules to a restaurant opening. It's just me—and Evan." She threw a cautious glance over her shoulder as if she expected the infant to come out and defend her from the big bad wolf at the door.

"Lili asked me to stop by with some cake samples for the wedding." He thrust his bag of tricks in her general direction in case words alone weren't enough to explain his presence. It wouldn't do if she thought he might be stalking her. "I must have got the time wrong," he added, though they both knew he hadn't. It sounded as though Lili could give her aunt Sylvia a run for her matchmaking money.

Avoiding the bag, she stepped back and waved him in. He gave the situation a millisecond delay before his curiosity overrode his rising annoyance at Lili's machinations. When would he have another chance to see where Jack lived? Passing through the long hallway flanked by arty seminude photos, he tried to suppress his excitement at being in his brother's home.

He placed the bag on the kitchen island and waited to see how Cara would play it.

"Can I get you anything? A drink?"

"A glass of water would be nice."

While she poured the water from one of those water filtration setups, he drank in the surroundings. The kitchen was, in a word, *da bomb*. Of course, Jack would have something supersonic and this was a chef's wet dream. All state of the art, gleaming stainless steel. A space that God would be happy to cook in. Joined with the living room in an open-plan style, Shane imagined that the design was right up Jack's alley. He talked a lot in the restaurant when he cooked, and no doubt, he'd want it that way at home. Cooking for his family, giving them a play-by-play of what he was doing or how last night's service had gone down.

She handed off the water glass and he took a long gulp.

"What did you bring?" She flapped at the bag of samples, evidently impatient to get him out and on his way.

"A few options." He withdrew them carefully, each one in takeout boxes from Sarriette. "Lemon angel food with pistachio cream. Chocolate ganache with mint. Pineapple with a mascarpone frosting."

He had spent his day off baking in the restaurant's kitchen—he even had to start over on the pineapple after that lughead Dennis mistakenly turned up the oven temperature to preheat for flatbread—and now that Lili wasn't even here to taste it, he was not a happy camper. He would have preferred that her matchmaking efforts didn't result in him slaving like a navvy when he could have been...shit, what else would he be doing? Cooking at home and fantasizing about his neighbor-wife, that's what.

Said fantasy eyed the slices suspiciously like they might grow fangs, jump off the table, killer-spider style, and pierce her neck.

"Want to taste? The planner should have some perks."

The look she gave him felt like a swipe of her tongue over his lips, giving the distinct impression she'd rather be tasting him. Which made no sense at all, considering how she'd kicked him to the curb. He was just about to dismiss it as a figment of his lately muddled imagination when she yanked out a drawer, extracted a fork, and did something odd. So odd, he had to blink a couple of times to clear his vision.

She eeny-meenied.

She didn't say it aloud and she didn't do the little hovering jabs with her fork, but her eyes moved deliberately from piece to piece. Most people were instantly drawn to their favorite because their default setting was chocolate or because anything with angel food sent them into a full-on mouth-gasm. With Cara, it was as though she wanted it all but her scarcely leashed control required a method.

Eeny, meeny, miny, moe. Catch a cake slice by—Pineapple, you're it.

She cut off a sliver, a razor-thin slice that a bird wouldn't find satisfying, and he watched, entranced as it passed her full, glossy lips. By the second chew, she turned away to the sink and laid the fork down, but not before a triumphant wave washed over him. Because he'd seen her joy and knew he'd had some small measure in contributing to it. He might be a dud as a husband but he could still make a mean dessert.

"You don't want to try the others?" he asked, knowing full well what her answer would be. Lemon Tart was back from her sabbatical. There would be no more sampling.

"We should leave it to Lili and Jack to decide. Not bad, Doyle. Not bad at all." She smiled and it was like watching the sun set over Lake Michigan. A burnished glow, but with a hint of sadness because the day was over. Yep, he was feeling poetic.

The part of him that longed for her acceptance perked right up along with his dick. Compliments, especially hard-won compliments from his hot wife, turned him on to a near unbearable degree. He really should be heading out but he was starting to like the vibe.

On the kitchen island lay Cara's big binder, the one she carried with her everywhere.

"How's the planning going?"

"Not bad." She bit her lip. "Would you like to see?"

He'd rather sever his left testicle. "Love to."

She launched into a recitation of the planning, from odes to the flowers to a pros-and-cons rundown of the five different types of wedding favor she had in mind. Printouts and spreadsheets overlaid with colorful sticky notes spoke to her ruthless efficiency and organization skills. And her excitement. Her face lit up, her hands got busy, she became more Italian. She became more like the woman he had married. Good to know it wasn't only the alcohol.

She flipped to the seating plan and he placed his palm flat on the page.

"Sorry, I'm babbling," she said with a breathy hitch that hit him somewhere above his diaphragm.

"No, it's great." He nodded at the chart. "I just wanted to see if Uncle Aldo has been pulled out of the penalty box yet."

The upturn of her lips showed her pleasure that he had remembered.

"I'm looking into special oven mitts to keep his proclivities in check," she said, "but my main concern is that I'm drawing a blank on unique centerpieces for the tables."

Centerpieces. Now that was more his speed. "How did they meet?" He knew Jack and Lili's hookup in a bar had gone video viral, but he wasn't privy to the details.

"She hit him over the head with a frying pan because she thought he was trying to steal stuff from DeLuca's. She was dressed as Wonder Woman at the time." Her small head shake gave the impression *she* would never act so impetuously but they both knew better. Vegas had changed all that.

"Almost as memorable as our first night together."

The corner of her mouth crept up into a not-quite smile. "Almost."

"Well, all Jack's restaurants are named after herbs. You could do something with herbs that people could take away. Put them in British tea tins or Italian wine bottles for the ethnic link." He rubbed his chin, noting he needed a shave. "Or maybe sugar sculptures."

"Sugar sculptures?"

He scanned the countertop, looking for a piece of scratch paper. His eyes fell on a handwritten list that, on closer examination, looked like instructions for handling Evan: his favorite story, the temperature to heat the milk to, the name of his pediatrician. Judging by the misspelled words and transposed letters, it looked like Jules might have literacy problems.

On a blank sticky note, he sketched Wonder Woman wielding a skillet and hooking with her lasso a man who bore a distant likeness to Jack. He pushed it toward her. It felt like a negotiation.

With her forefinger and thumb, she drew on her plump bottom lip. "Sugar sculpture requires a lot of skill."

"I could make them." When she still looked skeptical, he added, "Would you like to see my résumé, Ms. DeLuca?" He made sure to pronounce it *Miz* and the lift of one perfectly shaped eyebrow told him she got the point. He touched his phone and pulled up some photos. "I did a lot of sugar work at Maison Rouge when we catered for private parties there."

The sweet warmth of her breath fanned his jaw as she leaned in to look at the photos. He cycled through them quickly so she'd get a feel for his capabilities until she ordered him to stop with a cerise pink nail tap on *the one*.

"I recognize this. It won an award for something."

"Best Design at the International Exhibition of Culinary Art." It had been over a year ago but even now, pride swelled his chest. Drawing on Renaissance art for its inspiration, his sugar showpiece took the form of an angelic woman emerging from a sea of multihued glass. That he was the youngest winner ever of the award wasn't too shabby either. And he hadn't needed Jack Kilroy to get him there.

"It's amazing, Shane." Her brow furrowed. "What the hell are you doing at Sarriette? You don't have any opportunity for this kind of work there."

Too true. Sarriette's events were Mickey Mouse affairs compared to Maison Rouge, and the dessert menu was simpler in keeping with Jack's back-to-basics vision. But Chicago held other attractions, one of which was invading every one of his cells with her dizzying nearness.

"I needed a change."

If her narrowed eyes were anything to go by, that didn't cut it. Ambitious people found it difficult to understand behavior that went against the grain of progress. She took the paper from him and overlaid his crude drawing with a few confident lines.

"It might look cool if Lili was busting out of her wedding dress while she got her superhero on. Like she's transforming." This thought sent Cara into a flurry of giggles. "You're full of surprises, Irish."

A fizz of something burst between them, making his pulse beat wildly but not unexpectedly. Cara had this effect on him. A combination of druggy highs and nervousness, a fix that would never satisfy. He knew what it felt like now and was beginning to understand its power and how he could rein it in, but even a shot of methadone was like manna to a junkie. He moved in closer and breathed in her perfume. Hot, floral, sexy.

"You're doing it again," she said.

Her words halted him cold. "Doing what?"

"That secret smile. Like you're remembering things I can't." She considered him and he felt the weight of her stare like a brick wall between them. "What did we talk about that night?"

Ah, she was still trying to figure out how she had let her

guard down. "The crazy bride, Vegas excess, your dream to be Chicago's next party queen—"

She blinked. "I told you that?"

"Yeah, you have big plans and you were excited about it. How you want to get top events for the restaurant, become the doyenne of party planning. You also talked about Jack and Lili and how great they are together."

"That sounds familiar." She looked at the drawing, her expression filled with a yearning that pinched his heart. Cara wanted things with a barely banked passion but fear—of what, he wasn't sure—bound her like one of her designer outfits. He saw it in Vegas. He felt it when they kissed after the line-dancing class. Even tonight when she had surveyed his dessert samples. What he wouldn't do to get her out of those fancy clothes and stoke those fires smoldering below the surface.

"I'm sorry about my behavior the night of the dancing," she said. "I was rude to you."

"This is a tricky situation and you want to put it behind you. Neither of us wants a marriage, LT. I get that." The unmistakable heart twinge he felt right then surprised him, but not enough to derail his train of thought. "So, it'll just have to be sex."

Her eyes fluttered wide and her mouth worked. "What?"

"We can just do a sex-only thing, like a married-with-benefits deal."

Gotcha. Oh, his little beauty wanted to laugh. Her lips twitched and his dick twitched at the thought of bringing a smile to her exquisitely melancholy face. She appeared to be mulling it over, so he went in for the kill.

"Until we can make it annulled-with-benefits." He waggled his eyebrows and pulled that brimming laugh out of her. *Zing.* Why did it feel better for being so hard won?

On the downside of the laugh, she said, "Speaking of which, I'm picking up the papers tomorrow."

"Hm," he hummed. There was the twinge in his chest again, a touch sharper now. This was good, wasn't it? Never had his life needed more clarity than it did of late, and fixing his marital status would go a long way to resharpening his focus.

She cocked her head. "Lili thinks I should take advantage of all you have to offer."

"I always liked that girl."

As quick as he had made gains, he lost them as another Cara brain check whipped them away. He imagined her calculating the statistical probabilities for disaster and coming up with ninety-nine point nine percent. This woman thought far too much.

"Shane, I'm flattered but frankly, you're not my type." She gave one of those I-don't-want-to-offend-you-but-I'm-gonna-anyway smiles. "You're much too nice for me."

It wouldn't be the first time he'd heard it and it made him angrier than a bull battling a bee swarm. It was the stuff of chick flicks and crappy sitcoms, how women love a bad boy and good guys finish last. Where in the hell did she get off calling him *nice*?

"Would you prefer I take baseballs out of kids' hands at Wrigley Field or trip old ladies in the street? You want a guy who's not nice?" Here he was defending "nice" when he wasn't feeling particularly nice. Time to kick this up a notch.

"Were you not turned on the other night?"

Her mouth gaped and even that looked good on her. Was there no end to the ways she could get his blood pumping south?

He filled in her shocked silence. "The other night, when you kissed me—"

"You kissed me!"

"Semantics. When you kissed me and licked my chest."

Flushing, she brought her palm to her cheek to cool it. "I know what I did. I don't need you to remind me."

Man, seeing her all het up did hot and dirty things to him. He moved in and gently tipped up her jaw. She shook under his touch but she didn't retreat.

"I think you do need me to remind you. I think you need to be reminded of all the passion and fire that exists beneath that cool exterior you show to the world. I bet no one sees that, do they? No one sees how out of control you get when the right button is pressed. Maybe it's just a whisper of my hand across your breasts…" He dropped his gaze to confirm that what he was saying had some effect on her and, yep, to look at her lovely cleavage. Through the erotically thin material of that dress, he found her nipples primed to hard points. "Maybe a breath close to your ear or my thumb gliding across your lip will set you off."

Her tongue darted, making her lips moist, almost begging him to swipe that pouty lower lip with the pad of his finger. Take a soft suck, a juicy bite. The air felt close, the sweet scent of the cakes, Cara's skin, and their choppy breathing combining to coat all his senses.

"Still think I'm not your type? Because your body says different. It's telling me that we would be very compatible indeed. I bet if I were to run my hand down…" He trailed his fingertips down the placket of her dress, between her breasts, along her clenching stomach, until he sensed with his fingertips the band of her panties. A sexy thong, his Braille-for-underwear skills told him.

"I bet I'd find you're as wet for me as I'm hard for you. Nice? Let me tell you, what I'm thinking about you is the opposite of nice."

In her eyes he saw desire: greedy, raw, and heart-wrenchingly pure. He also saw other, nameless things that scared and fired him at once. Suddenly this sex-only notion was sounding like chump change. He wanted more. He wanted the luxury of hope.

Somewhere along the way, her hand had crawled along his chest and now rested above his pec.

"There are also other benefits to be had here," he said.

"There are?" It came out in a hoarse whisper.

I get to smell you on my sheets. I get to think of new ways to make you smile...

"Fat-free treats."

That sent her skeptical gaze sideways toward the cake samples. "Um..."

"No, Cara. My mouthwatering, succulent...nipples."

She shrieked so loud it left a ringing in his ear.

"I know you want another shot at these tasty little suckers, woman, and if you're good, I'll dab them in chocolate frosting."

That sent her into further shrieks and a full-body vibration.

"After your disgraceful behavior last week, we'll stay away from church basements. Best not to risk damnation." He shook his head in mock censure. "For shame, Cara."

She lost it. A laugh-snort explosion that she tried to bury in the well of shoulder. "Shane, that's too much. Please stop."

No fucking way. Making her laugh had suddenly become the most important job in the world.

She tilted her head up, her full lips so close he had to swallow against the blitzkrieg of her sensuality. "I think I might have missed the nipple frosting section of your résumé."

"True, I don't have a lot of experience in that area, but girls do tend to get funny ideas about guys who surround themselves with sugary delights all day. I can't tell you how many times I've heard, 'You're a pastry chef? Let's whip out the double boiler and a can of Reddi-wip and get this party started.'"

Snorting again, she cupped her mouth. She had made that funny little sound in Las Vegas and then spent a lot of time trying to hide it. He loved seeing her let loose. A full minute passed as their joint laughter wound down and the proximity to each other became shockingly apparent. Her hand still splayed over his chest, warm and full of life as she breathed herself to neutral.

"I know you've been wondering how we got here, Cara. How we both could have done something so crazy." He caressed her hip, absorbing the shock of heat he found there. "This is what happened that night. This feeling."

He wished he could articulate it better but that was the best he could do. There she had stood in the middle of her family and friends, looking like the experience was entirely alien to her. Like she had been deposited there from the mother ship and didn't recognize a single person. Shane knew exactly how that felt—to not belong, to be unsure of your place. The night had been spent turning wisps of recognition into strings of connection. They got drunk, they shared stories, they laughed a lot. And then instead of letting it play out naturally, he'd had a shit-for-brains moment and acted on a crazy, drunken impulse. Not far off from dear old Dad, that. As loath as he was to admit it, life since his teens had coalesced around one thing: meeting Jack so he could resent him in person instead of from afar. That obsession ruled him and time with Cara had allowed him to forget about it, had freed him up to be a different person.

With her, he felt like the best version of himself.

From beneath her dark blonde veil of lashes, she looked right into his cracked soul. The urge to tell her everything scorched his mouth. A woman with a slanted connection to her family would understand. His wife would understand.

And then, because he was the unluckiest guy on the planet, her phone rang. Her gaze flicked to the screen, flashing *Mom* and a picture of Francesca.

She sighed. "She's calling to check up on me. The woman hates it when I muscle in on her babysitting gig."

"I hate when she does that, too."

"Ciao, Mom." She rolled her eyes for his benefit. "It's fine. All under control."

Oh no, it wasn't, and as soon as she got off that phone, he was going to show her just how out of control things could get. Stepping away to give her privacy, he wandered a few steps into the living room. Jack and Lili had moved in about six months ago and the place had long passed the comfortable stage to thoroughly lived in. A little cluttered, a lot messy, with baby toys, books, magazines. Except for the kitchen, which clearly came under Jack's purview—it shone and spoke to his neat-freak nature. They were both alike in that way. It was almost competitive between them how clean they could keep Sarriette's countertops.

A gurgle from a baby monitor on the couch's side table broadcast that Evan was awake. Glancing over his shoulder, he watched Cara, her hands making a series of swoops and whips through the air as she tried to explain something to her mother. "Yes, I know, Mom."

The baby fussed again, louder this time, and Shane's heart fisted at the thought of the little fella all alone somewhere upstairs.

"Mom, I really need to go," Cara was saying. She had

heard Evan's distress and now desperation marred her usually smooth features.

Shane raised a hand to let her know he had it and got a grateful look in return. He took the stairs two at a time and closed in on the sound.

Practically every inch of wall space on this level recorded Jack and Lili's life. While the downstairs gallery of images displayed what looked like Lili's more professional, artsy work, here, it was an ode to their happiness. Pictures of Jack caught unawares while cooking or shaving or just plain laughing. Lili captured as she woke up, looking bleary-eyed and beautiful, the compositions not as practiced because Jack was likely behind the camera. There were photos of Cara, too, some with Francesca, bald and stunning, some with other DeLucas at family parties. In those, his wife stood out, her blonde crown a shining beacon among all that brunette Italianness.

Right now, another beacon beckoned—a six-month-old crying for a spot of comfort. He stepped inside and found Evan snugly wrapped in a one-piece, his chubby cheeks heated and wet. Shane picked him up and laid him against his chest, making sure to support his little head in his palm.

"There, there, kiddo. What's all the drama?"

Evan heaved a breath, a herculean effort for his tiny lungs, and Shane was instantly transported back to an earlier time. He didn't remember much about his mother, but he would never forget the helplessness he felt when she died and he ended up in his father's care at the age of five. A dyed-in-the-wool drunk was ill-equipped to handle a child, but the Irish social services system with its Catholic underpinnings privileged familial bonds over a child's fundamental needs. His father could be sober and charming when called upon, especially in the face of a financial incentive such as an allowance from the government.

Shane walked around the room and after a few back rubs, they both calmed down, transferring serenity to each other in a weird osmosis. The room was chockablock with a sensory overload of color, still vibrant under the dimly lit shaft of light shining in from the hallway. The ceiling was a night sky of celestial light, pimped out with glow-in-the-dark star stickers. Aunt Jo's boys had one of those ceilings and as a kid, Shane had wanted it for his own bedroom. Packy walloped him into the middle of next week when Shane dared to ask for it. Toys of every shape and stripe ringed Evan's room, many of which were too advanced for an infant who probably couldn't sit up yet. But the message was clear.

Evan, you are loved.

Through the now steady sough of Evan's breathing, he inhaled the baby's scent and pondered the other smells that might come close. Baking bread, Sarriette's kitchen at full tilt, Cara...

On the dresser lay a photograph of Jack holding Evan with Jules at his side. Laughing and easy, perched on the corner of picture and perfect. Heart thumping so hard Shane worried it might wake the kid, he picked up the frame, needing the heft of it to convince himself it was real. The family Kilroy: tight-knit, happy, impregnable.

Pain and anger bit into his chest. What the hell was he doing here? He and Jack might share the same genetic code but that was where it ended. A biological connection that Jack didn't want to acknowledge, that he saw as a problem to be dismissed with a few thousand Euros and nary a backward glance. Shane should know by now that blood was no guarantee of happiness. Neither was meeting the eyes of a beautiful girl across a crowded bar nor the hope-filled resurgence of that feeling every time he spent a moment in her presence. He was raw and torn up inside, his smiles brittle and false.

Nice? They had no idea.

"Everything okay?" Cara's smooth tone penetrated his fog of bitterness. She stood in the doorway, a hazy mirage in a barren desert.

Blinking like it could right his balance, he reset the photo on the dresser and hardened his mind against all that soul-splitting love. He would make Jack's wedding cake and move on. Go back to London and jump in on that business opportunity he'd put off for so long. Living like this hurt too much; he'd already experienced a lifetime on the wrong side of the glass.

"Tell Lili I stopped by," he scratched out as he placed Evan in her arms. "And drop those annulment papers off when you get a chance."

Her teeth snagged on her fleshy bottom lip, and he turned away, annoyed with how much that affected him. He needed to cut her loose, cut them all loose, and finally get his body on the same page as the brain that had just got a clue.

Behind him, he heard a small noise of discontent, whether from Cara or Evan, he couldn't be sure. Shoving one foot in front of the other, he pushed through the gauntlet of photo love, only hauling in a breath when he reached the safety of the dark street.

CHAPTER 8

The natives were getting restless and her stand-in bartender was not making the grade.

As Cara watched Dennis-the-extern get more of a martini on the bar than in the glass (using one of the top-shelf vodkas, natch), she nibbled away at her lip gloss and then started in on her lips. Damn, damn, damn.

She checked her phone again, willing it to ring with the news she wanted to hear: her cousin Tad was winging his way on his Harley to this private event at Sarriette—a wedding rehearsal dinner—and bringing with him his cocktail-shaking skills along with his innate Italian charm.

When he got here, she was going to kick his cocktail-shaking, innately charming ass into the nearest wall.

She cast about the room, taking in the perfectly laid table, the beautiful peony-based centerpiece she had created, and the rather antsy-looking horde of guests who were waiting for their cocktail fix. At least the hors d'oeuvres were going over well, as long as you didn't mind a side dip of misery. Stoically, Cara suffered the sullen stares of Maisey as she passed basil palmiers and crudités around to the guests, most of whom were scarfing it down while the line for the drinks got longer. Dennis had insisted he had experience when she roped him in twenty minutes ago, but it seemed the only experience he had was with wiping the bar down, and he wasn't even very good at that. She really needed to get in there and sort it out.

Stooping to the small bar fridge, Cara pulled out a couple of bottles of champagne, and gestured Maisey over with a subtle motion of her head. Too subtle apparently, as Maisey chose to ignore her.

"Maisey," Cara called out above the pop of the Piper-Heidsieck Brut, running mental calculations of how many bottles they'd have to eat to appease their guests.

Maisey trudged over as if the world might come to an end, her jaw set *à la* moody teenager. Hard to believe the woman was twenty-five years old. The same age as—no, she refused to spare that man another brain cell.

"Please serve our guests with complimentary champagne..." Cara poured the bubbly into flutes. "And cheer up, honey. It might never happen."

Cara's phone rang and she answered with a hissed, "Where the hell are you?"

"Hey, that's no way to greet your favorite cousin."

Shit, he wasn't coming.

"Tad, what's your excuse? Did one of your lady friends break a nail?"

Tad sighed as if Cara was the difficult one. "I'm at the ER with Evan. He had a fever and Jules got worried."

Cara's stomach dropped. "Oh God, is he okay?"

"Yeah, he'll be fine. Doc says it's just a bad cold and not

meningitis or something worse. I was getting ready to come over but Jules called and it all happened so fast."

She breathed a sigh of relief. Was it possible she hadn't covered the little guy up properly last night and made him ill? Just further proof of how bad she was at all this family jazz.

"I'm going to stay with them," Tad was saying above Cara's internal admonishment. "With Jack and Lili away in New York, she's on her own. I'm sorry I couldn't call earlier but they don't let you use cell phones inside."

"Tell Jules I'm thinking of her."

"Sure. Hey, they're coming out. Later, cuz." The line went dead.

The tinkle of breaking glass signaled another Dennis mishap.

Five minutes later, she was close to whipping out the high-end grappa she kept in the bottom drawer of her desk for emergencies. None of the usual bar backs were picking up her calls and the temp staff agency she used said they'd call around but she shouldn't hold her breath. Frantically, she headed for Sarriette's front of the house to see if Aaron could spare one of the waiters. Wednesday nights in most restaurants were often slow affairs, but not here. Jack's insistence that the fine-dining experience remain in the ordinary punter's grasp with bargain basement prices ensured full houses every night they were open. Needless to say, hope was low.

Until she passed the employee locker room and hope took root in her chest. Through the open door, she spied Shane hunched over on the bench, massaging out some tension in the back of his neck. And he was naked.

Okay, that was a teensy exaggeration. Not naked, just shirtless. Gloriously and beautifully shirtless. His tightly loomed back muscles just about made her jaw bungee to the floor.

Her reaction now wasn't all that different to finding him in Evan's room last night. The little guy had been buried in Shane's neck—hmm-hmm, did Cara know the attraction of that. They looked so perfect together, like one of those popular man-with-child posters that were all the rage when she was in high school and now formed the backbone of half the boards on Pinterest. Some shirtless hottie holding a baby that was supposed to make a girl's ovaries overload with the sheer *aw* of it.

Except for the unfortunate chest cover-up, the scenario had hit all her weak spots. The baby scent always made her gaga, but superimposed with hints of Shane, it rocketed her senses past eleven. Freshly baked bread and raw male. A trifecta of perfection that felt so out of reach—food, child, man.

But her beating heart had jumped into overdrive at the sight of Shane as he held that photo of Jack, Evan, and Jules. His expression had been overcome with a parade of emotions. Pain and longing and fear, things she recognized because they were her constant companions. They looked all wrong on his face, as though they didn't know how to arrange themselves but just hung there, waiting for instructions. In that moment, she had realized she knew nothing whatsoever about him, and boy, did she want to. Before she could probe further, Shane deposited a pacified Evan in her arms and left with a bark to tell Lili he had stopped by. Oh, and don't forget the papers that separate us legally.

Just who exactly had she married?

"Cara."

The bone-deep shiver skating down her spine brought her back to the locker room and the man who turned her on by merely breathing. During her drift, Shane had stood and now faced her.

That recalcitrant lock of hair still fell over his right eyebrow and she itched to push it back and then take a tour with her fingers through his dark hair. Her plunging gaze pulled short on a silvery scar linking one strong shoulder to his collar bone. Raw circular welts peppered one corner of his upper chest. A pinkish-white swatch the color of old prosciutto trailed his left side. The product of a rambunctious youth? Perhaps.

Something about the sight of him made her itch to touch and explore. Only when he grasped her reaching hand did she realize that her wayward body parts had suddenly became the boss of her.

"I'm sorry," she murmured while he held her hand in a kiss to his skin. "I didn't mean to…"

Didn't mean to what? Grope his chest like it was within her conjugal rights? She had thought he couldn't be more attractive to her but, surprise, surprise, here they were. The hair, the chiseled jaw, the dark nipples—she could write a poem about those nipples—and now that ravaged prize fighter's body that spoke to a very womanly instinct. Could she ascribe her feelings for Shane to some sort of twisted maternal compulsion?

Not. A. Chance.

"What happened?"

A brush of pain crossed his face, and his next words were casually strained. "It can get rough at the pastry station."

"Oh, yeah?" she said, not wanting to push but needing to know something about him. Desperately wanting to know something personal about her husband.

"Just ancient history." The sweet glaze of his eyes hardened over like a crème brûlée sugar shell, and she wasn't sure if she was relieved or disappointed he'd taken the easy way out. "Did you need something?"

Yes, she needed. Her body raged with need.

"I'm in a bit of a bind. Evan got sick—"

"Is he all right?" Not letting go of her hand, he stepped in close. His pulse thumped beneath her fingertips.

"He's fine. Tad and Jules took him to the ER but everything checked out."

"Does Jack know?" Shane's voice sounded tight. No more fake casual.

"I'm sure he does. Jules would have called him immediately." She regarded him intently, uncertain how to take his concern, which seemed out of proportion. Perhaps there had been a spot of bro-bonding last night. "So Tad was supposed to help out upstairs and now he's not coming and Dennis is making a hash of it and..."

He moved closer—still shirtless, don't forget that; still holding her hand, can't forget that—and the words dried in her throat. She tried to keep her eyes focused on his face. It was a very handsome face above a very hot body.

"Do you know anything about tending bar?"

"You assume because I'm Irish I must know how to work a bar?"

"Oh, I didn't mean—"

"Cara, it's okay. I'm kidding."

Less than twenty-four hours ago, there had been steam and flirtation, laughter and connection. *This is what happened that night. This feeling.* But with his abrupt departure, she felt like she had been hurled back to square one, unable to navigate the nuances of boy-meets-girl. Even a joke had her second-guessing every thought, word, and action. They couldn't be married, but she'd had high hopes she would be claiming alimony in the form of Shane's body.

"I've got advanced degrees in mixology and bar chat," he said. "I'd be happy to help." His face lifted in a brazen grin and her heart lifted right with it. *Down, stupid heart.*

"Will what I'm wearing do?"

Reluctantly, she extracted her hand from his and gave him the up-down, then up. And another down, just to be sure. Those jeans that clung affectionately to his legs, the broad bareness above the waist. The maximum concentration of sex appeal allowed by law.

"Um, you look fine." So fine. "I can find you a shirt."

She tried not to sound too melancholy about that. A bare-chested Shane shaking a cocktail was a delicious fantasy she'd be dreaming about tonight and so would every other woman at that party upstairs. Best to cover up those pecs and biceps and tasty nipples...She'd blanket him in a burka if she had to.

A couple of minutes later, he was behind the bar decked out in a tight black button-down shirt stuffed into the waistband of his well-filled-out jeans. A very relieved Dennis hugged him like he was the Second Coming, and Cara mentally kicked herself.

Why hadn't she thought of that?

* * *

Not for the first time this evening, Shane's rich laugh drew Cara's attention and she looked over to see that same smattering of female guests who had elected to take their dinner in liquid form. At the bar, they drooled as her bartender poured cocktails and charmed them out of their panties. Not literally, of course, but anyone could see they were thinking about it. If this were a hotel or cheesy cruise, his pockets would be weighed down with room keys by now.

He laughed again at something one of them said. Just

doing his job, she knew. Still, something dark and unkind burned inside her and she held on to it, thinking about how she could use it later at the gym. Cara wasn't the kind of woman who tickled a guy's funny bone. She was too tightly wound, too self-conscious of how her body looked when she laughed, too aware of those embarrassing laugh-snorts. In Vegas, it had been different. Shane had made her laugh and dimly, she recalled returning the favor, but isn't everything funnier with vodka goggles? Now she was jealous because the husband she didn't want found other women amusing. It was so beneath her.

It didn't stop her from hating every single one of his skanky admirers with the heat of a thousand suns.

Shane caught her eye and made an almost imperceptible beckoning motion with his head. She stepped behind the bar.

"How are we doing?" he asked while pouring a finger of scotch into a couple of lowball glasses.

"Good. Desserts will be out any minute, and then the wind down. Should be done in thirty, forty-five max."

"Did you tell the kitchen—"

"To remove the chocolate tartuffo mousse cake from the fridge to get it to room temperature? Done an hour ago."

"And—"

"Mona knows to use the one-oh-nine tip for the lemon tart decoration."

"She always wants to use the smallest one," he said, half grumbling.

"I know. She got the message." Mona, Shane's second at the pastry station, was a bit of a flake but she knew her place.

Flashing that drool-worthy smile, he nudged his hip against hers. "We're bossin' it, then."

Yes, they were. Shane's calm, easy competence was the perfect complement to her high-energy flutter. The idea of them working side by side spiked her pulse before her mind was hijacked by wicked thoughts of teaming up for more pleasurable activities. Dialing back her libido around Shane was getting to be a problem.

One of his adoring fans propped her stupendous boobs on the bar. *Cheerio, libido. Nice knowin' ya.*

"Shane, honey, is this when you release the serpent?" Rack of Gibraltar slurred. Her less well-endowed friend, whose face bore all the hallmarks of chronic sun abuse, nodded her approval.

Cara's head snapped back in alarm. "Release the what?"

Shane let loose a chuckle, laden with Irish charm. From a glass jug, he poured a measure of water into each of the whiskey glasses. "The serpent has been released, ladies."

Cara could feel her mouth gaping and she was having a mighty hard time closing it. "What does that mean?"

"Well, the full flavor of the scotch is only released when you add water to it," Shane said. "In whiskey parlance, we call that releasing the serpent."

I bet you do.

The ladies sniffed, swirled, and sipped tentatively from their glasses. "It's good. Really good."

Leather Face pointed over his shoulder. "What about that bottle there?"

"The Glenmorangie Lasanta? Oh, that's a great one, too. Honey, caramel, and toffee notes. Soulful stuff." Reaching up, his shirt strained against his back, outlining every delicious muscle pulled taut. The stretch did marvelous things to his ass as well. One of the spectators wet her lips and blew out a long breath while her friend squirmed. That's when Cara noticed the gaps on the top shelf, each one formerly home to the three bottles of high-end scotch now comprising a tasting trio on the bar.

"Soulful stuff, indeed," Leather Face murmured while Gibraltar moaned. The woman actually moaned!

A very feminine urge burbled in Cara's chest. It was like she was the cool kid who had the inside skinny on the underground band, but now the word was out. Shane had gone mainstream and every Jane, Dee, and Sally was getting in on the act.

"The Glenmorangie is matured in white oak barrels before they finish it off in sherry casks." Shane opened the new bottle and grabbed a couple of clean glasses. "The quality of the wood is key, girls."

The girls, who probably hadn't been called "girls" since their heyday circa 1969, preened.

"Quality wood is key. Right, Suzanne?" Leather Face elbowed Gibraltar.

The woman's mouth had dropped open at a Shane chest-hair sighting when he bent over. "Uh-huh."

"God, Suzanne, I can't take you anywhere." Leather Face handed him a fifty dollar bill, making sure she brushed Shane's fingers as she did so.

"The bar is open, girls. No need to pay."

"That's for you, Shane," she said, her smile like a great white shark's in her basketball-orange face.

"The staff sure appreciates your generosity." He dropped it into a jar behind the bar, one that was already filled to overflowing with fives and tens. A couple of twenties, too.

Shane's lips curved as he met Cara's eyes. He winked at her.

Cara stifled her giggle as it hit her. The thought of Shane Doyle using his masculine wiles to get more tips was too, too funny.

Gibraltar leaned over, her scary breasts swiping the bar like some lewd bar wash. "Shane, do you do private parties?"

Shane swallowed and it was so damn cute. "Ah, no, I'm strictly a company man. No freelancing." He looked over their heads. "Desserts are out, girls. You might want to return to your table so you don't miss out on my lovely lemon tarts and decadent chocolate cake."

That earned him another jaw drop. "You made the desserts, too?"

"I'm a man of many talents."

Leather Face wobbled off the bar stool and snatched at one of the scotch glasses. "I hope they're paying you well."

"I'd pay him well," Gibraltar replied in a loud whisper. "To release *his* serpent."

In a gurgle of lusty giggles, they lurched back to the dinner table to load up on sugar.

Cara suspected her stunned expression might stop a clock. "Wow, Doyle, I never would have thought you had it in you."

Shane cleared away the half-drunk glasses and spilled the dregs into the bar sink. "Come again?"

"Using your body like that." Immediately, she cringed as the words left no doubt that she'd been enjoying the show just as much as the customers.

"I don't know what you mean. Are you suggesting I'd use this"—he gestured at his chest, then sliced through the air in a downward motion past his waistband—"to make a few extra dollars? What kind of a person do you think I am?"

Her cheeks smarted in mortification. "Oh, I didn't mean to imply—"

"Cara, I'm happy to be of use." A wicked smile played on his lips, and he leaned in close. He smelled incredible. "We make a good team, don't you think?"

She hoped her swallow didn't sound as loud to him as it did to her. "I do."

His gaze held hers for a beat too long and when he looked away she realized it hadn't been long enough.

I do? Had she just answered his question about their brilliant partnership with "I do"? She'd heard of women with pregnancy brain; she must have its hormonal cousin, "wedding brain." Ruffled, she surveyed the room, an action that came as natural to her as breathing. Surely someone needed her, but her vision was filled with content guests, not an upturned nose or searching glance in sight.

"We should be doing bigger events, don't you think?"

There he went again with the *we*. Her heart fluttered at that tiniest of words and all the hope it held. She turned back to find him considering her with that sexy, boyish expression he had a patent on.

"Jack doesn't really care about the events stuff," she said.

"Why not?"

"It's just not interesting to him. More trouble than it's worth."

"That's ridiculous." His brow creased in bafflement. "You do an amazing job keeping these rooms full practically every night we're open. We should be expanding. There's that place next door—"

"I know!" she interrupted, unable to rein in her excitement. Jack was always putting her off with wait-and-see and no one else ever expressed interest. She filled Shane in on her plan to get Penny Napier's Pink Hearts Appreciation Dinner and her hope that it would plant the seeds for the restaurant's expansion.

"Jack's not interested in catering, as he calls it. He says it'll dilute the product because he can't oversee everything to his exacting standards. You know how these egotistical chefs are."

"Present company excluded," he said with a so-help-her-God smile.

"Oh, right. You're nothing like Jack."

A shadow passed over his face before brightening to that easy expression she loved. The dark was interesting, though, and she wanted to know more.

"Unless you want to be."

"Unless I want to be what?"

"Like Jack. You've been angling to be part of his team for a while now, haven't you?" Lili had said Shane sent his résumé every month for a year, begging for a job at Thyme in New York, then pushed hard to transfer to Chicago, so enthusiastic was he to work with a great chef like Jack.

Shane nodded slowly. "I have." His voice didn't quite match his expression. He had wanted to say something else but checked himself at the last second. "I could learn a lot from him but I don't think I have the temperament to be an executive chef. I have the standards. I just don't enjoy bellowing at people."

She ducked her head to hide the cool little smile she could feel burgeoning. That's what she loved about Shane, how different he was from all the guys she knew: Jack, her father, most of the men she'd dated in New York. And while these days she was drawn to weaker guys who let her lead, she didn't see that in Shane. There was nothing weak about him even when he was acting like Opie Cunningham.

"Actually, I'd like to open my own pastry shop someday," he said with a cool little smile of his own.

In Chicago, an internal voice squeaked before it was steamrolled by her common sense. *There is no future here.* "I'm sure Jack would hate to lose you but he'd jump on that as an investment."

"I don't need Jack."

The words hissed through the air like a curse. It wasn't

the first time she had the impression that Shane had a problem with her future brother-in-law.

"Jack's invested in my family's restaurant and he's going to be a part owner of Tad's new wine bar. He has a good eye, but I can understand how you'd want to be your own man." Most people would jump at the chance to go into business with someone as resourceful and well-known as Jack. Shane's independence did him credit but there was definitely something else here.

Raucous hoots went up from the guests as Rack of Gibraltar defied gravity and pulled her top-heavy self to a stand and a shaky toast. Cara's estimate of thirty minutes to go might have been premature.

"I didn't mean to snap," Shane said, his voice as tight as a drum. His color was high and Cara imagined a cat-five hurricane brewing beneath his typically calm surface.

"Working with Jack didn't turn out the way you expected?" Cara prompted. Sometimes, it's a bad idea to meet your heroes.

"No," he said, lifting his eyes to meet hers. "He's not what I imagined at all."

Her skin scorched from his focus. Not a single touch, but she felt like she'd been rode hard and put away wet. When she had first met him, she thought she could read him. A sunny, carefree, bring-him-home-to-mama kind of guy.

Nice? What I'm thinking about you is the opposite of nice.

"I have some work to finish. I should get back to it." That bottle of grappa in her desk drawer would come in handy right about now. She retreated with a wobble on one of her four-inch heels, all while he continued to stare. A hot, invasive gaze that made her feel desired and wrong.

Deliciously, wickedly wrong.

CHAPTER 9

By the time midnight rolled around, the room was quiet, the guests had been bundled into cabs, and Shane was talking to himself. The flirtatious ladies had stopped by to make him an offer for some after-hours fun times. The phrase "Irish ham sandwich" was bandied about liberally. He just about managed to keep his shudders to a minimum as he politely declined.

Sometimes the accent was a curse.

Now he was closing out the private-room bar and gabbing like an old biddy with a wall of bottles on how he wanted to play the Cara situation. Because he definitely wanted to play.

Tonight, there had been no mistaking that flare in her eyes while he suffered the mental strip-down from those bar patrons. He'd not intended to make her jealous but between the moment in Jack's kitchen and her interest tonight, there could be no more doubts about their sizzling connection. Last night, he had fled Jack's house because the thought of falling for her, of falling for the whole lot of them, scared him half to death. But surely he could separate out this thing with Cara. His stunning wife might be a ten to his sketchy six—he'd definitely married up there—but why shouldn't they act on the heat between them and enjoy each other?

"Yeah," he said to the bank of liquor. "Why shouldn't we?"

"Watch out, first sign of madness." Cara's soft voice cut his not-so-internal debate short. With his back still turned to her, his body enjoyed the rustle of that silky blouse against her smooth skin as she settled in on a bar stool.

"Bartender, tell me all about releasing the serpent."

He reached for the Glenmorangie Lasanta and was rewarded with a low whistle.

"Work it, Doyle. Soulful stuff, indeed," she said, all mock sultry.

"Only the paying customers get to objectify." He poured two fingers of scotch, splashed it with water, and pushed it across the bar. "Need the spiel?"

"No, I was part of your rapt audience earlier. Toffee, honey, and caramel notes, not to mention the oh-so-important wood." She took a sip, then another longer one. "You going to let me drink alone?"

"I'll cut you off when the time is right but I won't partake. I'm not much of a drinker." At her skeptical squint, he added, "Except during wild and crazy stag parties."

"Worried I'll take advantage of you again?"

"Well, there's always the chance we might be renewing our vows before the night is out."

She laughed, a sound that pulsed in his chest and made him wish that he hadn't folded like a cheap suitcase when Cara said, *Hey, I have an idea.* If he'd denied that dark, greedy part of himself—the Packy Sullivan part—they could have started this out right.

You can separate this out, man.

"I didn't think I'd be able to see the funny side of this but it seems I've gotten past it." She looked at him from under her lashes. "Alcohol always helps."

In Shane's experience, alcohol only ever helped cowards become bullies and weak men dull their pain.

She nudged the glass toward him. "Another, barkeep."

Hell no. She hadn't even finished that one. They were not going down this road again.

"Did you have anything to eat since lunch? That chicken can't have filled you up much." With Jack out of town, he'd made sure to cook her meal to her requirements, though he'd jazzed it up with a little rosemary-lemon marinade.

"I'll eat something when I get home."

"I could make you something now. We'll pop into the kitchen and I'll be your chef slave."

He headed out, strangely gratified when she followed him without complaint. On the way to the kitchen, he grabbed a couple of stools from the main bar and put them against the countertop nearest the burners.

"Now sit and tell me what you'd like, and it'd better not be chicken."

Her expression was pained. "I don't usually eat this late. It messes up my metabolism."

"Once in a while isn't going to kill you." He opened the walk-in and called out to her, "Your wish is my command."

From inside the fridge, he could hear her noisy thoughts, which were finally punctuated with a small sigh of surrender. "Are there any morels left? I saw they were a special on the menu earlier." Amazingly, there were some left on a cookie tray. Nice black ones that would go wonderfully with…he looked around. Steak? Cara wouldn't be down with that.

"Will you eat eggs?" He popped his head around the door, eggs in his hands like he was getting ready to juggle them. "I think they'd be great with scrambled eggs." It was simple and uncomplicated, for his far from simple and uncomplicated wife.

She nodded. "Can I help?"

He put her to work whisking the eggs, handing off the ingredients she needed: a splash of milk, a pinch of salt, a couple of grinds of pepper. Meanwhile, he sautéed the morels in butter and cracked pepper until the honeycomb surface browned up to a golden caramel color. The rich, muddy scent filled the air around them.

Looking over, he found her paused midbeat over the eggs. She caught his stare.

"I'll mess it up if I cook them."

"You? You couldn't mess up anything if you tried."

"You don't know me very well."

But God, he wanted to. So much for keeping it separate. He removed the morels from the heat and transferred them to a plate. "Just put the eggs in here."

She poured them in carefully, as though she were dealing with molten gold, then stood awkwardly, almost childlike. The slender column of her throat bulged on a swallow. He'd never met anyone so nervous in a kitchen, not even Dennis-the-extern.

"You know," he said, moving closer, "cooking is as much about confidence as it is about skill." She tilted her big eyes up to his. "Sometimes you just have to play the part."

"The part of a cook?"

"The part of a confident, sexy cook. Don't be afraid to make a mistake and you probably won't." He pulled on the knot of her hair and enjoyed the sensuous unfurl from its constraint.

"There's nothing sexier than a confident woman in the kitchen. You're confident everywhere else, so there's no reason why you shouldn't be here, either."

"Okay," she said suspiciously, shaking out her hair.

He put a hand on her waist and felt a deep breath rack her body. "Do you mind if I..."

Without waiting for her answer, he undid the top button of her blouse and revealed that beautiful shadow in the valley of her cleavage. He let his knuckles graze the plump swell of her breasts while another unbutton produced a glimpse of the laced edge of her bra. Pink, sheer, devilishly designed to turn him to granite in zero point zero seconds. Pink was her favorite color and it was getting up there on his list as well.

"This is supposed to make me better at cooking eggs?" Her voice rasped a little, and it thrilled him more than he could have thought possible.

"A sexy cook makes sexy food." He trailed his hands down her sides and over the flare of her hips. "Your skirt's not short enough." It fell a couple of inches above her knees, and while her calves were amazing, her thighs were spectacular. He wanted more thigh.

The snugness of her skirt was no match for his hands. Eyes never leaving hers, he pulled it up at her waist and folded it over so it revealed more skin than it covered. She made a breathy noise in her throat and his dick jumped.

"How are those shoes feeling?"

"What?" Voice in a tremble, she looked down, bending forward enough to give him another healthy glimpse of her gorgeous breasts.

"I've been wearing them for close to sixteen hours. How do you think they feel?"

"Take them off."

She stared at him like he wasn't the full shilling. "That's against health codes—isn't it?"

"I won't tell if you don't."

Her eyes had been bright before but now they sparkled like stars. Something about what he had said appealed to a deep part of her, either the rule-breaking or the secrecy. Maybe both. Leaning her palm on his shoulder, she kicked them off, and they hit the metal-bottomed counter with a satisfying thud. Her toes shone a shimmery pink, like sanding sugar. He liked the toes.

"So now you've got me half naked and barefoot. You planning to knock me up next?"

"Patience, young padawan. Let's see how you do with the eggs first."

He spun her around and turned the knob on the stove, sparking the blue flame to life. Resting one hand on her hip, he passed her a wooden spoon with the other. "Now stir."

He kept one eye on the eggs and the other on her mouth as she broke up the glossy mixture with jerky strokes.

"It's not that hard," she said, catching her fleshy bottom lip by her teeth.

If you say so. All his blood had pooled in his erection and only sheer willpower prevented him from rubbing his body against hers. Unknotting her hair had released fragrant herbals that now filled his nostrils. Without her heels, she was several inches shorter than him so he would have to lift her up to get her to notch right in to the spoon of his crotch. While he pondered the logistics of that, he looked over her shoulder at the eggs that were cooking up quickly. They were eggs, and they had no clue that he needed more time breathing her in.

Bloody eggs.

"Your father didn't teach you to cook?"

"No, it was more Lili's thing. I wasn't really interested."
She sounded sad about the way that had turned out.

"You're doing a fine job there. So what do you eat at
home? Takeout from DeLuca's? Pretty handy living right
above an Italian restaurant." More than once, he'd stopped
in to get a bowl of Tony's famous gnocchi with brown butter
and sage. The stuff was cracktastic.

He felt her shudder right down to his toes. "God, no.
I've had enough pasta to last a lifetime. I load up on TV
dinners and Whole Foods salads. I'm so busy that it's easier to have a routine, not think about my eating. That way
I won't forget."

My eating. That was a curious way to put it, like it existed
outside herself. A separate entity.

"Forget? Don't you just eat when you're, you know,
hungry?"

"I've always been a picky eater so there isn't much that I
like. I tend to stick to the same things. I know it sounds boring but if I don't plan it, I probably wouldn't eat at all."

He was about to ask more when she jerked back into his
chest.

"This looks ready," she said, removing the pan from the
heat.

He would come back to that, but for now, he'd tend to
her nutritional needs. He plated up and set their meals on the
counter with a big glass of water. She'd have quite the head
on her tomorrow if she didn't start on the H$_2$O.

The first taste of the morel almost knocked him off the
bar stool, its buttery nuttiness too gorgeous for words. The
complex array of flavors—earth, butter, spice—was perfect
with the simplicity of the eggs.

"Good eggs," he murmured around chewing, giving the
cook her due.

"Good morels," she said.

He kept his focus on his own meal, unsure exactly why. She didn't eat with the crew, she didn't want to join them for a meal after the line dancing, she had looked positively panicked in her father's kitchen that day he went there for lunch. There was something odd going on, independent of the usual womanly obsession about calories.

Pushing her cleaned-off plate back, she looked up, a slice of sunshine lifting her face. "That was great, Shane. Thanks."

"Dessert?" Before she could balk, he was back in the fridge. There were a few lemon tarts left over but he took only one—the sharing of dessert was one of those rituals perfect for the creation of intimacy.

She raised an eyebrow when he placed the tart down. She had such pretty eyebrows. Dark blonde crescents that were usually pinched or hitched or in the process of becoming pinched or hitched. Holding the fork up, he signaled with his eyes.

"Cute, Paddy."

It took him a moment to get it. "When I put this on the menu, LT, I didn't know about your nickname with the crew. They seem to think you don't like them."

"Oh, I like them fine. I just don't eat well with others."

He waited for her to elaborate, but for once his usual ploy of keeping mum didn't get the result. It wasn't that Cara didn't like food so much as she didn't like the social part of it. Food and people were the problem, or one of the problems, yet here she was eating with him. He felt some small measure of victory in this, though he wasn't sure he had a right to it. Where Cara was concerned, he didn't have any rights.

He carved a piece out of the semihard disc, making sure

he got a decent chunk of the pastry crust. The citrus scent, faint because the tart was cooler than the optimum temperature, snaked its way into the back of his nose and ratcheted up his taste buds to mouthwatering levels. The sweet-tart combination as he scooped it off the fork invoked so much pleasure he almost forgot where he was. The barest moan escaped his throat.

Cara stared at his lips, then licked her own. "That good, huh?"

"I am." He grinned. "Tart's not bad either."

She took the fork from him and sliced a sliver off the top layer, careful to avoid the crust. He wanted to tell her both pieces should be paired together, but he'd never been one of those prescriptive chefs with instructions for how things should be eaten. Food was too exciting for rules. Instead he watched her, and hell was he glad he did. It never ceased to amaze him how a face could be transformed by the taste of food, especially something sweet. There was a reason why dessert is the favorite part of every meal, why people skip appetizers or store up their Weight Watcher points.

The reason was the look of pleasure on his wife's face.

He really needed to stop calling her that, but it sounded so right in his head. *Better make sure you keep it in your head, idiot.*

She licked the fork, then licked it again, this time with a graveled *unh* of satisfaction. When she looked up, she wrinkled her nose. "What?"

"I've never been jealous of a fork before now."

Smiling, she passed the fork back to him, and he looked at it, thinking he should dash it to the ground because it was getting more action from Cara's mouth than him. Not one to dwell on injustice, he got over it and helped himself to another bite.

On her next sip of scotch, her shoulders danced a shiver shimmy, which did marvelous things to her breasts. He pushed the water toward her and got an endearing glare in return.

"You're very talented, Shane."

"Thanks."

"It must be wonderful to be so good at something," she said on a sigh.

"Ah, sure, everybody's good at something."

She rubbed the lip of the glass. "I suppose."

"Now that doesn't sound like sexy, confident, cooking-up-a-storm Cara. You're good at a million things." *Kissing, nipple sucking, a hip sway that could topple governments . . .*

She gave it her careful consideration. "I'm good at managing things and people. It's not creative—I'm not bringing great joy like you with your desserts or Lili with her art—but it's necessary. Control is necessary. Otherwise, it's just chaos."

He understood that to a certain extent. He wasn't in Cara's league of extraordinary control but he knew all about sticking to a plan and keeping your eye on the prize. Or he thought he had before his life took a crazy left turn a couple of weeks back.

She plucked the fork from his fingers and helped herself to another lemony morsel. At this rate, he was going to have to eat all the pastry, which screwed up the ratio. The pain of being a pastry chef.

"You're much better than the last guy," she said on a swallow.

The last guy who had fallen victim to Cara. "He was no good?"

"Oh, he was good, just not up to your standard." She gave a crafty smile and took another sip of her scotch.

Not up to your standard. He couldn't let it go but he took back the fork first. If he couldn't grab her hips and grind his body into hers, then it was best to have something else to hold on to. "So he was a bit of a wash then?"

"Oh, I wouldn't say that. He was just a little too...tentative." She stole the fork from him before he had a chance to take his turn. Her tongue slid across her lips, catching a hint of lemon cream at the corner. Knowing too well how those plump lips tasted was torture, and tonight they wouldn't just be tart and sweet. They'd also have that smoky imprint from the scotch.

His heart hammered, the pulse finding full expression in his throbbing dick. He grabbed the fork back. "No one's ever accused me of being tentative," he said, then shoved in another mouthful so he wouldn't be tempted to embellish.

She downed the rest of her drink, and her eyes watered. A couple of blinks later, she had the fork out of his hand and was scooping up another bite of the lemon topping. Jesus, all that crust—

"No, you're about as sure as anyone I've ever met, Shane." She held his gaze, bold as brass. "Who taught you to cook?"

"My aunt Josephine. Well, she wasn't really my aunt, just a neighbor of my mother's." As a kid, he'd hung onto her apron strings in her warm, homey kitchen, begging her to teach him how to make soda bread and fruit cake even when his father had derided him as a sissy for taking an interest. She'd taught him all she knew and when she couldn't teach him anymore, he got a job after school at O'Connell's Bakery on Tullamore Street, and when he couldn't learn anything else from them, he'd gone to culinary school. "She was there for me after my mother died when I was a kid."

Compassion filled her big blue eyes. "What about your dad?"

"He was around in fits. Spent most of his time in the local pub or the bookie's betting on the gee gees." At her blank look, he translated. "The horses."

Thinking about his father shouldn't have hurt anymore, but he'd found himself engulfed by his memory these last few weeks. How could he not when faced with evidence of the man's fecundity in Jack? Those high cheekbones, the strong brow, the hard, angular jaw. Jack was John Sullivan's son through and through while Shane had taken on his mother's likeness. Not dark or brooding, it was easy for his father to reject a kid he claimed didn't look one bit like him.

Cara's slender finger traced the edge of the countertop, mesmerizing him.

"Is your father still around?"

He spoke around the knot like a dumpling in his throat. "No, he's dead now. About eighteen months. Early onset Alzheimer's."

"I'm sorry." She placed her hand over his. It felt warmer than he expected.

"Don't be. He was a prick."

When she looked shocked, he realized he had been trying to get a reaction from her. "It's just…" He squeezed her hand. "John Sullivan was a difficult man to be around."

"You don't have the same name as him?"

Damn it, big mouth. If that got back to Jack…He took a long, hard look at Cara. Her eyes glowed warm and sympathetic, a repository of secrets. She wouldn't talk about this to anyone.

"He never married my mother. Wouldn't even admit paternity until after she died and Jo came after him with a rolling pin and the threat of the courts." Sometimes Shane wished she'd stayed out of it because his father's manner of claiming came with a price. He may not look like him, but Shane had the scars that branded him as a son of John Sullivan.

Jo thought raising Shane would be the making of Packy, the feckless town drunk. That a child might soften and fine-tune him into a responsible citizen. Irish women of a certain generation still looked on men with indulgence. *Sure, wasn't the drink to blame? Wasn't he a demon when he'd had a few bevvies? He can't be held accountable.* And so on.

He had loved the woman and mourned her death three years back but there was only so much he could take of the apologia for the species known as *Irish homo sapiens drunkus.* And that he had allowed himself to lose control in Vegas was the ultimate insult. He was more like the old man than he wanted to think. All Jo's nurture couldn't overcome the nature.

Cara's soft voice brought him back. "It sounds like you had a hard time of it."

Releasing her hand, he balled his fist to stop the automatic reflex to rub his scar. "He was a small-minded, nasty drunk who didn't think much of a son who wanted to bake for a living. Women's work. Definitely not manly enough for my father."

"But you wanted to make it your life—it really speaks to you, doesn't it? Food."

He looked up, surprised at her question, but also not really. Cara was sharp. She saw things other people didn't notice. "Yes, it does. Food means a lot to me."

Cooking and eating with Jo and her big, noisy family had got him through the tougher times, though he would probably never have thought to make it a career until he found out about Jack. Knowing about his brother deepened Shane's commitment to food and created an invisible connection to a man he had never met. It seemed silly when he put it like that, but there it was. Only later did the resentment toward Jack set in bone-deep. Resentment he knew was downright absurd—how can you blame a man for not being around to save you if he doesn't even know you exist?

Cara's smile was a little crooked. "You sound like a DeLuca. They're all food-obsessed."

Interesting how she set herself apart from her family. "But not you?"

"With the DeLucas, it's expected that you glorify the gnocchi, bow down to the bucatini." She made a supplicant's gesture with both hands. "People who don't cook or bake are considered highly suspect in the Italian culture, especially if you're a woman. As for whether it's manly or not…A piece of your cake can hit a woman's sweet spot and take her to a higher plane. For some women, it's better than sex. If that's not the definition of what it means to be a man, then we need to find a better dictionary."

Shit, that booze must have gone straight to her head. Too late, he remembered that mixing morels with alcohol could have weird effects.

"I'd be the first to tell you my desserts have taken women to places unimaginable—sure, every night, I can hear the moans in the dining room from in here—but if you think a piece of cake is better than sex, then you've not met the right man."

Color suffused her cheeks, looking so pretty on her he ached to run the backs of his fingers against her skin to catch her warmth. The air was so thick with the sex and need sparking between them that he expected he might combust any minute. Or his jeans would.

Slipping off the stool, she treaded carefully to the sink

with her fork in hand. Something about her bare feet tugged
sharply at his heart. He wanted nothing more than to fuck
her senseless and hold her tight against his raging body.

But she was buzzed and she needed air. They both did.

"Come on, Cara. Time to go home."

* * *

You haven't met the right man. It had sounded like an invitation but then he followed it up with a stop-her-dead glare
and an order to go home. Had they not just done a spot of
sexy cooking-cum-sharing? How could she have completely
misread the signals again?

"I'll just grab my purse and car keys," she murmured,
keeping her head down while she futzed with her shoes.
Craptastic, now her feet had swollen too large to fit back into
their cages.

"Okay to the purse but you won't need your keys. You're
on the bike with me."

Her breath caught, and she was unsure whether she
should credit his steel-voiced presumption or the excitement
of knowing what her thighs would be gripping for the next
twenty minutes. She jerked her mind away from that thought
and let another slide in to take its place.

This doofus thought she was drunk.

"I'm perfectly sober," she said, meaning it. So she might
have taken an indecent slug of her grappa stash earlier to
calm her Shane-frazzled nerves, and a couple spoonfuls of
scotch had since branded her throat. But after eating, she actually felt clearer headed than she had in some time, which
was saying something considering the tumult her entire body
was undergoing.

"Go get your stuff," he said firmly. Bad-cop Shane was
back on the case.

A cloudless, moon-bright sky greeted her when she stepped outside to the empty street, the night air pleasantly cool against her skin. While she waited for Shane to set the alarm and lock up, she allowed a lazy gaze down her body. Damn, she was popping out of her blouse and her skirt was hitched so high spectators could skip the sights in France and go straight to her underwear. Hastily, she grasped at her undone buttons but froze when an agreeable weight fell on her shoulders. The scent of Shane's leather jacket, now warming her skin, reached her nostrils. How could a piece of clothing smell that good?

Not the clothing. Just the man.

"Put this on, it'll keep you warm," he said softly against her ear.

Maybe, but she knew what she'd rather be wearing. *Eau de Shane*, drenched all over her body. *Cut it out*, she told her brain, while her other body parts got the mutiny underway by appointing union reps to stand up to the management.

Obediently, she slipped into the jacket with his help. He spun her around and zipped her up slowly. Slow enough that there was no missing how his gaze lingered like a kiss on her half-exposed breasts. It was sexual but, as always with Shane, it was more. Every look held infinite promise.

Then he put that stupid helmet on her head and she knew the pain of all those extras who had played Stormtroopers.

"Do I have to wear it?" she whined.

"Your head is precious to me."

Oh, that was so...

"Lame." Not the politest reaction but when doubts as to whether you're getting lucky take over, one's mood tends to sour.

"I know, but it's true. I'm going to have to get you your

own helmet." His licentious gaze traveled down her body. "Need help with your skirt?"

"Excuse me?"

His grin was a wicked, slow burn, the first since he had trampled the sexy vibe back in Sarriette's kitchen. "Need help turning it into straddle mode?"

She stared but the charmingly crooked grin remained fixed on his face. Maybe he couldn't see her stabby eyes with the headgear. She shot a condemning look at the death machine, then hitched up her skirt a couple more inches with a what-the-hell. At this rate, she was fast on her way to a new career on the pole.

He threw a long leg over. She did likewise but a lot less gracefully, and then it was, *Ladies, start your engines*. A long, pulsing shiver coursed through her. She found herself excited, nervous. Horny.

Oh God.

"Hold on." He waited until she slid her arms around his waist and settled her body against his. Why did she have to wear the helmet? While the wafting leather-and-man scent was divine, she had a notion it might be better times infinity if she could lay her cheek against the snugly woven muscles of his back.

To her surprise, he headed east toward the city instead of taking one of the major arteries north to home. Though she had seen the Chicago skyline a million times before, this viewpoint gave it a new vibrancy, making it bold and bright, grandly epic, impossibly romantic. The wind lashed through his overlong hair and she wished she was brave enough to let go one hand to touch it.

Moments later, they were speeding along Lower Wacker Drive through the underworld beneath the city. The sounds of the bike echoed off the walls around them, the street above, the body that didn't feel like it belonged to her. They emerged onto Columbus heading for Lake Shore and the liberation of returning to aboveground shook her mind free, sprinkling her thoughts on the breeze whipping against her legs. Barely an inch of a breath separated her body from Shane's. She gripped her thighs tighter and thought she felt his stomach strain taut beneath her hands.

This intimacy should have scared her, but in truth it was a fakery. She was holding on for dear life so she wouldn't, well, die. Closing her eyes, she luxuriated in the moment and imagined what it might be like. Her real husband. Her real lover. Her reality.

They came to a smooth stop. Home at last and it was far too soon.

He didn't appear to be in a hurry to get off the motorcycle and she went with the flow, holding on but not as tight as before because that would have been weird. He laced his fingers through hers.

"Cold?" It came out gruff.

She shook her head, brushing the helmet across his back. In unspoken agreement, their joined hands moved over his rigid abs and his hard chest. As for who was leading the tour, she couldn't say. Okay, it was all her, but she held on to the illusion of a spirit forcing the play of her hands on the Ouija board of his body. When they reached his pecs, he expelled a sharp hiss that shot spears of want to her sex.

Reluctantly, she pulled her hands away from his warmth and removed the helmet. With ramshackle legs, she climbed off the bike. Would he take control like he had the night of the line dancing? Would she wrest it back? Would she want to?

He snaked an arm around her waist and drew her into his hard side. Dipping his hand to the curve of her butt, he gave a gentle squeeze and propelled her forward. In his eyes, she saw hazy lust that sent her bones on an unauthorized leave of absence. The helmet slipped from her shaking fingers. *Thud.*

"Sorry," she murmured.

"Not a problem."

No, sir, it was not. Soft at first, his lips moved over hers, teasing, testing her limits. Sweet, so sweet. Only when she moaned did he give it his all. A full-scale assault of such heat, she found herself clutching at his shirt and wishing she could climb all over him.

Cleverly, he picked up on her desperation and pulled her astride his thick, muscular thigh but instead of easing the ache between her legs, it inflamed it. He slipped one of those big, callused hands beneath the hem of her skirt to palm her butt cheek. His other hand anchored her head back so he could feed devastating kisses along the curve of her neck. There was panting and whimpering and shaking, all on her side, of course. Mostly, he was quiet and methodical. A real professional.

"Shane," she whispered against the velvet-rough of his cheek, needing to say something, anything. Terrified this lurch into abandon might result in her forgetting everything—her name, who she was, who she was trying to be. Her mind was like a metronome waiting to peter out. If only she could will it still and relax, let this play out and enjoy the newness of feeling alive for the first time in years.

"I know," he said, though he couldn't possibly know anything. She wanted him to know it all.

On the gush of a breath, she bit out, "I had anorexia."

The words sat up, waiting for some sort of response, whether from her body or from his mouth she didn't know. Mood-killer par excellence. She didn't move, not voluntarily anyway. A tremor started up in her thighs, still wrapped around his strong leg. The longest seconds of her life ticked by. Perhaps he hadn't heard her.

"And now?"

The strangeness of her position made her cells tingle in defense. Straddled over a man's thigh, perched on a motorcycle, exposed in the alley behind her home. Good God. She made to move; he held her fast with his hand still affixed to her butt.

"How are you now?" he repeated in a low voice that tasted of night.

Physically she was fine, so she told him that truth. "I'm healthy and I eat three meals a day, most days. Sometimes I snack. And, of course, I drink to excess."

He snorted, and the noise, so human and grounding, eased her tremble. "That you do. Is this why you don't eat with the crew?"

She nodded. "I know it sounds narcissistic but I feel like I'm being judged all the time, so eating in groups is difficult. I like food. I just have a hard time with certain things. Social situations. My fear foods."

His brow wrinkled. "Fear foods?"

"People like me don't hate everything we eat. We just hate what it does to our bodies." It felt easier to speak of herself like she was a member of some odd sect. Less personal. "Some foods are more difficult than others, like pasta. I know that sounds strange, but when I was a kid, pasta was all we ever ate. So much of it, and everyone would be stuffing their faces."

He looked thoughtful. "Food's important for families. It's how they connect, show their love. Usually so they don't have to talk to each other."

Damn straight. "If you're not into food in my family, it's hard to feel like you belong. I've never really felt that." It broke her heart to say it, not just because it was true, but because she couldn't fix it. She would always feel that sense of separation from them.

"There are other ways of belonging."

She sighed. "Not in my family. They have certain expectations."

Marriage, children, all those things her heart keened for. It was safer to pretend she didn't want them, to scoff at the twin yokes of marriage and parenthood. It kept the matchmakers at bay and shored up defenses battered by the sight of DeLuca scamps and the beautiful kids she volunteered with at the children's hospital.

"But they're such wonderful people. Surely, they understand what you've gone through." With the hand not surgically attached to her butt, he rubbed the small of her back in tight heated circles. "What you're still going through."

Her heart beat rabbit kicks against her rib cage. "They don't know."

The hand on her back stilled. The overhead light cast his features in a feral light. "Why not?"

"When it first started, I was ashamed. I knew it was wrong to starve myself but it was like a drug. A perfection drug. It was easy to lie and say I'd eaten over at a friend's, and once I got to college it was like every other girl had some weird food habit she was trying to hide. Secrecy has been my normal for so long. I've been working to achieve a new normal over the last couple of years, but it's also been a tough time for my family. My mom battled cancer, the restaurant almost failed. What's going on with me would just add to their worry. I don't want them giving me strange looks every time I pick up a fork or go to a bathroom."

"So you've told no one?" he ground out, his incredulity evident.

Other than a therapist in New York, which didn't really count because she was paying her to listen. She suspected one other person knew, but they had never discussed it. "No one."

Confessing to Shane was so liberating but her reasons were less benign than it might look on the surface. He had just told her how important food was to him and she had told him that it was important to her in another way. A con in the relationship column and now that he knew the truth, she could move forward in the knowledge that this was a non-starter. Every word out of her mouth propelled them closer to good-bye, more swiftly and decisively than any legal document could ever do. A man who made his living in the kitchen couldn't possibly be interested in a woman who was the absolute negation of everything he stood for.

Silence reigned. Friendly, effusive Shane had finally met his match but then men hated when women had weird hang-ups. Oddly, she had expected he would be sweet and distantly kind about it, not quiet and intense.

"You won't tell anyone, will you?" she asked after the pause had stretched to breaking point.

"Me? Sure, I'm the master of secrets." The words sounded jaded on his lips—he wasn't talking about their clandestine marriage. The pain on his face when he held Evan last night and when he talked about his father flashed through her. She suspected he kept a lot of things in and that maybe, like her, he had no one to confide in. His family was gone; he was a stranger in a strange town. Line-dancing classes could take you only so far.

"Thanks," she said, slipping off his thigh. She tried to hold on to the delicious moment of friction between her legs before the chill set in. A little parting gift to keep her warm later. Now that she had placed a pall over the proceedings, they could get back to studious ignoring of each other. She dug her nails into her palms to stave off the tears she could feel thickening her throat.

He let her stand but his large palm still molded a possessive splay on her butt cheek. Can you say *awkward*? The dim yellow glow of the security lighting accented the planes and contours of his face and illuminated a blazing expression in his eyes.

"I once went out with a girl whose father made a point of cleaning his gun whenever I showed up to take her on a date."

Bewilderment made her blink. *Say what now?*

"I'd be sitting with him in the living room and I'd ask 'How're ya doin', Mr. O'Connor?' and he'd give me a cold nod and then go back to shining up his rifle like it was his ... well, you know what I mean."

She nodded, not having the slightest idea what he meant.

He breathed one of those satisfied sighs that accompanies a pleasant memory. "She dumped me a month later because I forgot her birthday but not before I'd spent several nights on her old man's porch showing her a good time. She'd bite my hand to stop from screaming when she came. Once she drew blood. While Mr. O'Connor waited up for her in the living room with that clean-as-a-whistle rifle across his lap."

"Shane, what—"

"Nice try, gorgeous, but I don't scare so easily. This is happening."

A shockwave barreled through her. Shane Doyle just flat out refused to conform to her expectations. From the first moment, he had been ten steps ahead of her with a clairvoyance that bordered on ridic.

"You mean you still want to do this?"

"Get that beautiful arse of yours upstairs now or I'm going to fuck you over the back of the bike."

Well.

She recovered her composure enough to ask, "And that'd be a problem because?" She was quite proud of the businesslike tone in her voice.

An eyebrow scooted up as he climbed off the machine. Plucking the dropped helmet from the ground, he tucked a hand under her elbow and steered her to the street. "We've already been interrupted once before in public and I'm not risking a repeat. This isn't going to be fast, Cara. It's going to be long and slow and very, very hot."

Lord, that was about the sexiest thing she'd ever heard. It also scared the bejesus out of her.

As he practically carried her through the front door of their building and up the stairs, she had to remind herself not to get carried away. That was probably a downright impossibility at this point, but she needed to retain some sliver of a grip. She halted outside her door, and he bumped into her, or rather his big old erection did. Hello, sailor.

"It would just be a one-off," she said, turning to face him.

"If you say so," he said cockily, though her brain heard, *Yeah, that's gonna happen*, and her foolish heart cheered that he already wanted to sleep with her again.

Stop. It.

"And you can't stay overnight."

He gave a self-assured eyebrow lift. "Good thing I don't have far to go."

"It's just that with our situation—"

He applied his lips directly to the situation, namely the sensitive juncture of shoulder and neck. It felt like heaven. "Which situation would that be? The coworker situation? The neighbor situation? Or the marital situation?"

They had an awful lot of situations and that was before they factored in the I-once-looked-like-a-*Les-Misérables*-waif situation. It was nice of him not to mention it.

"We can be adults about this," she responded in a very adult tone, worried she was talking herself out of this before they'd even started.

"Yes, we can." He sucked gently on her earlobe, so tender, yet so erotic. "Very adult. Neighborly, too."

She felt a lusty giggle coming on. Never in her life had she acted so girly around a guy. Never in her life had she been so acutely aware of what it felt like to be a woman.

"We're just being good neighbors," she murmured.

"Just borrowing some sugar." He grasped her hips and pivoted her so she faced her door. "Now get inside before I make a fool of myself, woman."

She twisted back to the tune of his heavy sigh, thrilled at what a good sport he was being about it all. Only one more thing would make it perfect.

"Aren't you forgetting something, Riverdance?"

The dimple went nuts. "Don't worry, I've got condoms."

"No, not that." Turning back to the door, she threw her flirtiest glance over her shoulder. "The hat, Shane. Get the hat."

CHAPTER 10

Cara had never seen a man move so fast as the next thirty seconds blurred through her mind. That was all it took for Shane to grab his hat, throw her over his shoulder like a sack of Idahos, and growl, "Bedroom."

So hot. Not nice.

Now, in her white-walled bedroom, she lay on her Jonathan Adler duvet while Shane kneeled over her, exploring the hollow of her throat with torturous skill. And he was...slowing down. Way down.

Anxiety blazed through her. A little flirty banter in the hallway and she had thought, *Hey, girl, you've got this,* but now the flutters in her stomach were emerging victorious. Lying beneath six feet of unabashed masculinity should have narrowed her world to just the two of them, but it felt like her crazy confession was the third person in the room.

Why couldn't he just take her quickly and get it over with? Push up her skirt, which admittedly wouldn't have far to go (hooray for straddle mode), and ease the ache? Her deep, dark secret, the thing that made her a freak—Shane hadn't batted an eyelid. He was supposed to run for the hills, not sit there astride that hunk of hot metal staring at her like she'd just told him Cheerios were her favorite cereal. No dramatics, no offers to throw her a pity party. He just wanted her. Slow and hot.

"Cara, you okay?"

She blinked and refocused on the deep swirls of those chocolate-drop eyes.

"Fi-fine. I'm fine. It's just…it's been a while for me and I don't want to disappoint you."

He chuckled. "Seeing as how you've got me so hot I'm about to come in my pants, I think you should be the one worried about being disappointed."

Funny, that, but she couldn't make her mouth curve up. Damn, she used to know how to smile.

He leaned up and rested his weight on the bed beside her. "Would I be right in thinking you have some issues with how you look naked?"

She nodded the head that felt too heavy for her neck.

"I could probably tell you how absolutely fucking perfect I think you are, but you wouldn't believe me, would you?"

She nodded again, shocked at his pinpoint sensitivity. Anorectics never believed what anyone—friends, therapists, lovers—told them about their bodies. She had talked to counselors, consumed message boards, devoured books. She was smart enough to know her inadequacy was entirely self-perceived, but it couldn't stop her from constructing her own truths.

"Well, I'm fairly shameless, so how about I get us started?"

She swallowed. Yes, please, yes.

Standing, he tipped his hat up like he had just spotted

her from across a dusty saloon and revealed those sweet, caramel eyes. Her sexy Irish cowboy. Slow as molasses in January, he undid the buttons of his shirt. As he stripped it off, his eyes stripped her bare. The shirt fell to the floor but she couldn't say the same for her inhibitions. Not yet.

"Now you," he said.

Trembling, she unpicked each mother-of-pearl button of her sleeveless silk blouse and slid it off her shoulders, deliberately enough that she felt a tingle of desire as the fabric whispered against her skin. Her inner priss couldn't get on board with the slinky stripper waft to the floor, so she kept it in her lap. That blouse cost two hundred dollars, for Chrissakes.

Swatches of color darker than her rose-pink La Perla bra flushed his cheekbones.

"Let me take care of that." He held out his hand for her blouse and she gave it to him, expecting he would drape it over the corner chair tucked beneath her vanity. Instead he headed for her closet door.

He was going to hang it.

She wanted to say he didn't need to, but he had already moved inside and was surveying the neat-as-a-pin racks. The unexpected kindness made her gulp.

Bending, she reached for her shoe.

"Heels stay on," he said from her closet entrance, his voice rougher than before. A lot rougher, and she realized that the dip displayed her breasts to advantage. Good to know.

The slow scrape of his descending zipper sent a message of readiness to her brain and a host of follow-up texts to her sex. The bulge of his erection filled her vision. Completely.

"Now your skirt."

Wait...all she got was his zipper? Sure, there had been

a nice reveal and all, but still. At her hesitation, he grinned. *Get it off, Cara.* Oh hell.

Standing, she unrolled the waist he had reworked to hooker length back at Sarriette, then unzipped and peeled. She had no choice but to wiggle, an action that jiggled her breasts.

She might have done that on purpose.

His next inhale sounded harsh and that auditory confirmation of the effect she had on him was enough to cause a few respiratory problems of her own. She stepped out of the skirt and handed it off to him. Back in the closet he went, taking a moment to smooth out the creases.

She fell in love with him a little right then.

Since she'd started eating properly, she no longer had toast-rack ribs, and her breasts and hips had filled out some. While she would never consider herself shapely, standing there in her expensive lingerie, she felt close to sexy. Or maybe it was the way he looked at her, like he didn't know where to start.

She knew exactly where to start. That jagged thread of silver on his shoulder was number one. She tracked her gaze down to his flat stomach, to the cut indents at his narrow hips, to the open *V* of his jeans. His boxer briefs were slung so low she could see a nest of fur covering that part of him straining to spring free.

Whatever was on her face must have made her lusty thoughts obvious. With a provocatively slow motion, he pushed down his briefs a few lovely inches and revealed his erection. Oh, my. She gasped like it was her first time out.

"Watch," he said, as he took his hard length in his hand and started to stroke. Like she could tear her gaze away from the sexiest thing she had ever seen. Shane, touching himself, his beautiful hands gripping and pumping with a necessary roughness.

Take me now, Jesus.

Between her legs, wet heat bloomed, and she pushed her thighs together. He never took his eyes off her, trapping her between his slow, rhythmic stroking and his blazing gaze. It was so hot it left grill marks on her eyes. Her knees nearly buckled and the floor started to look increasingly attractive—anything to get her mouth closer to that unbelievably arousing example of male magnificence. She wanted to lick him dry.

Instead she licked her lips, which seemed to excite him more if the way his eyes turned from deep chocolate to a one hundred percent cocoa was any indication. His movements were still marvelously controlled, but his voice betrayed him.

"You gettin' there, Cara?"

Gettin' there? Oh, she'd missed her stop a couple of miles back. She licked her lips again, drawing his smile of triumph. That cheeky Irishman.

Stopping his stroke, he reached for her hand and pulled her close in a twist so her back was flush to his chest, his erection jutting into the base of her spine. He unhooked her bra and slipped it off, then wandered his hands down to her hips. Under his touch, they felt voluptuous and shapely.

Under his touch, she felt whole.

He started with exquisite little nips at her neck, then soothed every sting with his tongue. His thumb brushed the underside of her breast before his palm covered it entirely. So big and rough. The brim of his hat grazed her cheek as he kissed her shoulder, his open mouth hot, his tongue licking fire against her skin. Her breasts felt heavy, her nipples tight and painful.

Across her stomach, he stretched one huge hand and slid a couple of rough-cast fingers below the band of her panties. Withdrawing, he traced circles along her toned abs, then dipped his fingers past the lacy border once more. She rubbed her butt against his open zipper like a wanton cat at a scratching post. The tantalizing friction made her skin buzz. A little lower with his hand and she felt his sharp intake of breath against her neck.

He spun her around to face him. A dull red flagged his cheeks. "You're shaved."

She giggled, so loving his reaction and loving more how it released some of her nerves. "Waxed, actually."

Slowly, like he was unwrapping a gift, he peeled down her thong a few inches to the tops of her thighs. He watched his own hand palm against her bareness, the edges of his mouth twisting up. "Is it everywhere?"

"See for yourself," she said, feeling bold.

Foxy fast, he was on his knees, pulling her thong with him. *Now* he moved quickly. Before she could get her bearings he had pushed her back on the bed, tossed her shoes and thong over his shoulder like a plea against bad luck, and spread her wide. Embarrassed, she squirmed her discomfort and tried to pull her thighs together, but he pinned her hips fast with his big, blunt hands.

"Let me see," he demanded.

He pulled her toward him, then nudged her thighs apart and arranged her legs over his shoulders, exposing her completely. Oh God, oh God. His lust-stoked gaze stroked her core, drawing moisture in a pool between her thighs. It felt like minutes passed under his intense scrutiny, every passing second kindling her nerve endings to flame.

A carnal curve touched his lips. "I see now that the fashion princess coordinates her wardrobe with the most luscious parts of her body. Pink lips, pink nipples. Pretty pink pussy."

Desire felt hot and loose in her belly. It might have been the dirty talk, but it could just as easily have been the look of smoky want in those dark eyes. Parting her with his fingers, he stroked through and dipped a thumb in his mouth. The sucking noise he made was positively obscene.

His eyelids lowered. "You taste so good."

"Really?" She'd always had her doubts.

"Oh, yeah. And I should know. I'm a professional chef."

Her half-hysterical laugh morphed to a moan as he got busy again. Blood rushed to feed the throb between her legs. His fingers speared her, sliding in and out, making her so wet she *felt* pink. Bracing on her elbows, she looked down. She wouldn't have been surprised to see her center vibrating with a remorseless beat like a telltale heart.

As much as she enjoyed the sight of his cowboy self, seeing right into his eyes would make this a million times better. She pushed up his hat to get a better view of those brown blobs of gorgeous, then plucked it off and placed it on the bed beside her.

"Good thing I haven't shaved in a couple of days. This is going to feel really good for you, LT."

Oh. *Ohhh.* He was already licking the crease between her leg and hip, his bristled jaw raspy against the soft, sensitive flesh of her thigh.

"I don't usually do that."

His tongue slicked perilously close to her folds. "Don't do what?" It came out as "doe-doo-whah."

"Oral."

That got his attention. "Giving or receiving?"

"Either."

He laid his forehead on her hip, and she thought she heard him mutter, "Jesus, Mary, and Joseph."

"Shane?"

A couple of extra-long beats passed, and then his shoulders rumbled. The man was...he was laughing!

"Cara DeLuca," he said around a hoarse laugh. "You are determined to drive me over the edge. Explain to me why."

Because it was just so intimate and it took too long to get her relaxed enough to get to that flash point. Guys usually acted like it was the ultimate sacrifice, like she should be ready to explode as soon as tongue meets clit. Past experience told her she would only end up faking it. The Shane experience told her she might not have to, but she didn't want to take a chance that her hopeful fantasies might be evicted by awkward reality.

"It just bores me," she said in her most offhand manner. "Most guys don't have the patience."

Lights of challenge flashed in his eyes. She should have known he would see if that way. Deep down, she probably hoped he would see it that way.

"The Irish are a very patient race, Cara. We endured eight hundred years of oppression." He blew a wisp of cold air on her sex that had her straining against his secure hands. He said she was killing him when really every one of his actions had her close to dying with pleasure.

"If you expect me *not* to bury my tongue inside you after you offer up that beautiful, bare, pink pu—"

"Shane!"

He leaned in and inhaled like she was a fine wine. "Cara, you have a starving man kneeling before you. Are you going to deny him?"

She knew he wasn't starving—not literally—but in some cold corner of her mind, the idea of feeding Shane her body seized her. That she, of all people, could possibly provide sustenance to anyone synched her heart up in a beat with the thrumming in her core.

"Cara," he warned in the wake of her silence.

"Shane, I need..."

His gaze met hers, his eyelids at half-mast but wide enough to see his banked lust.

"What, Cara? What do you need?"

Your mouth, your heart, all you can give.

"Just do it." She aimed for bossy but it came out shaky. Please, please, *there.*

"I need specifics, LT."

God *damn it*, she was too cranked up to be properly mortified. "Eat me, you Irish idiot."

Grinning like he'd won a prize, he placed his mouth between her legs and applied an unbearably arousing suction. He swirled his tongue around her tight bundle of nerves, alternating with gentle and firm laps. Life she hadn't known existed before she'd met him pounded through her. It was torture and ecstasy and she never wanted it to stop.

She shoved his head closer to the pulsing heart of her. She ground against his mouth and yelled her desperate need. Filthy things. Words that made her body blush. His tongue...oh, his tongue. It plunged and licked, soft, hard, wet, wet. She released a cry, high in her throat that probably sent the cat running for cover two walls over.

Thirty seconds. She had come in less than thirty seconds. How embarrassing.

He stopped feasting between her thighs and replaced his tongue with his fingers. Levering his body over hers, his mouth hovered close, shiny with her arousal.

"Didn't expect you'd be so easy." In an instant, his self-satisfied grin vanished. "Cara, you're shaking."

Not so much shaking as vibrating, and she was unable to will her body still. There was an excellent chance she might have a heart attack on the spot.

"I was trying to relax you," he said, his voice stroked with worry. "Are you okay?"

"I'm just out of practice." That's right, tell the hot, young stud how bad the old lady is at all this, but truth was she had never experienced an orgasm like that. This new-to-her body was having a hard time coping with the bliss overload. Pleasure-stung, that's how she felt. Overstimulated, every sense and nerve heightened to a dizzying sharpness.

"We can take a break, if you like." He looked concerned, but his tone said, *Please don't want a break.*

She felt her face splitting into a grin. "Back to work, Doyle."

"Hm, I'll get right on that but first you need to know how good you taste when you come."

While those dynamic digits continued to stroke her nerve-strung flesh, he kissed her. A sweet, soft kiss that stole her breath and doubts and all semblance of common sense. Nothing new there. She had no idea if she tasted good on his lips but she knew this much: together they tasted amazing. Her own kisses turned urgent, begging him to match her. He did. He always did. Each stroke of his tongue tore her under, each return of his blunt finger resharpened her arousal.

Though she was lying down, his fingers inside her and his mouth working hers were her only points of contact with this world. Her legs felt like water. Her skin felt so raw it might peel off any second. He broke their kiss just as another quake racked her, lifting her hips off the bed, shattering her into a million tiny screams.

What the hell? Rarely did she come once, never mind two times. It was like every orgasm she had ever faked was getting its revenge.

"Hope I'm not boring you," he said, his grin sexily smug.

She tried to breathe herself to blasé. It took a couple of moments. "You're holding my interest. Barely."

He laughed, a hearty sound that painted the white walls of her bedroom cell in glorious color. That was Shane, a vibrant rainbow splashed over her monochrome existence.

"You were awfully noisy, love. I think you could be louder though."

She pursed her lips to hide the smile she felt building. "It'd have to be pretty spectacular."

"I can do spectacular. I've won awards. Hat or no?"

"Hat."

With an eyebrow waggle, he reached over and grabbed the hat. He adjusted it so it sat at the perfect angle over his eyes. So fucking sexy.

"And if you need an extra treat, my nipples are here for your pleasure."

Her laughing snort morphed into something long and hard. No man had ever made her laugh like this.

I know why I married you. You make me feel good. You make me feel.

"Love that sound, LT. Love all your sounds." He grinned. "Let's make some more. Scoot up."

She walked back on her elbows, watching wide-eyed as he made a sinuous crawl up her body, taking sensuous pit stops to lick and suckle at her navel and breasts. His teeth rasped across one tight bud, and then he latched his warm, wet mouth onto the other.

Spirals of pleasure tightened her skin and wound down her belly. The build began but she wanted him to be with her this time. When he raised his head, she pushed him to her side so she could spend a few moments exploring his body.

Not a hardship in the slightest.

Starting at his chest, she made ever-decreasing circles

with her hand, enjoying the twitches of his tautly loomed muscles. She licked and traced the silver-white thread on his collar bone, and took time to examine the rough topography of his body. Bumpy abrasions and scar-roughened tissue that, given his age, could only have happened when he was very young. Someone had done this to him.

That made her mad as hell.

His eyes fluttered shut and his breathing grew shallow. Low, desperate sounds hummed in his throat. She held off on touching his erection as every swoop of her hand across his abdominals made his cock tap against her stomach in a sensual rhythm.

Any other guy would have pushed into her by now but Shane remained still, letting her lead after he had thrown her for a loop. It was as if he realized she needed some small dominion over this, and having grabbed control of the situation early, he was happy to let her take the wheel.

That undid her completely.

Over his shoulder, she caught their reflection in the closet door mirror. Her mouth slack with desire, a pearly pink glow to her skin, her eyes alive. So alive. His jeans and boxers rested inches below his narrow hips, exposing the paler skin of his half-covered ass. Like he was so desperate to have her, full removal was impossible. Not even his boots! The image of his powerful, semiclothed body sliding against her completely naked one felt filthier, somehow, and it summoned her moan of approval.

He opened those big brown eyes and smiled. A huge, dopey grin that knocked her sideways and made her hand shake in time with her throbbing sex.

"Eyes front, soldier," he whispered.

"Look," she said, chinning over his shoulder.

He twisted around to look at the mirror. "Wow," he said,

awe deepening his voice. "That's so hot. It's like we're in a sexy movie."

A sexy movie. Why did every word out of his mouth land laden with boyish wonder? Even his filthier talk smacked of an innocent enthusiasm.

Gently, he pushed her back and knelt over her on all fours so they could both benefit from the erotic reflection. She stroked the head of his erection and spread the beaded moisture, cupping his girth and palming up and down through the slick slide.

"That's it, Cara. So good."

He thrust into her hands, his cock poking her stomach, every jerky motion ratcheting up her own desire. Alternating between holding her gaze firm, not-so-furtive glances to the mirror, and checking out the expanding situation below, he finally settled for keeping his sniper focus on her. She'd beaten out all that competition for his attention.

Impressive, girl.

"Condom. Pocket," he croaked.

From his jeans she pulled out a condom and in the time it took her to open it—yes, out of practice there, too—he stripped completely. Half-naked Shane was something. The full deal was something else. Leaning up, she rolled the condom on quickly, relieved she hadn't forgotten how.

"You ready for me, darlin'?"

"Lemme have it, cowboy."

He settled between her legs, bearing his weight on his elbows, then inched himself in. Slow and slick, filling up that empty spot inside her. Her body thrummed like a live wire, every cell a sensitive mass of nerve endings. This was what it felt like to be in the moment. Joy didn't require nearly as much effort when Shane was doling it out.

"I'll go gentle," he murmured.

She didn't need gentle. She needed hard and now.

About halfway in, he stopped. "You're tight—damn, so tight."

This shouldn't be all about her. For too long, it had been all about her. She wrapped a leg around his hip and dug her fingers into his hot Irish ass. "Take all you want, honey."

Their eyes locked and something passed between them. He thrust into her hard, stretching her full while his hands cupped her butt and held her in place for his pleasure. With each push, her muscles pulled, clamping down on his erection.

"Sketchy six," she thought he muttered, then louder, "We look good together."

She fed a sidelong gaze at the mirror and met him there. His body was all lean sinew; the muscles of his back flexed like cogs turning under silk. Hard against soft, fire against ice. He was wrong, though—they didn't look good together. They looked perfect.

"We feel good together." He withdrew and slid back in with a long, sensuous glide. "Tell me you feel it, too, Cara." His eyes bored into her, the real her, not her reflection. The no-longer-numb version.

This is what happened that night. This feeling.

"Yes, Shane, I feel it."

Yet again, control had switched to his side and she was beginning to wonder if it had ever left it. She slanted her lips, desperate for the angle that would satisfy. He responded in kind but it wasn't enough—it never could be. She could feel gravity disappearing as weightlessness descended, a floating sensation she didn't trust.

She tightened her sex again and was rewarded with his husky moan. His thrusts became more urgent, deeper, creating a river of sensation that flowed throughout her body and emptied into the delta between her thighs. Her head lolled back as she lost herself in him.

Limply, she collapsed and waited for his release. Usually she turned away when a guy came inside her, fearing his disappointment, but not now. She cupped Shane's jaw and held it as he poured himself into her with every thrust. His body strained just as hers relaxed into cottony softness.

"Again," he whispered.

"What?"

"Come again." His teeth dug into his lower lip, the tendons in his neck stretched tight.

"I don't think I ca—" But then he changed his position, like he was channeling *Cosmo* sex tips or something. His length now stroked her center in a quicker tempo and the tightening pressure in her belly hiked up all over again. So fast that she couldn't believe it. She couldn't believe him.

Again. She came again with a force that left her drowning, her body given over to a pleasure she didn't understand. That she wasn't even sure she had a right to. His groan mingled with her diminishing whimpers, and she held on to him as if she deserved him. Her sweet dessert for taking a walk on the wild side. Her reward for being a good girl and eating her greens.

She fooled her mind into pretending he belonged to her for this one marvelous night. She'd always been good at playing tricks.

* * *

Shane found interesting uses for the knee-high ledge in her shower—*it's wasted on shampoo, Cara*—and by the time they stumbled out, she was sated, pruned, and a little cold. Quickly, she wrapped herself in one of her fluffy bath towels and settled in for the show in her fogged-up mirror. Shane rubbing his skin dry was a sexy *digestif*, the perfect conclusion to a calorie-laden meal. She figured it had to be okay to ogle after what they'd done.

He had no shame about his body, and why would he? He was a fine, powerful machine, every part perfect from his mink-brown head through his sculpted torso and those legs, strong enough to hold any weight, even one as insubstantial as hers. Too soon, the moisture beads on his skin were absorbed by her high-quality cotton. Damn those expensive hotel bath linens.

She drew a deep breath and got to untangling her hair with a comb, all while spying how he wrapped the towel around his waist. It rested low on his hips. She wanted to kiss those hips. Then he put on his cowboy hat and she unraveled like a loose thread on a sweater. Shakily, she continued with her hair, wishing she had the courage to ask him to stay.

"Looks like we found out something else you're good at." He circled her waist from behind and brushed a light kiss on her rounded shoulder. "I love your shoulders. I think they're my favorite part of you."

She doubted he would have thought the same thing three years ago when her shoulder blades were sharp enough to slice through a tomato can. Those bony shoulders had been loved by Cara, and Cara alone.

Strong arms cradling her, he set his mouth to the tease setting with hot kisses along the curve of her neck. The hat tickled her temple.

"Shane, I need to dry my hair."

He took the comb out of her hand and threw it on the vanity.

"Shane!"

"*Shane!*" he mimicked. A pleasant weight dug into the

small of her back, reminding her of the resilience of youth. He couldn't possibly be ready to go again—could he?

"Cara, I have so many dirty fantasies about you. Taking you on the kitchen counters at the restaurant, on your office desk, in the alley behind Sarriette. Your tight arse in those tight skirts drives me wild. So wild." He bit down on her earlobe. "I can't wait to get inside you again. Feel you so hot and wet around me."

His lips trailed a path of sweet destruction along her jaw. She felt as though she was falling, plunging to a great depth. It was dangerous and delicious. Maybe once more to savor—

"How's your fridge looking?" he asked.

Her mind flip flopped like a landed fish. "Excuse me?"

Cool air hit the damp, exposed skin of her back as Shane stepped away. "Sex always makes me hungry. I'm going to need a sandwich to keep up with you for the rest of the night." Before she could snap her jaw back into place, he was already striding to her kitchen.

"Shane," she called out, thinking she should allay his disappointment as soon as possible—about the contents of her fridge and his prospects for the rest of the night. Following, her mouth returned to its default position, dropped and drooling, while she took in the sight before her. A big bear of a man in the very small kitchen she scarcely used. Those powerful shoulders flexed above a mountain of male. As luxurious as the towel was, it couldn't hide how his butt muscles bunched as he leaned into the fridge to do his hunter-and-gatherer bit.

"LT, where's the food fit for the man who just took you to the heights of passion? All you've got is salad and"—his burly frame hid whatever he picked up—"Greek yogurt," he finished sourly, as if its very Greekness had insulted him. The melancholy in his voice brought her close to a giggle.

On opening the freezer door, his shoulders sagged. "I hope you have stock in Lean Cuisine. You're going to have to get in some man food."

"Man food?"

"Bread, meat, cheese." He bundled her in his arms. It felt too, too good. "Cara, if you want me to keep you satisfied, you have to take care of me."

A crawly feeling crept across her skin. This was getting out of hand. "I'm not filling my fridge for you—"

"Sounds dirty. Keep it up." He dropped a light kiss on her forehead.

Reluctantly, she extracted herself from his strong, masculine hold. "Shane, this is it."

"That's okay. I've got something in mine."

"No, Shane, *this* is it."

"Ah, the night's not over yet." His caramel eyes turned smoky and deliberate, hinting at the good times that lay ahead if only she would lighten up. Farther down, the good times were making themselves known in a very definite manner.

"I already told you no overnight stays."

"But I haven't fallen asleep yet," he reasoned.

"*But,*" she said, dragging out the word and trying not to think of his excellent butt, "you will eventually, and probably on top of me like you did in... before." She couldn't even say "Las Vegas." So much for getting over it.

"I did not fall asleep on top of you. I held you with care," he said, indignant.

"I told you how it was, Shane. You agreed." She headed to the bedroom and busied her trembling hands—the ones that had already proved themselves tricky little turncoats—with picking up his clothes and boots. She might have taken a moment to inhale his shirt's rich, clean scent.

In the kitchen, he stood with hat on head and hands on hips. The hips she wanted to lick.

Stop. It.

"I screwed up, didn't I? With my demands for food?" His mouth turned down in regret. "It slipped my mind, or more likely you screwed it out of my brain. You're going to have to tell me more about this anorexia business."

That he had forgotten was the most wonderful thing he could have said but now he remembered and everything was weird again. She was no good at this. There were too many mines to navigate.

"It's not verboten, Shane. Of course you can talk about food. That's not the problem." The problem was the expectation underlying a full fridge, that she could feed and nurture others, or more to the point, that she couldn't.

"I thought we were having a good time here."

"We are." She shook her head, correcting herself. "We were. Now you go."

Her gaze fell to his towel, tented so high she could hang that sexy Stetson on it. The sight made her maddeningly moist, a word she hated with a passion but that was unfortunately apt. She stumbled toward the front door and, on legs like swaying reeds, waited for him to follow.

"Cara, are you seriously telling me that a woman such as yourself is going to be satisfied with just a couple of orgasms? I refuse to believe it."

Five orgasms, actually, but who was counting? She fumbled with the door. "Believe, Shane."

"Can't say I approve of this behavior, which is clearly against your self-interest."

Acting against her self-interest was old Cara. New, healthy, *sane* Cara had to eliminate anything and anyone who threatened her mental well-being. Shane Doyle was enemy number one as far as her rationality was concerned. So what if he claimed interest in her problems or made her feel good in ways she could never have imagined? Before long, he would bore of her weird habits and neediness, and by then, she would be in too deep. She was already half in love with him.

She threw open the door and held out his clothes. When he crossed his arms defiantly, she deposited them in the hallway. The memory of Shane hanging her clothes with kindness tried to take hold but she shoved it to the back of her mind's closet like a cashmere turtleneck in July.

"It's been great," she said sweetly to the man responsible for the most wonderful experience of her life.

He wore the least sweet expression possible. She would venture to say he was glowering except Shane didn't, as a rule, glower. Expecting further verbal resistance, he surprised her by laying one on her and leaving her scrounging for air.

"When's your next night off?" he tossed out like they had just finished a few rounds of gin rummy instead of...well, what they had done.

That confirmed it. *Out, damn Shane, out.*

With a wobbly hand, she pointed to his door. Sighing dramatically, he crossed her threshold and turned to say something else. Ah-ah, Mr. Gift of the Gab. She closed up shop.

Oh, wait. She opened up to find him standing in profile, keys in hand, apartment door ajar. His mouth formed a grim seal matching the stiff line of his body but lifted in a curve when he saw her. The lump of ragged fluff, that could only be called a cat if one were in a charitable mood, had escaped into the hallway.

"Vegas, get back inside," he ordered the cat.

He called the cat Vegas? The man was clearly determined to drive her over the edge.

No.

More.

He shot her a wry grin. "Come to your senses?"

From behind the door, she pulled out a manila envelope and shoved it at him. "Sure have. Sign, and get them back to me as soon as you can."

As his hand curled around the envelope, recognition dawned on his face closely followed by discomfort. Just enough to make her stomach turn over with guilt. Vegas, that opportunistic fur ball, saw the writing on the wall and slipped by her legs.

Shane speared a look of disgust at the ragged feline. "Traitor."

And because she was Cara DeLuca—ballbuster, Lemon Tart, and damn proud of her luxury hotel bath collection—she whipped that very expensive towel from his hips, and indulged in one last look at all that hard glory.

Then she hardened every part of herself and shut the door once more.

CHAPTER 11

Shane, you're up."

Jack threw a lazy look at Shane that still managed to appear pointed, letting him know it was his turn to preview tonight's desserts to the crew during family meal. Most of them were still nose-deep in the boss's King Edward mussels in saffron and white wine broth. That wouldn't last for long.

From behind his perch at the Sarriette bar, Shane pulled out the special sweet and laid it on the center table around which most of the crew had gathered in the main dining room. He offered an intact one for presentation's sake, a helping of devilry the size of a hockey puck, and another one that was already segmented into bite-sized morsels.

"Chocolate ganache cake with a lemon-basil filling. I call it Bella Donna."

It was definitely a thing of beauty. For a while he'd been experimenting with cream fillings and this one was his best yet—a citrus-herbal combination that might be just as well suited to an Italian chicken dinner. But with the decadent richness of the Valrhona chocolate, new dimensions of flavor were released. This filling made the chocolate taste better, which was a feat in itself.

The crew agreed.

"Amazing," Aaron gushed, then clashed forks with Maisey as they both went in for another bite.

Mona shook her head despondently. "I may as well just give up. I'm never going to be this good."

The rest of the brigade muttered curses of appreciation interspersed with orgasmic moans. Mission successful.

"Looks like another winner," Jack said evenly. He was the only one not to have tried it, which irked Shane more than it should have. "But we don't give our desserts names. And isn't belladonna a poisonous herb?"

"A plant actually. It also means—"

"Beautiful woman," Jack finished, just as Cara swayed in wearing nosebleed heels and a skirt so tight Shane would need a crowbar to pry her out of it.

All turned to the perfect wave of her, their eyes filled with jealousy and admiration that most women as attractive as Cara would see as their due. But after last night, Shane was beginning to wonder about Cara's expectations and that tough-girl varnish she wore because when he held her in his arms, he had seen her fear and uncertainty. She hadn't wanted him to stay because it was easier to draw a line under it. Draw a line under them.

The memory of how she had come apart for him over and over was all the more special because she had trusted him with something so fundamental. He still couldn't believe she hadn't told anyone about her anorexia. He still couldn't believe she had told *him*.

And then he fucked it up by demanding sandwiches.

Their gazes fused, just like their bodies had last night,

and color fired her cheeks. Usually she would walk right by, parsing out that cool smile like a miser parts with pennies, leaving the crew to their assumptions. Lemon Tart, lesbian, stuck up. She didn't seem to care. But today she halted, her eyes shuttering in the face of his stare. He drank in those dark blonde eyelashes that fanned her cheeks like feathery crescent-shaped Madeleines.

"What's on the menu tonight?" she asked, easy-like, as if she shot the shit with the gang all the time. She picked up a crust of garlic toast, dipped it in the fragrant mussel broth, and raised it to her mouth. "Hm, you've outdone yourself with this, Jack," she murmured around her chewing.

"Pleased you could join us," Jack said, his expression curiously paternal. Strange, but that was the first word that popped into Shane's head.

Shane stood and gestured to his seat, at which Cara raised a perfectly plucked, or perhaps it was waxed, eyebrow of *Not this again, idiot*. She ducked her head as she sat and picked up a fork, her lips' upward tilt a private joke between them.

The crew had resumed their ribbing about some nonsense to which Shane was no longer paying attention. He couldn't hear or see anything else, not while Cara was slicing through his dessert and passing it between her lips.

He held his breath. She swallowed. He let it go.

"Nice filling, Irish."

"I aim to please."

"Color this girl a fan of your work." Her tongue swiped the corner of her mouth, a dainty little dip that made him smile and harden at the same time. "Nice to see someone doing something different with Italian flavors. Thinking outside the box."

"I've never been one for rules." He emphasized the last word. "I like to push the limits. See where it takes me."

There was a flash in those blue eyes, a warm-up from Arctic to Mediterranean. He gripped the back of her chair and watched the knuckle-white play of his hand. What would she do if he reached out and palmed the graceful curve of her neck, so bare and inviting? As bare and inviting as her sweet, pink—*don't torture yourself, man.*

Bending, he brushed his lips close to her ear. "One bite's not going to be enough."

In her tilted-up eyes, he read a startling determination. "You might like to push the limits, Shane, but some of us are all too aware of ours."

This morning he had done some online research about anorexia and learned that, while body image and self-esteem played a part, the need for control was just as important. Lately Cara had indulged in a few things outside her comfort zone: motorcycle rides, line dancing, sexy cooking lessons, marriage to a complete stranger. Framing this with rules was her way of taking charge. Moderation in all things—food, sex, life—kept her on the straight and narrow. But if she was going to overindulge, by God, it should be with him.

She floated to a stand and again all eyes rested on her. "Have a good service, everyone."

"Enjoy girls' night," Jack said. "And try not to leave my fiancée catatonic on the sofa."

"Aww, Jack," Cara purred. "Sounds like you're worried the vino will loosen her lips and we'll end up talking about you and your huge...talent. Let me assure you, Lili and I exhausted that topic within thirty seconds of your hooking up. Now all we talk about are your shortcomings."

On that final poke, she was five long strides to the door while the crew hooted, more in disbelief than anything else. High and mighty Cara joking around. With a grin and a head shake, Jack clapped his hands and ordered everyone to places.

Shane scooped up a couple of stray plates at the bar and tried to calm his organs the hell down. Pissed off, confused, and horny about summed it up. A one-off she had said, but then she walked in wearing that second-skin skirt—which she knew he loved!—and had the audacity to flirt with him while eating his dessert. The one she had inspired. Rich and decadent. Citrus Italian. His *bella donna*.

Was she feeling lighter of heart because she'd had an awesome night of hot lovin' from Yours Truly or was her improved mood down to something else more unsettling? Maybe the fact that she had seized control of a tricky situation—again, Yours Truly—and put it behind her. Not just drawn a line under the problem, but struck it through. All he had to do was sign those annulment papers and make her Shane-free dreams a reality.

Looked like one of them had this separating-it-out thing down pat, and it sure as hell wasn't him.

* * *

Cara slipped into a seat at the island in Lili's kitchen, her olfactory glands pumped and primed. Was it really possible that food smelled more appetizing now that she'd finally had a decent orgasm? If only she had known.

"What are we eating?"

Lili popped the cork from the red and grabbed a couple of wineglasses from the rack above the island. "One of Jules's pizza experiments. Roasted summer squash, thyme, and buffalo mozzarella. Some of her stuff is amazing. I swear she could give Jack a run for his money."

"Jack would take all the credit. The Kilroy genes."

Lili snickered. "You know it."

She poured a healthy measure of Montepulciano and slid the glass in Cara's direction. It had been a while since they'd had a girls' night in or out. Not since . . . sigh, Vegas. Acutely conscious of what had happened the last time she went off the sobersides reservation, she held off on taking a sip in case she let slip any of her secrets, specifically her matrimonial ones.

Pulling out her binder, Cara let the soothing power of a nicely organized set of papers wash over her and set her straight. *My precious.* Some people had odd sexual fetishes; Cara had office supplies.

"So, I've got the city permit for the photographs at Buckingham Fountain. And I'm still waiting on a quote from one of the carriage providers, but this is what I'm thinking." She flipped open to the transportation section, where she had printouts of the antique coaches. Several printouts.

"Now, we could go with something Jane Austen style." She pointed at the open-topped carriages that all screamed *Masterpiece Theatre*. "Jack would probably look good in a topcoat and Mr. Darcy sideburns."

"Oh, yeah," Lili said with a naughty giggle.

Before Lili could wander off track to lusty thoughts of ripping Jack out of his breeches, Cara swiftly moved on to her intended target. "But I think the Cinderella carriage would be best all around. Especially with the dress I have in mind."

"Cara," Lili started. "This all seems a bit over the top. The whole princess thing isn't really my style. A bit too Disney."

Her words turned Cara's spine rigid. Didn't Lili realize it had to be perfect?

"It's your wedding day. Hopefully, your only wedding day. You want it to be memorable and dreamy and so amazing everyone will be sick with envy. You want people to go away thinking that it was the most gorgeous wedding they ever attended."

Lili stared, and Cara realized she had been doing her high-pitched babble thing again. "I do?"

"Of course you do." Cara shifted uncomfortably in her seat.

At the buzzing of her phone, Lili's gaze slid sneakily to the screen. The message sent her into a husky laugh and she turned it around for Cara to see.

Make sure Cara gets quality European doves. No white-trash North American ones.

From her future brother-in-law, the comedian.

"Hey," Cara said, trying to be a good sport about it all. "I thought he wanted something special. I thought you both did."

Lili's expression was probably aiming for sympathetic but it got stuck on pity. "We do. He's just kidding. You're doing a great job."

They had four weeks and everything seemed to be crashing in on her like a tsunami. St. Jude's was booked, the reception would be held at the InterContinental on Michigan Ave—Jack, ever the romantic, insisted they spend the wedding night there so they could relive the memory of their first time in the sack—and DeLucas scattered across the globe were preparing to descend. But all the things that would make it perfect—the outfits, the favors, the intimate touches—were still to be worked out. In short, it was a bridal bouquet away from catastrophe.

"We still need to get you a dress."

Usually the dress would have been ordered months in advance but Lili claimed not to like any of the ideas Cara had offered. At this rate, they would have to get something off the rack and pay a premium to get it altered in time.

Her sister smiled. "Don't worry, I'm wearing Mom's."

"You can't." It was out of Cara's mouth quicker than it took the thought to form.

"Why not?" Lili's brow drew into a *V*. "If you're worried it won't fit me, don't be. Sylvia's going to let it out at the seams."

Though her mom was certainly a couple of sizes smaller than Lili, Cara's first thought had not been that it might be a tight squeeze on her sister's bodacious curves or that Cara already had six appointments at bridal shops early next week.

Her primary thought? *That was supposed to be my dress.*

As a girl, she had spent hours holding her mother's gown up in front of the mirror, then several more roping Lili and her cousins into the make-believe weddings starring Cara as the most beautiful bride who ever lived. It was old-fashioned, with a sweetheart neckline and a scalloped hem. Almost hippie-like in style, not really chic at all. But Cara had loved it and mentally called it as her own all those years ago.

Heart in chaos, she focused on the walls, dressed with Lili's beautiful art, and tried to shake off the bookend images of an innocent girl with her best days ahead of her and a stupid woman who made a foolish mistake. The years in between had guaranteed she'd have no use for that dress, so it was churlish to begrudge Lili the joy of wearing it. There'd be no white wedding for Cara, only a quickie followed by an annulment.

"You okay?" Lili asked, her brow ridged with concern.

"Fine. Just thinking about all we have to do."

Lili compressed her lips. "I don't have to wear the dress. It's just…Mom offered, and with the shortened time frame, it seemed like a good idea."

Cara forced her smile bright and her eyes wide to keep the unshed tears at bay. "Lili, it's a great idea. I made some appointments but I'll cancel them. One less thing to do."

Her sister looked like she wanted to say something else but the oven timer went off, saving Cara from further awkwardness. "Could you let Jules know the pizza is ready? She's putting Evan down."

Heading upstairs, Cara used the time away from Lili to get a handle on her emotions, though walking through the hallway of photo love on the next level made her pulse quicken again. More fuel for the raging envy monster inside her. *Get a grip, girl.*

From Evan's room came Jules's low murmur and a couple of steps farther in confirmed she was reading *If You Give a Mouse a Cookie*. A favorite with the kids on the oncology floor at the children's hospital where she volunteered, Cara could recite it from memory. But not Jules. Maybe she was trying, but she stumbled over certain phrases. *Milk mustache. Nail scissors.*

Cara stuck her head around the door and found Evan fast asleep, his sweet breathy sighs filling the room. Jules sat slumped in the corner armchair, the book open in her lap, her face a mask of frustration as she read aloud the page about the mouse wanting to hang his picture on the refrigerator with Scotch Tape. When Cara's father had read it to her all those years ago, they laughed at the absurdity of a mouse wanting to hang his picture. It still made her smile.

Jules took a deep breath and skipped over the word *Scotch* to *Tape*. Mouth in a downturn, she snapped the book shut and stood quickly.

"Hi," Cara said softly so as not to startle her. "Pizza's ready."

Jules gulped audibly. "Oh, right, thanks." As she returned

the book to the super cute canary-yellow bookcase, Cara couldn't help noticing that her hand shook.

"You okay?"

"Sure," she said but her smile was thin and watery. She raked her fingers through hair that looked like it'd already been thoroughly tousled. "I know he's far too young for that, but I want to be ready when he's old enough."

"No harm being prepared, I suppose," Cara said, confused as to why a book aimed at three- to five-year-olds needed to be studied in advance.

"You see . . ." Jules rubbed a spot on her wrist. "It won't be long before he wants to read along with me, so I'm getting a jump on the classics. Before he jumps ahead of me." Her adoring gaze fell on her son. "I have dyslexia and I'm trying to improve my reading. Jack hired a tutor for me."

Oh. Cara recalled a set of instructions the night she had babysat for Evan. Half the words were misspelled and looked like little Evan could have written them himself if he had sufficient motor control. She also recalled her callous conclusion that it was a good thing Jules lived with Jack and Lili because she didn't have much going on between her ears.

Her heart sank at how she had misjudged this girl. She had no idea what she had gone through, but she'd whipped out her Judge Judy gavel all the same and pronounced. Jealousy at how Jules had easily slotted into the DeLuca family had played a part, but mostly it was because she never seemed to struggle. She had won the life lottery: girl-next-door looks, a healthy child, the unconditional love of her family. But all this time, she had been bearing her own painful burden.

Cara rubbed Jules's shoulder, feeling awkward. Seemed it

was her default setting these days. "I'm sorry I haven't been very welcoming to you."

Her eyes flew wide. "Oh, not at all. Your family was there for me at the worst possible time."

"Yes, but *I* haven't been a good friend. I've been kind of wrapped up in my own stuff."

Jules smiled sweetly, making Cara feel like the worst bitch on the planet.

"We're all the centers of our own universes, aren't we? Though, once I got pregnant, it wasn't long before I realized how my priorities had to change because soon I would have a new center for my universe. I had to make an effort to open up, to Jack, especially. Ask for help because I couldn't do it on my own and if I wanted to be a good mum and sister and friend, I needed to trust people." Her smile shone so brightly that it lit up the twinkly night sky on the ceiling above their heads. "No woman is an island and all that."

The truth of that struck Cara like an arrow to her heart. Last night, she had shared something with Shane, starting with that shameful part of her, and now the thought of having to go back sat like an elephant on her chest. Old, furtive Cara slipping away from the family table so she could get rid of what she had eaten. Sneaky, desperate Cara getting up two hours before God—or Il Duce, same difference—so she could exercise in secret. Her body might have healed but those clandestine habits die hard. She couldn't tell anyone about her anorexia but the yearning to confide that other skeleton in her closet battled to break free.

"Cara, are you all right?"

"No. No, I'm not." She leaned over and stroked Evan's hair, marveling at his perfection from his watercolor-pink cheeks to his tiny, perfect toenails. "I married Shane in Las Vegas."

Jules's hand flew to her mouth. "Get. Out."

"That's what I'm trying to do." She sighed. "I should start at the beginning."

* * *

"So," Lili said, her gaze unfocused after her third glass of wine. "Shane."

Cara swallowed, then realized that might look like she had something to hide. Which she did.

Jules tilted her eyes up over the glass of red she'd been nursing for the last two hours. Her knowing look summoned a moment's regret that Cara had spilled her guts before dinner. She had sworn her to secrecy and, given Jules's proven ability to hold secrets of her own, Cara had no choice but to trust her.

"Yeah, Cara," Jules said with a wry smile. "We want very specific details, and if you need a pen and paper, I'm sure we can provide."

"Don't know what you're talking about," Cara said, shooting for haughty. "He's my neighbor."

Lili blew out a well-oiled raspberry. "Gina was leaving DeLuca's and saw you arriving home last night on the back of Shane's bike. She said you were showing so much skin she's surprised you didn't get pulled over by Chicago's Finest. Fess up now."

Busted. "Jeez, she's the worst gossip," Cara muttered. "It was just a one-time thing."

"What, no good?" Jules asked. "He looks like he'd be good." She leaned in, ready for girly confidences. "I mean, we all know there's nothing better than young, virile cock."

"Stitch *that* on a pillow." Lili moved Jules's wineglass away. "I'm cutting you off. If your brother could hear you now."

"Are you kidding?" Jules looked put out. "You know I've barely drunk a drop, not while I'm breastfeeding."

Cara started to giggle uncontrollably. "Oh God, she's right. He was like the Energizer bunny. Just when I thought I was done, he started right up again." She fanned herself, then took a bite of her now-cold pizza, one of the best things she'd tasted in ages. Giving herself permission to enjoy life had opened her taste buds to the max, including her taste for young, virile man flesh.

"The only reason I'm walking straight is because I made him leave right after."

Two sets of startled eyes glared at her.

"You kicked him out? Girl, that's cold." Glumly, Lili shook her head and placed her palms on the coffee table. "So, he could go all night but was he any good?" She pounded each word out for emphasis.

Jules took Lili's half-full glass of wine away from her.

Cara felt her lips part, but no words took shape. It seemed appropriate to acknowledge Shane's quality in reverential silence. Truth be told, her body hadn't recovered. Close to twenty-four hours should have been enough to dull the hormone high and bring her crashing back to earth, but she was still a raging bundle of energy. This morning, when she stepped beneath her shower spray, a host of erotic images flowed unbidden through her mind.

Not exactly unbidden, though. Completely bidden.

Then this afternoon, walking past the crew, she couldn't stay away from his orgasmic chocolate dessert or ignore the blatant invitation in his cocoa eyes.

Shane was turning out to be irresistible.

The hush was broken by Jules's heavy sigh. "I need to be rogered good and proper."

Lili and Cara burst out laughing.

"What about Tad?" Cara asked, grateful for the opportunity to deflect from her own alternately amazing and sorry love life. "I thought you two…"

"No, no." Jules waved her hand, then waved it again for emphasis. "Tad and I are a nonstarter. He's made it very clear we're just friends."

"Or Jack has," Cara said. "I think he warned Tad off."

"Wouldn't surprise me," Jules said morosely. "My brother is so over the top."

"He means well," Lili said automatically, falling back on her role of peacemaker mixed with a shot of stand by your man.

"You do know you're marrying Dad, don't you?" Cara said to her sister. "Dad with a British accent."

Lili's mouth worked indignantly. "I—I am not. Jack's nothing like Dad." She turned to Jules for support.

"She's not wrong," Jules said, breaking into a grin. "But you can handle him."

So true. Jack instilled confidence in Lili and she reined in his excesses and gave his life focus. Wasn't that the recipe for a perfect match? Two people filling gaps and bringing out the best in each other. She had no idea what she brought to the table, but she had to admit that Shane did for her what no other man had ever done.

In starving her body, her heart had wasted away but since that sexy Irish cowboy had swaggered into her life, it felt full again. Crazier still, he wanted more of her, even after her confession. Of course, how convenient a booty call she would make…over her desk, in Sarriette's kitchen (to hell with health codes!), a quick knock on the door across the hall.

But then, like all good things, it would end and pain would fill its place. There would be spying through her peephole as he brought dates back, surreptitious watching to make sure he wasn't around before she left her apartment.

Hell to the no. She had an addictive personality and Shane Doyle was a drug she could not afford. Getting out before she had her heart handed to her on a pike was the best decision she could have made.

CHAPTER 12

I'm wearing the wrong shoes," Cara said to Lili's back. "You could have told me where we were going."

"But if I'd done that, you wouldn't have come," her sister threw back, the words faint as they were snatched by the unseasonably cool breeze whipping across the flattened grass of Lincoln Park. They had parked the car on Cannon Drive and were now squelching their way toward the south end of the park, having left the paved path a while back. Last night's May shower had muddied the ground and with every step, the spikes of Cara's Cole Haan boots sank like golf tees into a field of jam.

In the distance, she spotted a bunch of men clustered in a very cozy lump, their arms latticed across each other's backs.

Rugby. She groaned.

"Oh, be quiet," Lili threw out, not uncharitably.

By the time they'd made it to the sideline, the man huddle had separated and one poor sucker had scrabbled about six feet before three others tackled him to the earth. Very civilized.

Lili nudged Cara in the ribs. "Jack's been at me to come see him play, so here we are."

"Why is it 'we' and not just 'you'?"

Her sister raised a tricksy brow and nodded in the direction of the field. Cara followed her gaze until it landed on...Mason Napier.

"Wait, Mason Napier plays rugby with Jack?" If he already knew Jack, why the hell was he trying to wrangle chef's tables out of her?

"Who?" Lili's face scrunched up in query. "No, that guy's on the other team. I draw your attention to Shane 'O'Steamy' Doyle."

That six-foot leprechaun, also known as her husband, emerged from behind Mason. Covered head to toe in mud, he practically blended in with the brown puddles but all that filth couldn't cover those thick, muscled thighs. Lust rooted her to the spot, but then she looked down and saw that she was actually rooted to the spot. She extracted her heel from the jellied earth.

Jack spotted them and trotted over.

"Sweetheart, you came." He threw a grime-streaked arm around Lili's waist and pulled her in for a deep kiss, then turned a suspicious eye on Cara. "I wouldn't have thought this was your scene, Cara."

"All my idea," Lili confessed. "She hadn't a clue, as evidenced by her inappropriate footwear."

Someone called Jack into the game. "We're going to the pub for a plateful of grease after, so don't go anywhere," he said, backing up.

"Wild horses wouldn't drag me away," Cara said, before adding in an undertone to Lili, "Why am I here again?"

Lili slid the sole of her boot along the grass in a vain attempt to wipe off a gob of mud. "I thought it might be fun to get some air."

Cara cast about the park, her gaze unavoidably drawn to Shane, who somehow looked taller, the dirtier he was. He also looked sweaty, the mud matting the hair of his arms— well, she couldn't see that level of detail but that's how she imagined it. He was definitely going to need a shower after this.

Stop. It.

She delivered her most condemning look to Lili. "You're going to have to give up some time. I'm not interested in Shane."

"Why not?"

"You were right. He's not my type at all. Too much of a puppy dog." A vision of Shane's amber eyes drilling into her as he...drilled into her was usurped by the hurt version when she shoved those annulment papers at his hard chest.

"So who was it?" Lili asked darkly.

"Who was what?"

"The guy who turned you into a man-hating drone." She frowned. "You used to want things. Love, marriage, the fairy tale."

Thrown by Lili's assumption, Cara fought for balance. She didn't hate men; she just knew she didn't have it in her to make one happy. There was a big difference. "Just because I'm discerning does not make me a man hater."

Lili *hmphed*. "So someone like Blonde Ambition, he's more your style? He's good-looking, I suppose."

Cara glanced in Mason's direction and got a wave in return. She stitched on a smile.

He *was* good-looking, all Teutonic efficiency and exquisite engineering distilled into six feet and change. Successful, a go-getter, the kind of guy she had always thought she would end up with when she dreamed her girlish dreams.

Beside him, Shane looked like he had stepped out of a coal mine, his muddied skin as dark as his mink-brown hair. Her piece of rough, her scruffy cowboy. Too easygoing, too young, all wrong. Yet when she assessed the two men before her, only one of them made her heart beat dangerously fast. Only one of them made her smile and freed up the knots in her brain. Only one of them made her unreasonably hopeful. And it wasn't Mason Napier.

* * *

Shane had forgotten how dirty rugby was, especially when you hadn't a clue what you were doing. By the time he had figured out the lay of the land, the land had figured out him. After only twenty minutes on the field, the soft ground underfoot was very familiar, as was the elbow of the big lummox he had been assigned to mark. He already had enough reasons to hate this guy with the perfectly pressed rugby strip and the boots so new they squeaked when he stepped back, usually onto Shane's feet. Then he started waving at Cara. That she had smiled back was not inspiring a boatload of confidence.

The cool nip in the air had vanished as soon as he saw her slender form amble up to the sideline with Lili. She wore white jeans that looked like a canvas waiting to be spattered, so flush he imagined he'd have trouble getting his hand inside the waistband. Oh, but how he'd love to try. Pity his services were no longer required—sexual, husbandly, or otherwise. Now she was here waving at this streak of shit.

There was a lull as one of the guys got medical attention up near the goal line.

"So you know Cara?" he asked his mark with as much disinterest as he could summon.

Two Left Feet squinted at Shane, evidently torn on whether he should divulge this top secret information.

"Yeah, I know her. She's done some volunteering for my mother's cancer charity and we've socialized a bit." His eyes narrowed further. "And you know her how?"

I'm her husband, bozo. "I work with her."

He offered his hand. "Mason Napier."

Shane took it, making sure to smudge some mud into the guy's palm. "Shane Doyle."

"Irish? You guys know your rugby."

"You could say that," Shane said curtly. He didn't mean to sound so cagey but he had his answer about how this guy knew Cara and he wasn't in the mood for small talk. Unfortunately, Napier was blind to the smoke signals.

"Cara's quite the girl. Lots of guys I know want to date her."

Though a volcanic bubble burned his skin, Shane held his tongue. Napier nodded slowly, like Shane had said something. Gobshite. The whistle blew, signifying the resumption of play, and Shane started a slow jog down the field, waiting for the ball to come his direction. Napier stuck to him like Shane's mud was magnetic.

"Is she seeing anyone right now?" Napier asked.

"Yeah, I believe she is."

"She's a beautiful woman," he said, his voice jumpy from the gallop. "I'd love to take that to pound town."

That halted Shane so fast he almost got whiplash. "She's with someone."

"Really?" Mason sped up as the ball filtered across the line heading to the goal. Shane maneuvered to his left to intercept the pass that was two players away.

"She's taken. I'm sure," Shane said, about one second before he stepped between Napier and the ball, got an elbow in the face, and became the filling in a sandwich with the ground on one side and six hundred pounds of muscle on the other. The wet pop and searing pain in his shoulder happened simultaneously, and everything went black.

"Shane! You all right?"

He opened his eyes tentatively to see Jack bent over him, his eyes wide with concern. Shane tried to get up—operative word, tried—but his whole left side was on fire.

"Fuck, that hurts." He made another attempt to get up just to be sure. Yep, still hurt.

"Don't move. Doc's coming over."

"Doctor's already here?" Shane muttered, confused. "How long was I out?"

"You weren't; you just blinked. Doc's on the team." Jack broke into an approving grin. "Sport of the oppressors, right?"

That dragged an excruciatingly painful laugh out of Shane.

A big guy with a beard who had introduced himself earlier as Max stepped in and started poking around. It didn't help. Shane groaned and twisted to his good side.

"Sorry, man. You zigged while I zagged," Napier said from far above like a golden god. Wanker.

"Shane, are you okay?" Cara knelt in the mud—God Almighty, in those snow-white jeans—and grasped his hand. "Sorry, stupid question."

"No, it's not stupid. Thanks for asking." Their gazes held, hers as wide and blue as the sky over her fair head. "You'll ruin your clothes, gorgeous."

She squeezed his hand and . . . it didn't make him feel better in the slightest.

"Shane, look at me."

Milk-pale, she stared and he stared back. For a nanosecond, a Cara-induced endorphin rush flooded his brain. Then Max threw his shoulder back into the joint and he bit his lip hard enough to draw blood.

* * *

"You need to ice it and keep it immobilized," Doctor Max said as he walked Shane back to the sidelines. "Can someone help you get home?"

"Lili can take him," Jack said behind them. "Where's your stuff?"

Shane pointed to where he'd parked his bike and stashed his tracksuit and backpack.

"Jack Kilroy, do not even think about riding that bike," Lili said. "You don't know how."

"Sure, I do. Been taking out Tad's Harley for spins every now and then." He ran a muddy finger along her jaw. "And don't think I don't know you've been doing it as well after I told you I didn't approve."

Lili looked affectionately bored, and then shot Shane a sly smile.

Shane's heart turned over, revealing its underbelly. Lately, he had realized he had a major problem, apart from the Cara situation. Not only did Shane like his brother, but he was foolishly letting his mind wander to a future with the whole stinking lot of them.

More than once, Lili and Jules stopped by with Evan for family meal at Sarriette, and Shane had to tamp down his excitement at being part of something bigger than himself. Lili continued to invite him over to her parents', though he'd made his excuses. There was something off about breaking bread with the in-laws who hadn't a clue about his true relationship with Cara.

Of course, a future that involved Cara's family but not Cara was a place his mind didn't want to visit.

Doctor Max was still talking. "It'll be a couple of weeks of pain. Best to check in with your doctor on Monday. I'll write you a script for ibuprofen—the good stuff, not the drugstore candy."

"Thanks." The pain was fading to a dull ache now so maybe he wouldn't need the pills or the doctor. Doctors had never been on his Christmas card list.

"How're you feeling?"

He turned to find a chalky-faced Cara, her jeans mud blotched. Those dirty knees cheered the hell out of him. "I'll live, but it might be a while before I dance again."

That pulled a smile from her. A luminous one that turned up his pain with the realization that he couldn't have her. It was good to be reminded of it.

"Think I might need to skip work tonight, but I'll call Mona and make sure she's good to go," Shane said to Jack, who had returned with his backpack. He fished for the key to the bike and handed it over.

"Take all the time you need." A muscle twitched in Jack's jaw. "That Napier was bang out of order."

"I'm sure it was an accident," Cara said quickly, and Shane tried not to get too annoyed that she was defending that piece of crap.

"Whatever, it was a dick move." Jack opened the door to his SUV and handed the keys off to Lili.

"I'll drive him," Cara said, taking his backpack from Lili. Three sets of eyes fell on her, and she flushed to the roots of her golden hair. "He lives across the hall. It's on my way."

"Cara, he's going to need help," Lili said, darting a sharp look at Jack.

"No, I won't," Shane muttered to no one in particular.

"You will," Jack said. "You're not going to be able to take that shirt off without assistance."

"I'm not completely useless. Come on, Shane," Cara said, pulling his bad arm.

He let out a growl as a hot poker of pain streaked through every muscle and tendon.

"Oh, sorry," Cara said.

"Are you sure?" Lili looked at her sister, concern etched on her face.

"I can do it," Cara replied emphatically.

Shane tried to grasp the undertone here but honestly, he was in so much pain that he didn't care who drove him.

Fifteen minutes later, they were home after a quick pit stop to pick up drugs and an unwinnable argument about the necessity for a sling. (I don't need it. Yes, you do. Repeat.) He hovered outside his door.

"Thanks for the lift. I just need my clothes." He gestured to his backpack clenched in her hands.

"I'm going to clean you up."

"I'm fine. I can take it from here." Irritation mounted in his throat. He felt stupid and embarrassed and not a little annoyed at the lot of them because he liked them and they were being kind.

"Shane, you go in. I'll be there in a minute." She turned away to her own door.

In the bathroom mirror, he assessed the damage. A goose egg that still had some growing to do shaded his right eye. At least it had stopped bleeding. The skin over his ribs—what he realized now with every tortured breath were likely cracked ribs—felt tight and raw like it had been scrubbed with a wire brush. Just the mere idea of taking off his shirt sent him into a paroxysm of pain. After an embarrassing struggle with the childproof lid of the prescription meds, he knocked back a couple of pain pills.

The bathroom door nudged open a couple of inches and Vegas, that treacherous little bastard, poked his head around the door. Or a very different version of Vegas. Jesus, Mary, and Joseph, the cat looked sleek and groomed and, fuck almighty, pretty. Around his neck, a pink—*pink!*—leather collar encrusted with sparkling jewels pronounced him the newest member of the sissy-kitty club.

Sucking in an agonizing breath, Shane scooped up the scrawny bag of bones with his good arm. "Where'd you come from and what did they do to you?"

"I thought the patient could do with a visitor. Rupert's missed you." At the sound of Cara's voice, the disloyal bundle made a fuss to be free.

"Who's Rupert?"

"Roo for short." She shot a sly glance at the cat, now playing figure eights with her bare legs. She had swapped out the needs-laundering jeans for a pair of skimpy shorts that revealed almost every sexy inch of her golden thighs. Clearly trying to send him to an early grave.

He scooted his mind back a step. "Roo?"

A soft tickle of a laugh escaped her lips. "Just kidding, Potato Head, but I sure had you going."

She was making jokes now? He looked down at Rupert-slash-Vegas for an explanation. Shane had heard of this. Animal therapy for people who needed to lighten up. Maybe a couple of days with a fluffy critter had removed that stick up her very fine arse.

She picked up Vegas and stroked him. "The cat beautician tried her best to work with the rough patches. Came out well, didn't he?"

He grunted noncommittally. Something had most definitely changed. She seemed easier, lighter, and while he liked edgy could-lose-the-plot-any-minute Cara, he also loved this side of her. His wife was a very complicated woman and that turned him on big time.

The image of a sheaf of annulment papers sitting on his dresser flashed through his brain.

Yep, still turned on.

"Sit," she said, dropping the cat to the floor. He did. So did the cat.

She grabbed a face cloth and soaked it in the sink. Starting with his forehead, she wiped gently at the mud and grime, also wiping away any hopes he had of pushing her from his thoughts. Methodically, she worked on his exposed skin above the neckline of his shirt, before kneeling to remove his boots and socks.

The sight of her bent in supplication sent his body into a predictable turn of events. Zero to rock hard in two seconds flat. Must be some sort of record. The soft, wet warmth of the washcloth felt marvelous on his calf, though he could get just as clean in the shower. Cleaner. Because if she continued in this vein, the whole situation was heading for filthy.

"So that guy who decked me said he knew you. Charity work or something."

"Mason's mother is the woman I told you about, the business I want to get for the restaurant. I also do some volunteer work with her foundation."

"What kind of volunteer work?"

Color stole up her neck. "I help organize some of their fund-raisers. Charity runs. Other stuff."

"Other stuff?"

"Just reading to kids at the children's hospital," she said softly, her gaze no longer meeting his.

Well, well, well, you could have knocked him over with a pastry brush. Just when he thought he had this woman figured out she threw him another curveball. What should he say to that? *Well done, you?*

Instead he said the doucheiest thing he could think of.

"That Napier bloke wants to fuck you."

She didn't even break her rhythm. "He said that?"

"Pretty much. Apparently he has friends who want to fuck you, too."

"Maybe he was just thinking of a way to distract you so you'd lose your focus on the game."

The pain in his shoulder turned sharp with the knowledge that she was right. That shit head had read Shane's interest in Cara and played him like a fiddle.

Feeling like more of an idiot by the minute, he asked, "So he's not your type then?"

"God, no. The man probably calls his own name when he comes."

That pulled a deep laugh from him and he sucked up the pain because it was worth it. Cara could be so serious but when she said something outrageous it was usually the funniest thing he'd ever heard.

The warm cloth over his thigh sent sensuous shivers through his body. He stilled her hand, clamping down on his tongue at the stab of pain that rocketed through him. If she went any farther he was going to do something stupid, like wrestle her to the floor and break a couple more ribs in the process. "Cara, you don't have to do this. If you help me with my shirt, I can take a shower."

Looking up, her eyes read soft and pure, yet determined. She wiped his knee with the warm, wet cloth, and his thigh clenched. His imagination journeyed to her losing the scrap and moving her fingers as high as they would go. His dick stiffened in readiness for the hand...that dropped back to his calf.

Silence stretched between them while he searched for something to say. It had been nowhere near this difficult before they went sheet diving.

"What was all that about with Jack and Lili?"

She halted her ministrations. "All what?"

"They were making weird faces like mimes when you volunteered to take me home."

"I'm not really nursemaid material. They were probably worried I was going to dislocate your other shoulder getting you here."

"Seems a bit extreme."

She got up to start the shower and though it hurt to turn, he did it anyway because he was a man and what felt like a couple of cracked ribs wasn't going to stop him ogling her peachy behind.

"They have good reasons," she said. "I haven't been around much when people need me."

"What people?"

"My mother. She got sick a couple of years back and I ran for cover. Lili stepped up, so she's understandably suspicious of my ability to take care of anyone other than myself." The bitterness in her voice surprised him.

"You seem to be doing a good job so far with me."

Ignoring that, she pulled off her sweater, revealing a white, stretchy top with straps that were thinner than the lilac bra cupping her perfect breasts.

"So you're feeling better?" she asked.

He started laughing, though it hurt like a heart attack because the timing of her question was so perfect. *It's gettin' hot in here. Oops, there goes my sweater. You feelin' better now, baby?*

She made one of those *you're incorrigible* noises. "I didn't mean that, perv."

"Yeah, but that's where my mind went. I'd feel better if you took that skimpy top off. Do the sexy-nurse bit right."

She traced a lazy finger along his jaw. "This isn't happening, Shane."

He couldn't help dropping his gaze to his lap. "Oh, I beg to differ, gorgeous."

Her laugh bounced off the tile, full and musical. That sweet, sexy scent she wore amplified in the heat from her body and the room. He toyed with the idea of pulling her hair out of its coil or palming the swell of her breast fighting for containment in that white top, but his hands were wet and he had already dirtied up her jeans. Really, he just wanted to get her wet in every place wetness felt good.

"This isn't happening," she repeated as she inclined her head closer. She moistened her lips, lips that were so close to his mouth he could tip forward and—

Get a wet washcloth in the face. She was a little rough, too, but she made up for it by combing her fingers through his steam-dampened hair, setting his scalp on fire with that gentlest of caresses. The painkillers were doing their job, dulling his ache to a low-grade throb. A throbbing of a much higher intensity was making itself known farther down, a burning ball of pressure that unfurled and flooded his groin.

He felt her breath like a whisper on his neck as she lifted his muddy shirt at the hem.

"If we get it off your good side first, it'll probably be easier."

They managed to pull it off with a minimum of fuss and less pain than he expected. Cue the shrieking.

"Shane, this is awful!"

A sidelong glance in the mirror revealed dark red splotches

across his torso, though the burn scar that covered his right side had these new brands beat in the ugly stakes.

"I'm fine."

"No, you're not, he-man. You need to see a doctor."

"No doctors." The idea of sitting in the ER chilled him to the marrow. He had already wasted too much of his childhood in hospital waiting rooms, lying about why he was there. Children are marvelously adept at keeping secrets, and Shane had honed that skill into an Olympic sport.

She was looking at him strangely because of his terse declaration. He backpedaled and dug deep for his charm.

"Not to worry, love. It looks worse than it is. I've cracked ribs before. Time and drugs—that's what it takes." And the ability to leave the past where it belongs.

Frown deepening, she ran a finger along his old scar. Apparently his charm was off today.

"You can tell me things, too. I'm not nearly as self-absorbed as people think I am."

She didn't sound convinced, and he wondered if she truly believed in her depth or how far she had come in her recovery. All he knew for certain is that he didn't possess one iota of her emotional bravery.

His father had used him as his punching bag for ten years until Shane was big enough to hit back. He had suffered the man's boot on his neck, shards of glass in his shoulder, broken arms, fractured ribs. He had felt words that hurt more than all those injuries put together. *Useless, worthless, good-for-nothing. A mistake.* The Alzheimer's did nothing to soften John Sullivan. It just blessed the old man with a blissed-out forgetfulness and sharpened every one of Shane's memories to jagged points. Honed his resentment toward Jack for not being around as well, which he knew was downright irrational. Nothing could be gained from a visit down that rocky road.

Cara's compassion pushed all his buttons or the ones that had yet to be pushed. His cock was fully engaged, but now his heart was lifting in reaction to her concern. He squeezed her waist gently, immensely gratified at the smudgy finger-prints he left on her immaculate top.

I claim you, Cara DeLuca-Doyle.

Annulment papers on the dresser, idiot.

"Don't worry about me, love," he said, smiling through.

That earned him a resigned noise. Charm offensive some-what successful.

"Stand up," she said, her hands on his shoulders. When he did, she used the upward movement of his body to slide her fingers down his sides, carefully avoiding the rawest welts. She slipped her fingertips inside the elastic of his shorts, their bagginess unable to hide the burgeoning situation down below.

"This is where I go solo," he said.

"Shane, I've seen it before."

Not like this she hadn't. His cock was a rampant weapon and if it didn't find some relief soon, he might not be respon-sible for his actions. The pain should have put a damper on the situation but the mere presence of Cara would make a dead man's dick lift a coffin lid.

Rein it in, boyo.

"That's not the problem. If I let you go any further, I'm going to have to dip into my fantasy bag."

"Oh, which fantasy would this be?" she asked like his dirty little list was familiar to her.

"The one where you bend over that sink and I plunge into you to the hilt."

She spared a glance for the sink. "Do I get any say in this fantasy?"

"It's my fantasy, LT. And in it you're screaming like a porn star and your primary participation involves telling me how much harder you want it."

The pat on the chest she gave him was patronizing, to say the least. But it also felt affectionate, like the look Jack and Lili shared while they bickered about riding Tad's bike. Shane hoped to God Jack knew what he was doing on the Dyna Glide.

"I guess I can't stop you from having your little old fantasies. Fantasies so rarely become reality, though." Her fingers lingered on the waistband of his shorts; her gaze stroked his mouth.

"Cara, the only reason this particular fantasy isn't turning into reality is because I'm likely to end up in the emergency room if I take it where I want to go."

Her expression was one of infinite patience. Oh, she was a cool one. "Shane, the only reason this fantasy of yours isn't turning into reality is because I've made it clear that we're not happening."

"So you have, yet here we are. With the nursing and the jaw stroking and the heat between us you can't deny. Not even a woman as controlled as you pretend to be."

So much for reining it in—all he'd done is turn himself on even more. He didn't need to look in the mirror to know his expression raged with an incongruent mix of pain and desire.

She stepped back out of his burning orbit and picked up Vegas. "I guess I'll leave you to go solo, then." Her voice was low and raspy, transmitting right to his groin. She took another look at the very clear evidence of his arousal and blinked rapidly.

He hooked the back of her neck. Another blade of pain shot through his left side but he stayed the course.

"I'm going to be in that shower thinking about you. Feel free to stick around and listen. Or anything else that takes your fancy."

Her sharp snatch of breath stole his own breath away but it could just as easily be those cracked ribs. He kissed her softly; any more fervently and he'd probably pass out. The cat made a pissy noise at being caught in a semicrush between them. *Suck it up, kitty.*

"I'll need help getting dressed later. And making lunch. And then getting undressed. So don't go far." He shucked his shorts and pulled back the curtain. Grimacing at how much it hurt to bend, he gingerly adjusted the shower tap all while potently aware of her heated gaze on his back.

Out of the corner of his eye, he saw both her appreciative survey of his body and her exit reflected in the mirror. Dangerous hope unfolded in his chest, but this time, he didn't push it away.

CHAPTER 13

Vegas jumped out of her arms, leaving Cara free to massage her temples in circles over her tight skin. It had taken every inch of her dwindling willpower not to strip down and step into that shower with Shane. If she had, they might have both ended up in the emergency room.

Psych consult needed for female presenting with acute nymphomania.

Those caramel eyes, the blatant desire lurking within, and his mouth—whoa, he could kiss. As soon as his lips touched hers, she was sucked into Shane's world, where it was sweet and hot and oh-so-sexy. A world she wanted to live in, and sleep in, and have freaking babies in.

She should leave. Run away like she always did when things got uncomfortable, but beneath that dirty-talking sex god, there lived a man in pain, and not just physical. He wore a deep emotional wound that not even that golden smile could hide.

In his Spartan bedroom, home to a dresser, a futon, the

ubiquitous cowboy boots, but no photos or anything personal, she pulled open drawers, searching for clean clothes. She had tried to go gentle when undressing him and he had responded with his macho *nothing to see here* act, but there was no reason why he should suffer any more than necessary. Sweatpants with an elastic-banded waist and a zipped-up hoodie would be a less painful alternative to a tee and jeans. She laid them out on his bed.

The manila envelope she had shoved in his hands three nights ago lay innocuously on his dresser. Still smooth, not a wrinkle in sight. Clearly, he hadn't been carrying it folded up in his leather jacket or regularly unsheathing the papers while he wrung his hands with indecision. Perhaps he hadn't given it much thought at all. A sneaky peek revealed her neat signature cutting a lonely script across one dotted line versus a blank where Shane's John Hancock should be. Almost three weeks later, they were still married and she wasn't freaking out.

Could she possibly be enjoying this crazy situation she found herself in? Was she actually thriving on this roller coaster of emotion? Good grief, she was. She was more than tall enough to go on this ride, and damn, she was starting to like what was happening here.

Enough to stick around and make lunch. She was going to make lunch for her debilitated husband. What should she make? What *could* she make?

Not a lot.

Placing her ear to the bathroom door, all she could hear was the rush of water, but her imagination supplied the video. Shane getting all slick and soapy, running his big, strong hands over his hard chest and taut abs. Moving his hand farther down and down—

Okay, lunch.

Offering a TV dinner or a tub of yogurt to an award-winning chef wasn't going to cut it. Cara was a product of a food-loving culture, worked with chefs every day, and had two hands that admittedly she would much rather employ washing the broad, muscled back of her wounded soldier. Surely a capable, kick-ass woman like herself could come up with something.

The cat brushed by her legs and meowed.

"Yes, Vegas. To the kitchen."

A few false starts later, they were on their way. While the aroma of melting cheese filled the air with its comforting warmth and pleasant associations, she fed the cat from a bag of unappetizing pellets she found in the pantry.

"Hey." At the sound of Shane's voice, her stomach gave a swoopy loop.

He'd managed to pull on the sweatpants she had laid out on the bed and had gotten halfway with the hoodie, which dangled off one shoulder like a pathetic matador's cape. Dripping wet bangs stabbed his eyes. It was the saddest, most beautiful sight she'd ever seen.

With as much care as possible, she helped slide the empty sleeve up his arm. She suddenly felt shy around him as though her attempts at domesticity had turned her into a diffident housewife. Fumbling with the zipper—clearly her brain didn't approve of this action—she watched in mounting disappointment as the metal teeth interlocked inch by inch on the slow slide up his chest. Too soon, he was indecently covered.

Criminal, just criminal.

She grabbed the sling off the table and applied it with a growing confidence in her new nurturing abilities.

His eyes shone bright, part amusement, part challenge. All devastating.

"Something's burning."

Sure was, honey. Scorching heat licked flames across her skin, but of course he was referring to his pain and not the heat wave rolling through down south.

"Your shoulder still hurts?"

"No," he said. "Well, yes, but I meant that whatever you're cooking is burning."

"Oh shit!" She turned quickly and removed the pan from the stove. The rather poorly constructed cheese sandwich was golden brown on the upturned side. She was uncommonly proud of that one side but it did little to alleviate the fact it would not be so pretty on the other.

"I messed up. I was trying to go with your advice."

"My advice?"

"There's nothing sexier than a confident woman in the kitchen."

His lips twitched and he eased himself into a chair at the kitchen table. "Serve up that bad boy, then."

She plated up and tried to ignore the acrid smell that accompanied its slide out of the pan. How was it possible to mess up a grilled cheese sandwich? Evan could do this. Jeez, the cat could do this.

"I could make something else."

"This'll be grand." He raised his smoldering dark eyes to hers and locked his gaze in place. "I'm very pleased you stayed, Cara."

He said it quietly, so her heart really shouldn't have overreacted like a wild animal trying to escape her chest. Their eyes held for a scary couple of heartbeats. Her whole world distilled to this moment, a one hundred proof shot of emotion ripping a high-octane path through her veins.

A loud knock on the door surprised her and forced her to

break the magnetic link. She opened it to find Tad and Jack. Crap on toast.

Her cousin held up a takeout bag from DeLuca's. "Lili called in an order for the patient." Without waiting for an invitation, he strode into the apartment. Jack followed with a similar, cocky gait. Immediately, Tad made himself at home, doling out her father's famous gnocchi with brown butter and sage onto plates.

Shane caught Cara's eye. "I'm good, Tad. Cara already made me lunch."

Tad did one of those cartoon double takes that he probably thought was hi*larious*. "Cara cooked? And it's edible? This I gotta see."

Shane took a big bite of the grilled cheese and chewed confidently. It might have been her imagination but his strained smile was less an effort to weather his bodily pain, but more a struggle to react graciously to the worst thing he'd ever had the misfortune of eating.

"Hmm, this is"—he rolled his tongue around his mouth and she saw the exact moment when he realized what he was getting himself into—"really good."

Her gorgeous, blarney-spouting liar of a husband.

Maybe she had been a little adventurous with the ingredients. There was a wedge of brie in his fridge, so she thought, why not? And because he was a gourmet chef, and oh no, would not be satisfied with a plain old cheese sandwich, she had added a few flavorful extras. Like pimento peppers. And Dijon mustard. And a smattering of capers because her mother used them all the time.

Tad scrutinized the sandwich in Shane's hands and emerged skeptical. He lifted his gaze to Cara.

"So C, thanks for the design and marketing workup for the wine bar. I really liked your idea for the furniture." She had filled another one of her thick binders with décor ideas and promotional strategies for Tad's new venture. One of her notions was recycled wine casks for the table tops. After reading through his business plan, she had high hopes for its success, along with its value as a location for private parties.

"No problem."

Jack handed over the key to Shane's Harley with a wry smile that said he'd enjoyed the ride.

"How're you feeling?" he asked Shane.

"Could be worse. Drugs are starting to kick in."

Jack grabbed one of the beers Tad had brought and popped the cap. He lolled against the counter, a position he was no doubt familiar with, having lived here with Lili for about six months.

"I had a chat with Mason Napier after you left Lincoln Park, Cara."

Cold dread poured over her. She raised an oh-really eyebrow and waited for him to elaborate.

"He seems to think we're running a catering business. That we're going to be hosting some party"—he flapped his beer-free hand and Cara braced herself for the notorious Jack Kilroy fireworks—"for a hundred people."

"We can do it," she said with more confidence than she felt.

That pulled a strained smile from him. "Cara, in case you haven't noticed, we run a very high-end, fine-dining, bordering-on-Michelin-starred establishment."

"And you hired me to be your events manager," she countered, her hackles on the rise. This had been a long while coming, and while she'd prefer not to do it with Shane and Tad watching on, it was time to have it out.

"Mason Napier...Mason Napier choosing *us* is an event. A nod from him would send business into the stratosphere.

We'd be the first choice for every party, every charity do, every shindig on the Chicago social calendar."

He huffed out a breath. "Cara, I admire your moxie—"

"Did he just say moxie?" Tad asked around his gnocchi chewing.

"Sure did," Shane said. "Time warped right back to 1934."

Jack shot filthy looks at the chorus, then went on. "I admire your moxie but that's not what we do. I hired you to manage small events in our private dining rooms. Events my current, handpicked team can handle at the same time as regular service. I've done these big parties at my other places in London, New York, Vegas. Quality control is a nightmare. I can't risk putting my name to frozen food and temp staff just to make a quick buck."

Even after a year of lying low, Jack's sensitivity about his spin around the hamster wheel of fame was still fresh. Having suffered the slings and arrows of the tabloids and the accusations of hackdom by chefs he respected, he still smarted at the thought his name could ever be associated with an inferior product.

"Jack," she said in her best Cara-cajole. "So you hire a few more people. Trusted people."

He was already moving down the list of cons. "And what about the space? We'd have to close for this one event and I know you won't want to stop there. Are we supposed to shut down every time we have numbers higher than what we can manage upstairs?"

"There's the place next door," Shane said.

Thank you, Shane. She didn't need to look at him to know his Irish eyes were twinkling.

Jack ignored him and kept his imperious gaze trained on Cara. "You're still angling to take on that lease?"

She lifted her shoulder in an indeterminate shrug as if it wasn't the first thing slamming her brain each morning when she woke. After Shane. She spent a couple of foolish moments letting Shane take a starring role in her fantasies first. Then she got serious and hit the gym.

"It's been vacant for six months. Someone's going to take it."

"In this economy? Cara, I don't want to be a purveyor of fast food. That's not what we're about here."

"What about Wolfgang Puck?"

All eyes shifted to Shane who had just thrown out that gem.

"What about him?" Jack asked warily.

"He does big events all the time." Shane flicked a go-with-me glance at Cara.

"Right, the *Vanity Fair* Oscar party, for example," she picked up. Wow, Shane was on fire. She paused to let it sink in with Jack. *One, two.* "Don't you want to be offering that kind of service in Chicago?"

"Wolfgang Puck?" Jack said. "He sells soup. In supermarkets." But he sounded more intrigued than annoyed. Nothing like a little friendly chef competition to stoke those fires.

"I'm sure your soup is better than Wolfgang Puck's, Jack," she soothed, trying desperately to ignore Shane's dimple winking at her from around his fingers. That dimple was going to be the death of her. "Just think of how Chicago is crying out for this kind of service."

"Cara," Jack said, half exasperated, but then his face transformed with a wide grin.

Turning, Cara found Lili, who had just walked in and now leaned in to kiss Jack.

"Your fiancé is an absolute Cro-Magnon," Cara said. "He's completely prehistoric about his business."

The tense line of Jack's shoulders slackened and he smiled at her sister, his eyes lurking with intent. "She likes me Cro-Magnon. It works for her."

"I'm trying to make us the go-to destination in Chicago," Cara hurried on, before Jack's brain turned to baby food in the presence of Lili. "It's bad enough you charge midlevel prices when you could be asking for twice as much."

"You know why I do that. I want anyone to be able to eat at Sarriette, not just the Mason Napiers of this world." They'd had this argument so many times she could recite it in her sleep.

"But in the meantime the Mason Napiers, and more specifically the mothers of the Mason Napiers, have needs that we can serve. Penny Napier's stamp of approval would be—"

"Penny Napier?" Lili interrupted. "You mean Penny Napier, founder of the Pink Hearts Cancer Foundation?"

Cara nodded. "She has that annual dinner every December and Mason said we could cate—um, host it if we had the space."

"We should do that," Lili said to Jack.

Jack let out a weary sigh. "Sweetheart, it's not so simple."

Lili curled her body into Jack's side. "I'm sure you could work something out between the two of you. You're both such go-getters."

"Oh, shush," Jack said, but Cara was already enjoying the sweet buzz of victory. She really should have roped Lili into the fray sooner. And Shane.

Who was now the subject of Jack's glare. "I suppose *you* think this is a good idea."

"Not bad," Shane said casually. "You could design the menus, and there'd be any number of chefs who'd jump at the chance to cook to your specs."

"And you'd have Cara running the show," Tad said.

"Zombie apocalypse, Jack," Lili added, grinning.

"What the hell does that mean?" Cara asked, her gaze flitting around the kitchen for answers.

Jack delivered a half smile. "I might have once remarked that come the zombie apocalypse, I would want to be on Team Cara."

"That's the nicest thing you've ever said to me, Jack."

Everybody laughed, even Shane, though the wince that crossed his face told her it must hurt like hell.

Cara's excitement threatened to overwhelm her as the idea of a business—a family business—took hold. There are other ways of belonging and maybe she had just found hers. Her mind racked up frequent-flier miles racing through the possibilities. Top chefs like Jack and her father. Lili in charge of photography. Tad, their wine expert. Shane's magical creations would slot right in. Shane as part of her family business.

Wow.

Thinking now might be a good time to call it a day, she shot a significant look at her new ally.

Shane gave an exaggerated yawn. "Thanks for coming over, guys, but I think I need to lie down for a while."

As the visitors headed to the door, Lili's gaze slid to Vegas. "Where'd the cat come from?"

"He belongs to Shane," Cara said, though that pink collar bore all the hallmarks of a Cara-style intervention.

"Hmm," was Lili's multivolume response as she stepped into the hallway. She turned back, mock surprise on her face. "Oh, you're staying?"

"I'm just being a good neighbor," Cara said, ignoring her sister's smirk.

She let Jack and co. walk a few steps before calling out

the kicker. "We haven't actually sealed the deal yet. Mason wants a chef's table for dinner next Saturday night."

Jack's expression soured. "Oh, for fuck's sake."

She closed the door, leaving him to Lili's soothing hands.

"Told you we make a good team," she heard behind her, so close she shivered.

Heart skimming the roof of her mouth, she called on all her resources as she turned around to greet Shane. *Don't jump him, don't jump him.*

"We do," she said, backing up until she met the unyielding barrier of the door.

In his sling, he should have looked helpless and ripe for a Cara smooch assault, but as usual, he managed to completely undo her to kitten weakness with his nearness and strength.

"Pity about this." He patted his trussed-up arm. "I'd do anything to have both hands free right now."

"You would?"

He tilted his head and his gaze raked her body top-to-toe. "I hope you're good at taking instructions, LT. Because you're going to have to follow my orders to the letter."

Instructions. Orders. Images of doing anything he asked assailed her diminishing calm. *Touch me, Cara. Right there, baby. Now yourself...*

"What did you have in mind?"

His smile was dirty, hot, and slow. "I'm going to teach you how to cook."

CHAPTER 14

Come Monday, Shane was in so much pain that he had no choice but to visit a doctor at Cara's insistence. Because she had a meeting with a potential client, she assigned Jack to drop him off at the Rehabilitation Institute of Chicago to see an orthopedic surgeon she knew through her numerous contacts. Shane suspected she had created a new binder to organize his recovery, or at minimum a spreadsheet.

In the car, Jack and Shane chatted about the wedding menu, then lapsed into comfortable silence until about six blocks out when Jack spoke up again.

"I hear you might be leaving us," he said, keeping his eyes on the road ahead.

"Where'd you hear that?"

"Cara said you have plans to open your own pastry shop."

That Cara had spoken to Jack about it bit into his neck, but then he hadn't actually sworn her to secrecy, had he? Still, it confirmed his gut instinct not to confide anything more personal. "It's just an idea. Nothing's settled."

"If you need someone to invest, you know where to turn."

What? Shane had been saving for the last six years and didn't need the money, but the joy coursing through his body numbed the pain dead. Of course, it wasn't just because of Jack's offer. Without knowing how he got here, Shane had come to the decision that he planned to stay in Chicago for as long as he was welcome. He could open his business here. He could live above DeLuca's. He could be with Cara.

"Why would you be interested in that? It's small potatoes for someone like you."

"The winner of the Best Design at the International Exhibition of Culinary Art? The guy whose creations cream the thongs of all my female customers?" Jack's brows drew together in a chevron. "Uh, that's why I'm interested in that. Don't get me wrong, I'll miss you in my kitchen but this way I still get some benefit out of you. I'm nothing if not self-serving."

Jack had to have known about it, but he had never once referred to the design award, which Shane had put down to some keep-the-help-from-getting-cocky dynamic. The drugging effect of the joy was wearing off, but Shane embraced the sweet ache. He wanted to remember this feeling forever.

"Of course," Jack went on, "I'll need a favor from you."

Too easy. "What's that?"

"I was thinking you could contribute a recipe to the book I'm cooking up with Tony. We've already got some great desserts—Frankie has this amazing zabaglione—but we could do with something with a bit of a wow factor. That chocolate cake with the basil-lemon filling..."

"Bella Donna." Beautiful woman. Italian flavors with hints of tart in a rich, decadent casing. "I'd be honored," Shane said, his chest too full with emotion.

"Good." Jack turned off Superior Avenue into the drop-

off zone for the hospital. "So how's Cara? She seemed awfully worried about you."

Non sequitur? No chance.

"She's just being a good neighbor."

"She cooked for you."

Crickets.

"None of my business?"

"Something like that."

Jack fed him a sharp look. "Don't hurt her, all right? She
means a lot to me."

Shane blinked away his surprise. "And there I thought
you were looking out for *me* when you warned me off before. Isn't she supposed to be a ballbuster?"

"Tales of her testicular terrorism might have been exaggerated. She's..." He looked like he was choosing his
words with the precision of someone selecting a cupcake
with the perfect amount of icing. "She's not as tough as
she gives off."

Shane's heart disintegrated to mush because he knew it
was true. Cara wasn't tough at all. Every new minute with
her revealed new vulnerabilities, and not just hers.

"She's not tough, but she's not exactly easy either," Shane
said, feeling the situation out.

Jack strummed the steering wheel. "Of course she isn't.
She's a DeLuca woman. If she's amazing, she won't be
easy..."

"If she's easy, she won't be amazing," Shane finished in
the words of the great Bob Marley, a poet ripped from the
world before his time. Along with his heart turning to overly
wet dough, an unwelcome twinge in Shane's gut acknowledged the twin negatives of annoyance and jealousy. Jack
knew about Cara's anorexia.

"Thanks for the lift," he said, no longer in the sharing

mood. He opened the door and climbed out, which, given his useless arm, was harder than it appeared.

"Want me to stop by in an hour and pick you up?" Jack asked.

"Nah, I can take the train."

"Need a couple of bucks for your fare, rookie?"

"Bite me."

Jack laughed and went on his way.

Sunlight dappled the blue-gray water out over the lake as Shane left the doctor's office forty-five minutes later. The ortho surgeon had strapped his ribs and told him to not even think about pounding the dough for a while. They'd had a good laugh about that one. The upshot was that Shane couldn't work at Sarriette for at least two weeks while the ligaments in his shoulder healed.

Inevitably, his thoughts strayed to Cara, Jack, and the rest. They were being so bloody nice to him and he was being so bloody... deceitful. There was no other way to describe it. Here he was wedging his way into their lives under pretense. The longer he left it, the deeper he sank. The deeper he sank, the more he wanted it. The more he wanted it, the more impossible it seemed.

He wanted it all. Sunday lunches with the DeLucas, playing uncle to baby Evan, catching a beer with Tad. Acknowledgment from Jack.

Not just that, but acceptance as a fully fledged member of his family. He had always thought he could muddle through with no one. Since Jo passed on and Packy settled his feet under the bar at the great brewery in the sky, it had been easier to keep all his relationships superficial. Friendly, yet distant. That was how the cockamamie plan was *supposed* to play out. Get along with everyone, do his work well, satisfy his curiosity about Jack. From the interviews and the episodes of Jack's cooking shows, Shane had a few ideas on what his brother would be like. Cocksure, arrogant, not a little vain...well, he was all those things but he was also a stand-up bloke.

Rarely had Shane allowed his mind to wander to an actual truth-telling showdown with Jack but when it did, there were fireworks. Jack would go into a ballistic rage and Shane would feel vindicated, the prophecy fulfilled. Then he could move onto his new business, onto something of his own. He could live his life free and clear. But now all he could think of was the people he would leave behind. Jack, the crew at Sarriette, the DeLucas.

One DeLuca, in particular.

He wanted to be part of something real—a real brother to Jack, a real husband to Cara, a real person—but acknowledging it wouldn't make it happen because therein lay the rub.

He had out and out lied. To Jack. To Cara. To everyone. He had snuck in like a thief and sat at the family table, thinking he could purchase their affection with smiles and charm and pastries. He could blame Jack for not being the total dickwad Shane had expected. He could blame Cara for losing her mind in Las Vegas and making him lose his. But he knew who was really to blame. Shane was the only person here in full possession of all the relevant facts and he had blundered in with an exit strategy worth shit.

How could he tell these people he'd come to care so much about that he had flitted from place to place looking for somewhere to call home? That he couldn't settle as long as he knew his brother was out there—existing? He hadn't even known himself until now. Jack would think he was on the make. The man was already offering to invest in Shane's business and carve out space in his cookbook.

As for Cara? Every single moment they had spent together would be tainted by his lie. Every motive would be suspect.

With the truth, it would be over and he wasn't ready for it to be over. Not by a long shot.

Walking away from the lake, he headed toward the train stop four blocks west and tried to enjoy the sight of girls in summer dresses, which in all honesty was not too difficult. His shoulder might be shot, but the rest of him was working just fine. At the intersection, his gaze attached to a pair of very nice ankles in very high heels. Up his eyes sauntered to a heart-shaped behind in a tight skirt below a ramrod-straight spine that tapered into a kissable neck. A couple of wispy tendrils had escaped her chignon and lay listlessly against her skin. He wanted to lick up one side of her banging body and down the other, then work his way in.

"Hello, Mrs. Doyle," he whispered against her ear.

She turned, her eyes softening as they fell to his banjaxed arm supported by a sling.

"Hey, what did the doctor say?"

"Rest up for a few days," he said, underplaying the injury's severity. "Don't be afraid to ask for help from friends, Romans, noncountrymen. Or women."

"The DeLucas aren't Roman," she said primly. "We hail from Fiesole, just outside Florence."

"I love Fiesole. Great pizza town."

At her golden laugh, his heart squeezed. *This is what happened that night. This feeling.*

"Where are you headed?" he asked, knowing the answer. Their walk across the street took them within a couple of blocks of the Michigan Avenue retail mecca. Cara's world.

Her brow went from smooth to lined. She snuck a glance over her shoulder, drawing his attention to a colorful array of ocean-inspired artwork hanging in floor-to-ceiling windows.

The large frosted logo, a handprint over a ball, announced the entrance to Lurie Children's Hospital.

"Is this where you volunteer? Reading to the kids?"

"Yes, and I'm running late." She stepped away, her slender frame now fraught with tension. Throwing another furtive glance over her shoulder, she turned back with her teeth firmly embedded in her lip. "Would you like to visit with me?"

Hell, yes.

Five minutes later, he was signed in, badged up, and sitting in the White Sox Play Area, sixteen floors up in oncology. Bright, inviting, a complete one-eighty from the soul-sucking hospitals he'd spent too many hours in after another "accidental" fall. Along the windows with panoramic views of the steel-blue Lake Michigan were the patient rooms. Doctors and nurses swayed in and out, and every briefly opened door revealed a child hooked up to equipment that no kid should ever have to see, never mind be connected to. As easy as it would be to succumb to melancholy and despair, there was none of it on show. The staff was all smiles and laughs through what he knew must be heartache. Perhaps they'd become inured to it. He knew something about that.

"You okay?" Cara was giving him that look where she was trying to decide what his game was. His charming mask had been slipping lately and she was seeing more of him than anyone ever had. He needed to be more careful.

"Sometimes it upsets people to see kids like this," she added gently.

He reached for his smile. There it was. "I'm grand."

Shane sat in an overstuffed chair and was immediately surrounded by a crowd of upright kids who acted like having cancer was a walk in the park. Well, more like a wreak-havoc sprint with the odd break to play with (destroy) one of the myriad toys that dotted the tyke-level tables. He shouldn't have been surprised that these kids, even sick ones, would have a lot of energy. That's what he loved about them. Their awe-inspiring resilience.

Besides, he needed all his surprise for the woman at his side. His wife was like a Jedi master with the little blighters. Once the more energetic ones had worn themselves out, she called them to order for a story. Something about a mouse and his sugar-induced shenanigans—the details were sketchy because his senses could scarcely process the scene before him.

Cara wasn't just complicated; she was a complete mystery. He had no idea that bearing direct witness to her passion would affect him so much. Rapt, all the kids listened as she worked her storytelling magic. A sallow-skinned bald boy, aged about five, climbed onto her lap halfway through and looked at her with plain adoration. Something inside Shane clicked and locked. *Right there with ya, kiddo.*

The story came to its conclusion and the kids started whining. Bloody kids, never satisfied.

"I want you guys to meet my"—Cara paused and cocked an eyebrow—"friend, Shane, who works as a pâtissier. Does anyone know what that is?"

The kids shook their heads and eyed Shane, holder of the mysterious occupation, with juvenile suspicion.

"That means he's a pastry chef," Cara continued. "Basically, he eats cakes all day."

"Is that why he's so big?" This from a blonde cutie who looked like a budget version of Cara.

Cara nodded gravely. "Yes, Lizzie, it is. He just eats and eats. Still growing, I imagine."

A few shockingly inappropriate comebacks came to mind, but he remembered his audience.

"What happened to his arm?" the admirer in her lap asked. The little mite's concern pinched his chest.

"He was playing a silly boys' game in a muddy field and five men sat on him."

"More like fifty," Shane corrected.

"Silly," Mini Cara said.

"Very silly," Cara agreed.

Several female staff stopped by to say hello and give him the twice over. Judging by her recall of life snippets about Jenny's five-year-old starting kindergarten here or Patricia's recent gallstone removal there, it was clear Cara was a regular. It was also clear that her work was valued. That she was valued.

An hour later, the kids were redistributed to their parents or doctors, and Cara and Shane were on their way. A sneaking suspicion played in his mind that no one in her family knew about this side of the many-faceted Cara.

"You're a very surprising woman, Mrs. Doyle."

Her face bloomed and brightened, and then he became aware of the unsettling fact it wasn't blooming or brightening for him. A tall, dark, and, probably by some objective standard, handsome doctor stopped and flashed more teeth than strictly necessary at Cara.

"*Hola, mi cariña*. You look great," Dr. Hot Stuff said. He kissed her cheek with lips that lingered a touch too long. With a superhuman effort, Shane managed to suppress a growl that he was a million percent certain would have come out sounding like "Mine."

"Hi, Darian," she said. "Thanks for the heads-up about the board position."

"Well, you're a shoe-in after all your work around here.

It just needs Madame Napier's approval." He expanded his gaze to Shane and thrust out his hand. "Darian Fuentes, a friend of Cara's."

Shane stiffened his spine, though it hurt like hell, and grasped the outstretched hand, though that hurt like a motherfucker. "Shane Doyle, Cara's husband."

Cara gasped. Man, he was in trouble. It was worth it to see the bafflement on the good doctor's face.

Dr. Hot Stuff's hand went limp. "Congratulations, Cara. I had no idea."

Shane released the hand. Victory was his. "It was a whirlwind romance. Swept her off her feet." He patted his bum shoulder. "Still recovering, in fact. She's very physical."

He didn't need to turn his head—probably would have hurt anyway—to know that he wasn't just in garden variety trouble. More like shit creek approaching, paddle in smithereens.

The guy took his leave and Shane stepped into the open elevator, his shoulder radiating pain throughout his arm and back. Worth every second. When his eyes touched Cara's, she just sighed like he was an overgrown child to be indulged and tolerated with the rest of the kids in her care.

"Don't worry, LT, that ugly, nasty doctor won't bother you again," Shane said.

She gifted him an eye roll, and it felt like she'd fashioned it just for him. Yeah, he was a goner.

* * *

They stood beneath the concave underbelly of the Bean and looked up, searching out their reflections.

"There we are," Shane said with the enthusiasm of new-found discovery. He pointed off in another direction with his good arm. "And there."

How did they make it so smooth? Cara wondered. Inspired by liquid mercury, the Cloud Gate sculpture in Millennium Park, affectionately known by Chicago's denizens as the Bean, was a miracle of engineering. A seamless, elliptical wonder that reflected and distorted the city's skyline. Underneath, the surface of the Bean's navel showed a multiplicity of views like a fun-house mirror.

Shane was supposed to be resting up. Cara was supposed to be wrestling with the wedding seating plan that would need UN observers to keep the peace. In the elevator at the children's hospital, Shane had asked her what tourist trap she had yet to visit and she had countered with "all of them." It was her right as a Chicagoan. She didn't have to do the sights.

"Good thing you're wearing that red top so we can spot ourselves," Shane said.

The milling crowds under the Bean made it difficult to distinguish one spectator from another in the smaller versions of themselves, but her cherry-red blouse popped out like "Where's Cara?" From a distance, they looked insignificant and fragile. Close up, the visions were contorted—bendy Cara, curvy Cara, skinny Cara, blobby Cara. It wasn't real but it still unnerved her.

"In this dimension of warped space, the solid is transformed into the fluid, so deconstructing empirical space and calling to mind the manifold possibilities of abstract space," she said in her best schoolmarm.

Shane looked at her, surprised. "Oh, yeah?"

"That's what it says on the Internet." She held up her phone.

"Sounded pretty sexy."

"It did?"

"Yeah, all those big words. I'm imagining you giving a lecture in your tight skirt and brainy-girl glasses—"

"I don't wear glasses."

He touched his fingers to her lips. "Shush, don't ruin it. There's a pointer involved and then you pull your hair out of your bun when you get to an exciting part."

The temptation to suck his fingers into her mouth almost engulfed her. Luckily, he removed them before things got X-rated. Mouth dry and finger-free, she glanced down at her screen. "When I describe the omphalos?"

He moved in closer. Close enough to slide his unslinged arm around her but he still held off. Tease. "The phallus?"

"No, the omphalos. It's Greek for 'navel.' That's what they call what we're looking at." She gestured up. "The navel."

"You look really cute today," he said, his gaze smoking over her.

"Thanks," she whispered, unreasonably pleased that he called her cute instead of hot or sexy. There was a tenderness about it that turned her insides to liquid.

"Do you mind if I…" He did that a lot—asked "Do you mind if I…" and then went ahead and did whatever the hell he wanted. Gentleman in charge. He reached around and pulled her hair out of its knot. His fingers brushed against the nape of her neck as he teased her hair out. "I like your hair loose."

Her heart skittered like a flat stone across the lake. "Oh, okay." As if she had a choice in the matter.

Still watching her with that smoldering gaze, he shoved her hair tie into his pocket.

"Did you just steal my scrunchie?"

"Just to put under my pillow. It's not creepy or anything."

He coasted his knuckles up and down her arm, an electric lick of fire, before finally settling in a hover near her hand. He was waiting for her to make the next move. She placed her hand in his and squeezed. Immediately, he returned the pressure, a sublime jolt that traveled up and out to every pulse point of her body.

"Your family doesn't know about your volunteer work, do they?"

Oh. She had not been expecting that. The vibe had gone from sexy to serious in an unrecognizable instant. Caught off balance, she said the first thing that came into her head. "They wouldn't understand. They'd think I was just trying to make up for my sins."

A long beat passed before he spoke. "That's a very harsh word, Cara." His gaze was filled with compassion and she had to look away, though she still held on to his hand. "Is this because you weren't around when your mum was ill?"

The noise of children, pushing and laughing and playing, sent a wave of sadness breaking over her. She usually felt this rawness for a few hours after her visits with the kids at the hospital, or the Frequent Fliers as they were known. Under the Bean, one little boy, no more than five years old, pulled his older sister's hair. So heartbreakingly sweet.

"They caught the cancer fairly early but my mother still had to go through surgery and chemo and radiation therapy. Looking at her was like seeing myself when I was at my worst. Bones poking through skin, the dark circles under her eyes. I knew she had no choice and it shamed me because *I* had a choice. For years, I chose to do that to my body. To treat it like a science experiment because I thought it would make me more loveable."

She swiped at the tears but they were already falling too fast. "I bailed when I was needed and let Lili do all the work. I was always too busy with the TV show I was producing, with the important, glamorous life I was faking. It was the most selfish thing I've ever done."

He released her hand to capture her now unstoppable tears with his thumb. Warmth and comfort pulsed through her at his touch. "You had to take care of yourself, Cara. Make yourself better. No one would fault you for that."

Ah, but she could. Every. Single. Day. "I should have been here," she choked out around a sob.

"And now you are here, doing an amazing job with Lili and Jack's wedding." How sharp of him to realize one prong of her atonement was Lili's big day. Her husband was quite the smarty-pants.

His thumb brushed over her lips. "Managing the little things helps you take care of the big things—is that how it works?"

She nodded. "Something like that, but I feel like I'm hardly coping or managing at all. Every day—" *Is a struggle,* she wanted to say. If it wasn't, she could take this feeling she had whenever she was with Shane and thread it through her life.

He made a sound of disbelief. "You think you're not coping? Cara DeLuca, you are *so* kicking butt. It's like you're tailor-made to recover from an eating disorder."

Her shocked laugh loosened something in her chest. What an odd thing to say. "How'd you make that out?"

"Ah, sure, don't I have a theory?"

She inched closer, craving his heat and strength. Craving him more than her next breath. "Okay, tell me this theory of yours."

"Well, whoever's up there watching us down here, whatever higher power you believe in, he—"

"Or she." Surely a female deity was involved in Shane's creation.

He nodded wisely. "Or *she* assigns problems for reasons. So you got this perfectionist gene but you also got this inner strength, this ability to overcome anything with sheer Cara cojones."

"Cara cojones?"

"Yeah, or *coglioni* in Italian." He smiled. "I'm multilingual. So, because you have these special Cara balls, you're in the perfect position to kick the arse of any problem that comes along. You've already made anorexia your bitch. That's not to say it's easy, because it isn't, but you've done this amazing job so far. And it means you will continue to do an amazing job. You're Cara DeLuca. You can do anything."

He sounded like the fortune cookie message of every body image and self-help book she'd ever read, and still her parched brain soaked up his hokey platitudes like an arid swatch of desert. Cara DeLuca might not be able to do anything, but Cara DeLuca Doyle definitely could.

"So the control-freak-perfectionist gene that contributed to my anorexia is also why I'm able to recover from it so spectacularly?"

"Don't mess with the theory, Cara. What's important to remember is that now you've come out the other side you don't have to keep up that tough-girl façade any longer. Pretending to be something you're not is an awful lot of work."

She heard his weariness, and when she looked into his deep, chocolatey eyes, the sadness in them tore through her. *I'm the master of secrets,* he had told her once. Perhaps one day, he would peel back that armor of charm and let her in.

"Cara, you don't have to wolf down my pastries or throw your clothes on the bedroom floor. You just have to be yourself. I know you're not ready to do that with the rest of them, but there's no need to pretend with me."

Her heart exploded on the spot and repaired itself in the same burning instant. How did he do that? How did he see right into her? While strolling down Sunset Strip with her hand wrapped in Shane's safe grip, she had felt solid, and not like she could be blown away by a gust of Nevada wind. Now with Shane's words, she realized that maybe she wasn't so crazy to want good things.

The thickness in her throat prevented any response, but neither did he seem to expect it. In returning their attention to the Bean, her hand found his again. Fun-house Cara didn't look so strange after all.

CHAPTER 15

A little twist," Cara said, bending once more to her task.

"'S fine," Lili said. "It's been fine for the last thirty minutes."

Shane shot a glance at Jack, whose only contribution for the last half hour had been a knowing eyebrow hitch at regular intervals. *DeLuca women.*

Though they had moved into Sarriette's dining room, it was almost as warm as the kitchen, which meant the chocolate icing would start sweating any moment. If they didn't get the shot soon, he'd have to start over. Lili got back behind the complicated-looking camera set on an eye-level tripod, and clicked several times.

Shane's Bella Donna chocolate ganache cake was now part of the gallery of photos that would adorn the pages of Jack and Tony's cookbook. He had never felt prouder.

It was the perfect end to a perfect day spent cooking and laughing with Jack, the DeLuca girls, and the crew at Sarriette. With his arm stuck in a sling, Shane was useless in the kitchen, so he spent his time dispensing orders to Jack and Mona, and enjoying every second of it. He even got to choose the music! The rest of the crew had gotten an unreasonable kick out of it as well; per Derry, Jack was now "Shane's bitch." Jack had grumbled but he didn't disagree.

Shane owed it all to Cara. At first, he was worried about her talking him up to Jack but he comforted himself with the knowledge that all Jack's offers came Shane's way because he had earned it. He was talented and he deserved his place in Jack's kitchen.

"Despite the fact you've done nothing but piss me off all day," Lili said to Cara while she packed up her camera equipment, "I'm still prepared to let you buy me an expensive adult beverage tonight."

"No can do," Cara said far too quickly. "I've got something else on." She made a point to look anywhere but at Shane. *Real subtle, LT.*

Lili certainly didn't have a problem with looking at Shane. "How about you, Irish? Will you be around to keep me company while my man earns the big bucks?" She raised an eyebrow in challenge. "I know you can't work with your gimpy arm. Probably not much you can do."

"You'd be surprised what I *can* do, gimpy arm and all, but alas, I'm busy tonight."

"Hmm." She gave him the DeLuca stare down but didn't press.

While Lili placed a lens in a soft case, Cara caught his eye with a smile that might have flattened a lesser man. True, he was busy tonight, and true, the reason for his busyness was spelled C-A-R-A, but neither hanky nor panky were part of the equation. Since that day in Millennium Park, they had been hanging out and watching movies with the cat curled up between them playing chaperone. He was teaching her to cook and once the film's closing credits rolled, she was headed to her apartment and he was headed to a cold shower. By the time he'd toweled off, the hum of the vacuum two walls over was just winding down. He was clean, her apartment was clean, everyone was a winner. He would have liked to remind her there were plenty of things they could do that wouldn't hurt his shoulder—Cara on her knees came to mind—but the anticipation was so damn sweet.

He also had another reason for holding back on reinstituting the good times. Gnawing guilt. As the physical pain in his shoulder lifted, the weight of his lie filled the void. But the only way out was forward. Keep up the pretense. He was a ninja at it, and sure, wasn't what he had now almost as real? A job he liked, friends who liked him, a woman who wasn't easy but then he had never done easy.

Shane wasn't given to flights of fancy nor was he prone to let his imagination get a jump on his common sense, but he'd felt a change in his relationship with Jack. It was subtle—an opinion sought here, a shared anecdote there. All the ordinary hallmarks of workplace camaraderie, but it coursed through Shane's veins like jet fuel. Jack actually liked him. Shane shouldn't have been surprised; he was very likeable. And being liked by your boss—your friend—was a helluva lot better than being hated by your brother.

What would be gained by telling the truth but a place outside the glass, looking in? He hadn't liked it out there. This way, he had one foot in the door and he could feel the warmth of the hearth on his face. Giving it up to return to the chilled shadows was not an option.

Jack and Cara had moved off to the bar with "The Binder" and curiously, Lili didn't make a move toward them. Shane approached her with two forks. Sighing, she took one from him and dug into the subject of her latest photographic masterpiece.

The grim set of her mouth brightened as soon as the chocolate morsel made contact with her tongue. He allowed her a moment to savor all that rich, dark goodness.

"You okay?" he asked.

"I am now." Eyes closed, her face teetered on the edge of ecstasy. "Have I told you lately that I love you, Shane?"

"Watch your mouth. You're *el jefe's* lady."

She slid a sidelong glance at Jack and Cara, now in a head huddle at the bar. "And you're a saint."

"How'd you make that out?"

"Your boss is a tyrant and the woman you may or may not be sleeping with is a control freak of the highest order."

He could feel a smile tugging at his lips. Lili was no dummy.

"It takes a certain personality type to handle them. We've got the knack." He scooped up some of the Bella Donna and cleaned his fork with his mouth. "How come you're letting them run roughshod all over you for the wedding?"

That netted him a dark look. "No, I'm not."

"I get the impression you're not into the big do, that you'd rather something more low key but you're doing it to please Jack and Cara."

She rolled her eyes. "Neither Jack nor Cara know how to do low key."

"That's for sure."

They both laughed conspiratorially.

"Seriously, though, if you don't want it to be so crazy, you should speak up."

She sighed. "I want them to be happy. It's one day and it'll make them happy."

"Yeah, but it's your day, too."

She considered this. Lili was like Cara in that respect: she thought awhile before she spoke. "When we were kids, Cara used to make us all enact her big wedding day. She'd wear Mom's dress and round up all the cousins and neighbor kids. She had more husbands than Elizabeth Taylor, scrapbooks filled with magazine photos, tons of ideas for her own future wedding. No one ever said no to her and that was when she was nine."

Shane knew all about how hard it was to say no to Cara. It was why they were in this mess, the mess he was beginning to enjoy more each day instead of less.

"She's always been a romantic, just like Jack." Her lips shaded a smile. "Am I scaring you yet?"

He felt an answering lurch in his chest and he forced humor into his tone.

"God, no. Guys love hearing about wedding-obsessed females." Cara might have been a romantic once, but not anymore. Not for herself. Something had broken inside her.

Lili drew her eyebrows together in a frown. "I'm not sure what changed. Whenever I ask her about dating, she brushes me off. I feel like something bad happened with a guy that's put her off the whole shebang."

Trusting her instincts more was a great start, but until Cara confided in Lili and her family, her healing would be incomplete. Like a bad break where the bones refused to knit together properly, her heart would stay fractured as long as she held on to the soul-crushing secret of her anorexia. And yes, he was fully aware of the irony.

Lili went on. "She's got it into her head that she'll never experience the fairy tale, so if it makes her better, if it makes them both better to have this one day, then who am I to stop them?" She cocked her head. "I guess what I'm saying is that you have your work cut out for you, Shane."

If she's easy, she won't be amazing ... With a woman like Cara, there was some assembly required to make a relationship work, but he had the best hands in the business.

"I've spent close to six weeks in Jack Kilroy's kitchen and survived." He grinned. "Think I'm up for the challenge of Cara."

* * *

Letting herself in quietly, Cara stole across the hardwood floor and then stopped short at an achingly familiar sound. Not quite muffled by the pitter-patter of his shower, Shane was happily butchering a Carrie Underwood tune.

Shane in the shower. Oh boy.

A scratchy cry snagged her attention and she looked down at its source. The greedy third in their cozy little triumvirate gave her the big green saucer eyes and mewled again. Like all cats, he felt the world owed him a living.

"Hold on, Vegas, I'm going to feed you."

She opened the tin of gourmet cat food—soufflé with wild salmon, garden veggies, and eggs—and emptied it into his bowl. Vegas dived in and left his faux affection for Cara in the dust.

After washing her hands, Cara got busy with her real mission. Ten minutes later, the coffee was burbling, the skillet was hot, and Shane's amazing brioche was soaking up the cinnamon-nutmeg eggy mixture he had introduced her to a few days back.

Since Shane's injury three weeks ago, they had been circling each other like wary lions on the African savannah. He showed her how to cook more than eggs—she had since added rice salad and sautéed eggplant to her repertoire—and she repaid the favor by keeping her hands to herself. He no longer needed help getting his shirt on or off but they both kept up the pretense. Every time she saw his battered body, she wanted to graze and mold him with her fingertips but something unwritten had occurred between them. She knew if she touched him properly, or improperly, all hell would break loose.

"Hey, neighbor." His graveled rumble sent her good parts into a quiver.

"Hey," she answered, not turning around. Not yet. She wanted to soak up the scent of him first, that clean, male spice that made her world smell and taste a million times better.

He clucked. "Woman, I told you the cat should eat only dry food. You're spoiling him."

"Kitty needs a treat every now and then."

She turned to get hers. As sure as she knew she was crazy as a cat lady, she knew he'd be his shirtless, jeans-wearing, hotter-than-hell self.

Bingo. Sinful as the devil and twice as dangerous. As he approached the business end of the healing process, the patchwork of hurt skinning his taut torso was now a light ochre. The contusion over his brow had deflated, leaving a smudgy bruise in its place. Languidly, he stood in those low-riding battered jeans, accessorized with nothing more than testosterone and a smile.

Yum.

He closed the gap between them and leaned over her with a sniff, his hand lying casually on her hip. *Lower, honey, lower.* She was a little damp from her morning run and heading for wetter climes any minute.

"Ah, *pain perdu*," he murmured. "Smells good."

"French toast, mister. You're in the U S of A now."

He switched to lean against the counter and she got the full Shane experience. The shower-softened hair, the towel tossed casually over one broad shoulder, the mysterious scar trailing down the other. Had a man ever looked this good in the morning?

"Nervous about tonight?" he asked.

She nodded, almost wishing he hadn't mentioned it. After postponing twice, Mason Napier was finally stopping by to eat in Sarriette's kitchen and make her beg for his mother's business.

"I just need it to make something happen," she said quietly. "Getting a shot at this would kick-start the next phase. I know I'd be good at it."

Shane smiled, a little wry, a lot sexy. "The woman who, up until a few weeks ago, only had a recipe for ice cubes to her name? Well, look at her now. She can do anything."

Embarrassed at his praise, she turned back to the slathered brioche slice, now browning up nicely in the pan. Shane was right, though. She had this. She looked around the kitchen. She *so* had this.

"Sit down, Shane. Breakfast's up."

"Love it when you get your 'tude on and make me eat, LT."

With not a small amount of shock, she realized that she loved it, too. Looking after a big, strong man, even though he didn't need it and she had really just inserted herself into his life, felt strangely like what she was meant to do. Holding her breath, she watched him take a bite of the golden bread, now covered with a dollop of crème anglaise and the orange-maple syrup Shane had made yesterday.

"Amazing, Cara. We'll make a cook out of you yet." It was overdone on one side but he hadn't said a word.

She slid in beside him and took a few bites of her own. Part of her recovery involved regular affirmations that eating was morally neutral and that there should be no guilt associated with it. Learning to cook and knowing what went into her meals, whether it was calorie-laden or not was so empowering. If she ate something a little bit wicked, it was her choice. She controlled the fork.

Shane was digging in with gusto and she had to focus on her plate when all she wanted to do was stare at him. The idea that they could just leave things the way they were lapped at her brain like the tide. She hadn't pushed the signing of the annulment papers and it had seemed awkward to bring it up. More awkward than being married but that was neither here nor there. Each day with Shane, each new wave of surf, sucked her in deeper.

She no longer wanted to guard her heart. She wanted to fall.

A comfort level she never thought she would experience with another person had set in during the last few weeks. When he wasn't showing her how to cook, they watched TV and movies, and he told stories about the places he had traveled. France. Morocco. Australia. Exotic and not so exotic locations. But the more he trotted out tales about hostel horrors in Brisbane or bungee jumps off bridges in South Africa, the less she felt she knew him. All his stories were charming yet weightless as if he had a never-ending supply of anecdotes to shield his deeper pain. She knew his father had abused him emotionally, probably physically, and she wanted him to feel as safe talking to her as she did to him.

"I've got something for you," he said around his chewing. He stood, reached behind the ragged sofa, and pulled out...oh my God...a helmet. A shiny, black motorcycle helmet with a pink curlicue design. Her heart thrashed so hard it threatened to leap out of her chest.

He placed it on the table. "Mine's too heavy and you need your own."

In her hands, it felt as light as air, and she wondered

how it could protect her skull. *Your head is precious to me.* She knew Shane wouldn't get her something cheap and that her safety would be his primary concern. Looking up, she found him staring at her with a look of such intensity that it dismantled her brain. The most powerful surge of emotion crashed through her that she couldn't catch her breath.

Heart, meet pike.

"It's fantastic," she said faintly.

Only when his shoulders relaxed did she realize how tense he had been. "This bloke in Tokyo paints them by hand. I didn't want to get something anyone else could have, so I sent him the design and he worked it up. It's personal to you. See?" He pointed at a florid swoop that, on closer inspection, revealed *Cara* in curled lettering. Twisting it, he showed the letters *L* and *T*, almost hidden in the loopy swirls.

Tears threatened and she blinked to force her calm. "It's beautiful, Shane. Thanks so much."

"Lili asked me to lunch again at your parents' this Sunday." He folded his arms across that vista of human scenery she fantasized about twenty-four seven. "What do you think about catching a ride with me?"

Showing up on the back of Shane's Harley wearing a helmet he'd had custom designed for her would definitely set tongues wagging. Cara and a man old enough to be her... younger brother. Two plus two makes two point four children. Was she ready for the DeLuca cannons?

"Someone might think something's going on."

"Someone might think right." He leaned in close, his breath warm and syrup sweet against her cheek. "People already have a good idea. The earth has continued to rotate on its axis and no one has died."

"True," she said noncommittally.

He looked thoughtful. "Lili thinks you had your heart broken and that's why you're so down on relationships."

"You talked about me with Lili?" She didn't like the sound of that at all.

"Just generally," he said. "Wedding stuff, mostly. Maybe you should talk with Lili more."

"We talk all the time."

After a couple of heartbeats, he raised an eyebrow. *You know what I mean.* Another pause, longer this time, weighted the air between them.

He frowned. "I hate to see you lose this opportunity to get closer to your family. Being honest with them about what you've been through would be a good start. Forgiving yourself would be an even better one."

He made it sound so easy, but then that was his gift. Did he think she could snap her fingers and everything would be hunky-dory? It was bad enough she couldn't be around when her family needed her, but the truth would not fly. Vanity and weakness had turned her guilt into a tangible, choking thing. Forgiveness required greater strength than she was capable of.

Rather than answer him outright, she sidled up to her good old pal deflection. "So what would *you* say is going on here?" Okay, more like out of the frying pan.

His smile was knowing. "Well, let's see, shall we? There's nursing and cooking and interminable *Mad Men* marathons." He waved at Vegas, curled up and sated beside his bowl. "There's a cat."

They considered the cat for a few seconds.

"It's not my fault you can't appreciate the fractured gender and social politics of the sixties," she chided. "And I've watched all your Paul Newman films. Quid pro quo."

"Still can't believe you'd never seen *The Sting*," he said as if it were the saddest thing in the world.

There was a pause as they reflected on the momentousness of that.

Standing, she placed her plate in the sink. Her heart made an all-points jump around her chest as she geared up to make her decision. *Here goes nothing.*

"Guess I'll have to get my skirt into straddle mode."

She barely had time to register the scrape of the chair before two beefy forearms curved around her waist and two hot lips lay down tracks on her neck. There was joy in his kiss. She had made him happy. She wanted to spend forever making him happy.

In a few startling seconds, he had hoisted her onto the kitchen counter and settled between her legs.

"Shane, your shoulder—"

His mouth cut off her protest; his tongue jump-started a revolt throughout her body. His obvious arousal indicated he was ready, to hell with his shoulder.

"Cara, my beautiful Cara," he murmured softly against her neck. "You've no idea how hard it's been not to touch you these last weeks."

Tell me about it. "You were injured, Shane," she said firmly. She splayed a palm on his chest and pushed him back a few inches. "The things I have in mind for you require you to be at a hundred percent fitness. You're not the only one with a fantasy list."

Eyes smoky with lust, he cupped her butt and dragged her flush against his hardness. He never dropped his stare, just peeled up her running jacket without bothering with the zip. She raised her arms to help. With the backs of his hands, he rubbed his knuckles across her nipples, still covered by her T-shirt. The friction brought the tight buds to tender points.

She wandered her hands over terrain she had memorized close to a month ago and where she'd been planning return trips in her dreams ever since. Her fingertips rose and fell along ridges and scars. Icy dread scrambled her insides as her brain made the final leap. Those circular contusions the size of pencil erasers... *Were those cigarette burns?*

Oh, Shane.

The press of tears burned her throat. "What happened here, honey?"

She wanted to pretend the nanosecond of stiffness she felt under her touch was in her imagination. It would be so easy to pass over it and reap her reward, but too often, she had let his charm buy his way out of serious conversations about his past. Shane had an awful lot of long-healed scars, his father was a mean old drunk, and doctors were not his favorite people. Didn't take a rocket scientist.

"Just a fight when I was a kid." His lips returned to their hot interrogation of the sensitive spot below her ear.

"What kind of fight?"

"The kind that leaves scars." More shivery kissing ensued.

Leave it. Don't push. "Did it have something to do with your father?"

Body in a clench, he left off his sweet assault. Agitation rolled off him in waves.

She held his face in both hands. "Shane, you can talk to me."

"There's nothing to talk about." His tight, fierce stance told a different story. "Not all Irishmen are tragic, melancholy figures despite what you may have read in the literature."

He smiled at his joke, but she recognized it for a fake. It was the same smile he used at Gina's wedding when Jack asked him to make his wedding cake. The same one he had plastered on when they visited the kids on the cancer floor. A smile of distance.

Evidently, that comfort level she felt with him was a mirage. Being there for people was more Lili's forte; Cara wasn't the kind of woman whom people trusted. Feeling foolish for having tried, she pushed back and off the counter. She put her energy into stacking dirty plates.

"Ah, LT, don't say you're disappointed that my childhood wasn't as dreadful as you hoped?" He stilled her arm. "I ran away to the circus and ended up on the wrong end of a lion tamer's whip. How's that?"

Wasn't it enough that he had shunned her attempts at emotional intimacy, did he have to mock her as well? God, the man had some nerve telling her to open up to Lili and her family. There was something incredibly disingenuous about a guy who chose to shroud himself in mystery giving advice on the spiritual benefits of honesty.

"Forget it, Shane."

"Cara." He took a noisy breath, filled with condescension. "It's not relevant to us."

"How can you say that? You have this font of stories yet there's always that part of you hidden from me." She knew those scars came with a less-than-charming tale that not even a raconteur like Shane could spin. "I've told you all there is, Shane. This soul-baring business works both ways."

He let go a breath that ruffled the damp strands curtaining his left eye. "What happened before we met doesn't matter. It's history. I refuse to let the past dictate my future."

Such a strong, yet meaningless, statement. How many times had Cara spouted off something similarly trite to motivate her forward, to shake off the shackles of her insecurities? She put the dishes in the sink, their petulant clink suiting her mood to a T.

He filled her silence. "All that matters is that from the minute I saw you, I've wanted nothing more than to worship your body and make you mine. We're good together. Forget about how we got here and let's just enjoy the destination." His voice was rich and soft to match the melted chocolate-drop swirls of his eyes. His warm, male scent made her dizzy with want but she refused to let him divert her like some easily distracted magpie.

"Do you think I'm too much of a princess to handle your problems?"

The muscles in his jaw bunched. "I think you're reading too much into stuff I told you about a man I don't particularly care for."

She touched his arm, trying to transfer an ease she didn't feel into a body that didn't want it. "Shane, I'm here for you—"

"Cara, just bloody leave it." The change was sudden, shocking. His eyes became flat discs of rage and his words whipped across her like a lake wind in February.

She'd fallen for a man who was stronger than anyone she knew. He was the rock she could lean on, the sponge that absorbed all her crazy and squeezed it out of existence. There was no denying that she had more baggage than the cargo hold of a 747 and now she was taking ownership. She was ready to let someone else climb aboard, but he didn't have enough faith in her to share his own heavy burden.

It took her a moment to realize the chill she felt was his body's removal from her personal space, a tacit invitation to take her leave. He wouldn't even look at her.

We're good together. Every step away from him slashed those words to pieces. She left as quietly as she came. Worse, he made no effort to stop her.

CHAPTER 16

For years, Shane had been the man with the plan: perfect his craft and become an incredible pastry chef, all with the aim of putting distance between himself and the father he hated. He had ignored the badgering voice in his head telling him that he didn't have to do it on his own, that he should seek out his brother and claim the connection between them. Women hadn't figured much. Keeping it casual worked for him. People inevitably let you down.

Then he met Cara.

Seeing her cooking at his stove in those sexy sweats of hers had grabbed him by the throat. When she turned, his whole future flashed before his eyes like something out of the bloody *Waltons*. Gorgeous kids with Cara's smile and blue eyes, big noisy dinners with his brother and his family, a life he had been pretending he didn't want because even thinking about the possibilities of failure made him want to shrivel up.

He loved her, plain and simple. It might have started

when he offered a beautiful woman his seat and then spent the night prying a reluctant laugh out of her, but today it had ended with his ludicrous evasion. Here he was urging her to be honest and he couldn't even confess to the most important fact about his origins. Her finely tuned defense mechanisms sensed all that was wrong with him. How messed up he was inside, how his smiles papered over his lies.

Can't charm your way out of this one, boyo.

She wanted to know who he was and where he came from. Who his people were and how he became the man he was. They were reasonable requests, but Shane had no doubt what would happen if he opened up about his father.

He wouldn't be able to stop. It would all come out in a vomiting stream of pain—the "accidents," the put-downs, the fucking unfairness of it all, ending with, *By the way, you know Jack Kilroy? Bloke's my brother.* Get your popcorn popping for the fiery train wreck that ensued. Confessing his sins might scrub some of the scabbed-over blackness from his heart, but it wouldn't get him Cara.

He took a long look in the restroom mirror at Sarriette and tried to see the resemblance to John Sullivan. It was slight, but it was there around the eyes. He definitely looked more like his mother, which was why his father had despised him. Shane was just a reminder of a drunken rut behind a pub in a one-horse coastal town. The bastard never let him forget it, either.

"Hey, boss," Mona said when he'd made it back into the kitchen. "We need a lemon tart and two pot de crèmes for the chef's table."

The chef's table. Unable to resist the siren call, Shane looked over to the recently installed four top in the corner of Sarriette's kitchen. The space was too small for it but he could understand the appeal. The intimacy, the heat, the bustle—there was something very heady about the whole experience. Napier had brought a couple of loud, braying suits who were already three sheets to the wind by the time they swaggered in a couple of hours late. They'd left their manners at the last bar, too, their boisterous hooting sucking all the energy out of the kitchen.

Cara sat with them, practically painted into a plunging, backless emerald dress with shimmery threads that winked beneath the kitchen lights. Under any other circumstances he would be enjoying the hell out of her in that dress but he was too pissed off. Napier's posse were enjoying it, though, judging by how they ogled and panted like wolves in heat. Refusing to meet Shane's gaze all evening, she played her hostess role to the hilt with simpering smiles and that tinkling laugh.

"Boss?" Mona urged. "You okay?"

Shane turned back to his second and absorbed the concern on her face. All throughout service, he'd been snapping at her about every tiny thing, from her supposed inattention to the icing details to the misshapen bread rolls she had whipped up earlier that afternoon. One of them had looked like a dick, for Pete's sake. He didn't really need to be here tonight—contrary to his nitpicking, Mona was turning out to be a great addition to the kitchen—but he'd told Cara he'd have her back while she worked her magic on Napier. That was before he'd run into the proverbial buzzsaw back at Chez DeLuca-Doyle.

Another raft of booming laughs echoed from the chef's table, now ill-harmonized with Cara's musical giggle. Sure, she was working the client but did she have to enjoy it so much?

His personal space diminished to nothing and he turned to find Jack at his shoulder.

"I think maybe you came back to work too soon," he said, his eyes full of challenge. "You're liable to overdo it."

"I feel fine," Shane spat back. He rolled his shoulder for good measure and relished the ache. Better to focus on that than what was happening twenty feet to his left.

More grating laughter drew his attention and his next glance over made him madder than hell. One of Napier's crew had placed a grubby mitt on Cara's silky forearm. Shane jerked forward, only to have Jack place a firm hand on his bad shoulder. Pain shot through him. Jack saw it but he didn't care.

"She can take care of herself," he said evenly.

Jack's crystal ball powers were on the money tonight. Cara deftly removed the guy's hand without missing a beat of the spiel she was delivering to Napier.

"You and I need to talk after service." Jack headed back to the pass to expedite the outgoing dishes.

Shane fought for dominion over his emotions. If he didn't look at that guy pawing over Cara, then it couldn't hurt him, but what you don't know is just as bad. Wasn't he living proof of that? He'd come to Chicago because what he didn't know about Jack had threatened to destroy him. Look where knowledge had got him.

Twisting back to the pastry station, he found Mona with the desserts plated, ready to put them up on the galley for service.

"I'll take those." He picked them up and headed to the chef's table. The laughter continued as he set the desserts down, the group clearly used to ignoring the help. Looking up, Cara held his gaze, then blinked him out of her mind.

"Ah, dessert. Best part of the meal," Napier said, switching on a man-to-man smile. "How's the shoulder, Doyle?"

"On the mend," Shane gritted out.

"I know what the best part of the meal is," Napier's lecher pal said. His bloodshot, wooly gaze slid across Cara's chest and made her jump. No, that wasn't right. It was the meaty palm sliding up her thigh that sent her five inches into the air like a scalded cat.

A well of anger bubbled in Shane's chest but before he had a chance to act on it, Cara took a hold of the loser's offending hand and occupied it with a dessertspoon.

"You're going to love this pot de crème, Michael," she said with a Cara-bright smile. "Sarriette's pâtissier is a genius."

Over the spoon, the sloshed sot squinted at Cara, seeking inspiration for his next move. As the woman had a consistent track record of inspiring drunken men to crazy acts, Shane was unsurprised when the moron dropped the silverware and took a face-plant in her lovely cleavage. Neither was Shane surprised when he took it upon himself to wrench Cara out of her seat and punch the guy in his slack mouth.

Cara grabbed at his arm—his bad one, of course. "Shane, I had it under control!"

Michael, or whatever the hell his name was, rubbed his mouth and tried to sit up straight. Shane lunged and the guy raised his hands up in frightened surrender. "Hey, man, I'm sorry."

Shame sat leaden in his gut. What was wrong with him? Behind him, the only sounds were a stovetop sizzle and judgmental silence. His gaze scanned the scene before him—smug disapproval on Napier's face, fear in the muddied eyes of the guy Shane had just struck, annoyance in the set of Cara's mouth.

You're no different than him. A brute bully, all twisted up inside.

Words of regret hovered on his lips, but a rough pluck on

his collar rammed his apology back down his throat. Within seconds, Shane was hurled through the door of Jack's office, his collar still attached to a strong hand with a few locks of hair thrown in. Shaking him off, Shane turned to face the boss.

"Get your hands—"

"Shut the fuck up," Jack said before turning and storming out.

Shane rubbed the nape of his neck and took a few more deep breaths but he couldn't seem to fill his lungs. He'd just assaulted a customer and Jack was going to sack him. In that moment, Shane realized he didn't care one iota.

Less than three minutes later, the door opened and he braced himself for a fight. Jack walked in, followed by Cara, Napier, and...that was it. Cara's ice-blue eyes snapped to his, then returned to Napier.

Shane felt his hackles rising. "Where's your handsy pal?"

Napier smoothed hair that didn't need smoothing. "Popped him in a cab. Mick could never hold his liquor. Almost as bad as you Irish boys." His chuckle sounded gold-plated.

"We Irish boys don't like it when women are disrespected."

Cara shook her head and looked to the ceiling, clearly unappreciative of Shane's "hands off our women" comment.

"Mason, we can't apologize enough about what happened. If Michael needs anything, please let me know." If Michael needs anything? Like free rein over the glorious, golden skin of Shane's woman, perhaps? Her voice was smooth and soft, and every word shredded Shane's nerves. "I hope this little blip hasn't put you off considering Sarriette for future events."

"I'm sure I can persuade Mick not to press charges but

I think, at this point, you should be more worried about the negative publicity. If it was to get out that one of your staff is in the habit of losing it at the drop of a hat..." He trailed off suggestively.

"I'll quit if it makes you feel better," Shane said.

"No, you won't," Jack shot back without missing a beat. "We're happy to host the dinner and cover all the costs." He offered his hand, clearly in a hurry to put the whole sorry mess behind him.

"That's very generous of you," Mason said, his mouth twisting up in a half sneer, half smile, like he couldn't make the full sneer-to-smile conversion. Their new client held on to Jack's hand like a limpet. "But I'll need something else."

Jack looked at his captured hand in distaste, and withdrew it with a jerk.

"I'm getting married in November and I want you to design a menu," Mason said, ignoring Jack's animosity.

"Congratulations," Cara said with false brightness. "I don't remember seeing the announcement."

"It's going to be low key. Just four hundred guests."

Shane repressed an eye roll. Another bloody wedding. Is that all anyone thought about? A lengthy pause followed as Jack and Mason sized each other up.

"I don't do weddings," Jack said. "I get a lot of requests, but this place and my family take up all my time."

"I thought you might say that," Napier said with a smirk. "Several people told me it couldn't be done, but when Cara came to me with her bid for the Pink Hearts dinner, I figured you might have changed your mind. My fiancée sent me out with clear instructions to get your cooperation. Women, right?" He gave an almost embarrassed shrug as if the whole thing was terribly out of his control. His gaze flicked from

Jack to Shane, and back again. "I think you could break your rule this one time, don't you?"

This one was a slippery little bastard all right. Jack looked like he wanted to break more than his rule, though judging by his current mood he would be perfectly happy with either Shane or Napier on the other end of his fist.

"I'm sure we can work something out," Jack finally managed. Shane could tell every single word killed him.

Hands were shaken, good-byes exchanged. Shane held back, not wishing to be any part of Napier's bargain, especially as it was down to him Jack had been put in an untenable position.

"Look after that shoulder, Doyle," Napier said as he walked out with Cara, who still refused to look Shane's way. "And your temper."

Left with Jack, Shane jumped into his defense. "That lout touched Cara."

Jack glowered. "And I was about to step in and take care of it."

Shane suspected his face had frozen in astonishment. "When was this magical intervention going to happen? Were you planning to wait until he had two inches of dick out? Four? Maybe a testicle sighting? That *your* kitchen in there and you let a customer paw all over one of your employees. Great job, fearless leader. What happened to the guy who punched how many paparazzi when they got up in his sister's face? Who went ape-shit on the whole Internet for insulting Lili?"

Jack had the decency to look uncomfortable. "I usually draw the line at thumping a guy in my own restaurant. Christ, I told you to stay away from her."

Shane forced his fists to play ball and folded them under his arms. "I'm getting sick and tired of you telling me how to conduct my personal life. I'll see whoever the hell I want, and if you don't like it, you can go screw yourself."

Jack visibly started. "Oh, that's how you want to play it? You know, I don't get what your game is at all, Doyle. Help me understand why an award-winning pastry chef would give up a job with Anton Baillard? Why, if you're so desperate to work here, you already have your next gig lined up?"

He paced to the desk and back. "I called Baillard this afternoon and you know what he told me? He begged you to stay at Maison Rouge, offered you twice as much as you'd be earning here. Why would you give that up for lower pay and a smaller kitchen? It's not as if I know anything about pastry."

"You know enough," Shane said, as if that was the most important fact in Jack's speech. Talk about burying the lede.

Jack scowled. "I didn't even want to hire you, but Laurent said you kept needling him about transferring here."

Shane's heart plummeted to his gut. Had he heard that right? Jack hadn't wanted him to work here? His follow-up question was interrupted by Cara's return.

"I had no idea he was going to pull that stunt," Cara said to Jack.

"Who? Napier or your thick-as-a-plank boyfriend?"

"He's not my boyfriend."

His heart bled into his chest. Jack didn't want him to work at Sarriette, and now Cara had pretty much denied their connection. Could he blame her after everything that had gone down between them today? There was no place for him here, no space at the table. A curtain of frost had descended over the glass.

"Do you think we're in the clear?" Cara was saying to Jack, all while doing a bang-up job of ignoring Shane. "He could sue us, destroy the entire business."

Jack stopped pacing and gave a dismissive wave. "Napier will keep his word. No one's getting sued, though the possibility of punitive action is still very real." He glared at Shane.

Shane had had it up to his neck. It was bad enough he had wormed his way into Jack's kitchen when he wasn't even wanted, but to be dismissed by Cara was doing his head in. He wasn't Jack's brother. He wasn't Cara's *anything*. He was nothing.

"If you're going to fire me," he said to Jack, "just get it over with instead of holding it over my head like the Almighty. That God complex you've got going on is really starting to piss me off."

"Shane," Cara began in that coaxing tone she used on Napier, though she iced it with condescension. "Jack's not going to fire you."

Jack held up his hand. "Not so fast, Cara."

Screw this. "You know what? I'll save you the trouble of having to think up any imaginative punishments. You can stuff your job."

Shane crashed out into the hallway. He knew he'd messed up, but damn if he was going to kowtow at the great Jack Kilroy's feet. He would rather suck out the grease traps with his mouth than apologize to that shithead.

* * *

"Shane!" Cara watched him pound out toward the front of the house, only to narrowly miss one of the harried servers.

"Leave him," Jack said. "He just needs to cool down."

Well, that was a given. Just when she thought she had a handle on what she was dealing with, he blindsided her all over again. What had he been thinking back at the chef's table?

"You're not going to accept his resignation, are you?"

Jack gusted a long sigh. "No, I'll talk to him tomorrow and sort it out."

Stepping back inside the office, Cara felt the tightness in her chest receding. What a catastrophe. It was bad enough she had to shine up her silver tongue for Mason when her heart was in shreds after her fight with Shane. Then, having to put up with that drooling idiot and his wandering digits was a nightmare, especially when all she could feel was Shane's impression of a snarling junkyard dog just a few feet away.

As for closing the deal, she should have known it had been far too easy. Mason was no more interested in his mother's charity dinner than Cara was in the outcome of the World Series. He had used her desperation to bag Penny Napier to get the true prize: former celebrity chef Jack Kilroy to preside over the food at his nuptials. While there was no way he could have planned tonight's events, it had certainly worked out to his liking. He might have inherited most of his gleaming wealth but the man was clearly a shrewd businessman who knew how to make a deal. Or craft one out of nothing.

"Jack, I'm sorry about what happened with Mason."

"Yeah, so am I. I should have stepped in sooner and put a stop to it. Shane was right."

She had meant Mason's methods, but to say she didn't feel a little thrill at Shane's defense would be a lie. For now, she needed to refocus on things not Shane. Mason's ambush wasn't the ideal way to win hearts and minds, but she was going to run with it all the way to the goal line.

"Now we have the Napier business, we can make a proper plan."

Jack scrubbed a hand across his mouth and looked at her

squarely. "This charity dinner isn't going to kill me. His wedding, on the other hand...I'll do it to get us out of this jam but it'll be the only one."

Her heart stuttered. "Jack, this is the perfect opportunity to launch us properly into bigger events. It'll bring in a ton of business."

He met her plea with a sigh. "Cara, you know I've been resisting. Well, it's just I wasn't completely honest about why I don't want to take on the burden of an extra business."

No, no, don't say it. It might be a burden to him but it was everything to her. She needed this to start something, but she could feel it slipping away with the blood draining to her toes.

"Once Lili and I are married, we want to start a family."

She could have sworn the room tilted. "Oh, I see."

"I don't want to be one of those parents who's never around. I can't leave Lili a single mother while I'm out making more money than necessary. Kids need both parents and setting up another business or expanding this one is not part of the plan."

So Jack had been bitten by the domesticity bug, and Cara couldn't blame him. Who doesn't want to cozy up with loved ones, spend quality time with the kids? Jack had grown up wild with a single mother, and later a neglectful stepfather, but he loved Lili, Jules, and Evan with a terrifying passion. Family was everything to him. At almost ten years older than Lili, it was understandable he'd want to get cracking on the next generation of genius sooner than later.

"Does Lili know about your plans to knock her up on your honeymoon? Thought she wanted a career," Cara joked, the words hollow and distant. *Her sister would have a baby soon.*

"She does know and she'll still have the chance to do anything she wants career-wise because I'll be around to share the parenting. I'm not farming my kids off to strangers. I don't want to miss a minute of them growing up."

Cara's heart clenched. Her sister was a very lucky girl.

"Why didn't you say something?"

He grimaced and took a moment before he responded. "There are occasions when I feel like we're rubbing your face in our happiness."

Shock sloshed over her. Sometimes she forgot how well Jack knew her. Sometimes, she felt like he was the only one who did until Shane.

"I'm fine. I'm—I'm in a better place than I have been for a while."

Instead of looking mollified, his expression hardened. "That wouldn't have anything to do with a certain hot-headed pastry chef, would it?"

She fixed him with a stare and lined up her excuses. *It's casual. A one-off. I don't need a man to make me happy.* The words clotted like heavy custard in her throat.

"That bad, huh?" Jack asked.

Legs shaking, she sank into the leather sofa. "I thought I could control it. There are a million reasons why it can't work and every one of them is a doozy. But when I'm with him, all the reasons fade away."

"Ever think that maybe you're just falling for that stupid accent of his?"

"It has occurred to me." She tried to smile, but her mouth got stuck.

Jack sat beside her, those stark green eyes intent. "He seemed out of sorts tonight. Yes, he had provocation, but that didn't seem like the Shane I know."

"We had a fight earlier. He doesn't say much about himself and I was trying to learn more about him." And instead of talking to her, he chose to exorcise his demons with the easiest target—a slobbery, grab-ass drunk. "I'm just not sure where he stands."

Concern drew Jack's lips into a tight seal. She had never been sure when he figured out her food issues or even how much he knew, but he knew enough. Every day, he made her plain old chicken dinner with care and precision (15 spinach leaves, no more, no less!) and now, as she held his gaze, not of pity but of support, she counted herself blessed that he was an arrogant ass to boot or she would have fallen in love with him years ago.

"I think after tonight it's clear where he stands," he said. "Guy's crazy about you."

And she was crazy about him, not just crazy, but hopelessly in love. She loved him because he didn't balk at her weirdness. She loved him because he brought life-affirming color to her world. Shane saw that her sum was far greater than her parts. He saw *her*.

She had been trying to keep her life ordered and neat so she wouldn't drown, or worse, drown in someone else. Since that night in Vegas, she had viewed Shane as a millstone around her neck when really he had been a life preserver, keeping her head above water. But now he needed her. He needed to see that she had strength and buoyancy enough for both of them.

"You like Shane, don't you?" she asked, suddenly defensive of her man.

"He's a great chef, fits my team like a glove, reminds me a little of myself at his age. Especially the flying off the handle part."

She made a scoffing noise. "When you were his age? You were still going nuts on people last year, Jack. How about an answer that's not all about you?"

He slipped a loose strand behind her ear. "Yeah, I like him, but I feel as though there's a lot more to him than meets the eye. Still not sure he deserves you but he would be very lucky to have you, Cara."

He gifted her a smile that reminded her of... How odd she'd never noticed it before, that crooked kink of his mouth just like Shane's. On her husband's face, it skewed softer, less carnal, but it was delightfully bent all the same. Jack's ancestry was Irish so maybe there was something to be said about the green genes. More likely, she just had her husband on the brain.

On the brain and in her heart. The heart that was full, healthy, and ready for the challenge of anything.

Watch out, Shane Doyle, your hot Irish ass is mine.

CHAPTER 17

At 4:10 A.M., Shane pulled up into the alley behind his flat and turned off the engine. Cara's girl car was parked in her spot, and he stared at it awhile, looking for clues. Perhaps it was situated a few more inches than usual to the right, a sign she might have been upset when she came home. Or perhaps, he was seeing things that weren't there. Wouldn't be new.

Eating the miles on his bike as far as Indiana hadn't done much to temper his boiling blood or summon up any more palatable conclusions. Jack's dismissal and Cara's denial of their relationship had eviscerated him. There were no real connections here; he was just a neighbor, an employee. A former employee. Time to move on.

As he ascended the stairs, he did a mental inventory of things to wrap up in Chicago. There wasn't much. Just clean out the fridge, pack his duffel bag, and make sure the cat was sorted. He was going to miss that bloody cat.

A door opened, but not the door he was expecting.

Cara stood in his rugby shirt, framed by the light from his apartment, blonde and fragrant. Something very primal stirred within him. His shirt. His flat. His woman.

"Where have you been?" she demanded, her brow crease even more pronounced. "I've been calling and texting you all night."

"I left my phone at work." He had crashed out of Sarriette, wearing his chef's jacket and trousers. Not caring a whit for the ride that grew colder the farther from Chicago he got, he'd abandoned the jacket at the side of the road. The symbolism wasn't lost on him.

"Sorry I messed up your meeting with Napier."

Her face contorted with exasperation. "Shane, you defended me against that drunken moron. I didn't appreciate it at the time, but I was upset about the prospect of losing Mason's business. I've been worried about you all night."

"You needn't bother."

"I want to bother, Shane. You're worth bothering about."

No, he wasn't. He was unwanted, unneeded, not useful to anyone. *Worthless, good-for-nothing. You're just a mistake.* All the rage he had tried to expel on the road rose to sensitize his skin.

At her step closer, he held a hand up in plea. In desperation.

"Don't, Cara. Because if you do, I won't be responsible. I'll..." He'd what? He would use her body to assuage the dark pulse, to subsume every broken need and desire.

She ignored that and ate the gap between them. Her hand on his chest sparked an electric pulse that rocked him. Anchoring her body with one hand on his hip, she pulled back at the neck of his tee and ran her finger along the silver-white strand on his collar bone. It should have soothed. Instead the phantom memory embedded in the scar tissue burned.

No one knew what it had been like. No one cared to know. It had lived inside him for so long, buried so deep in inky, liquid blackness that there was no way for it to break the surface. He couldn't tell Jo. She wasn't his real aunt and she had six needy kids of her own. He would have ended up in some place for the unwanted, miles away from the warmth of her kitchen. Foster care didn't smell like baking bread or apple-cinnamon coffee cake.

His brother should have been there.

Even now, that crazy thought filtered through, his childish rescue fantasy. Jack hadn't known he existed and Shane hated him for it.

"Shane, all you've ever done is be there for me. Let me do the same for you."

Christ, she had no idea what she was asking, how his greed was so encompassing. How his envy knew no bounds. He shook his head, willing words he had never said aloud to climb his throat. Still, they refused to come.

Her eyes widened, her face stricken by his muteness. She took his silence as an invitation to look at him. To look into him. He didn't care what he was showing her because if he couldn't speak, maybe she could see.

Those soft, wicked hands of hers pulled at the hem of his shirt and pushed it up. Just like that night outside the church, except there was none of the urgency, only care. Her fingertips touched his ugliest memory, the one that mottled the skin on his right side. He had thought feeding his father might sober him up; instead of turning on a deep-fat fryer for chips, he probably should have made a sandwich.

In those stunning blue eyes—Cara blue—he saw how far she had come on her journey. He had no illusions that he'd helped in any way. He only wished he could be as brave. She peeled off his shirt for better access and the elimination of that barrier unlocked his voice.

"He drank a lot and sometimes he lashed out. This one..." He took her hand and placed it over that painful memory engraved into his collar bone. "One day when I was eleven, I was cleaning up and I moved a bottle I thought was empty. It wasn't and he got angry. Pushed me into a glass cabinet. It was an accident, really."

The words stained the air, impossible to scrub clean after all these years, but Shane still refused to condemn him entirely. Without his father, there would be no Jack. Without Jack, he wouldn't have met Cara. He had to believe there was a reason for the pain.

Ignoring the liquid sympathy filling her eyes, he plowed on. *This one, that one.* They all held stories that felt looser with the telling, or more likely, it was the unbridled compassion vibrating off Cara that made the words trip off his tongue so smoothly.

"He didn't recognize me in the end. I visited him a few times, but he thought I was someone else."

"Who?"

Who else? The final twist of the knife was Packy calling out Jack's name. "Someone he had done wrong by years earlier. He wanted his forgiveness."

"Maybe it was his way of asking for yours," she said.

"Maybe." So much hurt in that one word he almost rolled his eyes at the chasm of self-pity he had opened up. He didn't want to think about the tangled reasoning behind a sick old man's final ravings or why in the end, Jack was Packy's abiding memory. He didn't want to think.

Leaning in, she kissed the scar on his collarbone, just a chaste graze of her lips along that symbol of his dark self and his soul cracked open. He gathered her in his arms and kissed her like it was the first and last time. Her fists bunched against his chest before they unfurled and flew to his hair. Her mouth scorched a trail across his and when she opened her lips fully, a throaty moan heralded the thrust of her tongue.

Desperately, he tore off her shirt, *his shirt*, and found her naked underneath, completely open to him. He kneaded and owned that perfect arse, those perfect breasts, because she *was* perfect, even if she didn't think so. His kiss was an apology for the sins she didn't know about, his hands on her hips an appeal for forgiveness.

Her mouth became more ardent, her tongue an insistent engine of torture. She ground her pelvis into his until he folded and roared his need.

Lifting her so she was wrapped around his hips, he set her against the wall, grinding into her until he was mindless with hope and desire. She moved her hand to where their bodies joined and pushed down his pants, releasing him. The new soundtrack was a medley of passion. Sucking, whimpering, moaning. The friction of their bodies, then the slick, liquid sound as his erection slid against her wet, wet heat.

Take her inside. Back up and make love to her in a bed. Anything but this lava-hot body meld in the no-man's land between their homes. It seemed suitable, though, an appropriate place for a relationship that defied labels. Before he could articulate that or make a move one way or the other, she wrapped her small but lethal hand around him.

"Take what you need, Shane. I'm all yours."

That launched him like a missile. He slid into her—no mercy, not gentle, what she wanted and what he needed. Her silken muscles grasped at his erection like her life depended on it. Pleasure coiled in his gut, winding so tight that the thought of release instilled ecstasy and dread. He wanted it.

He feared its end. Closing his eyes, he went with the age-old rhythm, pumping deeper and harder, each smooth motion punctuated with the erotic slap of flesh on flesh.

Any moment now...oh Christ, he held on to the perfect feeling and forced the messy emotion out of his mind. The part of him that wanted to tell her he loved her so much and that he was nothing without her. Her whimpers stretched to moans that stretched to, well, they could only be called screams. Cara was loud, and he loved it.

Lost in the heat of her, the feel of her, he held on tight until she crested to orgasm. Another second and he followed her over in a crash of sensation, fireworks bursting behind his eyelids, their noisy passion a symphony.

Then silence. Blissful, exquisite silence.

The cat purred.

Locked as one, a few moments leached to a couple of minutes. His cock was still hard inside her, powered by emotional versions of little blue pills. The twang in his shoulder said he should lower her to the ground, but leaving her was an impossibility.

"We didn't use a condom," she said.

So, that was it. It had felt good before, but slipping into her unholstered had taken that one over the top.

"Cara, I'm sorry. I just lost it there. I'm clean, baby. I swear."

She kissed his eyelids softly. "It's okay. Me, too. And it's the wrong time of the month for anything to happen."

What if he'd knocked her up and wasn't around to take care of her and their child? With every passing moment, it felt like he was turning into his father. The drunk who used alcohol to excuse his piss poor decision making. The deadbeat who wasn't around to raise either of his sons properly. But he wouldn't be like him. He refused to be like him.

"I don't regret it," she whispered.

"What?" he asked, assuming she meant the mind-blowing unprotected wall sex.

"What happened in Vegas."

Her words reached inside and placed a clamp on his heart. *Yes, baby. Don't stop. Give me this.* He immediately turned rock hard again.

"Something happened between us, Shane. Something is happening between us now."

Hell, yeah, it was. Without realizing it, he had nudged his erection farther inside her inviting sheath. He was in the zone and he wanted to memorize the GPS coordinates so he could get back there. He loved her enough to lie about who he was. Did he love her enough to tell the truth?

"I wouldn't mind if something else happened. If we had a baby." He touched his forehead to hers. "Do you think you'd like to have a baby with me some day?"

A flash of something crossed her face and for a moment, he wondered if he had engineered another stunning miscalculation. But then she smiled at him, one of those heart-fracturing smiles that would have put him in a puddle of longing if he wasn't already in a puddle of lust. Lust mixed with longing, a lethal combination that destroyed him.

"Yes, Shane. I would."

He hadn't dared to hope, and now his heart leaped so high it could clear the Chicago skyline. This was what he wanted. Connection, family, Cara.

"You mean it, Cara?" He pumped her slowly, rhythmically, all while keeping his eyes pinned to hers. Every upstroke was heaven, every downstroke a dream.

"Yes, I mean it," she gasped.

"Don't say it if you don't mean it, gorgeous."

"Damn it, you crazy Irish peat-bog dweller," she said in that bossy tone he loved. "I mean it."

She hadn't said it, but he knew she loved him. Complex, messy, beautiful Cara loved him. Tonight he had spoken aloud words that had never known the air, so these new words of love would wait. At least, until he had done what he needed to do.

In her eyes, he saw everything he felt. Hope burned bright, blazing through his body, immolating the skin of the past. Every thrust, every moan freed his mind from indecision. Maintaining the lie might keep her, but he could no longer live in the half-light. Tonight was perfect, but perfection wasn't enough.

Tomorrow, it might continue or it might end. There was no more middle ground.

CHAPTER 18

Shane wanted Cara more than he had ever wanted anything. More than acknowledgment from Jack. More than a kind word from his father. If he remained silent, he could have her, but the deceit would chip away at him. Chip away at them. Knowing Cara loved him should have felt like a sweet relief, but he couldn't enjoy it until this was done.

Under the warm rays of the early morning June sun, Shane walked the few blocks over to Jack's house. It didn't look so welcoming this time round and Shane felt like more of an interloper than ever. Lili answered, her face brightening on seeing him. Damn. If she was here that meant—

"Shane," she said, warmth shining off her as she pulled him inside.

"I thought you were going for the final dress fittings with Cara."

Shane had already texted Jack to say he was on his way over. Cara was supposed to be out with Lili and an audience was the last thing he needed. From the kitchen, he heard soft murmuring and baby talk. He told himself it was Jules cooing at Evan but his body knew his woman's sweet nothings.

Lili's eyes flashed mischievously. "We were, but we got delayed. I'm so glad you're here."

"Is Jack still pissed off?" he asked, holding back in the hallway, needing to get a heads-up on his brother's frame of mind.

She smiled, but her eyes held trouble. "He doesn't like when people take advantage. Back in his fame days, he went through a lot of that and this Napier guy practically blackmailing him—well, that's got him pretty annoyed." She shook her head, realizing how that might sound. "But it wasn't your fault, Shane. You just got caught up in it."

Just got caught up in it. Cara, Jack, all this love and family he craved like a drug. He strode into the kitchen to find Cara feeding a bottle to Evan. She turned to him, those blue eyes wide with joy. *This.* This was what he wanted and it was time to man up and take it.

"Hey," he said around the rock of emotion in his throat. He kissed her on the forehead because anything more passionate rang inappropriate while she was cradling an infant. Once, he might have been ready to bang her in the grounds of a church but even he had his limits.

"Hi, Shane," he heard Jules behind him. He hadn't even seen her when he came in, so blown away was he by Cara. They had spent the rest of the night exploring and branding each other. That rule she had about not putting in her mouth anything she didn't know the full calorie count for? Broken. Time and time again.

"Jack's just finishing up a conference call with London and New York," Lili said, slicing through his love-lust fog. "In the meantime, we have something to show you."

She gestured to a sheaf of papers on the kitchen island.

As he drew closer, it dawned on him that they were the galleys for the cookbook. His heart rate sped up.

"May I?" he asked, his fingers itching to touch them. To see his recipe in print.

"Of course," Cara said, standing to meet him, her arms now infant-free.

Stifling his tremble, he flipped the pages through recipes for gnocchi and veal meatballs, duck confit and zin-braised short rib. The desserts would be listed at the back but it seemed rude to skip straight to them, like ripping apart the packaging on a birthday gift before you'd done the polite thing and opened the card first.

He could feel his girl's warmth at his side, her scent almost overwhelming him and sending him to his knees. Finally, he reached it—the last one!—and let his eyes drink in the gorgeous sight. The image was so real, so lifelike, that the taste of chocolate filled his mouth and he felt the silky slide down his throat. At the end of the recipe, a line proclaimed him the creator in small text. Absolutely brilliant.

"Photo came out well," he said past his tightening throat.

Cara slipped her hand into his. "Look at the last page."

Ah, this wasn't the last page after all. He turned it over to reveal the cover in full, saturated color. *Learning Italian: Lessons in Family and Food,* by Jack Kilroy and Tony DeLuca. He swallowed hard. With Shane Doyle.

Holy shit.

"My name's on the cover." He looked at Cara. "But it's only one recipe."

Her smile was the slyest, sexiest thing he'd ever seen. "But it's the best recipe."

"What do you think?" Jack's deep voice intoned behind him.

Shane turned to face up to his future. "I'm chuffed, but you didn't have to do this."

Jack's lips thinned to invisibility. "I know."

Cara had done this. She had persuaded Jack to add his name. The air snapped with tension, evidently palpable, judging by the significant looks exchanged by Lili and Cara.

"How's my favorite French sex bomb?" Lili asked, her arm circling Jack's waist.

"Laurent says *bonjour*. He's still claiming you made a terrible mistake by choosing me and he's planning to object at the appropriate time in the church."

Lili's eyes glittered. "It'll be too late by then."

One of those special glances passed between them. "Yes, it will." He turned to Shane, face as hard as the granite countertops. "What's on your mind?"

"I'd like a word."

With a short nod, Jack grabbed a couple of beers from the fridge and headed out back. Shane considered whispering to Cara that he loved her, just so he could draw strength from her smile, but it would be a jinx. He followed his brother onto the large wooden deck ringing the back of the house in an L-shape. Steps led to a green expanse, intercut with paving stones, wild grasses, and low-lying border plants. It was more unkempt than Shane would have expected.

As if picking up on Shane's thoughts, Jack said, "Jules spends a lot of time out here. She's planting an organic vegetable garden." He pointed at the corner where green leaves sprouted above the topsoil. Looked like cabbages, carrots, and an assortment of herbs.

Jack handed off the beer. "You here to ask for your job back?"

"Nope."

"You here to apologize?"

"Not on your life."

His brother laughed, long and rich. "You've got a pair of brass ones, Shane. I'll give you that." He took a swig of his beer. "Listen, I'm sorry about last night. I was pissed about Napier and I shouldn't have taken it out on you. Defending Cara was a good move and I was just hacked off at the outcome."

"I suppose I should have thought first, but the guy made me see red."

"Guys like that always do." He smiled, a return to his usual good-humored self. "So we're good?"

"I need to talk to you about something else."

Jack's face fell. "Shit, you're quitting on me for real, aren't you? Look, let me explain what I meant about not wanting you to work at Sarriette. You don't seem to stay long at any one job, and initially, I didn't want the hassle, but—" He fanned his hand on the deck railing. "You want to know why I took you on, Shane?"

Shane nodded. He wanted to know more than anything.

"It wasn't because of your big award or the fact that you seemed to have a bee up your arse about working in Chicago. About six months ago, I visited Thyme one night for dinner with Lili. Although I'm still technically an investor, it belongs to Laurent now, so I don't feel right walking into the kitchen, especially when he's not there. The server said you were off that night but if you had been on, I would have waltzed right in and told you that your pear-almond crostata was the best dessert I had ever eaten. I knew I had to have you on my team in Chicago as soon as there was an opening. So if I've given you any doubt that you're welcome at Sarriette, then I apologize."

Shane took a draft of his beer and battled to get his emotions under leash. "I appreciate that. I'm not here to quit—again—but after what I tell you, you might change your mind about wanting me on your team."

He placed his beer down on the patio table and drew in the deepest breath he'd ever pulled. Maybe he could get it out in one snatch because if he had to breathe again, he might not remember how.

"You know how I've always wanted to work with you?"

Jack's lips curled up. His brother had a vain streak and since not being the center of attention, he enjoyed hearing that people admired him. A guy of Jack's talent and stature should get sick of the adulation but Shane suspected he fed off it.

"Well, there's a bit more to it. You see, we have a history. You and me."

Jack delivered a slow nod like he was trying to comprehend. "All right."

"Once you asked me where I grew up. I wasn't entirely honest. I'm actually from Quilty."

"You mean where my mother came from?" He had Jack's complete attention now.

"Yeah, your mother. And your father."

"Did your family know my mother?" Jack's gaze drew to curious slits, and Shane imagined that quick brain working overtime, connecting dots, drawing conclusions. "Or my father?" He said this more slowly and with an unmistakable hard edge.

"Actually, it's simpler than that," Shane said. Simpler? He was only trying to explain the most difficult thing he'd ever had to say. His mouth felt like an ash pit. "Your father is also my father. We're brothers."

Jack stared back, his thoughts working circles around his face, figuring it out. "You're John Sullivan's son?"

Now it was Shane's turn for the slow nod. He wanted to close his eyes, but he didn't want to miss this.

Jack's grip tightened on the beer bottle so hard Shane worried it might be crushed. A deathly pallor had descended over his face, appropriate considering he had just seen a ghost.

"I know this is a shock," Shane said, "and I expect you have a lot of questions."

"Yeah, I've plenty of questions." But he went silent instead of putting voice to anything. Silent Jack was never a good omen.

A few taut moments ticked by, and it occurred to Shane that perhaps Jack didn't buy his story. "I have proof. Documentation."

"I believe you," Jack barked, then clamped his mouth shut once more. More pained seconds passed. *Fuck, bro, say something.*

"Is everything okay?" Lili called out, drawn by Jack's raised voice. She peeked her head around the door.

"Fine," Jack said in a voice so tight it could smother.

Lili stepped onto the deck, alarm on her face. "What's going on?" She touched Jack's arm and her eyes widened.

No one spoke a word.

"Someone needs to tell me what's going on right now," Lili said.

"Lili, go back inside," Jack said, his raw stare never leaving Shane's face.

She turned to Shane. "Shane, what's going on?"

It should be Jack's news to give but the connection was just as much Shane's. After running from it for so long, he needed to claim it fully even if his brother wasn't ready to share.

"Jack...he's my brother. By blood." He added that last

bit in case there was any confusion that this was some sort of weird bromance thing.

Lili wrinkled her nose. Shane watched Jack and all he could see was an unscaleable cliff face. All he could see was the only person who mattered right now.

Her startled gaze ping-ponged between the two of them before landing on Shane. "This is for real."

Shane nodded.

"What do you want?" Jack asked, his eyes fixed and flat. "Or should I say how much do you want?"

Lili gasped. "Jack!"

"Well, that's what this is about, isn't it? Did your father send you?"

"He's dead."

"Good."

Man, that was cold. "I didn't come here expecting anything. I was just curious to find out more about you."

"So you sneaked around, getting me to trust you. To like you."

Yes, a million times yes. "I know it looks bad—"

"It looks like you're a chip off the old block. That's how it looks."

"Jack, listen to him." Lili placed a hand on his arm and he shook it off.

"When I think of everything I did for you. A job, a home, the book."

Fury raged through Shane like a monsoon. "I earned all of that. You didn't know shit about me except for my skills and I got every single one of those things under my own steam. You weren't around and I managed just fine on my own."

A muscle throbbed in Jack's jaw. He'd never admit Shane was right, no matter what Shane said. His mouth worked to form his next argument, and Shane braced himself for another rash of accusation.

"What about Cara? Is that why you've been all over her? Another way to insinuate your way into my life?"

"Cara has nothing to do with this."

Jack's mouth curled up in a sneer. "She doesn't? Yeah, you got a job in my kitchen because you're good, but she's done nothing but sing your praises since you got here. Telling me I should use you for the cookbook. I should invest in your business. You're a lot more subtle than your old man. I might have respected you more if you actually asked me outright instead of getting a woman to work favors for you."

"Jack, calm down," Lili said.

"That's not how it happened," Shane said, his voice rising with his pulse. Blood hammered in his eardrums. "I didn't ask Cara to do a thing for me. Funny how everything boils down to how it affects you. You're not much different from dear old Dad in that respect."

Jack's expression was thunderous, not unlike their father in a rage.

"Well, you'll be happy to know that in his final days, you were all he cared about," Shane choked out. "All he wanted was your forgiveness. So you win, Jack. You win everything."

The force of that last speech ripped holes in Shane's chest. He slumped against the railing, all his life force ebbing away.

Jack stepped back, scrubbing a hand across his mouth. "I'm done here. And you're done in my kitchen. In my building. In this town." He stalked off into the house.

Lili threw Shane a helpless look and touched his arm gently. "Shane, stay here. He just needs to calm down." She took off in pursuit of his brother.

That arrogant, fucking prick.

Coming in, this was exactly what Shane had expected, wasn't it? Big-man Jack Kilroy would get in a big-man snit and would only see how it affected him. Another Doyle with his hand out. The consummate user, the man on a mission to take. Letting himself get close to Jack had been his undoing because a man with an ego as big as all outdoors didn't have room for anyone else, especially the son of the man he hated.

He had to leave because Jack was right about one thing. Shane was done.

Going back through the house was not an option, so he stomped through the side gate that led to the street of two-million-dollar properties and suburbia in the city.

"Is it true?" Cara's tight voice shimmered on the warm air. He turned to find her teary-eyed and vulnerable, all color drained from her face.

He shrugged and barely registered that his shoulder was acting up again. "Yeah, it's true. He's my brother."

"No, is it true that it's been all about Jack?"

A hot mass of rage burned in his chest. Yes, this had been all about Jack. That British streak of shite always managed to make it all about him.

When he didn't answer—when he couldn't answer—she asked, "When did you find out?"

At whatever she saw on his face, her mouth fell open. "You knew all along. When we met, you knew and...oh God, you married me." The last couple of words were barely audible above the strangled sob caught in her throat.

"I can't talk about this now."

A flash of heat fired across her face. "Oh, you can't? Well, I want to talk about how you used me to get closer to Jack. Is that why you married me?"

The pain in his chest sang sharp. He knew his next words could only come out harsh but he didn't care. He was done. Done with the whole lot of them.

"Cara, it's not always about you. There are bigger things at stake here."

"Bigger than being married? Bigger than being in—" Her mouth clenched shut. *Bigger than being in love?* That's what she was going to say.

"For God's sake, Cara, call your lawyer. We're not even married anymore. I gave you exactly what you wanted."

Her lovely lips formed an *O* and color lit high on her cheekbones. It was cruel but right now, he hated himself more than he loved her.

She straightened like she was picking herself up, a mental hitch of her pants. Under any other circumstances, he'd be admiring the hell out of her but his rage was all-encompassing. His bitterness was too important.

"Good luck, Shane. I hope you get all you want."

And with a click-clack of those killer heels, she was gone.

CHAPTER 19

Fuchsia, cerise, magenta.

Moss, teal, celadon.

Luxurious fabrics in dazzling hues cocooned Cara as she sat lotus style on the floor of her favorite space, her walk-in closet. An ode to her successful recovery. Her sanctuary.

What else could she ever need? Cara didn't do relationships. She didn't do people. She was cool, in charge, Lemon Tart.

Bullshit.

What could be gained by staying married? she had asked Shane that day in her office all those weeks ago. *The marriage you wanted, Cara.* And yes, she had wanted. Somehow he had seen her desperation and the jealousy of Gina that shaded every joke about her bridezilla cousin. He had seen it and figured out a way to use it for his advantage.

He needed to stay close to Jack, to burrow his way into her big Italian family, and Cara had shot her arm in the air and screamed, *Me, me, me!* As if she were back in school, craving approval from her teachers. So desperate for a man to love her, she had fallen hook, line, and blinkers for this man. The worst man.

On the way home from Jack and Lili's, she had called her lawyer and pulled him out of his golf game. Marty confirmed the annulment would be forthcoming any day now. The delivery of the papers coincided with the day she and Shane visited the children's hospital together. Which was also not long after she had suggested to Jack that he think about investing in Shane's business and wouldn't that Bella Donna recipe make a nice close to the cookbook? When she was finally of no use, he had cast their marriage aside and given her what she wanted from the start.

Her independence.

Now she was solo in her closet, back to square one, as the fabric-plush walls enveloped her. Negative square one, really, because she was about to be bad. Terribly bad.

She didn't even like Sara Lee. When you've worked with top chefs like Jack Kilroy—when an award-winning pastry chef like Shane fucking Doyle is inspired by you to create a decadent dessert—your palate has a hard time going back to the rough stuff. But the grocery store two blocks away only had Sara Lee carrot cake, so needs must.

And oh, how she needed.

She needed to get it back. The control, the numbness, whatever it would take to move her through this pain.

With trembling hands, she opened the box. Twenty-one servings, three hundred and ten calories apiece according to the nutritional information. More numbers to define her. She sliced a fork through the clean frosting until it met resistance from the semifrozen cake beneath, then drove through to the bottom and scooped it up. Carefully, she slipped it past her lips and chewed.

Hmm, not bad. Sara Lee must have improved the recipe since the last time she had tried it. She swallowed and didn't even wait the requisite twenty seconds before going in for the next bite. That was the strategy she used to slow down her eating so her brain would get the message she was full, but she didn't need that now. Today's strategy was chain eating. Just shovel it in, chunk by desperate chunk.

Two minutes later, a quarter of it was gone. Five servings, over fifteen hundred calories. Blinking in shock, she raked her fingers through her hair. *Sticky fingers.* Her hands... *good God*...her hands were covered in cake and frosting. Spongey fragments studded her hair. Apparently she had abandoned the fork and started pawing the cake into her mouth. Apparently it had taken her just one hundred and twenty seconds to turn into an animal.

Her vision blurred and a sob escaped her throat, but the pain still clawed sharply at her chest. More, more, more. Only more could make her feel less.

With every morsel, she ingested the hurt, longing for the moment when detachment took over. Desperate to disengage, to get to that place inside herself when she would become invisible, where no one could see her. Her organs should be ossifying by now, her lungs collapsing, her heart turning to marble, but still she could feel.

The fabrics pressed in on her. Form-fitting skirts, arranged like colorful file folders, cataloged her failure. Exquisite blouses scorned her as she choked down another mouthful. Her body, this weak amalgam of flesh and bone and blood, had been her project for so long, and these gorgeous costumes had been her reward. What good were they now? Just pretty packaging for an ugly shell of a woman. Unmistakable evidence of overinvestment in the depleting asset of her body.

The lifestyle you ordered is no longer in stock.

In her haste to get more cake into her mouth, a clump of cream cheese frosting landed on her Betsy Johnson blouse, the coral silk top Shane had hung with such care. Her usual instinct would have been to grab a wet cloth, but her instincts were worth shit these days. Her instincts had lied, led her to trust, fooled her to love.

Standing like a sugar-dazed drunk, she fingered the blob of frosting and smeared it into the delicate material. An electric shock sizzled through her. *Ah, yes.*

Gratification.

That cream BCBG skirt, the one she found on sale at Nordstrom? *Smear and smush.* Her favorite Marc Jacobs blouse with the pearlescent buttons? *Rip those suckers off.* And when the initial assault didn't satisfy her bloodlust, she rent it seam from seam. Those lethal feet, her kickboxing weapons, had nothing on her killer hands. She shredded and tore and destroyed with claws like Freddy Krueger.

Only beautiful people deserved beautiful things.

It still wasn't enough. Frantically, she sought out new targets for her self-disgust. On the highest shelf, a shopping bag lay tucked away, minding its own business.

Leave it alone.

But it called to her like she was the dumb blonde drawn by a strange noise in the basement, except this was worse because she knew exactly what she would find. Exactly what she needed to take this self-pity fest to the *n*th degree.

Unlike the strong palette of her glamorous wardrobe, the outfits in the bag were all watercolor pastels: powder blue, candy pink, lemon chiffon, mint green. The cutest sailor outfit you ever saw, a dress for a baby princess, onesies with detachable booties. Items she couldn't resist on her shopping trips, those rare times when hope had triumphed over fear for a few crazy moments.

She'd even bought an "I ♥ the Cubs" T-shirt for the little slugger of her dreams. It had beckoned to her heart from the window of one of those tawdry souvenir shops on Michigan Avenue near the Art Institute. Now, the sight of it folded her in half with pain and brought renewed tears to her eyes.

The gap between can and should was so wide Cara wondered how she'd ever had the nerve to dream. Her, a mother? What if she passed all her weird behaviors on to her kid? What if she couldn't feed him because she freaked out at the sight of baby food or started worrying that her toddler had put on too much weight? Shane would have been the check on her crazy. *Do you want to have a baby with me some day?* Why would he say that if he didn't mean it?

It was too, too cruel.

Her beautiful sister, Lili, with motherhood stamped all over her ample curves, would have a bouncing, bonny baby soon, and Cara would be the best aunt in the universe. She already had gifts.

Her gut churned, the battleground of her body fighting the agony and the cake. Nausea flooded her mouth. She was going to be...She stumbled to the bathroom and made it just in time. With every retch, she puked away her hurt until the numbness took over. *Finally.* Relief that her body had made the decision for her washed over her, but she knew if it hadn't, she would have forced the issue anyway.

Old Cara would have taken charge and purged the pain the best way she knew how.

* * *

She had no clue how long she spent getting acquainted with the cool bathroom tile floor, but staying in this pitiful heap forever was not an option. On noodle legs, she pulled herself to a stand, washed her face, and brushed her teeth. *What now?* Go somewhere, anywhere, get away from Chicago. Hide out until Jack and Lili's wedding in less than two weeks.

As she extracted her suitcase from under the bed, a knock on her front door startled her. She went as still as a statue. Maybe if she stopped breathing, he wouldn't know she was here.

"Cara, open up. It's Lili."

Her heart sank. She tried to convince herself disappointment felt close to relief that her sister stood on the other side and not her... What the hell should she call him now? Her ex-husband? Former lover? Rat bastard?

Yeah, rat bastard had a nice ring to it.

In the mirror on her closet door, she blinked at her reflection. Pale, tear streaked, a touch unglued. So no change, then. She pinched her cheeks, drawing color that made her look like a sad old clown.

Deep breaths. She had been burying her shit for years, so she had this. She opened the door to the concerned faces of Lili and Jules.

"Did you find Shane?" her sister asked.

"What?"

Lili frowned. "You ran out of the house so quickly, I assumed you were going after... You've been crying!" She grasped Cara's arms and got up close and personal. "What's happened?"

"Nothing...I..." But the lie wouldn't come. Lili's sympathetic gaze only added further salt to Cara's raw misery. She had barfed her last remaining defense and flushed it down the toilet.

"Sit down," Lili said, the caregiver in her taking over. "Jules, get the grappa. Middle kitchen cabinet."

"On it," said Jules, already beelining for the booze.

Cara let Lili guide her to her white leather sofa, the pristine centerpiece of her all-white living room. Just another example of her effort to maintain control. Had she really thought she could bring a kid into this Cara-perfect world that looked more like a padded cell with every passing second?

Jules set the bottle of grappa and three glasses on the coffee table. In a mournful moment of silence, she poured and they all knocked back a shot of the potent brandy liquor. Cara took a few seconds to relish the burn on her empty stomach.

"How's Jack doing?" she asked.

"He's with Evan," Jules said. "He needs some time with his favorite little man."

"You want to tell us what happened?" Lili asked, her heart-shaped face marred with worry.

What happened? There weren't enough words in the dictionary to describe what had happened. The sound of her ragged breathing filled the silence while she screwed up her courage. Cara could no longer avoid her sins.

"I married Shane and I fell for him. Or maybe I fell for him and I married him. God, I don't know."

"What?" Lili shrieked. "Did you just say married?"

"I'm so sorry, sis. I don't think I did it to upstage you, but maybe I did. Maybe I'm just an ice-cold bitch who can't bear to see anyone else happy."

Lili's face screamed her shock. "Why are you saying that? Why would you even think that? Start from the beginning. Vegas?"

Cara nodded. "I was drunk..."

Her sister shrugged in agreement. Well, duh.

"But not that drunk. I asked him to marry me, Lili. There

was something there. Some knowledge that passed between us over the shots of vodka. Something that said, this one, this time."

Blaming Gina's bitchiness, the roofie in Cara's envy cocktail, had been her go-to position, but there *had* been more. She had liked how he made her feel. She had liked the person she was when she was with him. And maybe, she wanted to hold on to that feeling and see if she could scrimp and save and stretch it to another day or week or year.

Lili fed a skeptical glance to Jules, who thankfully managed to look surprised at hearing news she already knew. "But you had just met him."

"I know, but the minute I stepped in that bar, it was like seeing hope. At first, I thought it was just my tired feet talking. Oh, look, one of Jack's pals has some manners and is offering me his seat. But he had that cute smile and winking dimple, and he listened while I talked about Gina and how ridiculous she was. He told stories and held my hand. Four hours later we were man and wife."

It sounded so ridiculous she would be laughing if her heart wasn't deadweight in her gut, dragging all her organs with it. They had started this thing under the influence, in the fakest city in the world. How could she have thought it was real?

Lili shook her head with passion. "It's just a drunken mistake. You can get an annulment."

He already did. He annulled their marriage behind her back.

"I got the papers. I gave them to him, but then he was there, everywhere I went, and it was like a sign that he was supposed to be in my life. Listening to me. Fussing over me. Caring about me. We've even been looking after the stupid cat together."

"A cat?" Jules murmured. "That's some messed-up shit right there."

Cara buried her face in her hands. "But it was all a lie. He used me. He only wanted Jack." Just the same as with Mason Napier, stupid, needy Cara was merely a means to an end.

"I still can't believe it," Lili said. "Shane and Jack. It's mind-boggling."

"And weird," Jules said. "Only a few weeks ago, I was talking about how hot he was and it turns out I was lusting after my sort-of-brother." She shuddered.

"You're not related. And you're certainly not helping." Lili squeezed Cara's hand. "I've seen how he looks at you. I've heard how he talks about you. There's something there just like you thought." She didn't sound convinced, but Cara loved her for trying all the same.

"He's a liar, Lili. He wooed me with that stupid brogue. Well, you'd know all about that." Her sister had a permanent lady boner for Jack's British accent and dirty French talk. Cara slid a sidelong glance at Jules. "No offense."

Jules waved a hand magnanimously and wisely kept her British-accented pie hole closed.

"He used all his Irish guile and charm to trap me."

Lili opened her mouth to speak, and Cara raised a hand. Man-hating list making was in progress. Do not disturb.

"He took advantage of my insecurities. My hang-ups about food."

Befuddlement clouded Lili's face. "Your what now?"

"Sis." Cara's hands shook and she grasped Lili's to help her to calm. Shame rose like bile in her throat but she pushed it back down. "I used to have anorexia."

Her sister's expression blanked to chalk. "No, you didn't."

Cara let the news settle, all while her heart and lungs flew apart with the pain that her sister couldn't see. Had never seen.

"You just worry about your figure," Lili said, the edge in her voice pronounced. "Like all women."

"No, sis," Cara said, every cell poised to explode. God damn it, she was the one who was supposed to be in denial. She didn't need to hear it from her sister. "I had anorexia. I'm in recovery now but it's been a tough road. With Shane, I felt like someone new. Not control-freak Cara who has to have everything in its proper place, who's so self-absorbed in her strive for perfection that she can't be of any use to her family. To you or Mom."

Poor Lili looked like she'd been poleaxed, a little like how Cara must have looked two hours ago upon learning the man she loved had used her. And not too far off from how Shane had looked in the aftermath of Jack's rejection. She steeled her spine. This was *her* pity party and Shane Doyle was not invited.

"But why didn't you tell me?" Lili asked faintly.

Why didn't you figure it out? How could it be that after a few weeks, that rat bastard, Shane, knew her better than her own family? Every half-eaten lunch, every missed dinner, every early morning trip to the gym—surely Lili could have guessed that something was wrong. But the five years between them was a chasm that had served to keep Cara's secret safe. Lili was battling her own demons while being bullied in high school while Cara took her shame with her to college in New York. Maybe later, Lili could have pulled her aside on one of her infrequent visits home to Chicago and asked if the Skeletor look was really in vogue in the Big Apple, but blaming her baby sister wasn't going to help either of them through this.

"I didn't tell anyone. A while back, I hit a point where

I said no more. I realized I was missing out on so much and I wanted to be normal." She looked around her sterile living room, mentally comparing it to the comfortable clutter of Jack and Lili's, complete anathema to her inflexible personality. "I wanted what you and Jack have with each other. I wanted to be the one in Mom's wedding dress with Dad walking me down the aisle. I know I've never fit in but maybe that would help. Make me more of a DeLuca."

The tears started to come hot and fast, the leak unstoppable. "I've been so jealous of everyone. Gina, you, even Jules because of Evan. I wanted kids. Not just be the glamorous aunt, but to have something of my own, something real. A man, a family, a future."

Her girls wrapped their bodies around her from either side.

"There, there, love," Jules said rubbing her back. "There's no need to be jealous of my uterus. It's got me nothing but trouble."

Cara managed a watery laugh-snort and Jules joined in. Lili was still reeling from Cara's revelation, a million questions vying for voice on her face. Usually so quick to joke, she was having a hard time finding the funny in all this.

"But there's nothing to stop you from having all those things," Lili said, her eyes filling with tears. "You're my amazing big sister. You can get any guy you want. You can be anything you want."

"I'm the one stopping me, Lili."

Lili shook her head in disbelief. "I figured something must have happened but I assumed it was a guy. I always thought you had it so perfect."

"I did. I was Miss Perfect. These days, I'm Miss Recovering Perfect." Despite her meltdown in the closet. That speck on her record would eat at her for a while but she would rise above it. She had already come too far.

She wiped a tear rolling down Lili's cheek. Who would have thought she'd be the one offering comfort? "I know this sucks but I'm going to get through it. You wouldn't believe how much I've toughened up in the last few months. Best of all, I won't be married anymore and I won't have to see him."

Her husband's—her soon-to-be ex-husband's—parting gift.

Lili looked uncomfortable. "Well, I'm not sure we can guarantee that. After all, he's family."

Cara shot up straight, explosion imminent. "You mean Jack's going to just let him sneak his way in? After how he tricked us?"

Her sister's discomfort gave way to resignation and she turned to Jules.

"You know Jack," Jules picked up. "He gets his boxers in a twist and then he calms down. He's not going to turn Shane away, not when he has all these unanswered questions. Whatever Shane's done, he came here with the intention of making a connection with Jack."

Right, because he clearly hadn't come to make a connection with Cara.

CHAPTER 20

With legs like sacks of flour, Shane climbed the stairs to his apartment late in the evening. His arse was numb from too many hours on the bike, his heart bloodied from the morning's events. He had cocked up royally but then that's what he had been doing from day one. Now he was ready to fling himself on Cara's mercy.

On hitting the landing, his stomach dropped to the carpet. A pair of long legs encased in denim stretched across the hallway, the lower half of an unexpected sentinel.

His landlord. His boss. His brother.

Jack's hand curled around the neck of a three-quarters-full bottle of Jameson, nestled in his lap. At Shane's attention-grabbing cough, his eyelids fluttered open, and he drew his chin up with a squint.

"Where the hell have you been?"

"Out."

Pulling himself upright, Jack blinked a couple of times and gave a raggedy shake of his head.

"You drunk?" Shane asked.

"Not enough to marry a complete stranger."

Shitski. Jack might have come to say his piece, but right now Cara was Shane's number-one priority.

"I need to see Cara first."

"She's over at my place with Lili and Jules." Jack raised an eyebrow to let Shane know that he'd better be all right with that. "You ready to do this?"

Was he ready? He'd been ready for twelve years and now he was ready for a fight. He threw open the door and headed to the kitchen. After grabbing a couple of glasses, he turned to find Jack placing the whiskey bottle on the kitchen table like the start of a frat-boy drinking game. Only when Jack had sat did Shane sit himself.

A minute to compose was needed, for both of them, and it came in the form of Jack pouring the drinks. Shane hid his grim smile. Jameson had been their father's tipple of choice. Just perfect. He knocked back the whiskey and his eyes smarted from the fumes. It needed water but his muscles had slumped to fill the shape of the chair. There'd be no standing for a while.

"You don't look like him," Jack said.

"I take after my mother."

Thoughts raced across Jack's face, and Shane knew exactly what he was thinking. Jack was the spitting image of John Sullivan and it pissed him off to no end.

"I'm sorry about what I said. About being glad he was dead. That was uncalled for."

"It's okay. He wasn't easy to like and you didn't owe him anything."

Jack breathed deep. "When?"

"About a year and a half back. Alzheimer's."

"So just before you started looking for work at Thyme."

He studied the amber liquid in his glass. "He called me a few times and told me he was ill. I never called back."

Shane heard his own rough intake of breath. "Nothing you could have done. It took a while to diagnose because he drank so much no one saw the difference. He went downhill very fast."

The words Shane had thrown out back on Jack's deck hung between them. John Sullivan had died with Jack's name on his lips, but Shane understood his brother would need time to absorb that and what it meant. Shane hadn't quite come to terms with it but he was getting there.

Jack strummed the table in an impatient tattoo. "I think this is the part where you explain why you kept this to yourself, Shane. How long have you known about me?"

"About twelve years. You were just getting well known. Remember those morning TV spots you did on the BBC?"

Jack's eyes widened with the knowledge of how long Shane had kept his secret. "Three minutes to demonstrate how to make *coq au vin*. Bloody daft."

Sure, let's talk about food. "He told me then. At first I thought he was lying—he was one for the tall tale and he was drunk, morning and night, but the more I saw of you, the more I realized it was true. I wanted to reach out but I was only thirteen. You were the bomb. Successful, famous, you had everything. Why would you be interested in some snotty-nosed teen you didn't know from Adam?"

Jack didn't fight him on it. He knew Shane's instincts had been right.

"I was already interested in cooking, but once I started keeping tabs on your career, I decided that was my future, too. I wasn't thinking that it would be a way to get to know you. I didn't have a plan. It just made me feel closer to you. My hot-shit brother."

Through the abuse and constant put-downs, he had held on to that illusory connection. It had sustained him through some crappy times. Even his illogical hatred of Jack for not being there to save Shane had sustained him.

Shane's pain must have been etched on his face because Jack's next words were softer. "When you got older, why didn't you look me up?"

Shane sighed. "I wanted to, but he had already contacted you looking for money. He said you didn't want anything to do with him, and while I knew you didn't even know about me, it was out there. He'd set the terms and dirtied the water. The first thing you thought when you found out was what was I after." But that wasn't the only reason. Really, he was scared shitless that Jack wouldn't be interested.

Guilt clouded Jack's heavy-lidded eyes. "But I've gotten over it pretty fast, Shane. You know me well enough by now to see that I blow up and calm down in all of five minutes." He stood up quickly, too quickly, and gripped the table for balance. For a moment, Shane worried he might pass out, but instead Jack flipped on the tap at the sink and wet the back of his neck.

"So what changed your mind? Why are you telling me now?"

"Cara. I couldn't lie to her anymore." Lying to her was worse than lying to himself. She was as much a part of him as his scars and bruises, and her bravery demanded he match her.

"I don't even know where to start with that. I mean, for shit's sake, Shane. Married! Did you do that to get closer to me?"

A bolt of rage shot through Shane's chest. "Right, because getting my long-lost brother's fiancée's sister drunk and"—Jack opened his mouth and Shane raised a condemning hand—"convincing *her* to ask *me* to marry her is such a brilliant plan. That doesn't make a lick of sense."

Jack looked a touch shamefaced at his accusation. "Jesus, Shane, you've wasted a lot of time."

"It hasn't been wasted," Shane said, truly believing it. He had to because the alternative—that he could have been a part of something real years ago—didn't bear thinking about. "I was perfecting my craft, learning to be the best. I wanted to get to know you as an equal, not as a giddy apprentice or some user with my hand out looking for favors. I couldn't show up without something to offer."

His brother scrubbed his hand through his hair, just like Packy, and Shane looked away.

"I don't need you to offer anything. You're family. You're my family. That's more than enough."

His heart filled to a dangerous bursting, making his blood surge and his hands shake. He took a sip of the whiskey to calm his nerves. The glass was empty. He didn't want to argue with Jack, who always thought he knew best. He didn't want to admit that he might have strategized all wrong and played his cards poorly. Better to push that away and leave it for another day. For now, Jack knew, and it felt like they had a future, but without Cara it wouldn't be anywhere near as bright as it could be.

He felt a sting to the back of his skull and it took a moment to register that Jack had cuffed him a good one.

His brother plopped back in his seat. "That's for being an idiot."

Downright fraternal.

The long, satisfying moment of silence that followed was interrupted when Vegas hopped up into Shane's lap and made a sound like the start-up of an old, broken-down lawnmower. Jack eyed the cat shrewdly and poured them both another drink.

"So. Alzheimer's," his brother said, setting the bottle down. "Let me guess. Genetic?"

"One or both of us have a degenerative mental condition to look forward to."

Jack raised his glass. "Thanks, Dad."

Shane started laughing, and God, it felt good.

CHAPTER 21

The heavy knock on the door sent a corresponding *thump thump* through Shane's bloodstream, but when he pulled it open, disappointment set in. Only Jack. A week ago, the thought of his brother showing up unannounced at his door would have thrilled Shane. Since moving to Chicago, he'd had plenty of time to get used to the annoying parts of Jack's personality—the pushy, know-it-all, paternal aspect he exhibited with everyone—but having to put up with him as an official relative was more than he could bear, especially in his current mood. Bloody families.

"What?" Shane snapped.

"Already bored with me, bruv?" Jack asked, his voice tinged with that British mockery he practiced so well.

Shane stood back to let him in, not that Jack needed an invitation. When he wasn't pumping Shane for information about LBJ (Life Before Jack), he was being annoyingly chipper about the whole Cara situation. Which was a disaster.

All his calls went straight to voice mail. Lili told him

she'd gone to New York to decompress and visit with friends and Jack told him to give her time. *This is Cara we're talking about,* he reasoned.

Yes, it was. Cara, the woman he loved and wanted to hold and explain what an arsehole he'd been. The situation he'd found himself in might have appeared insurmountable, but he could have found a way. Only now could he finally admit that his tricky subconscious had spent his entire life planning this meeting with Jack. If he had been honest from the beginning, and shared that part of himself with her, then he wouldn't be in this mess. But all she could see was his heart-shattering betrayal.

Now Jack stood before him, not exactly smug, but cheerful enough that Shane wanted to punch him, to hell with the consequences. His brother took a seat on the ratty sofa, wearing that look that said he had all these fabulous memories of sex with Lili. Hooray for him. Bastard.

"Haven't heard from her," Jack said as Vegas jumped into his lap and made himself at home.

"Didn't ask," Shane said morosely.

"Still can't believe she asked you to marry her."

Of all the amazing things that had transpired the last few weeks, this was the part Jack had the biggest problem with. That Cara—rigid, buttoned-up, hardwired-for-control Cara—had actually done the asking. Shane tried to take comfort in the notion that maybe Jack didn't know Cara nearly as well as he thought he did. It was about the only comfort he could find in it all.

"Sure, I'm hard to resist," he said, trying to dial up his usual insouciance and missing by a country mile.

Jack made a noise of disbelief. "So you didn't think of saying, 'Hey, that's a great idea but how about we get to know each other first?'"

They'd already had this conversation but it didn't stop Jack from replaying it like a broken record. His brother had figured out fairly quickly the shape of Shane's buttons and he was catching up on twenty-five years of sibling torture.

Shane delivered his most skeptical look. "Are you telling me you didn't fall madly for Lili the minute you saw her? That you didn't know that she was the one?"

"I might have fallen hard but that doesn't mean I was dragging her down the aisle a few hours later."

Shane snorted. "Not for want of trying."

Jack gave that lazy smile of his. He couldn't deny it. "*Colpo de fulmine.* The thunderbolt. The DeLuca women are not for the faint of heart."

Shane sighed. "If she's amazing, she won't be easy—"

"If she's easy, she won't be amazing," Jack finished.

Shane's mind reached for the rest of it. *If she's worth it, you won't give up. If you give up, you're not worthy.* There was another line but it existed in a fuzzy place on the edge of his consciousness.

Jack was speaking again. "You know if I could make some changes, you'd be my best man, right?"

Shane stopped cold in the act of grabbing a couple of craft beers from the fridge. He didn't know, but Jack looked like he was going to explain.

"I've known Laurent for years, and the other people in the wedding party... Well, I can't exactly throw someone out to give you a spot."

Shane shifted uneasily. "I never expected that."

Jack leaned back and pulled at a loose string in the couch's tweed. "But I'd like us to do something together. Get away for a couple days. What do you think?"

"What about work? And your wedding?" It was only a

week away and there must be a ton to do, especially with the wedding planner out of the picture.

"I'm the boss, and while I know you think you're indispensable, we actually managed without you when you took your ballerina dive on the rugby field. You'll be back in time to make the cake." He smiled, so easy and natural, like he found long-lost brothers every day of the week. "Pack a bag. I'll pick you up at two."

Shane had something to do first. It wasn't going to solve anything but the itch to take action was making his skin break out in a rash. "Where are we going?"

Jack smiled slyly as he headed to the door. "Just some place we can kick back, get trashed, and talk about our feelings."

* * *

Abandon all hope ye who enter here.

That may as well have been carved into the Chihuly glass sculpture in the Bellagio lobby because Cara had finally realized her problem.

She was a completely spineless sucker.

How else could she explain why she had returned to the scene of the crime? When Lili had said she'd prefer a little sister time instead of some blow-out bachelorette party, Cara had grasped at it. But Las Vegas? What was she thinking?

For once, Lili was the organized one, with massage and nail appointments that usually fell outside her wheelhouse. And for once, Cara was grateful to have the load lifted from her shoulders.

Your shoulders are my favorite part of you.

Pfft.

"So Jack's okay with you gallivanting off to Vegas four days before the nuptials?" Cara asked while the very efficient nail girl jabbed a stick into her cuticles. *A little higher, honey. Aim for the eyes.*

Lili smiled. "It's good to spend some time apart. Make sure he appreciates me."

"Oh, he appreciates you. You're very lucky, Lili. I know I wasn't always so supportive."

"Well, when you think someone is just the most perfect example of sex-on-legs, it's hard to see the rest. You know how difficult it was for me to see beyond Jack's, um, assets." Her saucy smile faded. "But sometimes, it can take something big to see that maybe it's not just about looks and hotness. That there's a beating heart underneath all that sexy." She huffed out a breath, and Cara felt her own body go stiff in preparation for another see-reason speech.

"So Shane handled it all wrong," Lili said, "but he was working with what he had."

Jack and Lili had tried to advocate for Shane, and Cara knew the man had some feelings for her. But she could never be sure of his motives for marrying her, and in truth, it was his secret snip of the marriage bond that had flattened her. She had thought they had something special but now every moment they had spent together was tinged with suspicion.

He wanted connections, roots, all the stuff she had been running from forever. He wanted to be a DeLuca and a Kilroy, and boy, were they going to love him. Taking in waifs and strays was par for the course with her family; they could pick and choose the winners and not worry about the natural-born ones who failed to live up to the Italian code.

Shane didn't need her now that he had Jack and her family.

In the face of Cara's silence, Lili went on. "I can't believe you didn't have any clue. That he didn't even hint at it."

In those words, Cara heard her sister's own self-recrimination that she hadn't magically figured out her older sister had been starving herself as a lifestyle choice for the last fifteen years. *No, not a lifestyle choice,* her internal therapist rebuked. *Anorexia is an illness.*

"He never wanted to talk about himself. I knew about his father being a bully, but as for the rest..." Her stomach lurched in memory of how Shane had been hurt by his father. Jack's father. "I don't know, Lili. If he's going to lie about something so fundamental, how can I be sure that any of it was real?"

"Maybe if you answered the phone the next time he calls. Listened to one of his voice mails..."

Cara held up her hands, an action that did double duty in halting her sister's speech and allowing her to admire the pleasure-pink frosted tips. "There's nothing to talk about. Ancient history." Moving her hands under the nail dryer, she raised her most determined gaze to meet Lili's. No more self-pity. That look was so aging on her.

"Get your shoes on, Liliana. Tonight, I'm looking for my next ex-husband."

Two hours later, her sister emerged from the bathroom of their plush hotel room to Cara's gasp. The jewel tones of her ruby-red sheath picked up the natural shimmer of her olive skin and her sexy heels accentuated her shapely legs, making her whole body undulate in a sensual wave. Her hair was still as crazy as ever—no salon could manage that—but she was so gorgeous that Cara could only breathe her appreciation.

"Do I look okay?" Lili asked with a hitch in her voice Cara credited to the champagne. Jack had arranged for a bottle of bubbly to be sent to the room earlier and they'd both indulged in a glass or three in preparation for a night on the town.

"Stunning, Sis." She linked Lili's arm, determined to

keep a vise grip on her throughout the night. She might joke about picking up a new husband, but with her propensity for the idiot move, staying in Lili's orbit was the best strategy all round. "Let's do this."

As they stepped off the elevator, Cara's buzz crashed in a fiery ball of crap. Her cousin Tad leaned against a gold-leafed pillar looking tall, dark, and smart-assed. In a suit.

"What the hell are you doing here?" she demanded.

Tad raised an eyebrow in Lili's direction. "You haven't told her?"

"I was just about to. You're supposed to be in the bar, dummy."

Cara turned to her sister, confused. "What's going on?"

Lili pulled her away from the pile-up they were causing at the elevator bank.

"I'm getting married."

"Uh, hello, I know. I'm planning your amazing wedding. I'm your maid of honor." Definitely maid, now that she had confirmed her status with Marty. The annulment had been finalized this morning, but she was too numb to care.

Licking her lips, Lili shot a harried glance at Tad. "Actually, I'm getting married now. Tonight. Here in Vegas."

"What?" And then when the full force of it hit her, she added another resounding, "What?" So articulate.

"There's still going to be the big wedding with the carriage and the fountain and the three hundred guests, but..." Lili looked helplessly at Tad.

"We need you to calm the fuck down, Cara," he said.

"Tad!" Lili glared at him.

Cara double-glared at him and then turned back to her sister. "But you want the perfect day, Lili. The dress, the bridesmaids, everyone looking at you, wishing nothing but the best for you."

"Yes, but—but that's more what you want for me." She bit her lip. "I know you and Jack had this grand plan and I kind of got swept up in it. I'm still going to do that because Jack wants the big wedding. But I want it to be about us, too."

Stunned, Cara had no words. She had pushed Lili into a wedding she didn't want—oh, surprise, surprise. She had plenty of experience there. Some events planner she'd turned out to be, one who couldn't even intuit her client's needs. Instead of putting food on her feelings like normal people, she had put her dreams on them. She wanted the fantasy day for Lili, but of course she was living vicariously. Transference of your smashed hopes into another vessel. Psych-freaking-101.

"You mean Jack's here?" she asked stupidly. Of course he was here. "That's where you were last night. You were sneaking out to meet your fiancé!"

Lili had left the hotel room to get ice, but in no universe, not even one with a maze like the Bellagio's twenty-third floor, did it take twenty-five minutes to fill a bucket. The lying minx.

She had the decency to look sheepish. "Cara, the wedding is still going to happen on Saturday. It's still going to be as wonderful as you planned and no one else needs to know that Jack and I will have already said 'I do.' He's doing this for me because he understands that when it comes down to it, it's our day. Please say you understand." She wiped a tear from her eye.

A tight fist grasped Cara's lately brittle heart. "Lili, of course I understand. I'm sorry I've been so…well, me."

"No apologies." Lili hugged her, drawing her into the comfort of her soft, curvy body. "You need to forgive yourself, Cara," she whispered in her ear. "For everything."

Cara felt like she had been punched in the chest. She opened her mouth to say, *For what?* but closed it again, because hell, she wasn't that stupid. She had been ill and couldn't come home to help her mother. She had been ill and couldn't confide in her family. Keeping her secret had required so much more effort than finding it within her heart to accept that she didn't have to do it all alone. Her family loved her the way she was—control-freak, messed-up, far-from-perfect Cara.

Today, one marriage had officially ended and another one would begin. It was a good day.

Lili, in her shimmery red dress that made her look like a goddess, released her and smiled with glossy eyes. "Tonight, I'm marrying the hottest man on the planet with my favorite people as my witnesses." She linked Cara's arm and rubbed Tad's shoulder.

Tad smirked. "We're your favorite people? Knew it."

Cara smiled, relieved that it wasn't as difficult as she expected. "So if we're your favorite people, who's Jack got? Jules, I suppose, and…"

At Lili's grimace, Cara's heart plummeted to a splat on the carpet.

"About that…"

CHAPTER 22

You know I'm the one who's supposed to be nervous." Jack put his hand on Shane's shoulder, halting his fidget. "It's my wedding day."

Shane threw another glance around the chapel, a notably classier version of the one he'd gotten hitched in six weeks ago. White pillars, draped in flowing fabrics, gave it a heaven-for-hire ambience. Cara might have liked this—if she'd had a choice. His visual circuit led back to the double doors through which Lili and Cara would be entering any minute now. At least, he hoped Cara would be. By now, Lili should have dropped the M-bomb and Cara was either steeling herself for the nightmarish twenty minutes ahead of her or hightailing it to McCarran Airport as fast as her heels could carry her.

"You're not going to do anything stupid, are you?" Jack muttered.

Depends. "Like what?"

"I dunno, lie prostrate before the maid of honor begging for her forgiveness?"

The door opened, Shane's stomach flipped, and in walked...Jules.

He turned back to Jack and pushed his mouth into a facsimile of a grin. "I was thinking more along the lines of hijacking the toasts and making it all about me. See how you like it."

"As long as you don't ruin the ceremony."

"We're ready," Jules said to Jack, her eyes bright. She shifted her gaze to Shane. "Still not sure what to call you. Step-bro? Brother from another mother—and father?"

Shane coughed out a laugh. "You could just call me Shane."

Again, the door opened and this time it was...Tad. Who held Jules's withering glare boldly. Those crazy kids.

The flash of red that came through next signaled Lili's arrival. Shane slid a sidelong glance at his brother, whose face had broken into a grin big enough to power the Sunset Strip.

Behind Lili...no one. The door closed. Ah hell.

Immediately, it opened again and Cara stepped through, secreting her phone in her purse. Probably making arrangements for the next flight out. A few quick steps, and she had caught up with Lili and linked her arm. She looked beautiful, shell-shocked, like she wanted to be anywhere but here. And then she took one look at Jack and another at Lili, and her face transformed into sun. Nothing forced about it either, a genuine ray of brightness at how happy her sister and Jack made each other. If she was pissed about the surprise nuptials, she hid it well.

That was Cara. All class.

She refused to look at him. There was only so much magic Jack and Lili's joy could work. His heart broke into

a thousand ice shards, spreading a glacial chill across his
body, a return to the state he had been in before he met her.
He had made it to the other side of the glass but he hadn't
reckoned on the frosted veil separating him from the woman
he wanted more than anything.

Thirty minutes later, they were toasting the happy couple
in a private room at Mint, Jack's Las Vegas outpost in the
Paris hotel. Cara was speaking to everyone but Shane. Jules
was speaking to everyone but Tad. Which meant he and Tad
suddenly had a lot more in common than just their love of
Harleys.

"What did you do?" he asked Tad.

There was no missing the oblique glance he sent Jules's
way. In a single gulp, he downed his champagne and had
already grabbed another glass before he met Shane's eyes.
"Why does everyone assume I did something?"

"Because that's the way of the world, man," Shane said.
"Every day as part of your penance, just apologize to the first
three women you meet. That way, the balance of the universe might one day be restored."

"It'd take more than that, my friend." He directed another
dark look at Jules. "It's for the best."

Interesting. Tad seemed like one of the good guys, not
that it'd make a difference to someone as overprotective as
Jack. Big bro had made it clear in no uncertain terms that
Tad might want to invest in permanent body condoms so as
not to contaminate Jules.

"Can't believe you're letting Jack get in the way of a good
thing," Shane said.

That drew an expression of surprise from Tad. "You think
I'd let Jack Kilroy have some say in where I dip my wick?
No way. Believe me when I say this is better for all con-
cerned."

He didn't look convinced. In fact, he looked downright miserable.

"You okay?" Shane asked.

Tad's eyebrows snapped together and then just as quickly separated as if he had flicked an internal switch from pissed-off-at-the-world to the carefree ladies' man everyone knew. It was quite the display. His grin stretched wide as he made eye contact with the perky waitress circling with a tray of bubbly. The one with breasts that would break a man's nose coupled with come-hither eyes and pouty lips.

"I will be very soon."

Taking a few steps forward, he cut her off before she got to Shane and launched into his good ole boy offensive. Shane caught Jules's deepening frown. She turned back to Cara who must have a crick in her neck by now, so valiant was her effort to ignore him.

What Shane wouldn't give to have Tad's ability to turn off his feelings like that. Better still, a time machine would come in handy. He wanted to hit the restart button and take a do over. Walk down the Strip with a beautiful girl, bring her line dancing in Chicago, look after a cat together while they figured each other out.

All the courting, none of the marriage. He wanted his wife back.

* * *

Midnight and Cara was back in the bar of the Paris Las Vegas Hotel. Alone again, natch. Six weeks ago, she had bundled the DeLuca ladies through the door and surveyed the room; now she was solo and had no expectations.

In the time it took her gaze to fix on him, he was already on his feet, gesturing to his seat. She sighed and headed over, the inevitability of it like pincers in her chest.

"You look like you could do with a drink, beautiful," the tall, dark stranger said. Sharply dressed. Smelled good. Not Shane.

"Sure," she said but her heart wasn't in it. All her bonhomie had been used up marking time through the reception dinner. She had soldiered through, and it had been evident that Shane was on the same wavelength. Get it over with. Grin and bear it. A couple of times, she had found him looking at her, his eyes a warm secret. But there were no more secrets between them, just a fractured history that could be tucked under the rug with a couple of signatures. Six weeks of joy and pain signed away and notarized.

She had wanted to talk to him but her feet couldn't move in the same direction as her heart. Come dessert and the final toasts, she had turned and Shane was gone. All that strength she had been harnessing over the last couple of months—strength that should have made her brave enough to chase him down—had evaporated into the ether.

"What brings you to Las Vegas?" Tall, dark, and strange cut in to her thoughts, his eyes flicking appreciatively over her teal Diane von Furstenberg wrap dress. Not a lot of women looked good in teal, but Cara's coloring allowed her to pull it off with style.

"A wedding."

"Great city for it." He added a smile. It was a nice smile, just not the one she wanted to see.

She took the seat TDS offered just as her phone rang with "Single Ladies" and a Chicago number she didn't recognize. That mockery of a ring tone would have to go. It was so 2008.

"Hello?"

"Cara DeLuca?" She recognized the nasal whine of a put-upon assistant. "Mrs. Napier is on the line. Please hold."

The only Mrs. Napier Cara knew was Penny Napier and why she would be calling Cara at one A.M. Chicago time was not immediately clear.

"Miz DeLuca," breathed a patrician, moneyed voice down the line. "I hope I haven't disturbed you but I understand that you're in a city that never sleeps."

"Yes, Mrs. Napier." Cara swallowed her surprise and tried to sit up straighter on her bar stool. "What can I do for you?"

"Well, I hear my son has been throwing his weight around trying to get Jack Kilroy to perform like a seal at his wedding. Let me say that his behavior is in no way endorsed by me. Little prick's been a thorn in my side since I pushed him out of my womb thirty-four years ago."

Good thing Cara hadn't ordered a drink because she might have spilled it all over her dress. For the love of Frank, what was happening here?

"Your name has come before me more than once in the last year, Miz DeLuca. I hear you know how to throw a good party and tell a good children's story."

Cara managed to draw enough breath to form a sentence. "I'm a very resourceful woman, Mrs. Napier." Maybe it wasn't her best sentence.

Penny chuckled knowingly. "We have to be in this day and age. No one's going to give us what we want on a plate. Got to make our own road." Burying three husbands was Penny Napier's road, and the woman had definitely run with it. The pause sat weighted and Cara imagined a conductor with a baton building to the cymbals crash. Her heart beat triple time.

"Sarriette can host the Pink Hearts Appreciation Dinner without the attached string of my son's wedding. When you're back in Chicago, make an appointment with my assistant and we'll talk about that and what else you're good at."

"Thank you, Mrs. Napier. Could I ask how you found out about your son's, um, bargain?" Somehow, she doubted Mason had boasted about it over eggs benedict with the Momster.

"Your chef came to see me."

Your chef. Cara's tongue was suddenly too large for her mouth. "Jack?"

"No, the gorgeous one with the dimple. Of course, I already knew about my son's ham-fisted tactics through my sources but your chef charmed his way past my assistant and then he wouldn't leave until I agreed to hear him out. I wasn't really listening to a word he said—the man is absolutely sinful and then he opens his mouth and it's like a choir of angels singing. He could have been confessing to murder and I'd still be nodding like a lobotomized nun."

Shane Doyle and his stupid accent, marauding his way through Chicago's glitterati.

"Anyway, Miz DeLuca, I'm sure you have better things to be doing than talking to me. Wicked, wonderful things."

Cara smiled ruefully to herself. Her wicked, wonderful days were long behind her. "It was very nice talking you, Mrs. Napier. Thank you and sleep well."

"Oh, I'll sleep when I'm dead, Cara. Good night."

Cara stared at her phone for a good minute. Rumors of her demise were grossly exaggerated. Once the wedding was done, she would sketch out a business plan for DeLuca Events (she'd need a new binder!) and would start working on her contacts to draw up locations, menus, and vendors. She could do this. The last few weeks had revealed *coglioni* she never knew she had. Cara *coglioni.*

How she wished she had someone to share her news with. She wanted to take this new strength, stop being afraid, and open her heart, but first she needed a very strong adult beverage.

Another chirp from Beyoncé put a crimp in her cocktail plans. From the screen, Lili beamed like Doris Day on her birthday, which was pretty close to how she had looked all night. Tall, dark, whatever angled her an impatient look.

She answered with, "Hey, shouldn't you be busy trashing that suite with all your acrobatic, monkey sex?"

"Consider it done, Cara," Jack rumbled back from the other end.

"What's going on? Have you put my sister into some sort of sex coma? Lili, Lili, are you okay?"

Jack chuckled. "Maybe you should be less obsessed with the sex life of your sister and worry more about getting your own love life in order."

She groaned. "Did you really call me at midnight on your wedding day to give me relationship advice?"

"Yes, Cara. Yes, I did. The sacrifices I make for my family."

His pride in joining clan DeLuca rang clear and she had to admit not a small amount of pleasure that he considered her in that way. In the background, Lili called weakly for help.

"Shush, sweetheart, I'll take care of you. Cara, you still there?"

Could they be any more adorable? "I'm almost ears."

"Open your mind, love, then turn around." He clicked off. For the second time that night, she stared at her phone. Was that it?

Slowly, she turned—she'd always had a flair for the dramatic—and met the warm, brown gaze of...TDS.

"Excuse me, do you mind?" She waved him aside; he went easy.

At the door stood Shane, and man-on-fire, he looked good. During the ceremony, he had worn a suit, all sharp lines that did little to contain his boundless energy. Now, he was back to his usual uniform of faded, overly washed shirt and jeans, their supple softness almost tangible above those boots. Always the boots. There was plenty of scruff affixed to more jaw than one man needed, enough to remind her of how devastating his explorations of her body had been. How he had claimed every part of her. How he still owned her, body and soul.

With all the lithe grace that made him an excellent dancer, he glided over, only breaking eye contact to take in TDS, whose brow was ridged with annoyance. She couldn't blame him. He had given up his seat and his return on investment was appallingly low.

"Not wasting any time, I see," Shane said. A scent as familiar as her own lit up every cell of her body.

"Gotta start somewhere. I kind of enjoyed the married life."

Shane grinned, that crooked line that she saw now was so like Jack's. Not just sexy and carnal, but knowing. It certainly knew her.

"You know this guy?" TDS asked, affronted.

"I have no idea who he is," Cara said, unable to tear her eyes away from the man she knew she would love until her last breath.

His shoulders, those annoyingly broad shoulders, relaxed, smiled even. He thrust out his hand to her. "I'm Shane and I'm an idiot. I make pastry for a living and I happen to be related to Jack Kilroy."

A tangle of hope and nerves duked it out in her chest. She grasped his hand, that warm, male grip that never failed to make her feel safe.

"I'm Cara and I'm a recovering perfectionist. I manage like nobody's business and I also happen to be related to Jack Kilroy."

"Small world. Do you mind if I?" Releasing her hand, he gestured to the tight square foot of space between her bar stool and the next occupied one.

Do you mind if I? As if that had ever stopped him. Gentleman in charge.

"Sorry to have taken up your time," she said to TDS, who was already skimming a look over his shoulder, alert for less troublesome possibilities. With a shrug, he swaggered off.

Shane grasped the bar rail and held her gaze. She waited for the charm and blarney to come flowing like honey out of his gorgeous mouth.

After a long moment of pinning her to the stool with those eyes as dark as a decadent chocolate ganache, he said, "I lied. About something incredibly important, but it wasn't just a lie to you or to Jack. It was a lie to myself. You've no idea how long I've denied who I was and what I needed." His Adam's apple bobbed with his emotion.

She had some idea. If anyone could understand the weight of a secret, the burden of denial, it was she. But she had been honest with him as soon as her heart allowed and now she compelled the treacherous muscle to cooperate in the face of Shane's anguish. His pain rolled through her, all the more sharp because of his strength in healing her these last few weeks. He had been her rock and it hurt not to touch him.

"Lili said you knew for years," she pushed out. "Since you were a kid."

He nodded. "It was complicated. I hated Jack because he wasn't around. Because I was left with my father when I could have been with my brother, which is completely irrational because Jack didn't even know I existed. And if he had, he wasn't going to take on some kid he didn't know from the back of beyond. He hated John Sullivan and I assumed he would hate me if he knew me, so I got busy hating him first."

Something clicked in her muddled brain, snatches of the pain he had confided in her mixed up with an accusation he had thrown at Jack during his come-clean in Chicago.

"The forgiveness your father was looking for when he was ill? It was from Jack, wasn't it?"

He nodded slowly, the hurt incised on his handsome face.

Oh God, how that must have crushed him. To have survived what he did only to have this cruel, sick man no longer recognize the son he had almost destroyed and seek absolution from the one who'd had a lucky escape. She could see now how confusing it must have been for him. Needing to find that connection with Jack despite all the resentment he felt toward him. Tears stung the backs of her eyelids, but letting go would be too self-serving.

"Shane, I'm so sorry," she managed to whisper.

"I know you are, Cara," he said, and she hoped he truly did. "Despite all the shit with my father, I still wanted to meet Jack. To be sure, you know?"

She nodded.

"I expected he'd be an arrogant dickhead—"

"Well, he is."

He laughed, the sound more sad than amused. "Yeah, he is, but I liked him. I wanted to keep on hating him, but I couldn't. And then I fell for the whole lot of you and I wanted to be part of your family."

"So you just wanted to get close to Jack? To the rest of the DeLucas?" She could feel a headache bursting behind her welling-up eyes.

His smile was grim. "No, that's not it. I'm not explaining myself very well. I had no intention of forcing myself into Jack's life. My plan was to satisfy my curiosity and move on after a couple of months. Meeting you, Cara, knowing you, changed me. It made me realize that I wanted it all. I didn't want to live on the outside anymore."

She knew the pain of that kind of longing. She still knew it. But then he threw it away when he ended their marriage without telling her.

"When were you going to tell me you signed the annulment papers? Congrats, we're no longer married, by the way."

His brow knitted. "After the day we spent together with the sick kids and at the park, I wanted to start fresh and move forward without all the baggage of Las Vegas. The only way was to give you the annulment you wanted but then we were spending all that time together, and you never brought it up. There we were, getting along like a house on fire, like we were actually married and liking it, but I'd signed the papers and ended our legal relationship. And that's all it was. Just words on a piece of paper. What matters is what we felt that night and how we built on it for the last six weeks."

He moved closer and gentled her jaw.

"I can't change what happened, Cara. I know I screwed up. I should have told Jack sooner. I should have come clean with both of you."

Yes, he should have, but she could see why keeping it in was easier. We fool ourselves into holding onto the pain because the alternative—that we might get too used to days without it—would likely drive us mad with hope.

She sucked in a ragged breath. "Tell me why you said yes, Shane. I have to know." The thought that something so randomly chaotic had laid siege to her life was too difficult for her to comprehend. She knew why she asked him. He made her feel. Surely he knew why he said yes.

He held her face with both hands, his touch so agonizingly gentle that she trembled.

"Cara, my beautiful Cara. Have you any idea what you did to me that night? That you destroyed me the minute you walked through that door? I said yes because I'd found something unexpected. A woman who seemed to have this off-center relationship with everyone around her, but who had a laugh that warmed me from the inside out. This girl who should not be giving someone like me the time of day, but who made funny noises at my stupid jokes, held my hand like she meant it, and made me wish I could be man enough to deserve her."

His hands slid to her shoulders and he touched his forehead to hers.

"Jack is the reason I walked into your life, Cara, but you're the reason I stayed."

Her heart beat so erratically that she worried she might die. Just fall down dead on the spot. "Oh."

He looked offended at her underwhelming response. "Yeah, oh. Sure I sobered up and realized that what we did that night was hovering on the city limits of Crazy Town but I never forgot the feeling. Every time I was with you, I got that feeling. This gut pinch telling me it wasn't a mistake. It was supposed to happen. We were supposed to happen."

She knew that feeling. She had embraced it that night, the magic and freedom of acting on a wild impulse because it felt right. She had embraced it, and fought it, for the last six weeks, undergoing more highs and lows than the bar in a limbo contest. There had been ecstasy and pain, but through it all she had felt alive.

"You should have told me later. Over movie night," she said, unable to dampen the thrill she felt that he had somehow managed to turn this around. That blarney-talking peatbog dweller.

"Ah, so that's it. You're just annoyed because I didn't

spill my secrets. Women always have to know everything."
He smiled, both heartbreaking and sexy at once. "If I had
told you first, you would have insisted I tell Jack. I wasn't
ready. That kind of realization takes time."

Didn't she know it. She had waited thirty years to come
to hers and when it came to life-changing epiphanies, Cara
DeLuca had Shane Doyle beat six ways from Sunday. There
was no way in hell she was going back to old, unhealthy,
controlling Cara. New, healthy, a little bit wild Cara had so
much more to recommend her. She should wear teal more
often.

She slid off the bar stool. "How are those boots feeling?"

He looked down at his weathered boots, ones that had
taken him all over the world and brought him home to her.

"I've been wearing them all day but that's never stopped
me. How about those heels?"

She flexed her right foot, beautifully clad in a strappy
bronze sandal. "Not bad. I think I could make it a few hundred feet." Closing her eyes, she held out her hand.

A few, interminable seconds ticked by, but then warmth
flooded her as he curled his fingers around hers and joined
their palms together. Heat flared through her body and fired
all her neurons. *Ping, ping, ping. This is what happened that
night.*

This is what's happening now.

Jack had told her to open her mind, but she was Cara
DeLuca—Lemon Tart, Miss Recovering Perfect, zombie
apocalypse leader-in-waiting—and she could go one better.
She opened her eyes to color and joy and Shane's smile. She
opened her heart to love.

He drew her into him and enveloped her in his strong,
safe arms. "Do you feel it, LT?"

"Yes," she whispered against the sensual curve of his

lips. "I do." There she went again with marriage on the brain.

He raised her chin with his fingertips and stared into her eyes, all intense and romantic. "How drunk are you?"

"Absolutely hammered." On lust, on love, on life. She hooked her hand behind his neck and let her fingers play through his overlong hair. "I love you, Shane."

"Ah, sure don't I love you, gorgeous?"

His kiss turned her bones to jelly and she thanked her stars he was holding her fast through her pleasure-drunk haze. Once he had let her come up for air, he tipped an imaginary hat brim and delivered a cowboy squint.

"I do believe it's time to take a stroll with my good lady and see all the purty lights."

His American accent was terrible, but that was okay. Underneath it all, he had an even sexier one and a heart bigger than anyone she knew.

EPILOGUE

It was the most beautiful wedding cake Shane had ever seen—and tasted. After all, he had made it and he was a damn fine pastry chef.

He turned to the blonde bombshell by his side, who was doing a poor job of pretending she wasn't interested in the slice of sweetness adorning the fine china plate before him.

"LT, if you want some, just say so." Predictably, she had skipped the pasta course, but the chicken entrée, not plain but seasoned with a white wine and caper sauce, had met with her approval. Baby steps.

She rolled her eyes affectionately. "Oh, okay then. Just a bite."

With almost ritualistic care, he cut into the triangle of pineapple mascarpone and only when he was satisfied he had an appropriate frosting-to-cake ratio did he raise it to her mouth. Those lush lips parted, and she swiped her pretty pink tongue over them. Slowly.

"Stop it," he murmured.

"Stop what?"

She was determined to kill him. "You know what. Now do you want the cake or not?"

She opened that pert, sensuous mouth, accepted his offering, and licked her full, pink lips. He groaned. Shane went back and forth about his favorite Cara body parts, but her lips were definitely top three today.

"Whatcha think? Does it meet your exacting standards?"

"Not bad," she said around her chewing. "Should have gone with the Bella Donna, though."

Of course she would want the masterpiece inspired by her. He looked over to his brother, who was leading his bride in a spin around the dance floor, having just narrowly avoided Maisey and Dennis-the-extern. Jack danced better than he sang, which wasn't saying much.

"Unfortunately, the clients get to have some say in the matter, woman. You're going to have to get used to that."

"Freaking clients. Always gumming up the works." Leaning in, she swiped at his lip and dipped her thumb in her mouth. Jesus, that mouth. "At least I'll have you on hand to charm our future clients' socks off with that sexy brogue."

He grinned. "I'm supposed to be making orgasm-producing cakes, but if I must be trotted out like a sex puppet to sweet talk Chicago's cougar matriarchs and hot brides, I suppose I can suffer under those work conditions."

The details were still being sketched out, but DeLuca Doyle Special Events was expected to be up and running by the end of the summer. Working with his ex-wife, a marital status he hoped to rectify very soon, was more than he could ever have hoped for and he'd have the best of both worlds as he planned to stay on at Sarriette part-time.

"Centerpieces turned out well," Cara said, gesturing with her fork to his sugar sculpture of an Amazonian brunette clad in red, blue, and gold, capturing a man with her lasso. The happy couple had enjoyed that reference to their first meet immensely. Neither had it escaped Shane's notice that a couple of the pieces were already missing from other tables. Well, he'd won awards.

"That reminds me...don't move an inch." He hopped up and strode purposefully to the bar. Once back at the table, he placed a large white cardboard box before his puzzled woman. "Planner's got to have some perks."

With an abundance of caution, she flipped up the lid while he unhooked the interlocked side flaps so she wouldn't have to take it out and risk destroying the delicate work. He wanted to ensure no breakage so she got the full effect.

She turned to him, her eyes shiny. "Shane, it's beautiful."

"I thought you might like a souvenir of the last couple months, apart from the Vegas souvenir of a hot ex-husband." He gestured to the first figure on the sugary carousel: a man lying prostrate with a cool, elegant blonde standing over him in victory, her gravity-mocking heel flat on his chest. "Our wedding."

Her lips twitched. "This makes me look like a big game hunter and you look like the spoils."

"Shot through the heart, LT." The next set portrayed a line-dancing couple complete with boots and cowboy hats. "Our first date."

She sighed. "Funny how you're standing tall and proud and I'm hunched over like I might fall down any minute."

"Reality bites, Cara. If you want to prove me wrong, I can always chat with the DJ and get some country going. You could show us your killer moves."

She giggled. "These people aren't ready for the likes of me."

The rest of the sculptures covered further momentous

chapters in their story so far: the motorcycle ride that night she told him about her anorexia and they made love for the first time, Shane's painful conversation with a muddy field, the cover of Jack and Tony's cookbook (the detail for that one was a bitch). He had also created a strikingly close rendition of Vegas the cat.

"You've even got little Evan," she said, her finger gingerly touching the infant cradled in the arms of a blonde beauty.

"Not Evan. That's a memory we haven't made yet."

She blinked and looked at him, then back at the sculpture.

His heart expanded in his chest, pumping blood to everywhere that needed it. "I meant what I said, Cara. I want a child with you. In fact, I want a whole brood of little Paddys and Colleens and I'd rather not wait."

He hoped he hadn't overstepped the mark. He'd gladly hop on the next flight to Vegas but he knew Cara would need time to plan something she had been jonesing for since she was a little girl. At least she wouldn't have to buy a new dress; Lili had vowed that once she hit the honeymoon suite upstairs, she would pack up their mother's gown carefully to pass on to her sister. A new DeLuca tradition. Waiting a year to call Cara his wife—again—would be excruciating but if he had his child on the way, he might just about manage to bear up.

"With the new business..." She hesitated and looked at the sculpture again. "How would we find the time?"

"Come here to me, darlin'," he said and pulled her into his lap. She curled into the crook of his neck, fitting him so well he sighed at the perfection of it all.

"Have I told you how much I love these shoulders?" He lay soft, feathery kisses along the round of one of her gorgeous, creamy-gold shoulders.

Her expression was skeptical, but patient. By now, she was used to his winding way of explaining things. "You might have mentioned it."

"How they curve and slope and drive me crazy with lust?"

"You're lusting after my shoulders?"

"I am, but almost as important as being the objects of my crazed lust, they're also the strongest shoulders I've ever seen," he said. "You could lift sacks of potatoes on those shoulders."

"Shane..."

"No, listen up. They have to be strong because you're carrying the weight of the world on them. I'm here to tell you to let them just be beautiful once in a while." He kissed her slow and sweet, only unlocking his lips when she answered with a throaty moan.

"Now, look around you."

She scanned the ballroom, and he followed her gaze, drinking in the sight of his new family cutting loose. Tony and Francesca, Sylvia and Tad, Jules and Evan, Jack and Lili, even Uncle Aldo, who had flown in from Florence and got busy pinching as many plump arse cheeks as he could find. Two days ago, Shane had held Cara's hand while she shared with her parents the CliffNotes version of what she had suffered as a teen and a young woman. There had been waterworks and hugs and not one scintilla of judgment. The DeLucas were top people.

But his girl would always be hardest on herself, letting doubts about her suitability for motherhood beat her down. He was here to tell her she was Cara DeLuca, soon to be Doyle, and she had this.

"You're going to make an amazing mum, Cara, and remember, you don't have to do it on your own. You're a daughter, a sister, a niece, an aunt. Everyone loves you and will bend over backward to support you. Be my partner, my wife, the mother of my children, the love of my life. Let's take care of each other and build the life we always dreamed of."

She sniffed and her sapphire-blue eyes filled with teary love. "You're far too young to be so wise, Shane Doyle."

He thought about everything he had gone through, some of it his fault and some of it not. How they had both preferred silent endurance to sharing their pain with the people they loved. His girl wasn't easy, but she was amazing and if she wasn't ready for this, he'd wait. He wouldn't give up because she was worth it, and not giving up made him worthy of her love. That last line of Bob Marley's quote had come to him in the shower this morning, the one that had eluded him for a while.

Truth is, everybody is going to hurt you; you just gotta find the ones worth suffering for.

Opposing arguments fought the good fight on her face. Cara thought too much but that was one of the things he loved about her. The small crease between her brows vanished with a deep breath, and he imagined it affirming her decision and pushing away her doubts.

"On one condition."

"Anything."

"We start now." Those kissable lips curved up and she jumped to a stand. "We've got to beat Jack and Lili to the baptism font."

"Competitive? I like the way you think."

"And the kids will have Italian names. Giancarlo, if it's a boy. Sophia, if it's a girl. You're a DeLuca now."

Not just a DeLuca, but a Kilroy, too. Man, he was one lucky son-of-a-bitch. He stood and held out his hand. "Come on, then. Sylvia already told me those eggs of yours aren't getting any younger."

Whether her disapproving head shake was directed at his insolence or the crassness of her indiscreet aunt, he couldn't be sure. Grasping the waistband of his new monkey suit, she pulled him toward her. He had only agreed to wear it if he could also rock the Lucchese "Mad Dog" Iguana Lizard cowboy boots she had bought for him as an annulment gift. His ex-wife had marvelous taste.

Her gaze dipped to the slit that split the ankle-length dress to her thigh. Hot in pink, sexy as hell, every inch of her his.

"Good thing I chose the bridesmaids' dresses. Ready-made straddle mode should make the bike ride easier."

Drawing her flush to his rapidly hardening body, he extracted a hotel key card from his pocket. "Can't wait that long."

She rubbed her hip against him, exacerbating an already tricky situation. If he didn't get her between crisp, cool sheets *tout de suite*, this wedding would be remembered for more than the stunning centerpieces.

"Always ready to go, aren't you?" she asked in that serene tone he knew masked one fiery, passionate woman.

"Always ready for you, gorgeous."

Beautiful Lili DeLuca is too busy working at her family's restaurant to follow her own dreams...until she meets sexy chef Jack Kilroy. Can he convince her to realize her own ambitions—and turn up the heat in his kitchen?

Please see the next page for a preview of *Feel the Heat*.

CHAPTER 1

She should have been safely ensconced in the apartment above her family's restaurant, scarfing down leftover pasta and catching up on the reality show glut bursting her DVR. Instead, Lili DeLuca was considering a three A.M. stealth mission down a dark alley, wearing shiny, blue Lycra hot pants and a star-bangled bustier. As ideas went, this one was as smart as bait.

Peeling off her Vespa helmet, she sent a longing look up to her bedroom window, then peered once more into the alley leading to the kitchen entrance of DeLuca's Ristorante. The door was still propped open. Light still streamed out into the night. Brightness had never looked so wrong.

A busy Damen Avenue could usually be relied upon to assure an unaccompanied woman that she was not alone. Wicker Park, formerly a low-income haven for underfed artists and actors-slash-baristas, had grown into a dense jungle of expensive lofts, chic eateries, and chichi wine bars. Between those, O'Casey's Tap on the corner, and the regular influx of suburbanite good-timers, the streets were always full and safe.

But not tonight.

The bars had dribbled out their last drunks an hour ago and by now, the 708ers were snoring soundly on their sleep number beds back in the 'burbs. Despite the stifling ninety-degree June heat, her neighborhood had never appeared so stark and cold. Living so close to work might have its perks, such as a thirty-second commute and the best Italian food in Chicago, but it was hard to see the upside in the face of that damn kitchen door, open like a gaping maw.

Maybe it was Marco. Her ex liked to use her family's business as his personal playpen, adamant that his invest-ment accorded him certain privileges. A bottle of expensive Brunello here. A venue for an after-hours poker game there. Even a chance to impress, with his miserable culinary skills, the latest lithe blonde he was wearing. He'd cooked for Lili once. His linguine had been as limp as his...

Sloughing off those memories, she refocused on her cur-rent problem. Six hours ago, the Annual Superhero Extrav-aganza had seemed like a harmless way to rehabilitate her social life and get out there (oh, how she hated *there*). Guilt-ing her into living was a favorite pastime of Gina's, and her cousin had persuaded her to attend with honeyed words.

Time to get back in the game, Lili. No, your thighs don't look like sides of beef in those shorts. The Batman with the wandering digits? He's not fat; he's just husky.

A husky Batman might come in handy right about now.

Leaving behind the safe hum of traffic, she crept toward the door. The garbage stench stung her nostrils. Something furry scurried behind one of the Dumpsters. A raucous riff from the Rolling Stones' "Brown Sugar" swelled and filled the space around her. Insanity had its own soundtrack.

You might be dressed like Wonder Woman, but that doesn't mean you should play the hero. Just take a look and then call someone.

She sneaked a peek around the door. Expensive kitchen equipment—*her* equipment—lay strewn with serving dishes, pots, and pans on the countertops. Renewed alarm streaked through her. This didn't look like the handiwork of Marco, who thought a *bain marie* was the name of a girl he'd like to date.

So much for the plausible explanation. Some shithead was burglarizing her restaurant to the strains of Jagger and Richards.

The next move should have been obvious, but her cinder block feet and racing brain warred all the same. Call someone. *Anyone.* Her father. Her cousin. That cute chocolate-brown-eyed cop who stopped in for takeout on Fridays and insisted she give him a buzz at the first scent of trouble. She swallowed hard, desperate to stop her heart from escaping through her throat. It settled for careening around her chest like a pinball.

A cautious sniff returned an astringent blast of bleach that competed with the lingering basil aroma of Friday night's dinner service. Trembling, she nestled her camera, an eight-hundred-dollar Leica, inside her Vespa helmet, then squeezed her phone out of the tight pouch at the side of her shorts. She started to dial. *Nine. One...*

Her twitchy finger paused on hearing something more eerie than heart-stopping. From inside the walk-in fridge, a voice bounced off the stainless-steel interior. High-pitched. Indeterminate gender. Singing at the top of its lungs. It was also completely out of tune.

She pulled open the screen door and quietly stepped inside. Damn feet had never known what was good for them.

Frantically, she searched for a weapon, and her gaze fell gratefully on the cast-iron frying pan resting on the butcher's block. She swapped it out for her helmet, appreciating how the new heft almost worked to stop her hand from shaking. Almost. Her blurred and frankly ridiculous reflection in the fridge's stainless steel should have given her pause; instead it emboldened her. She was dressed for action. She could do this.

Rounding the walk-in's door, she took stock of the enemy in a millisecond. Built like a tank, his back was turned to her as he reached up to the top shelf for a container of her father's ragu. For the briefest of seconds, the incongruity gnawed at her gut. A tone-deaf, ragu-stealing brigand? So it didn't exactly gel, but he was in her restaurant.

In the middle of the night.

Any hesitancy to act was wiped away by his stutter-step backward and the corresponding spike in her adrenaline. She hurled the pan and allowed herself a gratifying instant to confirm his head got the full brunt. Wolfish howl, check. Then she slammed the door shut on his thieving ass.

It had been quite a nice ass, too.

Good grief, where had that come from? It must be a relief because a drooling appreciation of criminal hot stuff was so not appropriate. She loosed a nervous giggle, then covered her mouth like she could smother that wicked thought along with her chuckle. Naughty, naughty.

Now what, shiny shorts? Time to call in the cavalry, but as she pulled out her phone, another thought pierced her veil of giddy triumph. By now, Fridge Bandit should have been making a fuss or bargaining for his freedom, yet a full minute had passed with not a peep.

Confident that the broken safety release on the walk-in's interior would keep him at bay, she laid her head and hands flush to the cool fridge door. Somewhere behind her, the music's boom-boom bassline meshed with the walk-in's mechanical hum. Both now vibrated through her body while the thump-thump of her heart tripped out a ragged beat.

Still nothing from within that cold prison. New horror descended over her.

She had killed him.

Fortunately or perhaps, unfortunately, the panic of that dread conclusion was dislodged by the fridge door's sudden jerk outward, sending Lili into a rather graceless meet-cute with the kitchen floor. Butt first, of course.

So someone had fixed that safety lock, then.

Her former comrade, the frying pan, emerged like a mutant hand puppet, soon followed by a wrist and a hairy arm before the whole package materialized. Vaguely, something big, bad, and dangerous registered in her mind. He held the pan aloft to ward off any imminent attack, but he needn't have worried. Still grounded, super powers severely diminished, she blinked and focused. Then she wished she hadn't bothered as the tight knot of fear unraveled to a cold flood of embarrassment.

"Jesus Christ, you could have bloody killed—" Fridge Bandit said. His mouth dropped open. Scantily clad superheroes flat on their butts often have that effect.

Thick, black hair, green eyes flecked with gold, and a face straight out of a Renaissance painting were his most obvious assets. Lili postponed the full-body browse because she knew she was in trouble.

It was *him*.

He touched the back of his head, a not-so-subtle reminder of her transgression, and placed the pan down with all the care of someone disposing of a loaded weapon. His casual wave at the countertop behind her cut the music abruptly.

Probably a skill he had acquired during an apprenticeship with the dark side of the Force.

"You all right, sweetheart?" he asked in the casual tone of one who doesn't really care for the answer. He pocketed an iPod remote and made a halfhearted move toward her. She held up the *I'm okay* hand. *Too late, buster.*

Lowering her eyes to check the girls, she exhaled in relief. No nip slips. She jumped to her feet, surreptitiously rubbed her sore rump, then cast a glance down to her red, knee-high Sandro boots for inspiration. Nothing doing.

You're wearing a Wonder Woman costume and you just went all-out ninja on one of the most famous guys in the Western hemisphere.

At last, she raised her eyes to his face, now creased in a frown.

"I'm Jack."

"I know who you are."

Lili figured anyone sporting a painted-on outfit like she was probably had, oh, a ten-second ogle coming her way. Her ego might have taken a shot along with her behind, but she knew she had started the evening looking pretty darn good. Hell, four out of five flabby-muscled Supermen at the party had thought so. With her overweight teens firmly in the past, she'd since embraced her size fourteen figure, and on the days she felt less than attractive—for every woman suffered days like those—she had enough friends telling her to own it, girl, revel in those curves.

So here she stood, owning and reveling, while simultaneously forging a somewhat unorthodox path for feminism with her own leering appraisal.

Jack Kilroy's extraordinarily handsome mug was already branded into her brain. Not because she was a fan, heaven forbid, but because her sister, Cara, was constantly babbling about its perfection, usually while nagging everyone she knew to watch the cooking show she produced for him, *Kilroy's Kitchen*. (Monday nights at seven on the Cooking Channel—don't forget, Lili!) A hot-as-a-griddle Brit, his star had risen in the last year, first with his TV show, then with his bestseller *French Cooking for the Rest of Us*. And when not assailing the public with the sight of his chiseled good looks on food and lifestyle magazines, he could invariably be found plying his particular brand of brash foodie charm on the daytime talk show circuit. He wasn't just smokin' in the kitchen, either. Recently, a contentious break-up with a soap star and a paparazzi punch-up had provided delicious fodder for the tabloids and cable news outlets alike.

The camera might add ten pounds, but in the flesh, Jack Kilroy was packing the sexy into a lean six-and-change frame. The matching set of broad shoulders didn't surprise her, but apparently the tribal tattoo on his right bicep did, judging by the shiver dancing a jig down her spine. It seemed so not British and just a little bit dangerous. Her gaze was drawn to his Black Sabbath T-shirt, which strained to contain what looked like extremely hard, and eminently touchable, chest muscles. Sculpted by years of lugging heavy-duty stockpots, no doubt. A pair of long legs, wrapped in blue jeans that looked like old friends, completed the very pleasant image.

Jack Kilroy was proof there was a God—and she was a woman.

"Is that your usual MO? Frying pan first, questions later?" he asked after giving her the anticipated once-over. He had used up his ten seconds while she had stretched her assessment to fifteen. Small victories. "Should I hold still and let you use your lasso to extract the truth from me?" He gestured to the coil of gold-colored rope hanging through a loop on her hip. If he expected her to act impressed by his knowledge of the Wonder Woman mythology, he'd be a long time waiting.

Maybe she was a little impressed.

"I thought you were stealing. I was about to call the police."

"You're telling me there's something worth stealing around here?"

Her body heated in outrage at his dismissive tone, though it could just as easily be down to the way his dark emerald eyes held hers. Bold and unwavering.

"Are you kidding? Some of this equipment has been in my family for generations." Right now, most of it had been pulled out from under the counters and was scattered willy-nilly on every available surface. "Like my *nonna's* pasta maker." She pointed to it, sitting all by its dusty lonesome on a countertop behind a rack of spices.

"That rusty old thing in the corner?"

"That's not rusty. It's vintage. I thought you Brits appreciated antiques."

"Sure, but my appreciation doesn't extend to food-poisoning hazards."

A protest died on her lips. Her father hadn't used that pasta maker in over ten years, so a zealous defense was probably unnecessary.

"So either I'm being punked or you're Cara's sister. Lilah, right?"

"Yes, Cara's sister," she confirmed, "and it's Lil—"

"I thought you were the hostess," he cut in. "Are frying pans the new meet-and-greet in Italian restaurants?"

It's three in the morning, she almost screamed. Clearly, the blow to his skull had impacted his short-term memory.

On cue, he rubbed his head and then gripped the side of the countertop with such knuckle-whitening intensity that she worried he might pass out.

"I'm the restaurant's manager, actually, and I wasn't expecting you. If I'd known *Le Kilroy* would be gracing us with his exalted presence, I would have rolled out the red carpet we keep on hand for foreign dignitaries."

She sashayed over to the ice cabinet and glanced back in time to catch him, his gaze fixed to her butt like he was in some sort of trance. Oh, brother, not even a whack to the head could throw this guy off his game. With a couple of twists, she crafted an ice pack with a napkin, and handed it to him. "How's your head?"

"Fine. How's your—" He motioned in the direction of her rear with one hand while gingerly applying the ice pack with the other.

"Fine," she snapped back.

"I'll say," he said, adding a smirk for good measure. *Oh, for crying out loud.*

"Is that *your* usual MO? I can't believe you have so much success with the ladies." The gossip mags devoted pages to his revolving-door dating style. Only Hollywood fembots and half-starved models need apply. They clearly weren't in it for the food.

For her insolence, she got a blade of a look, one of those condescending ones they teach in English private schools, which for some ridiculous reason they called public schools.

"I've had no complaints."

She folded her arms in an effort to project a modicum of gravitas, which was mighty difficult considering what she was wearing. It didn't help that every breath took effort in her sweat-bonded costume. "So, care to explain?"

"What? Why I've had no complaints?"

"I mean, what you're doing in my family's restaurant at this ungodly hour."

"Oh, up to no good. Underhanded misdoings. Waiting for a superhero to take me down."

Okay, ten points for cute. She battled a smile. Lost the fight. Palms up, she indicated he should continue and it had better be good.

"I'm doing prep and inventory for the show. Didn't Cara tell you?"

Of course she hadn't told her. That's why she was asking, dunderhead. "I haven't checked my messages," she lied, trying to cover that she had and her sister hadn't deigned to fill her in. "I was busy all evening."

"Saving cats from trees and leaping tall buildings in a single bound, I suppose."

"Wrong superhero, dummy," she said, still ticked off that Cara had left her out of the loop. "You haven't explained why you're doing this prep and inventory *here*." It seemed pointless to remind him of the lateness of the hour.

"Because this is where we'll be taping the show, sweetheart. Jack Kilroy is going to put your little restaurant on the map."

* * *

Good thing Laurent had stepped out because if he'd caught Jack referring to himself in the third person, he'd laugh his *derrière* off. That shit needed to stop. It was worth it, though, just to get this reaction. Wonder Woman's mouth fell open, giving her the appearance of an oxygen-deprived goldfish.

"Here? Why would you want to tape your stupid show here?"

Jack let the comment slide, though the snarky dig about his success with women had been irksome enough. Rather hypocritical too considering all that hip swaying and lady leering in his general direction.

"Believe me, it's not by choice. This place is far too small and some of the equipment is much too . . . *vintage* for what I need."

Contrary to his comment about the size and age of the kitchen, Jack felt a fondness bordering on nostalgia. The nearest stainless-steel counter was scuffed and cloudy with wear, the brushed patina a testament to the restaurant's many successful years. He loved these old places. There was something innately comforting about using countertops that had seen so much action.

Returning his gaze to Cara's sister, he speculated on how enjoyable it might be to hoist her up on the counter and start a little action right here and now. That costume she was poured into had cinched her waist and boosted her breasts like some comic-book feat of structural engineering, creating an hourglass figure the likes of which one usually didn't see outside of a sixties-style burlesque show. A well-packaged, fine-figured woman with an arse so sweet he was already setting aside fantasy time for later. His head throbbed, but the lovely sight before him was the perfect salve.

As intended, his "too small" and "vintage" comments set her off on another round of fervent indignation. The wild hand gestures, the hastily sought-for jibes, the churning eyes. Beautiful eyes, too, in a shade of blue not unlike curaçao liqueur, and with a humorous glint that had him trying not to smile at her even though he was incredibly pissed off at what she'd done. A woman—a very attractive woman—in an agitated state got him every time.

"This kitchen is not too small. It's perfect." She jabbed her finger at the burners and ovens lining the back wall. "We get through one hundred and fifty covers every Saturday night using this *tiny* kitchen, and we don't need the Kilroy stamp of approval. We're already on the map."

"I never said tiny, but I'm full of admiration for how you've utilized the limited space."

That earned him a response somewhere between a grunt and a snort followed by a surprise move toward a heavy stand mixer. Surely, she wasn't going to start clearing up? He put a placating hand on her arm.

"Hey, don't worry. I'll put everything back the way I found it."

She glanced down at his hand resting on her golden skin. By the time her eyes had made the return trip, she was shooting sparks. *Back off.* Hooking a stray lock behind her ear, she returned to her task—clean up his mess and make him look like an arse. A cloud of unruly, cocoa-brown hair pitched forward, obscuring her heart-shaped face and giving her a distinct lunatic vibe.

It would take more than a death stare and a shock of crazy curls to put him off. Teasing her was too much fun. "I'm pretty fast, love, and if you can move with superhero speed, we'd get it done in a jiffy."

Another push back of her hair revealed a pitying smile. "Don't ever claim to be fast, Kilroy. No woman wants to hear that."

Ouch.

Before he could muster a clever retort, the kitchen doors flew open, revealing Cara DeLuca, his producer in full-on strut. Neither the crazy hour nor the mind-melting heat had stopped her from getting dressed to the hilt in a cream-colored suit and heels. Laurent, his sous chef and trusty sidekick, ambled in behind her with his usual indolence and a tray of takeout coffee.

Cara's sister grumbled something that sounded like "Kill me now."

Sibling drama alert. Unfortunately, with a younger sister determined to drive him around the bend, he was in a position to recognize the signs.

"Lili, what on earth are you wearing?" Cara gave a languid wave. "Oh, never mind."

Lili. He had called her *Lilah.* Lili was much better. Lilah sounded like someone's maiden aunt. This woman didn't look like anyone's maiden aunt.

Cara's eyes darted, analyzing the situation. His producer was nothing if not quick, which made her both good at her job and prone to snap judgments. The crew called her Lemon Tart, and not because she was sweet.

"Why are you holding your head like that?"

Jack cast a sideways glance at the sister. He wasn't planning to rat her out, but to her credit, she confessed immediately. In a manner of speaking.

"I thought it was that gang of classic-rock-loving, yet remarkably tuneless, thieves who have been pillaging Italian kitchens all over Chicago, and as I was already dressed for crime fighting, instinct just took over, and I tried to lock your star in the fridge."

Laughter erupted from deep inside him, although he was fairly positive she had just insulted his beautiful singing voice. A muscle twitched near the corner of her mouth. Not quite a smile, but he still felt the warm buzz of victory.

"Lili, you can't go locking the talent up in a fridge," Cara chided.

"Or hitting it on the head with a frying pan," Jack added.

Cara's head swiveled *Exorcist*-style back to her sister. "She did what?"

Jack rubbed the back of his head, heightening the drama. "I don't think she broke the skin, but there'll be a bump there later."

Cara caressed his noggin and yelped like a pocketbook pup. "Oh, my God, Lili, do you realize what could have happened if Jack had a concussion and had to go to the emergency room?"

"It might have improved his personality. He could do with a humility transplant," Lili offered, again with that cute muscle twitch that he suddenly wanted to lick.

Laurent had been suspiciously quiet but now he stepped forward, and Jack braced himself for the Gallic charm offensive. As usual, his wingman looked bed-head disheveled, sandy-colored hair sticking out every which way. His bright blue eyes twinkled in his friendly face as he launched into one of his patented gambits.

"*Bonjour*, I am Laurent Benoit. I work with Jack." It tripped off his tongue as *Zhaque*, sounding lazy and sexy and French. "You must be Cara's beautiful sister, Lili." He proffered his hand, and Lili hesitantly took it while the corners of Laurent's mouth hitched into a seductive grin. "*Enchanté*," he said, raising her hand to kiss it. This netted a husky laugh, which was a damn sight more than Jack had managed in the five minutes he had been alone with her. Man, that Frenchman was good.

"Now that's an accent I can get down with," Lili murmured.

Jack sighed. While his own British voice accounted for much of his success with American women, over the years he had lost more skirt to that French accent than he'd eaten bowls of *bouillabaisse*. Laurent—brilliant sous chef, occasional best friend, and his most rigorous competition for the fairer sex—was the embodiment of the French lover. As good as he was in the kitchen, his talents would be just as well-suited to tourism commercials. All he needed was a beret, a baguette, and a box of condoms.

Jack's head still hurt and weariness had set in bone-deep. He was sure he had lost consciousness for a few seconds in the fridge and now he battled the dizziness that threatened to engulf him. Coffee. That's what he needed. Coffee and something to focus on. Something that wasn't curvy and soft-looking and radiating man-killer vibes.

"Any chance we can get on with what we were doing?" he sniped at Cara, more brusquely than he'd intended.

"Of course, Jack, babe. We'll let you continue." Dragging her sister by the arm, Cara marched her out of the kitchen with a portentous, "Liliana Sophia DeLuca, a word in the office, if you please."

Laurent stood with arms crossed, staring at the scene of departing female beauty. Jack eyed his friend. *Here it comes.*

"I think I'm in love," Laurent groaned. "Is she not the cutest *chérie* you have ever seen?"

A laugh rumbled in Jack's chest. "That's the fourth time you've fallen in love this year and it's only June."

"But did you not see her cute little nose wrinkle up when I offered her my hand? And that lovely *derrière*. What I wouldn't do for a piece of that."

"She might have 'zee lovely *derrière*,' but she's got a dangerous bowling arm." His fingers returned to the spot where the frying pan had connected. A bump was definitely forming.

Jack followed Laurent's gaze to the swing doors through which Cara and her sister had just exited. A sudden image of brushing his lips against Lili's and watching the pupils of those lovely eyes magnify in passion flitted pleasantly through his mind. It wasn't long before his imagination had wandered to stroking her inner thigh and inching below the hem of those tight, blue, shiny shorts.

Things were just getting interesting when the crash of a dropped serving pan knocked him back to the present. While Laurent muttered his apologies, Jack blinked to quell his overactive brain, the pain in his head briefly forgotten. Maybe he should apply that ice pack to his crotch.

Evie, his dragon-lady agent, had been clear. *Think of the contract, Jack. Keep your head down and your nose clean. And whatever happens, do not engage the local talent.* Right now, that imminent network deal was the rocket that would propel his brand into the stratosphere. No more rinky-dink cable shit. Instead he would spread his message of affordable haute cuisine to as wide an audience as possible and garner fame for all the right reasons.

Which meant grasping women were an unnecessary distraction, even a tasty piece like Cara's sister. He needed to forget about smart-tart birds with eyes and curves that would lead a good man, or one who was trying to be good, off the straight and narrow. After his last disastrous relationship, he wasn't looking to screw around with the help, even if she did have the best *derrière* in the Midwest.

* * *

Lili trudged after Cara into the restaurant's back office, her focus on the platinum-blonde cascade that swished from her sister's ponytail. After three careful swipes of the swivel chair with a tissue from her purse, Cara sat, smoothing her cream silk skirt as she went.

"Nice costume," she said with a knowing smile. "Jack seemed to like it."

The absurdity of that statement canceled out the deceitful thrill Lili had felt while pinned by Jack Kilroy's assessing gaze. She'd been right not to trust it. A man like that—too good-looking, too charming, too *everything*—needed constant female attention to keep his ego afloat. Memories of her ex were still fresh: she'd been there, done that, bought the T-shirt.

Her long sweater hung on a hook inside the door, and she threw it on. "Have you seen Mom yet?"

Cara examined her nails, an avoidance tactic Lili immediately recognized because she was rather fond of using it herself. "I spoke to her on the phone. She sounds in good spirits. I was planning to drop over a gift later."

Lili bit back a catty response. Cara's ability to ignore the unpleasant was legendary and lately had become a source of ever-increasing resentment between them. Why bother to visit when nothing says "Congratulations on beating cancer, Mom" better than a fancy gift basket, delivered weekly like clockwork? It was too late, or maybe too early, for a sister-on-sister confrontation. Besides, there was something about all that fragile beauty of hers that made it impossible to hate her properly. Lili needed to change the subject, though it would probably take some sort of power tool to chisel off the sour look she knew was cemented on her face.

"Cara, you could have warned me about the British Invasion."

Her sister crossed her shapely legs and picked some imaginary fluff from her tulip-shaped skirt. Size zero or two, Lili was willing to bet, though she looked a little plumper than she had on visits past. Cara's thinness was both an object of envy and awe, and Lili wondered how her sister retained such a rigid grip on her self-control. Occasionally, Lili speculated that Cara's distinctly non-Italian attitude to food could mean just one thing: her sister must have been adopted. If only.

She shrugged in that don't-hate-me-'cause-I'm-beautiful way of hers. "I talked to Il Duce last night and he's on board."

Il Duce was the nickname for their father, coined to reflect his startling similarity to a certain Italian wartime dictator. Lili might be the de facto manager while her mother recovered, but her father was supreme ruler. She shouldn't have been surprised that he'd make an end run on this. Standard operating procedure.

Lili knew she hadn't hidden her hurt reaction in time by the way Cara quickly adopted a softer tone. "It's a once in a lifetime opportunity for the restaurant. Remember I told you we had Serafina's on Randolph lined up for the taping next week? Well, yesterday we find out they've had to close for health code violations. Rats!" She waved her hands in the air as if she'd seen the vermin with her own innocent eyes. "We were scrambling to find an alternative and I suggested our place to Jack. To be honest, Jack's really grateful Dad can help out."

In the five minutes Lili had spent with Jack Kilroy, gratitude was nowhere in evidence. In fact, he had acted like he was doing *them* the favor, though in reality, that wasn't too far from the truth. Her earlier braggadocio about DeLuca's healthy numbers couldn't disguise the trouble they were in, a perfect storm of external pressures and internal entrenchment. They were lucky to boast eighty covers on a Saturday, never mind the buck and a half she'd tossed out back in the kitchen. Week nights were practically a ghost town. Classical Italian dining wasn't quite in vogue anymore and as amazing as her father's food was, it was getting harder to compete with the hipper, trendier eateries that had popped up all over Wicker Park. Lili had ideas for taking their game to the next level. Lots of ideas. But her autocratic father refused to play ball.

"What do you think of him?" Cara asked, dragging Lili's thoughts reluctantly back to Jack Kilroy. "He gives good handsome, right?"

Lili gave a noncommittal shrug that did little to divest her shoulders of worry. Her sister had been drinking Jack Kilroy's Kool-Aid ever since her New York company, Foodie Productions, began handling his show back in January. It had been a real coup for Cara to get the gig, and to hear her sister speak, the future of mankind was riding on it. Though how someone who despised food made her living producing food television was one of life's great mysteries.

In the interests of sisterly peace, Lili decided to feign some interest. "So why is he cooking in someone else's restaurant and not in a studio like the other hack chefs you see on TV? I'm surprised Lord Studly would be caught dead in a place like this."

"On occasion, Lord Studly is happy to lower himself to the level of the great unwashed." That accented voice swept over her like cut crystal. It really should come with a government health warning.

She turned and got the full blast. Wow, if he wasn't the incarnation of sin-on-a-stick. Focus on the face, she told herself as her photographer eye drank in more details. A smattering of freckles dotted across his nose. A scar on his chin that was probably airbrushed out of magazine covers. And beautiful eyelashes, like silken, inky strands fringing his green eyes. Live-and-up-close Jack was much more impressive than small-screen Jack. She wondered how he might fare under her camera's gaze. Very well, she suspected.

Too late, she realized she was gawping, but funnily enough, he was gawping right back. Braining someone with cast-iron cookware was starting to look like a viable pick-up strategy. She drew the edges of her sweater closer together.

The scratchy brush of the wool heightened the new sensitivity of her skin, which felt like sunburn under Jack's ferocious gaze.

He blinked and held out her Vespa helmet. "Yours, I presume?"

She took it with a shaky hand, relieved to see her camera and phone were still safe inside. "Thanks," she muttered, wishing he didn't turn her into such a gloopy mess.

"You rode a motor bike in that getup?"

"A scooter, actually. What of it?"

"Just building a picture in my head."

Oh, for . . . never mind. She swiped all expression from her face. "The show?"

"Well," Cara said. "Here's the premise." She leaned forward as if she were making a pitch to a Hollywood producer. "It's a cooking contest pitting Jack against a host chef in a cuisine he's not so familiar with. Jack's specialty, of course, is French, so he's going up against other cuisines, preparing a brand-new menu and serving it to real restaurant customers. He'll be competing against Dad, and whoever gets the most votes wins. Simple, right? The show's brand new. It's called *Jack of All Trades* and DeLuca's is going to be on the premiere episode!"

Lili settled in against the desk and switched her attention to Jack, who lounged against the doorframe with an easy devil-be-damned grace that said he was above it all.

Her father had won awards—*Chicago Magazine*'s Best Italian, two years running, albeit over ten years ago—and chefs came from far and wide to learn the secrets of his gnocchi. He was the true kitchen genius, not this jumped-up limey who coasted on his charm and cheek bones. Time to get her game face on. Never too early to start the trash talking.

"So, not so hot at *la cucina Italiana,* then?"

He appeared to be thinking hard about that, so Cara jumped into the pause. "There's also a twist. Jack gets to pick his own appetizers and dessert, but Dad chooses the pastas and the entrées for both chefs. And doesn't tell Jack until the day of the contest."

Better and better. Lili could think of several dishes that could pose last-minute problems. This might be fun. Her gaze traveled the long, lean body of British Beefcake. This might be a whole lot of fun.

"Oh, you're going down," Lili said, then winced as she realized that could be interpreted as flirty. So not her intention, especially as she sucked soccer balls at flirty.

Evidently he hadn't got the memo because his face lit up with a traffic-stopping smile. He probably had a million risqué comebacks on tap but he let that killer smile do all the work. Seeing it in person made a girl feel incredibly lucky.

He moved into the cramped office, inching closer like a jungle cat stalking something small and defenseless. While she was in no way defenseless, and no one would ever have characterized her as small, there was still something rather daunting about how he filled a space. Especially a confined space. A flushing tingle spread through her body and her nipples tightened. Although he couldn't possibly have seen *that,* he cocked his head and considered her as if he had. As if her body's reaction to him was the only possible response to a smile that dangerous.

"You think I have something to worry about?" he said in a tone that made it clear he had this one covered, honey.

Irritation over her hormonal meltdown turned her surly. "Oh, yeah. My father's going to take you to the woodshed, Britboy."

A slight twitch appeared like an errant comma at the

corner of his no-longer-smiling mouth. "Don't worry, sweetheart. I think Britboy can cook a bowl of linguine and melt some mozzarella over a slab of veal. Italian's not the most challenging of cuisines, no offense to your father, and any restaurant would kill to be featured on my show. It's a guaranteed seat-filler for the next six months."

Apparently she didn't just suck soccer balls at flirty; she sucked spectacularly. The great Jack Kilroy had just dismissed her and her family's livelihood as no longer worthy of his inestimable attention, and boy, did that stick in her craw.

"If you think it's that easy, perhaps you should stop by for dinner tonight. I think you'll find my father can melt cheese to rival any idiot-box chef. Oh, a hotshot like you probably won't learn anything about food, but you might learn something about hospitality."

He opened his mouth to speak and then seemed to think better of it. Good call. Stepping around her, he thrust a piece of paper at Cara. "Here's what I need. I'll start testing dishes tomorrow." Pronouncement made, he stalked out of the office with all the flourish of a Shakespearean actor marching off stage.

Lili shook her head in disbelief. "I know he's your boss, Cara, but that guy's got some nerve walking in here and proclaiming Italian cuisine easy. And you should have heard him dissing the kitchen and our equipment. Just who does he think he is?"

Cara picked a speck of invisible dust off her low-cut blouse and tousled her perfect, platinum-blonde hair. "That, baby sister, is your birthday and Christmas presents all rolled up into one sexy, hunk-shaped package."

Taking her love life off the back burner, Jules Kilroy joins an online dating site. But her best friend, Tad DeLuca, can't stand the idea of *his* Jules with another man. Even if he gets burned, Tad vows to turn up the heat this time...

Please see the next page
for a preview of *Hot and Bothered*.

CHAPTER 1

Tad DeLuca ground his teeth so hard he risked bone dust shooting out of his ears.

"It needs a part," came the latest utterance from under the hood of the pizza oven. Four little words that signaled a screwing over of the major variety was about to take place. Compounding the insult, the speaker, complete with abundant ass cleavage and just-for-show tool belt, crawled out from behind the oven, butt first, and adjusted his waistband.

Too late, dude, you're already the clichéd repair guy who can't seem to find a pair of jeans—or a belt—to fit him.

"That's what you said last week," Tad said patiently. Really patiently. "You installed the..."

"Temperature regulator."

"Temperature regulator, and said that should be it."

Over the oven guy's head, the pizza oven loomed, mocking Tad's foray into the world of business ownership. Flatbreads were one of the cornerstones of his new wine bar menu—or had been—and now he was thinking about his backup plan. The nonexistent one. Of course, a chef was needed to cook the menu, and the notable lack of one since his new hire had upped and quit this morning was yet another problem that needed urgent attention. The joys of being his own boss.

"It's not the regulator this time. There's a—" He said something incomprehensible and Tad tuned out. Three semesters of engineering coursework under his belt didn't really qualify him to talk pizza oven repair shop, but maybe if he'd stuck around college longer, he'd be on more of a conversational footing here. Unfortunately, thinking about his college days inevitably led to thinking about how they ended, conjuring memories that scorched him fresh to this day.

"How long?"

Still in an ungainly squat, Oven Guy rubbed the back of his neck while he caught his serrated breath. "A week. More like two."

God *damn it*. The man's eyebrow shot up as if Tad had spoken that aloud. He hadn't, but the pulverized bone dust blasting from his ears might have given anyone pause.

In less than a week, he was slated to open Vivi's in trendier-by-the-second Wicker Park, just a stone's throw from his family's restaurant and old stomping ground, DeLuca's. Going from bartender to bar owner seemed like a logical progression but fate hadn't been on speaking terms with logic for a while. His first location choice had burned to the ground before he signed the lease. He had been outbid on the second. But now it was all systems go. The wine cellar was stocked with favorites, old and new. Publicity was in motion and staff was in training. The menu had been worked out with his chef—now his ex-chef.

It had taken him a while to get here. Years of dwelling

on his mistakes and making excuses to stay stock-still. Letting people down was second nature to him, but *this*—he looked around at the gleaming, polished surfaces of his new kitchen—would be his way back in. Making Vivi proud might get him there.

A menu of delicious snacks would definitely help.

"Penny for 'em, babe," Tad heard softly in his ear. "Or should I just tell you what's going on in that charming head of yours?"

Smiling away his irritation at how shitty the day had gone so far, Tad turned to greet the girl-next-door blonde who could make it all better. Hair in a Muppet topknot, dark circles under her green-gold eyes, her shirt shapeless and wrinkled over baggy desert camo pants rolled to just below her knees. If it were anyone else, he would guess she had just tumbled from a warm bed where she had been well and truly serviced. But this was Jules Kilroy, his best girl but not his girlfriend, and who, as far as he knew, had never been on a date—or anything more—in the two years he had known her.

The smart mouth upturn of her lips couldn't disguise how tired she looked. Neither did it detract from her pale, fragile beauty, which had him itching to wrap his body around her and gather her tight to his chest.

Instead of focusing on all the reasons why he wanted to protect her, which inevitably led to the reasons why that was a terrible idea, he moved his gaze back to the safer territory of that smirk. When Jules wore that look, it was easy to remember why they had become friends in the first place. They had connected the moment she showed up in his family's restaurant, knocked up, beat down, and in need of a pal.

Some pal he had been. He jerked his brain away from that thought and dialed up a friendly grin.

"You don't want to know what's going on in my head. It's a whirling cesspit of debauchery that would make your hair curl."

She gave a discreet chin nod to Oven Guy, who had once more descended to all-fours to poke around the appliance mechanics.

"You're thinking there's nothing more attractive than the sight of a generous arse peeking out of denim."

He'd always liked that word. *Arse.* Or really he liked the way Jules's lips shaped it. Her British singsong accent hadn't diminished one iota in the time she had lived in the States. It wasn't one of those regal voices that sounded like her mouth was filled with plums, either. It was a good-time girl voice. A little husky, the kind of rasp you might get from screaming above the boom-boom bass at a club the night before.

Which wasn't likely. Up until her baby bump had made her conscious about shaking her booty on the boards, they had been quite the team on the dance floor. Now she had her hands full with her eighteen-month-old, Evan. The kid was adorable but those circles under Jules's eyes confirmed he was also a handful.

His phone buzzed and he checked it discreetly, unable to hide his frown at the sight of the last person in the world he wanted to talk to. When he looked back at Jules, there was no missing the blatant curiosity on her face. Usually there was a more engaging proposition on the other end of the line and Jules liked to tease him about his flavor of the month. Sometimes, they lasted two.

She tilted her head and he waited for her to get warmed up. Rarely took long. "How's the washed-up ballerina?"

"Retired Olympic gymnast," he corrected, referring to the gamine hottie he had been seeing the week before and who had now been relegated to Tad's past tense.

"Still pulling out all the stops on the floor exercise?"

That drew a laugh from deep in his gut. Jules had quite the cheeky mouth, and he enjoyed immensely their back-and-forth.

"It didn't work out," he said sadly.

"Oh, the poor thing. Marked down by the Italian judge." A slender finger touched her lips. "Or maybe not as flexible in her old age. What was she? Eighteen, fifteen?"

"Twenty-two. They just look very young."

"Taddeo DeLuca, when are you going to settle down with a nice-ah, plump girl and make-ah da bambinos?" she sang in a terrible stage Italian accent. For good measure, she pinched his cheek, an unapologetic nod to his aunt Sylvia, who devoted her non-Mass time to matchmaking for her un-attached nieces and nephews.

In his head, the answer to the rhetorical question rang clear as the Liberty Bell. Give him freedom or give him death. Drag him to hell before he hitched his ass to a woman for the long haul.

On his lips, something more flippant hovered. Maybe a joke about how his Facebook fan base would never stand for it or how no one compared to the fair, green-eyed beauty standing before him, but she had already redirected her good humor.

At Oven Guy, who had pulled himself to a lumbering stand and was writing up his chit of can't-help-you-a-damn.

"Hi, there." Her bright grin became impossibly wider.

Visibly startled, the repairman ran thick fingers through his hair.

"Uh, hello," he offered cautiously.

"Looks like hard work," Jules said, her eyelashes flutter-ing. That's right, fluttering.

Juliet Kilroy did not have a flirty bone in her body. Not

once had he seen her even talk to a guy with any intention beyond ordering a diet Coke with lime in a bar. Of course, as long as he'd known her, she was either pregnant or mom to an obstreperous kid, so flirting was fairly low on her list.

But it sure looked like she was flirting now.

With Oven Guy.

"So two weeks to get that part?" She loosed a breathy sigh and chewed on her bottom lip. Oven Guy's cheeks flushed and he stood up a little straighter, and damn if Tad didn't blame him. That lip snag thing was very cute. And very sexy.

Defenseless in the face of Jules's charm assault, the man's hands fell into a distinct caress of his tool belt.

Jules looked down at the belt with wide-eyed innocence as if the notion of belt stroking and all it implied had only just occurred to her. Slowly, she returned her gaze with a slide up Oven Guy's body.

"What are you doing?" Tad asked her and then wished he hadn't because his voice registered more peevish than curious.

"Practicing," she said without taking her eyes of the non-repair guy. "You don't know how much we'd appreciate it if you could get that part sooner. The pizza needs of the masses must be appeased." Was it Tad's imagination or did her accent sound a little posher than usual?

"Practicing what?" Tad asked, no longer caring how put out he sounded.

Ignoring him, she kept her green-gold gaze trained on her target.

"I could probably put in a special order," Oven Guy said, his blush now saturating his hairline. "Have it in a couple days."

"Lovely man," she said with a fire-bright smile.

Lovely Man returned a shy grin and backed out of the kitchen, muttering something about calling with an update the next day.

"Sorted," Jules said, rubbing her hands together in satisfaction.

"What in the hell was that?" Tad asked.

"It's a well-known fact that honey gets the bee. Do you want your special part or not?"

If it meant he had to witness that display again, that would probably be a whopping great negative. There was no good reason why Jules fake-flirting with some guy should have bothered him, except that it had and that was reason enough.

"Thanks," he said, trying not to sound like a curmudgeon and failing.

"You're welcome." She folded her arms beneath her breasts, an action that molded the shapeless material to her figure in a way he should not be noticing. "Where's Long Face?"

That was the nickname she had given to Jordie the chef, who usually wore the lugubrious expression of a man with the weight of Krypton on his reedy shoulders. The bastard hadn't sounded all that sad when he called to quit this morning. Tad filled her in on his tale of woe, glad for the distraction and gratified when she made sympathetic noises in all the right places.

Moving her gaze around the room, she rocked that look where she wanted to say something, usually some criticism about how he was mistreating his latest woman or the fact that he drove too damn fast on his Harley. As well as being one of his closest friends, she was unafraid of playing annoying sister and nagging mother hen.

"Out with it," he said, eager to hear what she had to say.

Her smart-mouth take on his occasionally imperfect decision making was often the highlight of his day.

"No working pizza oven, no vittles, and a dining room about to be filled with the harshest critics known to man. You're in deep doo-doo, mate."

Shit. In all the excitement, he had forgotten to cancel the trial tasting of his now nonexistent small plates menu. Luckily, the impatient herd about to descend on his fledgling bar was his family and not Chicago's rapacious food cognoscenti.

He had planned trendy accompaniments to go with the extensive wine list. Duck rillettes. Porcini and shallot flat bread. The expected selection of artisanal cheese and charcuterie. Items that didn't require too much effort and absorbed healthy markups. He might expand the menu later but he didn't want to overextend himself starting out. For now, it was all about the wine—especially today when there was no hot food on offer.

At least there were cold cuts. He strode over to the prep station and uncovered a couple of platters.

"Here, make yourself useful, wench," he said to Jules. "Take this out to the horde."

* * *

"What do you mean he quit?"

Jules lifted her head at her brother's sharp tone. Jack was going with the dark and disapproving thing he used to great effect, and giving it an extra twist because he also happened to be an investor in Tad's business. Tad would have preferred to go it alone but it was either bring Jack on board or wait another three years to accumulate enough seed money. Sometimes dreams involved compromises. Didn't she know it.

Her brother, aka Jack Kilroy, was one of those incredibly

successful restaurateurs with a household name even Pygmy tribes in New Guinea had heard of. In the last couple of years, he'd scaled back his multinational food empire and eliminated his TV commitments to focus on his grand passions: his Chicago restaurant, Sarriette, the go-to foodie destination in the West Loop and his wife, Lili, who was also Tad's cousin.

"He was offered a job on a cruise ship," Tad was saying about Long Face, the AWOL chef. "The *idiota* wants to see the world. I hoped you could spare Derry for a few weeks while I work on getting someone else in."

Jack's forehead crimped. Lending Sarriette's sous-chef to Tad for a month was not trivial, and but for the fact Jack knew a good investment when he saw it, Jules suspected her brother wouldn't even cross the street to piss on her friend if he were on fire. There had always been an unpleasant tension between them.

"We'll sort something out," Jack said after a long beat. "So we're not eating, but what are we drinking?"

Tad twisted the bottle in his hand to face the rest of his audience—Lili, her sister, Cara, and Cara's Irish husband, Shane Doyle, who was also Jack's half brother on their father's side. Long story.

"Doggie!" Evan squirmed in Jules's arms, reaching for the bottle with a picture of a friendly overgrown terrier on the label. Her toddler was a touch obsessed with dogs lately. The label's letters leapfrogged over each other, making little sense to Jules's literacy-challenged brain. Dyslexia could be a real pain in the arse.

Tad launched into his wine spiel. "This is a Chilean Pinot. Plummy, lashings of fruit, full-bodied. Goes well with zin-braised short rib flatbread." He met Jack's pointed stare. "Or it will when we have someone to cook it."

Tad poured tasting samples of the purple-red wine into stemware and passed them around. A little smile shaded his lips as he took a seat on the plush, chocolate-brown velvet couch, just one of three sofas ringing a low-to-the-ground stone table near the entrance. He had been planning this place for so long that Jules knew he couldn't help himself. His pride at how the bar had turned out was clear. It was beautiful.

The flickering votive lights sitting on the window ledges bathed the room in an ethereal glow, casting a shine over the cherry wood furniture. On the exposed brick walls, Lili's beautifully tasteful nude photos with nods to wine culture—models holding bunches of grapes in provocative poses, others with slashes of terracotta mud on their skin—were like a love letter from Mother Nature. Sun, earth, life. The kicker was the glass-walled wine cellar, which brooded behind the bar, a window onto the world of wine. Or at least that was the sales shtick the guy who built it had given Tad when trying to convince him to go with that design. Jules was glad he did. The shock of floor-to-ceiling glass staved off that air of pretension that often shrouded these types of places. There was an accessibility about being able to see right into the cellar from out here.

He caught her looking around and shared the secret smile with her. It was his dream, but he had talked about it for so long that she felt a small measure of ownership over it as well. He was unafraid of seeking her opinion and she was unafraid of giving it. Usually about the ~~skank~~ supermodel he was dating and how she didn't much like that (lilac) shirt he was wearing and *damn it, Tad, could you not walk into every room like a herd of African elephants? I've got a kid trying to sleep here!*

Underneath the sarcastic quips and snarky comments, the

deep affection was undeniable. Simpatico, that's what they were. It had been like that from the beginning.

Cara leaned in and sniffed Shane's glass, her hand falling naturally to her swollen belly. Five months gone with twins and already as big as a house. She should have looked tired and worn, but this was Cara, who always managed to project disgustingly radiant.

"God, I miss this," Cara said, burying her nose below the lip of the glass.

Shane snatched it away and took a healthy slurp.

"Sadist," Cara muttered, drawing Shane's generous kiss and Jules's mental sigh.

"Don't say I never do anything for you, Mrs. DeLuca-Doyle," he murmured against his wife's lips, the pleasure and satisfaction in his voice impossible to disguise. Cara had organized their dream wedding in a record-setting four months, their second nuptials in the last year. Another long story.

Jules turned Evan in her arms and lay his fussy head against her shoulder so she could take a sip of the wine. Yes, she was a terrible mother.

"What do you think, Jules?" Tad asked as the aroma of berries filled her nostrils.

"Warm, a bit spicy." *Like your lips.*

No, no, no. Where the hell had that come from? She had been getting along just dandy this last year, planting her head in her life as a busy mom, and trying not to dwell on that horrible night she had almost destroyed her friendship with Tad. One kiss, three seconds of horror, a year of regret. She had harbored illicit hopes fueled by a lack of sleep and new-mom hormones, but he shot her down. The right decision, she acknowledged now. Thankfully, they had recovered and got back on the friendship track, but every now and then a stray, wanton thought popped in to say hello courtesy of her inner bad girl trying to front a saucy charge.

Now, now, Good Girl Jules admonished.

Bad Girl Jules giggled naughtily.

Within seconds, she felt the telltale signs of baby drool on her shoulder. Excellent. There was nothing like a cut to the reality of motherhood to remind her of her obvious unsexiness.

She had left the house in a hurry. Nothing new there. People had told her that once she had a child, getting out the door would be the biggest challenge, between the need to remember everything and the last-minute tantrums of your kidlet. There was no time to take a shower or put on any makeup. People had told her that, too. Forget about running a comb through your hair. All that is secondary to the needs of your child.

Usually, she didn't mind but since she had moved out to her own place, the burdens of motherhood had started to weigh more heavily. For the last two years, she had been living a blessed existence in her brother's town house with all the human and financial support she needed. Early on, Jack had shared the child care duties, getting up in the middle of the night no matter how late he trailed in from the restaurant, and feeding Evan from the milk supply she had pumped earlier. When the blues came to visit, her sister-in-law Lili was there for her, listening to her griping and moaning. She had the best extended family in the DeLucas that any girl could ask for. She knew she was lucky.

She also knew she was lonely.

It sounded so ridiculous, this need to have a man's arms to hold her. Hairy, tanned, muscle-corded arms...

She was ensorcelled by Tad's forearms again. Her friend's forearms.

Could she help it if they were the model for the forearms she imagined cradling her as she slept? That when she thought of a line of ropy muscle and brawny sinew banded beneath her breasts while she stood at the sink washing out Evan's milk bottles, these were the ones that shot to the top of the list? Maybe it wasn't the sexiest fantasy—a man taking you while you tried to scrub that tough stain off the pot—but boy, a nice set of forearms can spice up the dreariest of tasks.

But did it have to be her friend's arms? So her circle in Chicago was small, and smaller still since she had Evan. Her family had no problem jumping in to babysit when she headed to the gym (for a smoothie) or picked up pin money while catering for one of Cara and Shane's special events, but meeting people—meeting men—was nowhere near as easy as it had been in London. Back then, she had been single, child-free, and up for most anything after a couple vodka tonics. She didn't miss those days, but she did long for the chance to feel sexy, desired, wanted. Frankly, she didn't know a lot of unattached, eligible men, except for Tad.

Unattached, perhaps. Eligible, not on your life.

Tad made a living out of blowing through women like he was in a race. Some of the stories he told her made her hair stand on end. Other body parts, too. She encouraged his sexy confidences—partly because it turned her on, and partly because Tad fascinated her. He was the kindest, funniest guy she knew, but he treated women like conveniences until they became inconveniences. He was bad news in a hot package, and just the sight of him made her soft parts quiver.

His attractions were myriad and obvious. The hot bod, the piercing blue eyes, the dark, wavy hair that framed his face like a wimple of sin. In his banged-up jeans and motorcycle leathers, he was sex-on-Italian-legs.

In the kitchen, they had joked around and it was good to be back to the easy vibe between them. Their friendship was precious, and that she felt comfortable teasing him about his vigorous love life again was a good sign. They were firmly ensconced in the F-zone—the friend zone—once more, and all was right with the world. And the occasional hormonal brain fart, where she started fantasizing about his forearms of all things, was just that. Occasional and hormonal.

He crinkled his eyes in a *You okay?* kind of way, and she battled to lose whatever frowny/befuddled/horny look she wore. Really, she needed to get a shot of Botox so her expressions around Tad could become unreadable.

Coming back to earth, she plastered on a smile for her family. As always, Jack and Shane were ribbing each other about who had the better palate.

"Your taste buds are ruined from all that sugar," Jack said. "You probably can't even detect salt anymore."

"You know taste buds deteriorate with age," Shane shot back, instantly defensive of his pastry chef credentials. Jack was nine years older than Shane and they had only recently connected, but the bond between them had been instantaneous. It was as though they understood the meaning of family on some cellular level.

"Now, now, ladies, you're both pretty," Lili said, catching Jules's eye with a *men* headshake.

"So, we have some good news," Cara said, all efficiency. She wasn't one for lazy afternoons of shooting the shit with the clan, preferring to keep everyone on task. "Shane and I got the Daniels wedding in May next year."

Everyone made noises of congratulations and raised their glasses. DeLuca Doyle Special Events had become the hottest party planning company in Chicago since its inception just over eight months ago. Getting the wedding of the mayor's son was huge, but then Cara never did anything by half.

"By that time, the babies should be a few months old," Jules said, unable to keep the awe out of her voice at the idea of Cara as Supermom. She'd always had a bit of a girl crush on the slender blonde who exuded sophistication and frightening competence. "How are you going to manage?"

Cara gave one of her knowing smiles. "This event will be big enough that we won't need to take on as many clients for the next year, but we'll probably hire someone to help with the business."

"Yeah, we will." Shane's expression was filled with loving concern. Cara was a whirling dervish when it came to work, and pregnancy hadn't slowed her down, much to Shane's chagrin.

"Well, we have some good news, too," Jack said, his hand moving naturally to Lili's hair. He was rather obsessed with it. "My beautiful wife's work will be included in the New Artists Exhibit at the Museum of Contemporary Art in September."

"Amazing, cuz," Tad said, leaning over to kiss her on the forehead.

"Yeah, I'm excited. And nervous." Lili was a bit shy where her photography was concerned but she was super talented. "And my hot chef husband just sold the rights on his latest cookbook to Japan, which makes it what now?"

"Twenty-four countries," Jack answered with a proud smirk.

"Have you checked the *World Almanac* lately?" Shane asked. "There are a hundred and ninety-six countries. That's a pretty low percentage when it comes to world domination."

"You haven't made it until it's translated into Farsi," Tad said.

"Or Yoruba," Shane added to Jack's eye roll and a chorus of laughter from everyone else.

Jules checked her sigh. They were all such a talented lot of buggers that it was mighty difficult not to feel like a complete and utter loser around them. Not once had she regretted Evan, who gave her direction and balance, but there were occasions she wished she knew what she wanted to do when she grew up. Being surrounded by rock stars sharpened her feelings of inadequacy to barbed points.

There had been a moment back in the kitchen as Tad recounted Long Face's departure story when she thought: *I can do that!*

Common sense had punched it back down where it belonged. She was an amateur among gilded professionals. Her small-time efforts making pizzas, preserving lemons, and futzing about in her organic vegetable garden were hardly the stellar credits needed to work in a real restaurant kitchen. Shane and Jack had been cooking since before they could walk. They had years of training under their belts. With her dyslexia, she could barely read the recipes, never mind the hassle of finding child care for Evan.

No, she was lucky. Filled with needs and desires, but incredibly lucky.

While she figured it out, she knew she wanted one thing. Moving into her own place was step one, and she had taken care of that a month ago. The thought of what she needed to do next terrified and thrilled her equally, but she had to step up. It was time.

And she was going to need the support of her friends and family.

"Um, I have an announcement of my own," she said as the good-natured poking ebbed and flowed around her.

All eyes fell on her, probably the first time that had

happened since the day she crashed a taping of Jack's old cooking show at DeLuca's Ristorante and dropped the pregnancy bomb on her brother and a passel of strangers who were now her family and friends.

The silence stretched. She hadn't meant to pause for effect—that wasn't her style at all—but now her next words took on an unwanted significance. Note to self: don't yell "stop the presses" when you want to slip something by the posse.

"Everything okay, Jules?" Jack asked, that familiar worry crinkle bisecting his brow.

She sucked in a bolstering breath and pushed it out quickly.

"I'm going to start dating."

Fall in Love with Forever Romance

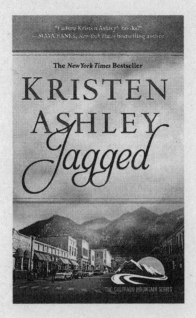

JAGGED

Zara is struggling to make ends meet when her old friend Ham comes back into her life. He wants to help, but a job and a place to live aren't the only things he's offering this time around... Fans of Julie Ann Walker, Lauren Dane, and Julie James will love the fifth book in Kristen Ashley's *New York Times* bestselling Colorado Mountain series, now in print for the first time!

Fall in Love with Forever Romance

ALL FIRED UP

It's a recipe for temptation: Mix a cool-as-a-cucumber event planner with a devastatingly handsome Irish pastry chef. Add sexual chemistry hot enough to start a fire. Let the sparks fly. Fans of Jill Shalvis will flip for the second book in Kate Meader's Hot in the Kitchen series.

Fall in Love with Forever Romance

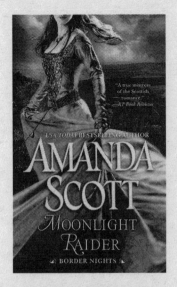

MOONLIGHT RAIDER

USA Today bestselling author Amanda Scott brings to life the history, turmoil, and passion of the Scottish Border as only she can in the first book in her new Border Nights series. Fans of Diana Gabaldon's *Outlander* will be swept away by Scott's tale!

Fall in Love with Forever Romance

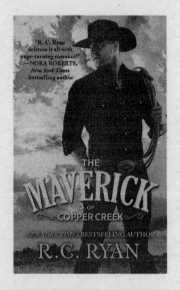

THE MAVERICK OF COPPER CREEK

Fans of Linda Lael Miller, Diana Palmer, and Joan Johnston will love *New York Times* bestselling author R. C. Ryan's THE MAVERICK OF COPPER CREEK, the charming, poignant, and unforgettable first book in her Copper Creek Cowboys series.

IT HAPPENED AT CHRISTMAS

Ethan and Skye may want a lot of things this holiday season, but what they get is something they didn't expect. Fans of feel-good romances by *New York Times* bestselling authors Brenda Novak, Robyn Carr, and Jill Shalvis will love the third book in Debbie Mason's series set in Christmas, Colorado—where love is the greatest gift of all.

Fall in Love with Forever Romance

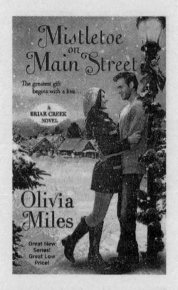

MISTLETOE ON MAIN STREET

Fans of Jill Shalvis, Robyn Carr, and Susan Mallery will love this charming debut from bestselling author Olivia Miles about love, healing, and family at Christmastime.

Fall in Love with Forever Romance

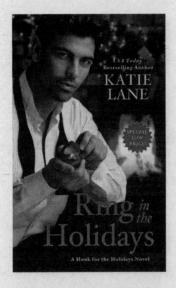

RING IN THE HOLIDAYS

For Matthew McPherson, what happens in Vegas definitely doesn't stay there, and that may be a very good thing! Fans of Lori Wilde and Rachel Gibson will fall in love with this sexy series from bestselling author Katie Lane.

About the Author

Kate Meader writes contemporary romance that serves up delicious food, sexy heroes, and heroines with a dash of sass. Originally from Ireland, she now makes her home in Chicago, a city made for food, romance, and laughter—and where she met her own sexy hero. When not writing about men who cook and the women who drool over them, she works in an academic library. For updates, excerpts, and recipes, visit her website at katemeader.com.

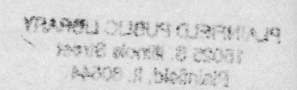